TRIPLE THREAT

TRIPLE THREAT

A SAMANTHA STARR THRILLER, BOOK 3

S. L. MENEAR

Book and cover design by eBook Prep
www.ebookprep.com

July, 2019
ISBN: 978-1-64457-085-2

ePublishing Works!
644 Shrewsbury Commons Ave
Ste 249
Shrewsbury PA 17361
United States of America

www.epublishingworks.com
Phone: 866-846-5123

"If you only knew the magnificence of the three, six, and nine, you would have a key to the universe."

NIKOLA TESLA, 1856 - 1943

"...I have created a Ball Lightning, which can be heard on the icy peaks of the Himalayas."

NIKOLA TESLA

ONE

December 21, Ramstein Air Base, Germany

I never dreamed my discovery in Hong Kong would trigger a covert race among the USA, UK, and power-hungry psychopaths. They're all searching for Poseidon's Sword, a metaphorical name for a powerful ancient weapon of mass destruction based on the prototype I found. And I sure didn't expect that *I'd* be the key to locating it.

Lucky me.

I had survived mortal combat with a six-eight Russian assassin, mostly through dumb luck. Several of my ribs were cracked in the process, but I'll heal—he won't. Not after I gouged out his left eye, shot him full of holes, and burned him to a cinder. Nicolai is definitely dead *this* time. Wish I could say the same for his employer, Lord Edgar Sweetwater. He escaped in his submarine right before the love of my life rescued me yet again.

My man, Laird Ross Sinclair, a handsome Highlander and captain in the UK's Special Air Service, was what any woman would consider the perfect boyfriend—tall and muscular with thick black hair, deep-blue eyes, and a confident swagger. The sort of man who was willing and able to step up and save the day, and me, any time. And he lived in his ancestors' castle in Scotland. It even had a moat and drawbridge.

I had been snuggled up with Ross in front of a warm hearth when a Delta team burst in and announced that the U.S. president and the U.K.'s prime minister had agreed that I must return to the States with the D-boys and assist the military in locating the WMD. They had a helicopter waiting on the front lawn.

And now here I was, standing on a dark tarmac in bitterly cold wind between a hard-ass Delta Force captain and a flirty young Air Force guy.

The loadmaster for a U.S. Air Force C-17 Globemaster gave me the once over, pausing a little too long on my chest. "Samantha Starr?"

I nodded as my cracked ribs throbbed with every heartbeat.

He read from his clipboard: "Five-nine, one twenty-five, blond hair, blue eyes—you match the physical description printed here, but I need a picture ID, preferably your passport."

I shrugged. "The last time I saw my passport, it was inside my backpack at a Harry Potter theme park in Florida."

He raised a brow. "Why didn't you get a replacement?"

"Well, after the drugs my kidnapper injected wore off, I was kinda busy trying to save two children and escape from an exploding island in the North Sea."

I made eye contact with the Delta captain whose team escorted me. The captain's job was to ensure I arrived safely at Dover Air Force Base in Delaware several hours from now.

"My boyfriend in the British Special Forces saved us."

The loadmaster smirked. "Yeah, right." He glanced at the Delta captain. "What really happened?"

The formidable soldier checked his watch. "What she said." He leaned toward the loadmaster. "I'm vouching for her."

"But I need—"

The captain's laser-beam eyes cut him off as the loadmaster gripped his clipboard like a shield.

"Put us on board."

Isn't it amazing what a glare from a scary alpha male can accomplish?

We climbed up the C-17's aft loading ramp.

I settled in for the long flight back to America. Hard to believe how many miles I'd covered in the past few days. When would this crazy nightmare end?

Flanked by beefy Special Forces soldiers, I squirmed in my upright seat, trying to get comfortable inside the cavernous cargo aircraft. Inward-facing passenger seats lined both sidewalls, and huge pallets filled the wide floor. It wasn't long before we roared into the late-evening sky over Frankfurt.

The steady hum of jet engines usually lulled me to sleep when I wasn't the pilot.

Not this time.

Pain knifed through my cracked ribs like multiple hits from a nail gun. The non-reclining seats didn't help.

I nudged the men sitting on either side of me. "Any chance you have pain pills or a flask?"

My escorts just frowned and stared straight ahead.

Lucky me.

The flight seemed to drone on forever. A few hours before dawn, we landed at Dover Air Force Base beside Delaware Bay. The D-boys escorted me down the aft cargo ramp into harsh winter air.

A brisk wind stung my face, and light snow swirled across the dark ramp, depositing lacy paisley patterns on the tarmac.

Ah, the familiar aroma of jet fuel perfumed the air.

Inside a giant hangar, the Delta captain rapped on a metal office door.

An army lieutenant opened it, and Old Spice wafted over me as a burly guy with a gray buzzcut stood ramrod straight and saluted the D-boys.

I recognized him.

He addressed the Delta team standing at attention. "Dismissed, gentlemen. Return to your unit."

His fancy U.S. Army uniform sported four stars with ribbons and medals. "Hello, Miss Starr. You may remember me from Ramstein Air Base in Germany. We met after your brother Mike's SEAL team rescued you from the Black Sun cult last October."

I offered my hand. "Nice to see you again, General Ryan."

He gently squeezed it. "Thank you for coming. May I call you Samantha?"

I glanced around the cold, gun-metal gray office with a tiny space heater in the center. "Everyone calls me Sam, and it's not like I had a choice about coming here." My shivers shot sharp blades through my chest.

"Sorry, Sam, but there's a WMD in play, and you seem to be the only person who can find it." He pulled out a chair. "Have a seat and let's talk." He nodded at his aide.

The lieutenant opened a briefcase and placed a recording device in front of me. He settled at the table and nodded at the general.

Ryan noticed me grimacing. "Haven't your injuries from Wewels-burg healed? That was back in October."

"Yes, but now I have several cracked ribs, courtesy of Nicolai Vasiliev."

"Do we know about him?" Ryan glanced at his aide.

"A Russian assassin—former Spetsnaz—employed by Sweetwater. He's noted in her dossier, sir." He slid a folder to the general.

Ryan scanned the room. "Is there anything we can give her for the pain?"

The lieutenant rifled through several desk drawers. "I've got whisky and aspirin." He held up a pill bottle and a fifth of Macallan.

I forced a smile. "A little of both, please."

Ryan poured three fingers of Scotch while his aide handed me the aspirin bottle. I shook out two pills to pair with the whisky and gulped them down.

Ryan sat back. "What did Sweetwater want with you, Sam?"

"Payback for last August." I eased into a more comfortable position. "Well, that and the WMD, Poseidon's Sword." I took another gulp.

Ryan's aide tapped the folder. "It's all in there, sir."

"I'll look at this later." Ryan turned back to me. "Do you know where that weapon is hidden?"

"I had to stop searching while my wounds from the Black Sun Master healed." I paused and ran the facts through my head. "Look for an electromagnetic dead zone in the Himalayas and search that ancient city our Navy discovered underwater near Cuba."

"All right." Ryan steepled his fingers. "I understand you have visions, usually of future events. Not my bailiwick, but tell me about any that might concern Poseidon's Sword."

"I had a vision in early October of a huge obsidian pyramid with three women standing back-to-back on a gold disc mounted at the top."

"Hmmm, and what did these women look like?"

"Triplets in their mid-twenties—a blonde, a brunette, and a redhead." I shrugged. "Actually, they looked a lot like me, especially the blonde."

"Is it possible she *was* you?"

"The name on her belt was Solraya."

He leaned forward, scrutinizing me. "Any other visions related to the weapon?"

"Um, yeah, I flew a charter flight to Hong Kong and had a vision that led me to a small curio shop. I found a sculpture there exactly like the black pyramid and women, but it was only two feet tall."

His eyes widened. "That must've been a shock, finding a replica of your vision."

"I was stunned." I sipped the smooth Scotch. "Of course, the pyramid in my vision was one hundred feet tall, and the women were real."

"So, we're looking for a weapon housed in a huge black pyramid?"

"I think so, and that sculpture turned out to be more than a work of art."

"You bought it?"

I laughed. "It was more complicated than that. I cradled it in my arms, astonished at the accuracy of every detail, including small crystals in the statues' hands. They lit up when I brushed off the dust with my fingers."

The general straightened. "Seriously?"

Another quick sip. "The shopkeeper, who introduced himself as Dragon Master, said he'd waited a long time for me to come. He called me Golden Twin, told me to keep the artifact, and gave me some cryptic advice. His words made me curious to discover my destiny."

Big mistake.

Ryan leaned forward. "What did he say?"

"His exact words were: 'Your destiny lies hidden in one teardrop on cheek of time, in rose-red city old as time. Follow dragon current and beware Vril wielded by Black Sun.' I later discovered the first two clues referred to the Taj Mahal in India, and Petra, the stone city in Jordan."

"And the rest?"

"Dragon current is another word for ley line, and Vril is the electromagnetic energy that flows through ley lines. The Black Sun Master learned how to mentally control it. Good thing he died in Wewelsburg."

His aide tapped the folder. "All the details are in there."

Ryan nodded. "The shopkeeper gave you the device? Where is it now?"

I emptied the glass, my rib pain dissipating into a distant memory. "I shipped it to a trusted friend, Ben Armitage. He's a professor of antiquities at Harvard."

The general hesitated, narrowing his eyes. "Do you know where he keeps it?"

I leaned forward. "It's inside a wall safe in an office above his garage. I asked him to keep it secret until we knew more about it."

He slumped back. "I was hoping you'd say he locked it away at the university."

"Why?"

"Professor Armitage was kidnapped last night. The safe in his office is empty."

"Oh, no." I felt like I'd been gut punched. "Do you know who's responsible?"

"I was hoping you might know." He shook his head. "It can't be the Black Sun cult. They were wiped out at Wewelsburg."

"You can bet Lord Sweetwater is behind this." I shifted my eyes to the aide and back to the general. "He's a rich arms dealer with a Napoleon complex."

Ryan nodded. "The report from the Brits focused mostly on your rescue. I'd like details of Sweetwater's escape from his island in the North Sea."

I closed my eyes a moment to flash back. "He left in his submarine, *Pelagic Predator*, right before all the bombs were set to explode."

Ryan leaned forward, his eyes intense. "What can you tell me about that sub?"

"He bragged it's 184 feet with an anti-magnetic steel hull and hydrogen/oxygen fuel cells for silent running." I shrugged. "That's all I know."

Ryan shook his head. "A sub like that would cost half a billion dollars."

"Believe me, Sweetwater can afford it. He's worth fifty billion British pounds."

Ryan gave me a hard look. "Does he have enough clues to find Poseidon's Sword without you?"

I hesitated. My answer could keep me in military custody and jeopardize my airline pilot career. "I doubt he'll find it without my help, but even if he does, he can't activate the weapon without me."

Ryan narrowed his eyes. "What're you talking about?"

"Ben told me ancient legends claimed scientists in Atlantis invented Poseidon's Sword." I paused, feeling light-headed from the whisky and wondering if he'd believe Ben's theory about me. "He's convinced my body carries a unique electromagnetic frequency identical to certain powerful women from Atlantis."

"Why would he think that?"

"My touch activated the sculpture, which he believes may be a small prototype of the weapon." I sighed. "Nothing happens when anyone else touches it."

Yep, lucky me.

Ryan straightened. "Does Sweetwater know you found the weapon's prototype?"

"He must know. The Brits told me he had a high-tech spy facility that monitored all my cell calls and texts."

Ryan shook his head. "We need to find him fast."

I frowned. "Won't his stealth submarine be hard to track?"

Gunfire and explosions interrupted our conversation. Staccato blasts from automatic weapons echoed inside the hangar.

"What was that?" I turned and glanced at the door as an MP crashed through it.

"General, we're under attack!" Bullets peppered the MP's back, and his face hit the floor in front of us.

"Bar the door!" Ryan shouted as he pulled out his cell phone.

The general's aide slammed the door, locked it, and shoved a heavy metal desk against it.

I checked the MP for a pulse. Dead.

Everything seemed to move in slow motion as I helped the aide flip our metal table on its side to use as cover.

I glanced around the spartan office. "Are there any weapons in here?"

"None." He piled chairs on the desk against the door as Ryan barked orders to base security on his cell.

I picked up the whisky bottle and turned to Ryan. "Can you use this to make a Molotov cocktail?"

Ryan nodded. "But I don't know how much good just one will do."

"We only need to hold them off a minute or two until armed soldiers arrive, right?" I handed him the bottle.

"Could be five or ten minutes. I'm guessing all the guards on duty are dead, and the barracks are on the far side of the base." Ryan unknotted his tie and pulled it off.

Bullets hammered into the metal door. Seconds passed. Something hard and heavy slammed into the door and broke the lock.

The general quickly rigged the whisky bomb with his tie as the fuse. He glanced at me. "Do you have a lighter?"

"Are you kidding? I'm not even wearing my own clothes."

Ryan turned to his aide. "Well, Lieutenant?"

"Sorry, sir, I don't smoke." He yanked open desk drawers to search.

Another heavy blow knocked the door open an inch.

I nudged the general and pointed at the old-technology space heater with the glowing wires. "Try that."

The desk slid inward under the heavy onslaught as the door against it inched open.

Ryan lit the cloth fuse against the hot wires and tossed the crude bomb at the men pushing through the door.

The Macallan bottle exploded on two intruders and engulfed them in flames. They rolled screaming across the office floor as the three of us ducked behind the overturned metal table. The stench of whisky and charred flesh turned my stomach.

General Ryan shielded me with his body as men in black combat gear rushed in brandishing AK-47s. One guy clubbed Ryan's head with a rifle butt and dragged his limp body off me.

Ryan's aide suffered the same fate. I assumed the intruders didn't want to risk hitting me with a bullet. Someone wanted me alive.

The leader tapped his watch. "Time! Get the girl." His cold, dark eyes were the only facial feature not covered.

I scooted up against the overturned table and tried to delay the inevitable, hoping armed troops would storm in. I kicked and punched them, nailing one guy in the face with my foot. Blood poured from his nose.

When a muscular man grabbed my right wrist, I sank my teeth into his hand and tasted blood.

"The bitch bit me!" He balled his fist to punch me, but another guy blocked him.

"Do you have a death wish? The boss said no injuries." He shoved the bleeding guy.

Four commandos dived on top of me and pinned me down. They zip-tied my wrists and ankles. A stocky guy threw me over his shoulder like a sack of grain and ran outside. My ribs exploded in pain as my chest banged against his hard back with every step.

An unmarked black helicopter with amphibious floats strafed a row of fighter jets parked on the ramp. Noxious smoke from burning jet fuel stung my nose and throat.

The stealthy-looking helicopter landed on the ramp, and my captor tossed me into a seat and belted me in. We lifted off and flew low over Delaware Bay.

The invasion and kidnapping probably had taken less than ten minutes.

We sped out to sea fifty feet above the moonlit Atlantic Ocean. Fifteen minutes later, the helicopter slowed, circled, and landed on the water.

I looked out the window. *Oh God, not again.*

A sleek black submarine drifted on the surface. The brilliant full moon illuminated *Pelagic Predator* emblazoned on the sail.

A crewman threw a line to one of the commandos, who tied us alongside the sub.

The same stocky man slung me over his shoulder and carried me aboard. My chest felt like it was being crushed in a vise, and I gulped air in fast spurts. Brisk salt spray prickled my face and burned my eyes.

Sweetwater strode across the deck and grabbed my left wrist. "You won't need *this* anymore." He snatched my DARPA watch with the automatic GPS locator signal and tossed it into the ocean.

"Activate the timer on the bomb and cut the chopper loose," he told a sailor. "Time to dive."

My stocky captor dragged me below like he was hauling a duffel bag.

I gritted my teeth and inhaled quick, shallow breaths.

The hatch thunked closed, and the narrow walkway tilted downward as the submarine plunged beneath the waves.

Moments later, a distant boom shuddered the sub.

Wish I'd never found that damn artifact.

TWO

December 22, Winter Solstice

Lieutenant Mike Starr and his SEAL team waited in their rigid hull inflatable boat on the Arabian Sea. Their covert mission in Pakistan had stripped Islamic terrorists of several key players.

Heavy cloud cover inked the night, and steady rain pelted the sea and drowned out other sounds.

Mike scanned the water with his night-vision binoculars. A nuclear submarine, SSGN-729 *Georgia*, would surface soon and recover his team.

Something moved behind the veil of rain.

A pod of orcas glided into view. Many of the killer whales were almost thirty feet, a little longer than the boat.

"Hey, guys, we have company. Orcas are checking us out." Mike scanned the whales. "Holy shit, a woman is riding one!"

"Your brain's waterlogged," a teammate said, rolling his eyes. "We're a long way from Sea World."

Another SEAL shook his head and laughed. "Poor guy probably hasn't been laid in a while. He's imagining women now."

Mike pointed. "She's right there and coming closer."

His men stared.

A killer whale stopped alongside them. The woman had her arms wrapped around its dorsal fin. Long red hair cascaded over her bowed head and black bodysuit.

She looked up into his eyes. "Mike, please save me...." Her voice faded.

Mike hesitated. *How does she know my name? Good god, she looks like my sister.*

A SEAL nudged Mike's arm. "She knows you. Get your ass in gear."

"Yeah, let's not upset her killer-whale buddies," another teammate said.

Mike pulled the woman up into his arms. She shivered, wrapped her arms around his neck, and snuggled against his broad shoulder.

He tilted up her chin.

"What's your name?" He searched her face for a clue to help him remember her.

She managed one word before she passed out: "Blaze."

The orcas scattered and vanished underwater seconds before a massive submarine surfaced, sending a wave into their boat.

Mike carried Blaze aboard with his SEAL team. A sailor passed around towels as they dripped on a metal walkway.

The captain pushed through the team and glared at Mike. "I wasn't informed a civilian would be with your team. Who is she?"

Mike glanced down at the beautiful redhead in his arms. "Her name is Blaze. She passed out before she could tell me more."

The captain eased closer and scrutinized the unconscious woman. "Was she part of your mission?"

"No, sir, we rescued her moments before the sub surfaced." Mike assisted a sailor as he wrapped a blanket around her.

The captain crossed his arms. "You found her drifting in a disabled boat?"

Mike hesitated and sighed. "Uh, not in a boat, sir."

"Come on, she wasn't swimming this far from shore, was she?"

Mike glanced at his men for support. "She was with a pod of orcas, sir. One of them carried her right up to our boat."

The captain's eyes widened. "Are you saying she was *riding* a killer whale?"

"Yes, sir, and my men saw it too." Mike turned to his team.

They nodded and chimed in, confirming his report.

The captain stood inches from Mike. "Why is she on my boat?"

"She said my name and asked me to save her." Mike met the captain's gaze. "And she bears a strong resemblance to my sister."

"How did she know you're Lieutenant Mike Starr? She could be an enemy spy or saboteur."

"She called me by my first name. Her exact words were, 'Mike, please save me.'"

The captain thrust his hands on his hips. "Lieutenant, do you know this woman?"

"I'm not sure, sir. She looks familiar, but I can't remember if we've met before."

"Well, she's *your* problem. I want her guarded every second until you're transferred to the aircraft carrier. Take her to sick bay and have her checked out." The captain strode back to the control room.

Mike gazed at the beautiful redhead in his arms and glanced at his men. "That didn't go so well. Get squared away and then somebody relieve me so I can change into dry clothes." He carried the unconscious woman to sick bay.

After showering and dressing, Mike returned to Blaze's cot. The doctor had started IV fluids, washed off the saltwater, and dressed her in loose-fitting clothes borrowed from one of the smaller sailors.

She slept for four hours on the submarine and during their transfer to the aircraft carrier.

USS LAWRENCE LEE

Mike stayed by Blaze's side as she slept in a small private room in the ship's hospital. He occupied the only chair and checked email on his smart phone. An hour later, a tall, blue-eyed man with a square jaw and a blond buzz cut walked in.

"Matt!" Mike jumped up and hugged his twin brother.

"Hey, Mike, I've got a lot to tell you about Sam and stuff that happened while you were on a mission." Matt grinned. "Who's the hot babe?"

"Her name's Blaze." Mike explained everything.

"Whoa, you found one of the triplets. This is unbelievable." Matt shook his head.

"What are you talking about? What triplets?"

"The weapon prototype Sam found had three statues standing on top of an obsidian pyramid." Matt explained how the statues resembled Sam. "They were labeled the Goddesses of Sun, Moon, and Fire— Solraya, Luna, and Blaze." He pointed at the sleeping redhead. "Blaze is the fire goddess."

"Well, she *was* riding a wild orca when I found her. You don't see that every day, but a real goddess shouldn't need to be rescued." Mike stroked her long red hair.

"She certainly *looks* like a goddess." Matt shook his head. "Too bad there's no such thing in real life. Could be fun having a goddess for a girlfriend."

Blaze woke and focused her emerald-green eyes on Mike's face. "Miii—" She coughed.

Mike held a glass of water to her lips. "Drink this. Your throat's dry from hours at sea."

She drained the glass, glanced at Matt, and smiled. "You must be Matt." Her voice was hoarse.

Matt's eyes widened. "How do you know my name?"

"Your sister, Sam, told me about you when I saw your brother at Wewelsburg Castle. Are you a SEAL too?"

Matt gave Mike a sideways glance. "No, I'm a fighter pilot."

Mike leaned in. "Blaze, I didn't see you at Wewelsburg Castle."

"No, but I saw *you* through Sam's eyes. My sisters and I were telepath- ically and psychically connected to her. We asked her to request that you wipe off the greasepaint so we could see your face." She smiled. "You were with two Scottish men named Ross and Derek. Ross is Sam's man."

"But why would Sam tell you *my* name?" Matt crossed his arms. "I wasn't there."

"When we saw Mike, Luna and I said we wished there were two of him." Her cheeks turned crimson. "Sam said Mike had an almost identical twin brother named Matt."

"Back up a second. How did you connect with Sam?" Mike sat on the edge of her bunk.

"We were trained to develop our psychic and telepathic skills, and we heard Sam yelling our names over and over in our minds." Blaze shrugged. "She was being tortured and needed our help."

Matt narrowed his eyes. "You helped a total stranger just because she asked?"

"She knew more about us than we did. She said our parents, Richard and Sheila Conor, were killed in a plane crash in the Himalayas, but we survived and are connected to an ancient prophecy about a weapon called Poseidon's Sword. Sam said she was being tortured because she looked exactly like my sister, Solraya. We had to save her."

"Hold on a minute. Are you saying you're a real goddess?" Mike arched his brow.

She hesitated. "No, but our captors raised us as though we are. It's a long story."

Mike exchanged surprised glances with Matt. "How did you save Sam?"

"We surrounded her with a powerful circle of electromagnetic energy. The evil man's energy couldn't penetrate the circle, but he kept trying. When he ordered his men to shoot her, we expanded the perimeter and stopped them."

Mike remembered the blue-white light from thousands of lightning bolts sparking outward in all directions inside the circular chamber in Wewelsburg Castle. Charred corpses lined the perimeter. He also remembered Sam had asked him to wipe off his greasepaint after the electromagnetic storm ended. *How could Blaze know all those details? Could her story be true?*

"I saw the energy circle, but how did you accomplish that telepathically?"

Before she could answer, Captain William Kingston strode in. Mike and Matt stood at attention. The ship's captain was tall and broad-shouldered with chiseled features, warm brown eyes, and dark-brown hair with silver sprinkled throughout.

"At ease, gentlemen. Introduce me to our guest."

"Captain Kingston, meet Blaze Conor. We think she's the daughter of our mother's best friend," Mike said.

"Welcome aboard, Miss Conor. I'd like to believe you're an American citizen with the best of intentions, but you must understand I'm responsible for the lives of thousands of sailors on this ship. I doubt you're a saboteur, but proof of your identity would make my job a lot easier."

"Maybe this will help. It's my most prized possession." She opened the baby locket on her bracelet and lifted out a computer chip. "Do you know what to do with this?"

The captain took the chip and turned it over in his hand. "I'll give it to our tech department and see if they can download it."

"I'd like to know what's on it too," she said. "I've had it since I was a baby."

"We'll analyze it and bring you a printout." The captain pocketed the chip. "Matt, stay with Blaze. Mike, come with me."

Mike followed the captain up to his private quarters after dropping off the chip at the tech center.

"Close the door and take a seat." The captain settled at his desk. "What I'm about to tell you is top secret. Your brother doesn't know because I was briefed right before I found you in sick bay. I didn't want to say anything in front of our guest, and don't tell your mother."

"You can count on me, sir."

"Your sister was kidnapped last night." The captain leaned forward, his voice sympathetic. "A mercenary team snatched her."

Mike sucked in his breath. "Do we know who ordered it?"

"We believe she was taken aboard Sweetwater's stealth submarine. Navy divers recovered her DARPA watch in 150 feet of water off the coast of Delaware."

Mike's face reddened. "Sweetwater will kill her."

The captain shook his head. "He needs her alive to help him locate and activate the weapon. He's probably holding Professor Armitage aboard also."

"Why do you think that?"

"Armitage was kidnapped earlier, and the weapon prototype is missing from his safe."

A Navy tech officer entered and handed the captain papers. "We got this from the chip, sir. My men are studying the components to determine the chip's age. We'll have an answer for you soon."

"Thank you, Lieutenant. Get me the date on that chip ASAP." He saluted and waved the officer out.

"What does it say, Captain?" Mike asked.

The captain's eyebrows shot up. "Blaze Conor is legit. Her late father, a former SEAL, founded Gold Trident Industries, which is now a multi-billion-dollar high-tech corporation. The document is dated twenty-three years ago."

"So maybe the other things Blaze told me are true. She claims she connected telepathically with my sister when Sam was in Wewelsburg. Maybe she can do it again and help us find her."

"I hope so. Our president is furious we lost her twice. If this gets out, America will be humiliated. We keep losing her, and the Brits keep rescuing her. We need a win on this, so don't tell your sister's Scottish boyfriend. We can't risk the Brits finding out we blew it again."

As if on cue, Mike's cell chimed with a text from SAS Captain Ross Sinclair: *Heard thru grapevine Dover AFB attacked early a.m. Is Sam OK?*

Mike showed his phone to Captain Kingston. "Sam's boyfriend just sent this. How should I respond?"

"Say she's in a secret location." Kingston shrugged. "Technically, you're not lying."

Mike tapped out the text, and Ross responded: *Good. Keep her safe.* Mike flashed it at the captain.

"Well, that's one problem solved, for now anyway. What more can you tell me about Blaze?"

"She admitted she's attracted to me. With your permission, I'll stay close to her and enlist her help." Mike tried to hide the worry in his voice. "She mentioned one of her sisters is interested in my brother."

"Where are her sisters?"

"I don't know. She woke up a few minutes before you walked in. I think she'll want to help us. She wasn't trying to hide anything." Mike

17

ran his hand over his blond buzz cut. "I need to get back there and talk to her before time runs out for Sam."

Captain Kingston copied the documents and handed them to Mike. "Take these with you and explain we need to keep the chip a few days for further study. We'll confirm if the chip is at least twenty-three years old."

"I think she'll welcome all this info on her family."

"All right, Lieutenant, I'm counting on you. Stick with Blaze Conor and keep me informed. Dismissed."

PELAGIC PREDATOR

Two of Sweetwater's mercenaries dragged me through the 184-foot submarine and tossed me into the brig two levels down. I noticed Professor Armitage was in the cell next to mine as they cut my zip ties.

"Ben, I'm so sorry they took you. Are you hurt?" I looked him over and didn't spot any blood.

He remained quiet until our captors left.

"Sam." Shock and exhaustion clouded his face as he stumbled over to the bars. "I thought you were in Scotland with your Special Forces Highlander."

"I was, until the U.S. military swooped in and took me. My flight landed at Dover less than an hour ago. I wasn't there more than twenty minutes when Sweetwater's team snatched me." I sucked in my breath and exhaled slowly, trying to relax my chest muscles and ease the pain. "Sweetwater must have informants inside our military."

"I'm not surprised. He can afford anything." He stepped closer to the bars separating our cells. "Are you all right? You seem to be in pain."

"I was hauled in here like a sack of potatoes—not good for my cracked ribs."

"Sorry, wish I could do something for you." He had a tone of defeat.

"I'm the one who should apologize. It's my fault they took you. If I hadn't sent you the prototype, you wouldn't have been dragged into this. Did they hurt you?"

"No, but they took the device when they kidnapped me." Ben lowered his eyes. "Sorry."

I looked around for hidden cameras and listening devices. None were obvious.

I stood as close to him as I could and whispered, "Ben, I promise I'll find a way to get us out of this sub. Tell me about the device. How did it set your house on fire?"

"You activated the small crystal pyramids when you touched them in Hong Kong. They were still glowing when the artifact arrived at my house."

"Hmmm, they stayed lit all that time?" I raised a brow. "How did you fire the weapon?"

"I turned the diadems on the statues' heads, and they released the crystals. I placed them in the slots at the statues' feet, and brilliant light beams shot up and merged into a single searing laser above the statues' heads. That laser burned through my ceiling, attic, and roof in seconds."

My mind reeled at the thought of a giant weapon made from that prototype. "How did you turn it off?"

"After some very tense moments, I tried pressing the diamond pyramids in the diagram on one side of the obsidian base, and the laser stopped. The crystals popped back into the statues' hands, and everything went back to normal."

I thought a moment. "Any chance that laser could burn through steel?"

He closed his eyes to relive the scene. "I think it could cut through anything. The immense power was terrifying."

"I have a plan. It's important to convince them they need both of us to operate it."

"What do you have in mind?"

"Our government wants the prototype. You can rest assured our Navy is searching for us. We need to force this stealth sub to the surface so the military can find us."

"If this doesn't go well, we'll be entombed on the bottom of the ocean." He ran his hand through thinning gray hair. "I'm not brave like you."

"Nonsense. Only a brave man could've kept his wits as a powerful weapon burned through his home. You've got the right stuff, Ben. We can do this." I gave him a reassuring smile.

"Your plan will only work if they ask us to perform a demonstration while we're still in this sub." He shook his head. "They might wait until we arrive in port."

"Sweetwater isn't a patient man. He won't wait." I reached through the bars and squeezed his hand.

Would my destiny lead me to enlightenment or continue to thrust me into danger? I decided to roll the dice and hope for a win.

USS LAWRENCE LEE

Mike entered the tiny room in sick bay and found Blaze and Matt chatting. She took a sip of orange juice and grinned at Mike.

"I'm glad to see you're recovering so quickly." Mike handed her the printouts. "That chip had lots of info on your family. Looks like you're an heiress."

She read the pages with hungry eyes. "Thank you. I was hoping the chip would lead me to my relatives." She glanced at Mike. "Where is it?"

"The captain kept it for further study but will return it soon." Mike gave her a warm smile. "Where are your sisters?"

"They're prisoners in a hidden enclave in the Himalayas. An evil remnant from Atlantis lives there."

Mike and Matt exchanged surprised looks.

A deep vibration coursed through the room and shook Blaze's bed. Her eyes widened. "What happened?"

"The ship just resumed flight ops. That vibration was the catapult flinging a fighter jet into the sky." Matt grinned. "You'll get used to it."

Her eyes lit up when a sailor walked in with a tray of hot food. An aroma of roast beef, mashed potatoes, and warm bread filled the room.

"Uh, we need to step out for a moment." Mike motioned for Matt to follow him. "Enjoy your meal. We'll be back in a few minutes."

They walked down the narrow passage to a place out of earshot where they could watch the door to her room.

"A fire goddess from an Atlantean enclave in the Himalayas? This gets more intriguing by the minute." Mike raised his brows. "I'm not sure what to think."

"I think I'd like to meet her sisters." Matt grinned.

Mike gripped Matt's shoulder. "Bad news, brother. Sweetwater kidnapped Sam. He has Professor Armitage and the prototype too."

Matt's jaw dropped. "Sam again? And Ben too?"

Mike nodded. "The skipper wants a tight lid on this, so don't tell Mom."

"That's one mistake I'll never repeat. Mom tends to share too much info. We should teach her the World War II motto: Loose lips sink ships."

"Kingston said the president is furious America lost Sam twice."

Matt clenched his jaw. "Do we know where they are?"

"We think they're in Sweetwater's stealth submarine, but we don't know where it's headed. I'm hoping Blaze can connect with Sam telepathically like she did at Wewelsburg. Maybe she can help our Navy locate her."

Mike stared down the walkway, his mind drifting back to the fierce battle in the Black Sun's castle in Germany. *How did she and her sisters create that electromagnetic maelstrom? Maybe she can disable Sweetwater's sub.*

Matt narrowed his eyes. "Before we ask for help, let's ask her how she escaped the enclave. That couldn't have been easy."

"Yeah, and it's a long journey from the Himalayas to the Arabian Sea. We need to be sure we can trust her."

Matt nodded. "Her story is beyond bizarre. We need proof."

"Yeah, how do we know the 'evil Atlanteans' didn't send her to retrieve their weapon?" Mike blew out a sigh. "But she seems genuine. I sure hope she's telling the truth. We need help finding Sam before it's too late."

"Let's see what she says." Matt led the way.

Blaze had cleaned her plate in record time. She dabbed her chapped lips with a napkin and smiled when the handsome, muscular twins entered.

"I've been wondering how you speak English so well. Is that what the Atlanteans speak?" Matt asked.

"They speak many languages. The Atlantean alphabet is similar to the English one. They had twenty-three years to teach me their vast knowledge. I'm fluent in twenty languages."

Mike sat on the edge of her berth. "We'd love to hear how you escaped from the enclave and made it all the way to the Arabian Sea."

"My sisters and I made a silk paraglider in secret. The cocoon for the pilot doubled as a sleeping bag. I glided down to a distant valley on a calm morning at dawn while the Atlanteans were holding a special worship ritual inside the obsidian pyramid. My sisters told them I was sick in bed." She yawned, sleepy after her big meal.

"Didn't they come after you?" Matt asked.

She shrugged. "I was far away by the time their three-hour ritual ended."

Mike crossed his arms. "You still had hundreds of miles to cover after you landed. How did you find transportation?"

"I took some jewels and gold coins from the Atlantean treasury and hired a man with a Jeep to drive me to the nearest airport. It turned out to be several hours away on narrow, winding roads." She sipped ice tea.

"Passenger flights were available there?" Matt asked.

"No, the airport was quite remote. The pilot of a small cargo plane flew me to a coastal airport in exchange for gold coins. I knew Poseidon would take care of me when I reached the sea." She said this in a matter-of-fact way, as though it should make perfect sense.

"Are you saying you swam into the Arabian Sea, and orcas carried you away?" Mike asked, incredulous.

"Don't you remember how you found me?" She tilted her head, looking surprised he would ask that when he already knew the answer.

"Well, yeah, but that's not something most people could or would do." Mike arched his brow.

"Riding orcas is not unusual for Atlanteans, and they think my sisters and I are goddesses. Their ancestors were one with the sea, and Poseidon is their god." Blaze drained her ice tea. "They taught me how to mentally communicate with sea creatures, and I learned how to swim in a mountain lake."

Mike glanced at Matt and asked Blaze, "What about that electrical

22

storm you caused in the Generals' Chamber at Wewelsburg Castle? How did you do that?"

"My sisters and I were trained to mentally harness the Earth's energy." She looked from one brother to the other. "Rivers of electromagnetic energy known as dragon currents or ley lines flow through the Earth in every part of the world."

Mike thought a moment. "The men you killed in the circular chamber were members of the Black Sun. Their leaders were reputed to have control over Earth's electromagnetic energy. They called it Vril."

"They were using Vril to torture your sister. As triplets, our combined abilities were greater than those of the Black Sun Master. We channeled our power telepathically and psychically through Sam to defeat him."

Mike nodded. "I saw the energy storm and the charred corpses along the perimeter."

Matt unscrewed a lightbulb from a nearby lamp and set it on the bed. "Can you make this bulb light up without touching it?"

Blaze smiled and focused on it. The bulb shined brightly and then shattered.

"Sorry, that was my first try with a lightbulb." She frowned at the broken glass. "Guess I zapped it with too much energy."

Mike stared at the shattered glass. "Could you disable a large ship?"

Blaze looked crestfallen. "Gentlemen, I would never do anything to harm your ship. I'm forever indebted to you for rescuing me."

"Sorry, Blaze, you misunderstood me," Mike said. "I have another vessel in mind, a submarine. It's a boat that operates underwater. You were unconscious when one picked us up."

Blaze frowned. "I don't understand what you want."

"Sam has been taken prisoner aboard a stealth submarine. We're hoping you can help us find it and rescue her—maybe disable the sub's power so they'll have to surface," Mike explained.

She sighed. "I want to help, but I'm afraid my captors will find me. My sisters and I would have to combine our powers again, but if I contact them, the remnant might sense our telepathic energy and discover where I am."

"Don't worry, our military will protect you." Mike patted her hand.

She bit her lip. "You're asking me to take a huge risk. I just barely escaped, and there's a lot at stake now for me and my sisters."

"What can we do to reassure you?" Mike asked.

She glanced up at the low ceiling, thinking. "I want an irrevocable written document from the U.S. government agreeing to rescue my sisters, declare us alive, restore our U.S. citizenship, and facilitate our inheritance." She crossed her arms. "That's the least they can do if they want me to risk everything."

Mike nodded. "Sounds fair. Matt will stay with you while I run this by the captain. He'll have to make the request."

"Thank you, Mike. I hope you understand that I must be cautious. My sisters are counting on me to save them." Her big green eyes moistened.

Mike glanced from Matt to Blaze. "No worries, I'll take care of it."

SEESCHLANGE

A Black Sun submarine captain studied red markings on the electronic chart table depicting the U.S. eastern seaboard. Instrument lights glimmered in the dim control room.

He ran his hand through his spiked platinum hair, pointed at the last mark, and spoke to his executive officer. "We know Sweetwater's sub was off the coast of Massachusetts when he snatched Professor Armitage and the prototype." He tapped the chart. "They cruised south and surfaced fifty miles off the coast of Delaware to take aboard the Golden Twin."

"*Jawohl*, Captain, but we lost them when they submerged. How will we find them again?" The young XO stared at the vast area covered by the ocean chart.

"Our researchers studied his maze of shell corporations and discovered Sweetwater owns two private islands on this side of the Atlantic. The one in the Bahamas is flat and surrounded by clear water." The captain tapped the chart. "Here."

"Ah, so no place to hide a large submarine like *Pelagic Predator*."

"His other island, seventy miles north of the Dominican Republic, is mountainous with only a tiny cove and beach. He must have a sub base hidden in the mountain with an underwater entrance." The captain plotted a straight line from Sweetwater's last known location to the island.

The XO focused on the small volcanic island circled in red. "Ah, I see, but can we catch up with him?"

"Our little submarine can run faster in silence than his behemoth." He patted the XO's shoulder. "His sub must run slower to hide from the U.S. Navy because it displaces so much water as it moves."

The XO thought a moment. "Should we intercept them at sea or engage them at their base?"

A smile. "We must remain flexible on the hunt."

"But sir, either way, they'll outnumber us twenty to one."

The captain's lips curled down, his eyes hard. "That's why we have a Vril Master on board."

The XO's eyes widened. "Of course, Captain." A smile crept across his face. "Vril never fails."

PELAGIC PREDATOR

The throbbing in my chest subsided after a few hours. Exhausted, I imagined I was back in Ross's arms, running my hands through his thick black hair and gazing into his deep-blue eyes. I fell into a restless sleep on the stiff cot and woke with a start at the clanking of a key in the lock.

Guards dragged Ben and me from our cells. The dark, cave-like passages seemed to suck the oxygen from my lungs as we weaved through the long submarine and finally stepped through a side door.

Lord Sweetwater, short, bald, and portly, relaxed in a gold-trimmed, throne-like chair. His stateroom resembled a cozy office lined with teak bookcases and furnished with teak and cordovan leather chairs. Vertical aquariums between the bookcases gave the room a Jules Verne vibe.

His sinister, dark-brown eyes focused on us. "Ah, Miss Starr, Professor, I've been looking forward to this." Sweetwater gestured toward the device on his desk. "Show me how to operate my prize or spend the rest of the journey in the torture chamber."

The guards shoved us into seats across from him, reawakening my rib pain.

Thirsty, I faked being hoarse and coughed. "A little water would be helpful."

"Where are my manners?" He turned to a steward. "Some bottled water for our guests."

I gulped the water, not knowing when I'd get more.

Sweetwater drummed his fingers on the desk. "Now, show me how this works."

"It might not be a good idea to operate this inside a submarine," I said, doing my best to feign fear.

I gambled reverse psychology would ensure we'd be forced to fire the weapon and not be blamed when it damaged the sub.

"Nonsense, I had a fire shield installed on the stateroom's ceiling. Testing this little prototype won't hurt my sub. Now stop wasting time." Sweetwater sat back and crossed his arms.

"How deep are we?" Ben asked.

"Three hundred feet." Sweetwater raised an eyebrow. "Why should that matter?"

Ben wiped his forehead with his sleeve. "It's just that I've seen this device in action, and I'd like to survive the demonstration."

"You're stalling. Get on with it." Sweetwater pounded the table with his fist.

"All right, but first clamp a vise to the desk and secure the proto-type," Ben said, licking his lips. "You wouldn't want it to fall while it's firing."

Sweetwater pointed at a guard. "Get a vise from the maintenance bay." He looked at me. "Explain how it works while we wait."

"My touch activates the crystals. That's all I know," I lied. "The professor figured out how to fire it."

Sweat trickled down Ben's face. "The process involves several steps. I'll demonstrate the firing sequence once the device is secured." He wiped his brow again.

A guard walked in with a large vise and clamped it to the desk. He cranked it open, placed the obsidian pyramid between the sides, and cranked them tight against it.

Ben glanced at me with wide eyes. "All right, Sam, activate the crystals."

When I touched them, they filled with brilliant light. I saw a brief vision of an island nation with pyramids, airships above, longboats in the harbor, and an angry volcano looming behind the city. In an instant, the vision vanished.

The submarine captain entered. "Lord Sweetwater, you asked me to alert you when we're thirty miles from the sub base. We're right on schedule."

"Thank you, Captain." He waved at Ben as the captain left. "Get on with it."

Ben glanced at me and twisted the diadem on the blond statue's head a quarter turn clockwise. Her hinged hands released the crystal, and he placed it in the slot at her feet, which slanted the crystal's tip toward her head. Once he completed the same steps with the other statues, blinding beams shot from the crystals and merged into a powerful white laser above the statues' heads.

The beam shot straight up through the fire shield and burned through the steel structure. Men in the section above us screamed. Sweetwater shielded his eyes, his mouth agape.

Ben and I slid our chairs back to avoid the dripping molten steel.

"Act like you're frozen in fear," I whispered.

"Act? Sam, I'm terrified." Ben cowered against the bookcase. "Any second now we'll be flooded with seawater."

"Relax, a small hole in the hull won't sink us if the sub surfaces," I whispered.

Water poured through the two-inch hole and gushed onto the laser, where some of it vaporized and turned the room into a sauna. Sweetwater faded into a dark shadow in the hot steam.

A klaxon horn blared, followed by a frantic announcement to hold fast while the sub made an emergency blow. I'd seen the movie, *The Hunt for Red October*, and knew they would pump high-pressure air into the main ballast tanks to force out water and lighten the sub. It was about to shoot out of the water like a missile and splash down.

Ben and I tried to hold onto the bookcase, but the violent maneuver sent us tumbling across the slanted floor. Hot saltwater splashed over us as we braced against the aft wall. We became weightless for an instant. Then the sub crashed into the sea, and we slammed onto the floor.

"Mission accomplished," I whispered into Ben's ear. "That laser is like a giant flare for our Navy. They're sure to spot us now."

"You *knew* this would happen." Sweetwater shouted through the steam. "Turn off that bloody laser or I'll shoot you!"

I grabbed Ben's arm and whispered, "Take your time."

Ben crawled across the slippery floor. "We tried to warn you." He struggled to stand beside the black pyramid in a downpour of hot water and a shroud of steam.

Sweetwater racked the slide on his Walther PPK pistol. "You've got thirty seconds, Professor."

"I'm doing the best I can." Ben wiped his face. "It's wet and slippery, and I can't see clearly in the steam."

"I can see well enough to shoot you. Best hurry."

I waded over to Ben. "If you shoot him, the laser will never stop."

"Then I'll shoot you instead—blow out your right shoulder joint."

"Stop, I'm turning it off." Ben searched for the pyramid-shaped diamonds embedded on one side of the obsidian pyramid as hot water swamped it. A diamond glinted, and he pressed it. The blond statue's crystal popped out of its slot and landed in her hands. Her fingers closed around it as her diadem rotated back to its original position.

The laser stopped. He pressed the other two diamonds as saltwater splashed his face. When all the crystals returned to the goddesses' hands, the brilliant lights extinguished.

As the steam dissipated, Sweetwater lurched forward and pointed his pistol at me.

"If the U.S. Navy finds us, you'll be the first to die." His voice sounded like the snarl of a vicious animal. "Guards, bind their hands and make them sit right here in the water. See to it they don't move." He hit the intercom button. "Captain, seal that hole and take us down!"

USS LAWRENCE LEE

Captain Kingston strode into Blaze's room with a big smile on his tan, chiseled face. Mike and Matt stood at attention.

"At ease, gentlemen. Good news: Our military spotted Sweetwater's submarine on satellite a few minutes ago. I suspect they were forced to surface. A powerful laser is shooting up through the sub's hull, just forward of the sail."

"They must've fired the prototype below decks," Matt said. "How long until they're intercepted?"

"They're headed to a small mountainous island that we believe Sweetwater owns. We're dropping in two platoons of SEALs." Kingston glanced at his watch. "They'll be on station in twenty minutes."

Mike clenched his jaw. "I wish I was going in with them."

Blaze bit her lower lip. "I hope Sam survives this."

"Don't worry, our SEALs will save her," Kingston said.

"Will they recover that laser weapon too?" Blaze asked.

Kingston raised a brow. "That's the plan. Why do you ask?"

"It's supposed to have statues of me and my sisters on it." Her eyes brightened. "I'd like to see it."

"Sorry, that device is top secret." Kingston arched a brow. "In fact, everything you know must be kept secret."

"You can trust me, Captain. I'm a loyal American." Blaze smiled.

Kingston crossed his arms. "Your family's jet crashed in the Himalayas twenty-three years ago."

She nodded. "Yes, on the winter solstice, my first birthday."

He took a stern tone. "The people who raised you are the only family you've ever known, and you expect us to believe you have no loyalty to them?"

"As I grew older, I realized they couldn't be our real family."

"What made you think that?" Mike asked.

"They look nothing like us. The women are seven feet or more, and the men are eight to nine feet. They have harsh, angular faces and lean bodies with long, spindly fingers. And they're cruel."

"Captain, has anyone considered the possibility those so-called Atlanteans might be from another planet?" Matt asked.

Blaze interrupted. "I'm certain they're from Earth. I've read their archives, which date back 200,000 years. They lived on the continent of Atlantis in the Sargasso Sea."

"What happened to them?" Mike asked.

"Over time, earthquakes swallowed most of the continent and left a small portion on the southwestern end."

Captain Kingston asked, "What caused their final demise?"

"A massive tsunami, followed by a volcanic explosion, caused a shift in the tectonic plates, and the island plunged to the bottom of the sea. The only survivors were already aloft in airships." Blaze held a solemn countenance.

"How many people were in the airships and where did they go?" the captain asked.

"The lead airship carrying the royal family, scientists, and dignitaries was the only one that escaped the pyroclastic cloud." She shrugged. "I don't like them, but I'm grateful they survived. Otherwise, no one would've been there to rescue me and my sisters when we were orphaned as infants."

She hesitated. "On another subject, have you received the written document I requested concerning me and my sisters?"

"It's in the works. I should have it signed for you soon."

An officer approached. "Excuse me, Captain, sir, but you asked to be updated about that SEAL mission. They're approaching the target now."

"Thank you, Lieutenant." Captain Kingston hesitated and stared hard at Blaze. "Mike, stay with Blaze. Matt, come with me to CIC."

Matt followed him to the Combat Information Center as the USS *Lawrence Lee* cruised back to the Mediterranean Sea.

THREE

PELAGIC PREDATOR

Shouts and noisy activity filtered down as seawater sloshed around us in Sweetwater's stateroom. He was above decks supervising the frantic rush to repair his submarine.

It took several minutes for the crew to temporarily plug the hole and enable the sub to submerge to a shallow depth and complete the short journey to Sweetwater's facility. I assumed it was underground on an island, similar to his sub base in the North Sea, where I'd been held prisoner with two Scottish children.

I guessed another fifteen or twenty minutes had elapsed when a jolt shook the floor—probably the submarine bumping against a dock. I prayed our Navy was closing in.

The stocky man who had treated me like a sack of grain waded toward me in the one-foot-deep water.

"Get up." He yanked on my zip-tied hands and pulled me up.

Another guard did the same to Ben. They shoved us ahead along dark passageways and up ladder-like steps to an open hatch. We climbed through it and stepped onto the broad outside deck.

I was right about the underground harbor. Flashlights and lanterns provided the only light in the dark chamber. Their electrical power was out. Good sign. Maybe our military had destroyed their power grid and were about to ambush Sweetwater's men.

"What the bloody hell do I pay you for? Get those generators back online!" Sweetwater roared at a man in a black uniform. "We need power to repair my submarine. Hop to it."

Our guards pulled us onto the pier, and another man carried the Atlantean prototype off the boat.

We had walked about fifty feet from the sub when screams erupted from below decks. Our guards stopped, and we glanced back.

Water around the sub began to boil, and steam billowed from the open hatch. A storm of short blue-white lightning bolts, like the ones I'd seen in Wewelsburg, danced across the hull as the stench of burning flesh fouled the air.

Sweetwater's men were so focused on his submarine, none noticed a small sub breaching the surface in the shadows on the far side. I spotted it because I was expecting our Navy. The submarine was about sixty feet long, big enough for a platoon of SEALs.

After a few minutes, the water around Sweetwater's sub stopped boiling, and the electrical storm on the deck ceased.

"Board my sub and find out what the bloody hell happened." Sweetwater gestured to a few men milling around. "You three, remain with the prisoners." He pointed at our guards and the man with the prototype.

Four men jumped onto the deck and screamed. Their boots and feet melted into the scorching metal, and they fell to the deck. Their clothes caught fire amidst their shrill screams. In seconds, flames engulfed their bodies.

I turned my head away from the carnage and looked at Sweetwater. He stood frozen with dropped jaw and wide-eyes, staring at the horrific scene.

I glanced at our armed guards. Laser dots covered their torsos.

"Ben, hit the deck!" I dived prone at our guards' feet.

He must've seen the lasers too because he didn't hesitate.

The guards were slower to react and fell dead beside us, blood oozing from multiple bullet wounds.

I glanced up and caught Sweetwater diving into the inky water. He never surfaced.

The only man left standing was the one near me holding the prototype in front of his body like a shield.

Distant shadows fired automatic weapons from their deck as the small submarine crept closer to the dock. I prayed they were with the U.S. Navy as I cowered on the pier and gulped air in fast spurts.

"Place the artifact on the pier and put your hands on your head. Now!" a deep, German-accented voice said.

The man complied, but they peppered him with bullets the instant he set the prototype on the dock. He crumpled into a heap beside me, his warm blood splashing my neck and cheek.

Oh God, Germans aren't in the U.S. Navy. They sounded like the Black Sun. How could that be? A joint raid by German GSG-9, Navy SEALs, and the British SAS killed all of them in Wewelsburg.

I gazed over my shoulder as their submarine docked behind Sweetwater's burned-out hull.

In seconds, black-booted soldiers surrounded me. Strong hands pulled me to my feet and shoved me to a tall, slender man with spiked platinum hair.

"Bring me the artifact," he commanded.

A soldier held the prototype between me and the leader.

"Touch one of the crystals," spiked hair said.

I obeyed, and bright light filled a crystal pyramid.

"Good, you are indeed the Golden Twin. Our Supreme Master is eager to meet you. I am Captain Hess."

A scary-looking guy with dark, beady eyes and a long, narrow nose stepped forward. "I am Second Master of the Black Sun. First Master was killed in Wewelsburg."

Goosebumps erupted on my skin as I recalled my nightmarish torture at the hands of the Black Sun Master in Wewelsburg Castle. I trembled despite my determination to remain calm.

Second Master curled his lips in a sinister grin. "Once you're secure aboard *Seeschlange*, you will tell me everything that happened in the Generals' Chamber at Wewelsburg. We'll have plenty of time for all the details. It's a long voyage." He nodded at the captain.

"Take her and the professor below," Captain Hess said to two of his men.

Faint sounds of distant gunfire filtered down as I descended the ladder-like steps.

Within minutes, we submerged and vanished silently into the vast Atlantic Ocean.

Yep, destiny is a bitch.

USS LAWRENCE LEE

Matt entered Blaze's hospital room with a clenched jaw and hard eyes.

Mike stood. "What's wrong?"

Matt hesitated and glared at Blaze. He turned to his brother. "The SEALs found Sweetwater's submarine in an underground base on his island north of the Dominican Republic."

"Good, did they rescue Sam and Ben?" Mike asked.

"They weren't there. Neither was the prototype." Matt faced Blaze. "But everyone on the submarine was killed the same way as the Black Sun members in the Generals' Chamber. They found their charred corpses welded into melted steel." He glared. "Well, Blaze, what do you have to say about that?"

Her jaw dropped. "Surely you don't think *I* had anything to do with it? I was with Mike the entire time, and I didn't know where they were."

"You and your sisters are the only ones capable. The Black Sun Master died in Wewelsburg with all his followers." Matt studied her reaction.

"How could you even think such a thing? My sisters and I saved Sam at Wewelsburg Castle. We're not your enemy." Tears ran down her cheeks. "Apparently, all the Black Sun members weren't killed. They must have another base." She crossed her arms and pursed her lips.

"She might be right." Mike faced his brother. "We assumed Wewelsburg was their only base. Could be they have another, maybe in South America. A lot of Nazis went there after World War II." He glanced at Blaze and back to Matt. "And Sweetwater? Is he missing too?"

"The men who weren't on his sub were found dead on the dock with multiple bullet wounds. No trace of Sweetwater, Sam, Ben, or the prototype. The SEALs found a tunnel under the dock that led to the opposite side of the island. Nothing but empty docks there. And the island's entire power grid was fried."

Mike shook his head. "Any boats, seaplanes, or helicopters leave the island right before the SEALs arrived?"

Matt shook his head. "Nothing on the surface or in the air."

"Well then, the answer is obvious." Blaze leaned forward. "Your sister and the professor were taken in another submarine. It's the only possible explanation, unless she knows how to command orcas."

"You'd better hope we can convince Captain Kingston you're right about the submarine." Matt shook his head. "So far, you're the main suspect."

Her eyes filled with tears again.

"Don't cry, we'll figure this out and clear your name," Mike said.

"I'm innocent, I swear."

"Maybe, but it would help if you contact your sisters and locate Sam. Our military will protect you from the Atlanteans. Besides, they're hiding in the Himalayas, far away from here." Matt patted her shoulder.

"All right, I'll risk it to convince you I'm innocent." She wiped her eyes. "And after we rescue *your* sister, I expect your military to rescue mine."

"Agreed," Mike said.

"Our government will want to find that enclave and bring your sisters home to America. Count on it," Matt said.

"I'll believe that when I receive their written promise." Blaze sat cross-legged on the bed and closed her eyes. "I'll need absolute silence and no interruptions."

They waited. After twenty minutes, she opened her eyes.

A smile. "We made contact with Sam. She's in a submarine called *Seeschlange* operated by the Black Sun. She said it's small, about sixty feet. They told her it's a long voyage to their destination where the Supreme Master is eager to meet her." Blaze straightened her long legs.

"*Seeschlange?*" Mike asked.

"It means sea snake in German."

"Where are they taking her?" Matt asked.

Blaze shrugged. "She doesn't know."

"Is Ben with her? Did they take the prototype?" Mike asked in rapid fire.

"He's with her, and they have the device. They made her touch one of the crystals to verify she's the Golden Twin."

"What's the Golden Twin?" Mike arched his eyebrow.

"It was foretold in an ancient prophecy. She's a non-relative who looks identical to my blond triplet, Solraya, and who carries a unique electromagnetic frequency. Your sister's touch activates the device."

"What does the prophecy say about Sam?" Mike asked.

"The Golden Twin is the key to Poseidon's Sword." Blaze touched Mike's arm. "Your sister is the Golden Twin. That's why the Black Sun wants her."

"Blaze, why did you break the telepathic connection?" Matt crossed his arms. "We had questions for her."

"I didn't break it. She did. Right before she went silent, she explained a Black Sun Master on board might render her unconscious if he sensed us talking." She bit her lip. "Then we won't be able to help her."

"So Black Sun Masters are telepathic and can intercept her conversations with you and your sisters?"

"No, but anyone who can mentally control Vril can detect all types of energy, including telepathic energy."

Captain Kingston arrived at the door with two master-at-arms guards. "You're in a lot of trouble, Miss Conor. Now would be a good time to come clean."

The brothers stepped in front of Blaze.

"We know what happened to my sister, sir," Mike said. "Blaze is innocent."

The captain crossed his arms. "All right, Lieutenant, let's hear it."

Mike briefed the captain on everything.

"Could be true, but there's no way to verify her story until we find your sister. Blaze might just be telling us what we want to hear," the captain said.

"I understand why you might think that, Captain," Blaze said. "I'll prove my innocence by assisting you in rescuing Sam and the professor and recovering the device. When Sam contacts me, I'll report it right away, but I want that document you promised me."

"All right, I'll work on expediting your paperwork, and I'll suggest sending assets south near the eastern coast of South America. The guards will remain outside your door." Captain Kingston turned to the twin lieutenants. "Take turns staying with her and keep me informed."

SEESCHLANGE

Ben and I were thrust into a dark cell in the bowels of the sub where the triplets contacted me telepathically. I was stunned to learn Blaze was on board the USS *Lawrence Lee* with my brothers.

"Ben," I whispered into his ear, "I just talked to the triplets through telepathy. The Navy knows we're in this submarine. They're looking for us."

He nodded and collapsed on the bottom bunk, looking exhausted but relieved.

I settled on the top bunk and stared at the ceiling while trying to devise a way for the Navy to rescue us without putting their sailors at risk from the murderous Black Sun Master. If the triplets overpowered him with their combined abilities, Ben and I would probably die too. A small metal submarine submerged in salt water was an excellent conductor.

In Wewelsburg, I was inside a tower in a huge stone castle, chained to the marble floor in the circular Generals' Chamber. I was safe in the center while the triplets scorched my adversaries along the perimeter. Our safety in this tin can was doubtful.

On the other hand, if we waited until we arrived at our destination, we'd have to deal with the Supreme Master, who might have as much or more power than the triplets over Earth's electromagnetic energy. What to do?

Too bad destiny couldn't speak. Last October, gold tridents had guided me down perilous paths of discovery I thought would lead to my ultimate destiny.

Where are my pathfinders now? How will I escape a suffocating hell in this cramped, cave-like submarine?

I had to rely on brief telepathic reports from the triplets to help me keep track of time. We were fed twice a day, approximately every twelve hours it seemed.

Several days passed without the dreaded visit from Second Master. I was beginning to think he'd forgotten about his threat.

The door lock rattled. So much for wishful thinking. I looked down from my top bunk as Second Master entered our cell. His cold, lizard-black eyes swept over me. *Oh God.*

His power absolute, he had no need for guards to accompany us.

"Golden Twin, come with me. Time for a nice, long chat." His voice hissed on "nice." He offered his hand.

I recoiled, not wanting to touch him. Chilly goose bumps erupted across my skin as I dropped off the bunk.

"Ah, you fear me, as well you should, especially if you're planning to lie. Tell the truth and we'll get along fine. Defy me and learn the true meaning of pain." He held the cell door. "Come."

My eyes the size of saucers, I glanced at Ben. I trailed Second Master to a spartan stateroom festooned with swastikas. He shoved me into a chair and settled behind a metal desk bolted to the floor. The small obsidian prototype of Poseidon's Sword rested on the desktop, the blond statue's face mocking me as she held the only glowing crystal.

"Tell me, what happened at Wewelsburg Castle?" He curled his lips in a humorless grin, exposing yellow tobacco-stained teeth.

I didn't want him to know the triplets' role because he'd block them from helping me again. But I didn't relish being tortured either. I'd have to be a convincing liar.

I started with the truth, intending to ease into the lies. "First, I was taken to the underground chamber in the tower where Master tortured me with Vril. He demanded I contact the triplets and convince them to disclose the location of the remnant from Atlantis."

"You called them telepathically?"

"I tried, but I couldn't make contact from underground," I lied.

"And then?"

"He blew out my ear drums—took two months for them to heal. The pain was excruciating." All true.

"That's nothing compared to what I'll do if you lie to me." Second Master stroked the Atlantean prototype. "What happened next?"

"I suggested he take me up higher in the tower where telepathic communication might be easier." A lie. Actually, I tricked him so the military could pick up the GPS signal from my DARPA watch above ground.

"He took you to the Generals' Chamber?"

"Yes, he chained me over the black sun in the floor and ordered me to contact the triplets. I'd never done it before and didn't know if I could, but he didn't believe me." More truth.

"Did you succeed?"

"No. He became impatient and tortured me again. It felt like I was being electrocuted from the inside out. The pain was unbearable, and I blacked out." All true, except I did contact the triplets, and I never blacked out.

"And when you awakened?"

"All the Black Sun men in the room, including Master, were dead."

"Who killed them?"

"How would I know? I was unconscious." *I hope he can't tell I'm lying.* "I later discovered Navy SEALs and British SAS soldiers had joined the German GSG-9 unit in a fierce battle with your people. Afterward, they unchained me and took me to the military air base in Frankfurt where I received medical attention." That part was true.

"But you must've seen the dead. How were they killed? Bullets? Explosives? I don't understand how they defeated a Black Sun Master." He raised an eyebrow, his tone suspicious.

"When I woke up, I felt dizzy and disoriented. I was in a lot of pain and could barely hear the soldiers. Dark shadows obscured the bodies of your men as I was carried out, and frankly, I didn't care what had happened. I assumed they'd been shot, but I don't really know." Another lie.

"Did you see what I did to Sweetwater's submarine?" He smiled.

"Yes, it was terrifying." I trembled.

"Then surely you understand my skepticism that your soldiers defeated our Master."

I licked my lips. "Is it possible he was so focused on torturing me that he didn't notice the soldiers' stealth attack?" I prayed my suggestion was plausible.

"Perhaps, but I doubt it. I think you're lying."

"I vividly recall the excruciating pain from the torture. I'd do anything to avoid *that* again. Please believe me. No way would I lie to you." I locked onto his cold gaze.

"There's only one way for me to be certain." He ran his tongue over his thin lips, like a lizard swallowing a spider. "I do hope you weren't planning to have children."

His dark reptilian eyes blazed, stoked by the fires of Hell, as he caressed the crystals held by the statues.

I glanced around the small stateroom—no weapons.

He studied the lit crystal. "Too bad *my* touch doesn't activate it. Torture is more exhilarating when I have the option to terminate the subject." He smiled. "And don't expect to avoid pain by passing out. I know how to keep my subjects conscious."

I suspected he'd torture me no matter what I told him. What a sick creep.

"If I tell you everything, you'll still torture me, so why should I cooperate?"

"Ah, Golden Twin, you *are* perceptive. Alas, the Supreme Master has big plans for you and wants you as undamaged as possible. That's why I'll give you one last chance. I doubt your Scottish lover will want a barren wife." His thin lips curled into a snarl. "Now tell me what really happened."

A crewman burst in and bowed. "Sir, you're urgently needed in the conn. An enemy submarine is stalking us."

Second Master jumped up. "Guard her until I return."

This could be my only chance to save myself and Ben. The crew was unaware of my expertise in tae kwon do.

"May I use the head while we wait?" I struggled to my feet, feigning weakness.

The guard hesitated and glanced out the door, giving me a second to deliver a hard kick under his chin. His head snapped backward into the metal doorframe. Dazed, he stumbled forward, and I thrust the heel of my hand into the underside of his nose and broke it. Then I slammed his head against the metal frame, knocking him out before dragging him behind the desk.

I had to act fast, so I activated the prototype's crystals and secured two of them in their slots. I'd wait until I found the control room before inserting the third crystal to fire the laser.

Second Master had turned right when he left, so I crept in that direction.

The glow of instrument lights beckoned me to the conn. I crouched in the open doorway and scanned the control room.

My primary target stood facing away beside the retracted periscope. His head was bowed in concentration.

Worried he would sense me behind him, I twisted the diadem on the third statue and almost dropped the crystal before locking it in. I stood and fired the weapon into Second Master's back.

His clothing burst into flames as the laser burned through him and two crewmembers. It left a two-inch diameter hole in the aft hull. I angled the laser upward and burned another small hole in the upper hull. Water gushed in and sprayed the room with seawater. I fell backward against the bulkhead.

"Captain Hess, order an emergency blow or I'll kill everyone!" As I spoke, the laser turned some of the water to steam and added to the chaos.

The captain turned to his XO. "Sound the alarm and execute the blow."

A klaxon horn blared as the executive officer announced, "Emergency blow!" over the speakers.

I braced against a corner and clutched the prototype in a death grip as the submarine shot up to the surface like it had been fired from a cannon, momentarily becoming airborne. My feet left the deck as the boat hung weightless for a millisecond.

When we slammed down, the weapon slipped from my hands as I pitched forward onto the floor. Water swirled around me as I struggled to grab it.

Captain Hess lunged at me through the mist.

I snatched up the weapon and angled the laser toward his head. The result will haunt me forever.

The crew in the small control room watched the top of their captain's head explode and his eyeballs dangle from nerve cords. They rushed me. I cut them into pieces with the laser and sliced narrow openings in the hull.

The stench of burned flesh fouled the air as seawater imploded from every direction. Nausea gripped my gut.

All the crew in the conn were dead, but I had no time to agonize over the carnage.

I sloshed through the turbulent water to Second Master's charred body, felt inside his pockets, and retrieved the key to our cell. I had to free Ben before we sank. Carrying the weapon would slow me down, so I took a chance and positioned it on the electronic map table with the laser shooting up through the hull like a flare.

I noted the course line on the map table: a base in the Antarctic under the Ronne Ice Shelf in the Weddell Sea.

Water churned around my hips as I slogged up the passage to Ben's cell.

I gripped the cell key. "Don't worry, I'll get you out of here." I unlocked the iron door and pulled it open.

"Watch out!" he yelled as a guard lunged from behind and slammed my forehead into the bars.

Dizzy, I lost focus, and my knees buckled. I collapsed into the water.

A heavy boot stomped on my back and held me down. Just when I couldn't hold my breath another second, the boot lifted. I gasped for air and stood. Ben was fighting the guard.

The men traded punches as I slipped beside the guard and rammed the cell key into his carotid artery. He sank to his knees, blood gushing from the fatal wound.

The boat slanted aft toward the flooding control room, and I worried the laser weapon would slide off the chart table.

"Hurry, we don't have much time." I swam through the rising water.

Ben sliced through the water behind me, kicking hard.

I barely managed to catch the device as it slid to the edge.

"Quick, deactivate this while I hold it," I said.

His fingers slipped on the wet obsidian as he felt for the diamond pyramids embedded in the side of the device. He struggled to lock the crystals into the statues' hands. Seconds ticked by while he secured the weapon.

Water lapped at my chin. "Let's get the hell out of here. The hatch is that way, and everyone else is dead." I clutched the prototype and led him to the ladder as the water engulfed us.

We rushed up onto the slanted outside deck with no time to locate life vests. I expected to see a big U.S. submarine waiting to take us aboard.

The sea was empty.

Oh God! Had Second Master killed all the Americans and sunk their nuclear sub?

"We have to survive until help arrives. I'm so sorry I got you into this mess, Ben."

"This isn't your fault. Besides, you know how I love ancient puzzles." He offered a brave smile.

"Help me hold the prototype." I faced him and braced my legs.

Water engulfed the deck as he turned to me. "No worries. I was on the swim team during my undergraduate years at Harvard. I stay fit in the university pool." He grabbed one side of the artifact. "Were you able to send a Mayday?"

"No, but I can call the triplets telepathically. They'll save us."

"Hurry, it'll be dark soon."

Treading water, I concentrated on making contact as the submarine slowly slipped into the South Atlantic. Our legs pumped hard as we held the heavy little pyramid between us.

We struggled to save the artifact as I desperately called the triplets telepathically.

The cold ocean sapped my strength. Was it my destiny to drown holding an obsidian anchor?

After ten minutes, I gasped and broke my concentration. "It's no good, we're exhausting ourselves." I looked into his anxious eyes. "We have to let it go."

"No!" He coughed up water and slipped under for a second. "Damn it, activate the laser so our military can find it if we drop it."

"The current might move it so that it'll cut us to pieces on its way down." I sputtered as a wave splashed my mouth.

"We'll probably drown anyway, but maybe the world won't lose an important artifact." He looked determined.

"No, we'll survive. Keep your lungs filled with air."

He slipped under and came up gasping as he clutched his side of the prototype. "Damn it all, I'm just too old for this. Activate the crystals."

As my touch lighted the first crystal, an orca surfaced between us under the artifact and seized it in its massive jaws. The killer whale dove beneath the waves, and the brilliant glow of the crystal vanished into the depths.

"Whoa, I sure didn't expect *that* to happen! I hope his buddies aren't hungry. Drowning may be the least of our worries." I treaded water with my last bit of strength.

"Oh God, they're circling us." He pointed at black fins slicing through the water. "You'd better make contact with somebody quick before we become their next meal!"

I closed my eyes and tried to block my fear as I concentrated on connecting with Blaze. I gambled I'd have better luck summoning one triplet as I mentally broadcasted what I'd done to the Black Sun Master and his submarine. Ominous silence filled my head.

I felt a monstrous killer whale beneath me and braced for the crush of his sharp teeth and powerful jaws. Instead, it lifted me onto its back as another one did the same with Ben. We held onto their dorsal fins.

Blaze's voice blasted inside my head. *"Stay with the orcas. Help is on the way."*

"What happened to the U.S. submarine?" I asked telepathically.

"Your Navy located the small submarine you were in, which was a relief because they were beginning to doubt me. Then the Black Sun Master used Vril to attack the nuclear sub."

"Oh no, did he kill them?"

"The U.S. sub is disabled on the surface about five miles from you. You saved the sailors' lives when you killed the Black Sun Master."

"Are they sending a boat to pick us up?"

"No, a British ship from the Falklands is speeding to your location. Sorry I didn't answer you at first. I was busy relaying information to Captain Kingston so he could arrange your rescue."

I rested my head on the orca's broad back. *"Thank you, Blaze, I've never been so happy to hear a voice in my head."*

Blaze's sisters, Solraya and Luna, joined us. *"Hey, we helped too. We sent the orcas to save you and the professor while Blaze worked with the Navy."*

"Thanks, we couldn't have survived without everyone's help."

"Is the device safe?" Blaze asked.

"We were about to drop it when an orca grabbed it."

"And now?"

"A killer whale dove with it, and I'm not sure where it went."

"Luna was in command of the orca with the device, right Luna?" Solraya said.

"I thought Solraya was doing that," Luna said.

"Well, I hope you two didn't lose it because the Navy will blame me," Blaze said.

"Command the orca to give me the device," I said.

"It's not responding," Blaze said. *"I can't locate it."*

I glanced at Ben. "I'm talking telepathically with the triplets. They said a ship is coming for us, and they aren't sure what happened to the artifact."

I saw the faint outline of a ship's bow materializing on the horizon. "I see a ship." I pointed.

"I hope the orcas will allow the crew to rescue us." He shivered. "I'd hate to be in the grip of those long, sharp teeth."

"Looks like destiny may have something else planned for us."

USS LAWRENCE LEE

Matt's cell chimed, and he glanced at the screen. Loren Starr, his famous romance novelist mother, was calling.

"Hi, Mom, what's up?"

"What in hell's going on? I just had a vision of my precious daughter desperately treading water with Professor Armitage. And killer whales surrounded them!" Panic shot her voice up an octave.

Dammit, Mom had another vision at the worst possible moment. Matt glanced at Captain Kingston.

"Mom, you can't tell *anyone* about this, especially Ross. Sam and Ben are okay. A ship brought them aboard a few minutes ago. That's all I can say right now, and if you repeat any of this, Mike and I will end up serving time in Fort Leavenworth. Seriously! I love you, and I'll call back when I'm allowed to talk about this." Matt hit END and gave his twin a worried look.

Kingston glared at Matt. "Lieutenant Starr, explain what just happened."

Matt rubbed his golden-blond buzz cut. "Captain, sir, I can't help the fact that my mother has visions. It runs on the female side of our family." He glanced at Mike. "She saw Sam in the water with Professor Armitage and the killer whales, so she called me in a panic. I had to tell her Sam's okay or she would've run to Ross and asked the Brits to save her. You heard what I told her."

"Can we count on her discretion?"

"The thought of us rotting in jail will keep her quiet." Matt met his gaze. "Of course, the Brits know about Sam now anyway."

"True, but the kidnapping hasn't been made public." Kingston clenched his jaw.

Mike joined in. "No worries there. Mom would never knowingly jeopardize our Navy careers. She'll keep silent now that she knows her daughter is safe."

"Which brings me to our next problem." Kingston turned his attention to Blaze. "The Brits sent two ships from their Falkland Islands—a big one to rescue the U.S. sub and tow it to port and a small, fast one to rescue Sam and the professor."

Blaze's eyes widened. "If the Atlanteans learn powerful nations know the truth about their enclave, they might feel forced to fire Poseidon's Sword ahead of schedule and kill millions of people."

"You're quite perceptive, Miss Conor." He shook his head. "The Brits wasted no time putting Sam and Professor Armitage on a jet bound for Great Britain. We're in negotiations with their prime minister as we speak, but we need leverage to secure their return and the Brits' silence. Can you connect with her again?"

"If she's awake. What should I tell her?"

"Say we're trying to keep this entire incident secret to avoid the embarrassment of the press learning the U.S. military lost her twice. Don't mention the Atlanteans. We'd also like her and the professor returned to us."

"What incentive are we offering the Brits?" Blaze arched her brow.

"A chance to interview you. Tell Sam you'd like to meet with her, her mother, and Professor Armitage at MacLeod Castle, and you'll allow two MI6 agents to join you and ask questions. Explain to her we want everyone to reveal as little as possible while appearing to cooperate."

"I'd love to meet Sam and her mother." Blaze beamed.

Matt interrupted. "You should give Sam an incentive as well. She wasn't happy about being taken from her boyfriend and forced back to the States."

The captain crossed his arms. "What do you suggest?"

"Include Captain Ross Sinclair in the meeting and give them a couple of days together before she has to return to the States." Matt grinned. "That should seal the deal."

Kingston nodded at Blaze. "Include that and let me know what she says."

"All right, but how will she explain suddenly knowing this?"

"She'll have to admit she connects with you telepathically, but tell her not to mention your sisters."

"Okay, give me a few minutes." She hesitated. "Just a reminder, I won't meet with them until I have the document guaranteeing citizenship for me and my sisters, including the other stipulations I requested."

Kingston nodded. "Understood. You'll have the document before you leave my ship."

East Falkland

Minutes after the crew pulled Ben and I out of the ocean, they wrapped us in blankets and strapped us into seats on a Lynx helicopter. The chopper lifted off from the helipad on the aft end of the ship and raced to East Falkland as the sun set behind us.

At RAF Mount Pleasant Airport, a British officer allotted us fifteen minutes for hot showers and dressing in the dry clothes provided. Four heavily armed Special Air Service soldiers escorted us to a Gulfstream G650ER jet and boarded with us. A man in a suit, probably a MI6 secret agent, waited on board.

He stood. "Welcome aboard, Sir Lady Samantha, Professor Armitage. I'm Trevor Chambers, here on behalf of the United Kingdom." He extended his hand.

"I sincerely appreciate the title bestowed by your queen, but there's no need for formalities here." I gave him my best smile as I took his hand. "I'd like to thank you and your country for saving me, yet again."

"I'm grateful for our rescue too," Ben said as he pumped his hand. "Please convey my gratitude to your superiors."

"It'll be my pleasure, and rest assured you're safe now. Her Majesty's Special Forces will protect you." He nodded at the soldiers. "We made the mistake of entrusting Sir Lady Samantha to the American military. I doubt we'll be doing *that* again. Our prime minister will guarantee her safety now."

"That's fine by me. I know I can always count on the SAS." *Especially my hot Highlander.* I beamed at the soldiers.

Trevor gestured to comfortable-looking leather seats. "Please be seated and we'll get underway."

Ben and I settled in as the aircraft began taxiing. Minutes after we secured our seatbelts, our sleek executive jet roared down the runway. We soared into the night sky and headed for Great Britain.

I closed my eyes and thought about recent events, starting about ten days ago when Nicolai kidnapped me from Orlando with Charlie and Emily. Ross rescued us from Sweetwater's island in the Orkneys, and then Delta Force soldiers swooped in and flew me to Dover. Two kidnappings and another rescue later, I was headed back to Great Britain.

The crazy timeline made me dizzy, like I was a silver ball bouncing around in a pinball machine. My brain felt as fatigued as the rest of me. I craved sleep, but it was obvious Trevor intended to interrogate me. I was a loyal American, but I owed a huge debt to the UK. I had to figure out how to keep both countries happy.

"As you might imagine, Sir Lady Samantha, I have many questions." Trevor's eyes gleamed with anticipation.

"And I'll tell you everything, but I need something to eat and drink first." I glanced at Ben. "We both do, actually."

"Of course, forgive me. We'll have plenty of time to talk. Even with favorable winds, it'll be about a fifteen-hour flight in this extended-range Gulfstream."

"Lucky for us we're in the only private jet that can fly that far non-stop." I smiled.

"Your meals are almost ready. Our steward has steak Diane with new potatoes and baby asparagus for you." He signaled the steward. "Would you like a fine red wine with your meal?"

A big smile. "Trevor, it's like you read my mind."

"Oh yes, that would go a long way to soothing my shattered nerves," Ben said.

In moments, linen-covered tray tables were installed in front of us, and our meals were served. The best part? The vintage bottle of full-bodied Chateauneuf du Pape. A glass of blended red wine had never tasted better. I sighed with contentment as the delicate flavor of spices and berries lingered on my tongue.

As I savored the meal, Blaze's voice blasted into my head. *"Sam, your government wants to make a deal with the UK. They want you and the professor back and the whole embarrassing episode kept secret. In return, they'll allow me to meet with you, your mother, the professor, Ross, and two men from MI6 at MacLeod Castle. We're supposed to seem cooperative, but tell them as little as possible, and don't mention the Black Sun."*

I answered, *"I'd love to meet you, and please ask Mike to escort you. I haven't seen him in a while. I'd also like some time with Ross."* I closed my eyes and enjoyed the smooth ruby wine.

"Good, I'd like spending more time with Mike, and they already agreed to give you and Ross two days alone together."

"How am I supposed to explain how I know about this deal?"

"You're allowed to tell them we communicate telepathically, but don't tell them you connect with my sisters too."

"There's a man on this airplane, Trevor Chambers, who I suspect is a spy in the British Secret Services. I'll run this by him. He'll probably have to call his superiors

before he can give me an answer. Contact me again in thirty minutes. I doubt I'll be able to stay awake much longer than that."

"All right. I'll tell Captain Kingston what you said."

I patted my lips with the linen napkin and turned to Trevor. "Brace yourself. This may sound crazy, but I just had a telepathic conversation with a woman named Blaze. She's the red-haired triplet whose statue is on the Atlantean prototype—the woman labeled the fire goddess."

That got his attention. He froze with his fork halfway to his mouth.

I love the Brits. Usually, they have excellent command of their emotions and facial expressions, but I had managed to disarm him.

He set his fork on the plate, dabbed his lips with a napkin, and sat back. "I beg your pardon, Sir Lady Samantha? Did you just say you had a telepathic chat with the Goddess of Fire?"

"Yes, Blaze is on board the USS *Lawrence Lee* with my brothers—I think in the Mediterranean Sea. She told me America wants to offer the UK a deal that includes interviewing her at MacLeod Castle." I gave him the particulars. "Blaze will contact me in thirty minutes for an answer."

His eyes gleaming, Trevor couldn't hide his excitement. "Excuse me while I make a call. There's an encrypted satellite phone in the cockpit." He hurried forward.

"Sam, did our government really ask Blaze to contact you?" Ben raised his eyebrows.

"Yep, the Brits hold all the cards, so the U.S. government had to offer an incentive for their cooperation. Our president wants to avoid the public humiliation of losing me twice in one week. And, of course, he also wants the WMD."

"Can't say I blame him for not wanting to look incompetent in the world's eyes, but I imagine the UK wants that weapon too."

"Let them sort it out. We get to meet Blaze, and we'll see Mom and Mike, and you'll meet Mom's boyfriend and my hot Highlander." I drained the last drop, and the steward refilled my glass. "Chateauneuf du Pape is exactly what I needed."

"I'm assuming they'll agree to the deal." Ben shrugged. "I can't imagine why they wouldn't."

I swallowed the final delicious bite of my steak as Trevor exited the cockpit door.

"Fingers crossed, Ben. Trevor's on his way back now." I glanced up at him.

Trevor settled in his seat and tried to keep a poker face, but I saw the smile in his eyes.

"On behalf of the UK, I've been instructed to accept your government's offer. We're diverting to Edinburgh. A helicopter will take us from the airport to MacLeod Castle where Laird MacLeod, your mother, and Captain Sinclair will be waiting for us."

"Wonderful! When Blaze contacts me, I'll ask her how soon she can be there." I raised my wine glass and lightly clinked it against Trevor's.

It wasn't long before Blaze's voice invaded my head again. *"Have they reached a decision?"*

"They agreed to everything. We're scheduled to land in Edinburgh about fourteen hours from now. Then it'll be an hour flight in the helicopter to Mom's boyfriend's castle. Tell Captain Kingston and ask him when you and Mike will arrive."

She answered a few minutes later. *"We'll land in Edinburgh the same time as you, and we'll fly to the castle together. I can't wait to finally meet you."*

I shared the news with Trevor.

Maybe chasing my destiny wasn't so bad after all.

I reclined my seat, closed my eyes, and fell into a deep sleep.

FOUR

Edinburgh

My breath formed brief puffs of mist in the chilly winter air as I waited on the tarmac for the military Gulfstream to lower its airstairs on the general aviation side of the airport.

Mike and Blaze disembarked. Moments later, I stood face-to-face with my destiny. We stared at each other, speechless. It was like looking in a mirror after I'd dyed my hair red and wore green contact lenses. Our size and facial structure was identical, and our hair was even the same length, except mine was golden blond. I felt like I'd found a long-lost sister.

Ben and Trevor hung back while Mike introduced me to Blaze.

"Sam, it's wonderful to finally meet you." She grinned and hugged me.

"It's great to meet you too." The warmth of her body reassured me she was indeed real. "I've seen your statues and your image on walls, but seeing you in person proves just how much we look alike. I'm amazed."

"And you look exactly like my blond triplet, Solraya." Blaze shook her head. "No wonder the Black Sun recognized you as the Golden Twin."

"Did you enjoy the flight?" I nodded in the direction of the military jet.

"Oh yes, the jet was much faster and quieter than the small cargo plane that flew me to the Arabian Sea." She grinned. "I loved it."

"And soon you'll experience a helicopter." Mike pointed at the Super Lynx. "It's a lot noisier, but the view is great."

He stepped forward and gave me a quick squeeze.

"Mike, I've missed you."

"I've missed you too, Sis." He arched a brow. "But what've you been doing, auditioning for a spot on my SEAL team?"

"What do you mean?" I tilted my head, searching his eyes.

"Lately, you've seen more combat than I have. What's up with that?" He crossed his muscular arms and grinned, always teasing.

"Not my choice, brother dear." I smiled at Blaze. "I'm lucky she was able to save us."

Trevor cleared his throat. "Excuse me, on behalf of the United Kingdom and Her Majesty, I'd like to welcome Miss Conor to Great Britain. Trevor Chambers, at your service." He kissed Blaze's hand.

"And this is Professor Ben Armitage." I pulled him forward.

"Miss Conor, I'm pleased to meet you, and I hope I'll have the chance to meet your sisters someday soon." Ben extended his hand.

"Thank you for helping Sam with the Atlantean device. You must be quite clever." Blaze smiled and squeezed his hand.

A British military officer approached. "Excuse me, but we only found luggage for Lieutenant Starr, Mr. Chambers, and the SAS team."

"That's because the women and Professor Armitage were fished out of the sea," Mike said. "What you see is all they have."

The officer scanned the group. "Very well then, the helicopter is ready to depart. You may board now. The SAS team will follow in a separate helicopter."

I strapped in, eager to see my mother, Duncan, and Ross at Macleod Castle. Soon we were skirting the eastern coast of Scotland.

About an hour later, I spotted Duncan's castle perched on a cliff overlooking the North Sea. We circled over the small village of Craigervie and settled on the lawn near the castle's front entrance.

My heart hammered my chest when I spied Ross jogging across the grass toward us as the blades wound down. His thick black hair swirled in the downwash. Seconds later, I was in his arms. The noise and nearby people faded as his lips burned into mine.

"All right you two, dial it down a click," Mike said with a chuckle. "Mom wants a hug." He tapped Ross's shoulder.

"Ah, young love—she's been gone ten days and look at them." Mom threw her arms open wide. "My turn."

After we embraced, she scanned me for new injuries as the helicopter carrying the SAS soldiers landed nearby.

"It's a bit noisy out here." Mom's boyfriend, Duncan, herded everyone toward his castle as the rotor wash swirled around us. "We'll make the introductions inside."

Duncan's butler, Baxter, wore his usual formal attire as he held the massive oak door for us. We entered the stately foyer where the polished stone floor reflected iron chandeliers hanging three stories overhead.

"This way, please." Duncan led us into the great hall, which was larger than a grand ballroom with a high cathedral ceiling braced with sturdy wood beams. Massive granite hearths at both ends of the long room blazed with crackling fires and helped the heavy iron chandeliers bathe the cavernous hall in golden light.

A twenty-foot Christmas tree covered with decorations and tiny white lights glittered in one corner. Centuries-old portraits of Duncan's ancestors lined the walls, and a hand-carved oak table that seated forty-four dominated the floor's centerline.

"Welcome to MacLeod Castle." He bowed. "I'm Laird Duncan MacLeod, and this castle has been in my family for hundreds of years, but don't worry, it has modern plumbing and heating." His eyes twinkled.

I took Blaze's hand and stepped forward. "This is Richard and Sheila Conor's daughter, Blaze." I turned to her. "Blaze, this is my mother, Loren Starr. She writes medieval romance novels set in the Scottish Highlands, and Duncan looks like the chieftain on the cover of her last book." I smirked.

Mom's jaw dropped as she gaped at Blaze.

Duncan broke the awkward moment by kissing Blaze's hand. "It's a pleasure to meet you, lassie."

"Thank you, I've been looking forward to meeting you, and Sam's mother, and Ross." Blaze smiled at Mom.

"Oh, Blaze, forgive me, dear." Mom hugged her. "It's just that you could be my daughter's twin if not for your red hair and green eyes. It's a bit of a shock." Mom took her hand. "Your mother and I were best friends. We had so much in common. I've missed her."

"I'd love to hear all about my parents." Blaze turned and smiled at Ross. "After that kiss you gave Sam, I'm guessing you're Ross." She grinned and extended her hand, careful not to reveal she recognized him from Wewelsburg.

Ross kissed her hand. "It's uncanny how much you look like Sam." He smiled and glanced from Blaze to me.

Mom embraced Ben and swiveled to Duncan and Ross. "Gentlemen, this is our dear family friend, Professor Ben Armitage."

The men shook hands.

"Thanks for your help when Sam disappeared in Petra. Your knowledge of ancient civilizations steered us to that hidden passage in the mountain." Ross touched Ben's shoulder. "I'm sorry you got pulled into that mess with Sweetwater."

Before he could respond, a man standing in the background cleared his throat. "Excuse me, I'm Nigel Kingsley, and some of you already met Trevor Chambers. We're with the MI6 branch of Her Majesty's Secret Services. As you might imagine, we have a lot of questions."

"We understand, gentlemen, but it's New Year's Eve," Duncan said. "Let's begin the evening at the dinner table with a delicious meal, fine wine, and interesting conversation." He beckoned us to the massive table.

Mom and Duncan sat together at the head of the table, and I sat at Duncan's left between Ben and Ross. Blaze sat at Mom's right, and Mike sat next to Blaze, leaving the men from MI6 facing each other.

Too bad neither of them looked like James Bond.

My mother glanced at Blaze and Mike over a sip of vintage Chateau Lafite Rothschild. "May I ask how you two met?"

Blaze glanced sideways at Mike.

"We met at sea, and Blaze was exhausted, so I brought her aboard

Matt's carrier to recuperate in the ship's hospital." Mike glowered at Mom to cue her to stop prying.

Oblivious, she pressed on. "Blaze, dear, were you injured?"

"No, but Poseidon took longer than expected to arrange my rescue. When Mike found me, I was weak and dehydrated." Blaze spoke as though referring to a mythological god of the sea was not unusual.

That was the comment that rendered Mom speechless.

I knew the spies from MI6 were hanging on every word, so I changed the subject. "Blaze, have you ever been in a castle?"

She tilted her head as though my question surprised her. "Well, yes, but not in person. This castle is much prettier than that *other* one."

The men from MI6 must've been getting more confused by the minute. They didn't know she connected telepathically with me at Wewelsburg Castle. This could turn out to be fun if we handled things right.

"Wait until you see the rest of it. All sixty rooms are fabulous. We'll take you on a tour after dinner." I grinned and sipped the exquisite red wine.

"I'd like that. It's obvious this castle has great significance," Blaze said.

Duncan arched a brow. "And how do you know that, lass?"

"Your castle is built over the intersection of powerful dragon currents. I believe the Brits call them ley lines." She closed her eyes momentarily. "I can feel the energy flowing around us." She smiled. "Throughout history, important structures have been built over inter-secting ley lines so the inhabitants could benefit from the powerful underlying electromagnetic energy."

"Well, I'm glad my ancestors got it right." Duncan furrowed his brows. "But how did they know where the ley lines intersected?"

Blaze paused in mid sip and glanced at all of us, looking perplexed. "Duncan, your ancestors *felt* the concentrated energy. Don't you?"

Duncan shook his head. "Sorry, lassie, I guess that ability has been lost to modern men."

"So...no one here can feel the dragon current?"

I didn't want to admit to anything in front of the MI6 spies, so I said, "I know I feel ecstasy when I eat chocolate. You will too, Blaze. What's for dessert, Duncan?"

Ross patted his mouth with a linen napkin. "Duncan, the prime rib was delicious, but I do hope you have something chocolate to calm the ladies." He grinned.

Duncan's sky-blue eyes twinkled as he glanced around the table. "We'll have chocolate brownies, warm from the oven, covered with vanilla ice cream dribbled with hot fudge and whipped cream. Loren planned it."

"Ooh, yummy." I nudged Ross. "You'll have to help me burn off those calories later."

He leaned over and kissed the top of my head. "Count on it."

As if on cue, Baxter served the divine dessert.

Nigel barely waited until our last bites. "As promised, we'd like a chat with Miss Conor, Sir Lady Samantha, and Professor Armitage." He glanced at Duncan. "Is there a room for privacy?"

"Of course. You'll be comfortable in the study. I'll show you the way." Duncan led us out of the great hall.

I pulled Ross aside and whispered in his ear. "Rescue me in thirty minutes. I don't want to get in trouble for telling too much." I nibbled his ear. "Tell Mike to do the same for Blaze."

He squeezed me and glanced at his watch.

Duncan's study was warm and welcoming, lined with oak bookcases full of leather-bound books, the stone floor covered with a wall-to-wall red Axminster carpet. A well-cushioned cordovan suite formed a semi-circle around a granite fireplace where a blazing fire added to the cozy atmosphere.

Baxter placed a silver tray holding five crystal goblets and a Royal Scot crystal carafe filled with mineral water on the coffee table.

Blaze and I flanked Ben on the sofa while Trevor and Nigel sat opposite each other in armchairs. Nigel switched on a recording device and placed it on the coffee table in front of us.

"Sir Lady Samantha, if you have no objections, we'd like to begin with Blaze Conor." Nigel faced her. "We know a private jet carrying your family crashed in the Himalayas twenty-three years ago on your first birthday."

Trevor interrupted. "We're past December 22, the winter solstice, so happy belated birthday, Miss Conor."

I made a mental note to remind everyone to do something special for her birthday.

She smiled. "Thank you. May I ask a question?"

The agents nodded.

"Why do you refer to Sam as Sir Lady Samantha?"

"Our queen created a new order of knighthood for women of extraordinary valor," Nigel said. "Sam earned the title Sir Lady Samantha, First Knight of the Order of Boadicea, after she saved nine noble blood lines from extinction and prevented a war in Northern Ireland last August."

Trevor nodded. "Our nation owes her our eternal gratitude."

"Quite impressive, Sir Lady Samantha." Blaze grinned at me.

My cheeks burned.

Nigel circled back on topic. "All these years, a flight attendant was thought to be the sole survivor of your plane crash. Now, here you sit, a healthy twenty-four-year-old woman." He glanced at Trevor.

"We'd like to know who reared you, where you've been living all this time, and if your sisters, Solraya and Luna, survived also," Trevor said.

Blaze hesitated, seeming to collect her thoughts. "I was raised in a secret enclave in the Himalayas by a small remnant of survivors from ancient Atlantis. My sisters are still being held there. The Atlanteans think we're the Goddesses of Sun, Moon, and Fire, and they trained us as such."

"Why do they think you and your sisters are goddesses?" Nigel asked.

"Our arrival was foretold 11,000 years ago. We arrived in their enclave on the predicted day, and we look exactly like the ancient drawings of The Three."

"Interesting." Trevor leaned forward. "I realize you were only infants then, but did you learn *how* you arrived there?"

Blaze tilted her head, thinking. "The Atlanteans said we were strapped into a self-contained survival pod that dropped into their hidden domain. They placed it in a special alcove in their temple."

Nigel leaned forward. "Have you seen it?"

"When we were old enough to understand, they showed us the pod. They said the large gold trident symbol on the side was proof we were authentic." Blaze poured a glass of water and took a sip.

"The trident was probably a coincidence. Your father named his company Gold Trident Industries in honor of the symbol for Navy SEALs," Nigel said.

Blaze shrugged. "I only know what they told me."

"What can you tell us about the Atlanteans, their appearance, intellect, unusual abilities, whatever comes to mind?" Nigel said.

Blaze looked up at the ceiling and frowned. "They're tall and slender with long, spindly fingers and angular faces with narrow noses. The women are a little over seven feet, and the men are eight to nine feet tall."

"Would you say they're good looking?" Trevor asked.

"I don't find them attractive. I suspect they've suffered from too much inbreeding over the centuries." She shrugged. "That sort of thing's bound to happen when a society keeps their existence a secret."

Nigel and Trevor exchanged glances.

"How would you describe their personalities?" Trevor asked.

She shivered and rubbed her arms. "Cold and aggressive with no empathy—hard task masters with no love or kindness."

I reached behind Ben and squeezed Blaze's shoulder. "Blaze, how awful for you and your sisters."

She bit her lip and nodded.

Nigel cleared his throat. "How did they manage to keep their community self-contained in the harsh climate of the Himalayas?"

"They harnessed Earth's electromagnetic energy to power their enclave and facilitate growing crops and raising livestock."

"They must be quite scientifically advanced," Trevor said.

"Their civilization has had 200,000 years to work things out. Too bad their war-like tendencies angered Poseidon so much that he sent Atlantis to the bottom of the sea." She shrugged. "You'd think they'd learn a lesson and be nicer people."

"About that, we understand they possess a weapon they call Poseidon's Sword, and they intend to use it to rule the world."

"The Atlanteans are evil, power-hungry monsters. They plan to use the weapon on the next winter solstice, as foretold by the ancients." Blaze leaned forward and gulped the rest of her water.

"Have you seen Poseidon's Sword? What does it look like, and where is it?" Nigel asked.

Blaze sucked in her breath and crossed her arms. "I've told you more than I should have already." She stood. "They have my sisters. I'm not about to risk getting them killed. Interview someone else." She rushed out and slammed the door behind her.

Nigel and Trevor stood, their jaws clenched.

"Gentlemen, do *not* go after her. If you make her angry, she could turn you into toast. The Atlanteans taught her how to mentally control Earth's electromagnetic energy, and we're sitting over a mother lode." I held their gaze.

The agents sat down.

"All right, Sir Lady Samantha, what happened in Dover?" Nigel checked the recorder.

"I sincerely appreciate my title, but for simplicity here, please call me Sam, refer to the professor as Ben, and allow us to call you Nigel and Trevor." I raised my eyebrows. "Okay?"

Nigel and Trevor exchanged uncomfortable glances and nodded.

"Very well, please answer the question, Sam." Trevor pulled out a notepad.

"We landed in Dover a few hours before dawn, and I met with General Ryan in a hangar office." I took a sip of water and described my kidnapping. "They were in and out in less than ten minutes."

Nigel leaned forward. "Where did they take you?"

"Sweetwater was waiting offshore in his stealth submarine. After rushing us aboard, they blew up the helicopter."

Nigel glanced at Ben. "Where were you when this happened?"

"In a cell on the sub. They snatched me from my home the previous day."

Nigel straightened. "Did they take the Atlantean artifact?"

A nod. "They knew it was in the safe in my study." Ben sighed. "Sorry."

"And where were they taking you?" Trevor jotted down more notes.

"No idea." I decided to take a chance and lie to please my government. "Look, we're not proud of what we did, but it was the only way to save ourselves."

I squeezed Ben's hand, and our eyes met. "Do you want to tell them, or should I?"

Ben hung his head. "You do it."

I bit my lip. "After several days in our cells, Sweetwater demanded a demonstration of the device. The prototype's laser burned holes in the upper hull and fried several of his crew, forcing the sub to the surface."

Ben nodded. "Our Navy spotted them on satellite. I guess they must've called your military base in the Falklands and asked you to send a ship for us."

Trevor broke in. "Actually, America sent a submarine, but it never made it there—problems with their nuclear reactor. We sent a ship to tow their sub into port and dispatched another ship to rescue you. What happened to Sweetwater's sub?"

"It sank with Sweetwater and his crew." I shook my head. "We hated killing so many, but it was them or us." A partial lie because it was actually the Black Sun's sub.

A nod from Ben. "We had no choice."

"And the Atlantean artifact?" Nigel pressed.

"We dropped it while treading water." Partly true. "At that point, we'd deactivated the laser for our safety." I shook my head. "We feel terrible about losing it."

Ben poured a glass of water. "It'll be difficult to find without the crystals illuminated, but I believe the U.S. Navy is looking for it right now."

"And the water is quite deep there." Trevor glanced at Nigel.

Their expressions indicated they believed us. Maybe we could pull this off after all. The Brits couldn't send a submersible to search for the artifact while our Navy was scouring the area—bad for diplomatic relations. No search meant they wouldn't discover the sub on the bottom belonged to the Black Sun. The Brits still believed the cult had been eliminated in Wewelsburg.

"Let's move on. Sam, tell me about your telepathic communications with Blaze. When did that start?" Nigel sat back.

"It was strange. She made contact the first time when I was in the jet headed to Great Britain. Hearing her voice in my head was weird and totally jarred me. She said she was on board the carrier with my brothers, which seemed even more bizarre. I was shocked."

"Was it the telepathy that shocked you or discovering Blaze was alive?" Trevor asked.

"Blaze being alive after so many years was a bigger shock than our telepathic conversation. My mother and I have sent each other visions when we needed help, but we've never actually spoken telepathically." I shrugged.

Trevor raised a brow. "Why were you so willing to believe her? It could've been a trick."

"My mother told me that Blaze's mother, Sheila Conor, had psychic abilities similar to hers, so it was reasonable that her daughter had them too. Besides, she knew a lot about my brothers, like she really was there with them." All true, except I first talked to her telepathically a few months earlier during my torture in Wewelsburg.

"Has she told you anything about her sisters?"

"Only what she told you about them being prisoners of the Atlanteans in a secret community in the Himalayas. She also said I look exactly like her sister, Solraya. She's the one with the blond hair." *Would this be enough to keep them happy?*

"And the third sister?" Nigel asked.

"Luna—she's raven-haired with deep-blue eyes. The sisters look exactly like the statues on the artifact I found."

"Ah, but we've never seen it." Nigel glanced at Trevor.

"You don't have to take my word for it. Ross saw their pictures on a wall in a chamber in Petra back in October when his team was searching for me inside the mountain. He also saw a statue of Solraya in the same chamber."

"Or it could've been a statue of you. Blaze said you and Solraya are identical." Nigel narrowed his eyes.

I crossed my arms. "Nigel, I think we can agree *I'm* not the sun goddess."

The door opened, and Ross walked in. "Sorry, gentlemen, but that's enough for tonight. Sam and Ben need some holiday fun. You can resume tomorrow."

Duncan walked in. "Join us for Dom Perignon Champagne in the great hall to celebrate the New Year."

Earlier, Mike encountered Blaze in the hallway after she stormed out of the study. Seeing him turned her scowl into a smile.

"What happened?" Mike asked.

"They started asking things I'm not supposed to tell them, so I said I was concerned I might be putting my sisters' lives at risk and walked out." Blaze grinned. "I did well, didn't I?"

Mike smiled. "Yes, now let's find a comfortable place to hide in case they come looking for you." He took her hand and led her up the stairs.

They ducked into a cozy sitting room on the second floor and closed the door. An expansive candelabra chandelier bathed the room in a warm glow, and a red-velvet loveseat, blanketed in soft shadows, completed the setting.

Mike guided her to sit beside him.

Blaze squeezed his hand. "Um, I need to ask a favor, but I don't want to make you feel uncomfortable."

His voice filled with concern. "Of course, anything."

"As you know, I was confined in an isolated village since I was an infant. As goddesses, my sisters and I were kept separate from the people there. We've not had any experiences with boys or men—no dating. We weren't attracted to Atlantean men anyway."

She sighed. "But now I'm in the real world, and I don't even know how to dance or kiss or do any of the things normal men and women do together." She touched his arm. "Maybe you could help me."

He gave her an encouraging smile. "Relax, I understand. What would you like me to teach you first?"

She hesitated. "Well, I couldn't help noticing Sam and Ross kissing.

They do that a lot, and it looks like they really enjoy it." She took a deep breath. "Teach me how to kiss."

He touched her hair and slid his fingers down to her face. "Are you sure you want to try this?"

She nodded. "Positive."

Mike kissed her forehead. "There are many forms of kissing. I'm not sure you're ready to kiss like *they* do. I mean, they've been together a while. That kind of passion isn't something you jump into. You have to take it slow, like this." He pressed his lips gently on Blaze's, his eyes closed. Then he pulled back, noticing her eyes were still open.

He smiled. "Uh, forgot to tell you to close your eyes."

"But I wanted to see what you were doing."

"And?"

"The kiss felt…good. Can we do it again?"

"Eyes closed this time." He cupped her face and felt her warm lips pressing hard against his. He pulled back slightly, but she leaned in.

"Time out," Mike said. "Do it softly."

"Softly, okay." Blaze moved in and kissed him just right.

She was obviously enjoying it, so he took her into his arms and held her close. Her rapid breathing told him everything as jolts of pleasurable energy shot through him.

Damn, this is going to be more difficult than I thought. Can't lose my cool. He pulled away. "You catch on fast. Still enjoying this?"

"Oh yes."

"Me too."

Her emerald eyes sparkled with a naughty glint. "I want to do it over and over until I'm really good at it, like Sam is with Ross." She reached for him.

God help me—haven't been laid in ages—too many missions. Geez, why does she have to be so damn beautiful? Better cool down, soldier!

But their passion escalated. Mike was about to thrust his tongue into her mouth when Sam called their names. He pulled away moments before the door opened. Their faces were flushed, but Sam didn't seem to notice in the dim room.

"Oh, here you are. What's going on?"

"We're hiding from MI6. Are they gone yet?" Mike asked.

"They just left for the Highlander Inn, and we want you to see something secret while we have the chance." Sam grinned. "Come downstairs. Everyone's waiting."

Ross, Ben, Duncan, and Mom were in the great hall when we walked in.

Duncan handed flashlights to Mike and Blaze. "You'll need these. We're going to a hidden chamber beneath the castle." Duncan slipped his hand behind a portrait, and a small door opened in the wall. "Follow me and be careful when we descend the steps. They tend to be a bit slippery."

We followed Duncan into a dark passageway through the stone walls to steep, circular stone steps carved into the cliff. We stopped in an alcove at the halfway point, two hundred feet above the North Sea, a place I'd been before with Mom, Ross, and Duncan.

Duncan faced us. "Shall we have Blaze give it a go this time?"

"May as well." I turned to Blaze. "My mother opened the hidden door after she discovered the gold hand above it, and weeks later, I opened it when they brought me down here. Chances are it'll work for you too." I pointed at a gold handprint embedded in the rock six feet above the floor. "Just put the palm of your hand on it."

At her touch, a deep grinding heralded the door opening.

Duncan tapped her shoulder. "Blaze, lass, you must enter last because the door will close as soon as you're inside."

Eager, Mike stepped in first, followed by the rest of us. When Blaze entered the chamber, the stone door closed with a thud.

Blaze spun around wide-eyed, looking at the life-sized pictures of her and her sisters and scenes from Atlantis. "I can't believe it. This looks like it's been here for centuries."

"I thought this might be a nice birthday surprise for you. I'm glad you like it." I grinned and gestured at all the painted walls.

"The redhead looks like Blaze, and the blonde looks like Sam," Mike said. "This is amazing."

Ben studied every image and beamed. "I've never seen anything like this."

"Wait 'til you see the hologram." I glanced at Mom. "I wonder if it'll show something different if Blaze activates the crystals."

Blaze tilted her head. "Why would it do that?"

"Because when I activated the crystals, we saw a different hologram than the one that displayed when my mother activated them. Give it a try." I pointed at the crystals held by the three goddesses whose luminous moonstone images were embedded in the wall.

The crystals filled with brilliant light when Blaze touched them, and a hologram appeared in the center of the circular chamber. It began with the three goddesses standing back-to-back atop a huge black pyramid. A blinding flash of light preceded a new image showing Atlantis rising from the sea and displacing massive walls of water that rushed outward in every direction. Giant sphinxes flanked the city's columned streets. White marble buildings covered the downtown area, and an enormous black pyramid stood sentinel in the background.

"That's not what we saw last time." I froze and stared.

Blaze seemed spellbound as the image faded and the crystals' lights extinguished. Tears rolled down her cheeks.

I put my hands on her shoulders. "What's wrong?"

"You saw it. My sisters and I died in a blinding explosion right before Atlantis rose."

"That's one interpretation, but the bright flash could mean something else." I hugged her. "Don't worry, one way or another we'll defeat their plan and save your sisters."

She bit her lip and sighed. "Let's go back up now."

"Of course, lass, just place your bare foot on the gold footprint embedded in the floor and wait until everyone is out before you leave the chamber." Duncan pointed at it.

Soon we were all headed up to the castle, where everyone gathered in the great hall for more Dom Perignon at midnight.

Blaze took me aside. "Do you think your mother and Duncan would help me claim my inheritance? I'd like to get the legal stuff handled before my sisters are rescued, assuming we don't die like in the hologram."

"Of course, they'll help. Do you have anything to prove your claim?"

"I have a computer chip from my baby locket with my parent's will and details of their holdings. It also has my personal data and my sisters'. And Captain Kingston gave me a printout of everything. I brought the chip and papers with me." Blaze opened the locket on her wrist and revealed the chip.

I took her hand and led to her to Mom and Duncan.

"Blaze needs our help to claim their inheritance. She has all the necessary documents on a computer chip." I pointed at her locket.

"I have an army of corporate lawyers that can pounce on this for you," Mom said. "We'll get the ball rolling right after the holiday. Don't worry."

"And we'll arrange for the CEO of Gold Trident Industries to fly here and finalize the paperwork. He's your uncle and will want his brother's children taken care of. And the U.S. government will be happy to assist you in exchange for helping them locate Poseidon's Sword and the Black Sun." Duncan smiled.

"Thank you. I'm eager to regain my citizenship and financial independence." Blaze hugged Mom. "Thanks for lending me your clothes and taking me in." She kissed Duncan's cheek.

After toasting to the New Year, we hugged each other and retired to our rooms.

I couldn't help noticing Blaze's somber mood as she slipped into her room. Not what I had hoped for her.

Ross locked my bedroom door and grinned. We fell onto the bed, consumed in a passionate embrace. We rolled around, tongues entwined, fingers fumbling with buttons and zippers. The room could've been fifty degrees, and I wouldn't have noticed. My full attention was on my hot Highlander.

FIVE

Lieutenant Derek Dunbar relieved the SAS team from the Falklands and stationed his men outside. He entered the castle to look for Ross, his commanding officer and best friend, and meet the mysterious guest they were supposed to guard.

The first person he encountered was a beautiful woman with red hair and green eyes. "Hello, Sam, what are you trying to do? Confuse Ross with a red wig and green contacts?" He grinned.

She focused on his face. "Tall and handsome with dark-brown hair and green eyes—you must be Derek." She extended her hand. "I'm Blaze Conor, pleased to meet you."

He stepped closer and peered into her eyes as he kissed her hand. "So, *you're* the mysterious guest we're guarding?"

She curtsied. "Goddess of Fire, at your service."

"How did you know my name?"

"Sam told me all about you. She thinks you're handsome, and I agree."

Derek sensed an opportunity. He had suppressed his strong attraction to Sam because she was Ross's woman. Now here was a carbon copy even more striking. He took her hand. "Let's pop into the study and have a private chat." He led Blaze into a nearby room and closed the door.

She smiled as she squeezed his hand. "I really liked it when you kissed my hand."

"So did I. Hasn't anyone ever kissed your hand before?"

"Not until yesterday. I was stuck in the remote Himalayas my entire life." She sighed.

"Sorry, lass, that must've been miserable." He kissed her hand again.

"The thing is, now that I'm free, I'd like to learn normal social behavior. I feel like an awkward teenager from a strange land, not knowing what to do. I've had no experience interacting with people other than my sisters and the weird Atlanteans."

"Didn't you date Atlantean men?"

"Dating was forbidden because they revered us as goddesses." Blaze shrugged. "I didn't find Atlantean men attractive anyway."

Derek sat back and searched her face. "I'm guessing you're in your mid-twenties?"

"Yes, twenty-four, as of the winter solstice."

"And you've never had a proper kiss on the lips?" Derek arched a brow.

"Not until last night when Mike started teaching me, but we were interrupted before we got to the tongues part." She hesitated. "I wanted to try kissing like Ross and Sam. They seem to enjoy it immensely." She tilted her head. "Would you be willing to give me a few pointers?"

Derek grinned. "Lassie, I'll teach you everything. Just follow my lead." He drew her into his arms and kissed her gently. Her enthusiasm encouraged him.

She leaned back and inhaled. "You're really good at this. Kiss me again." She reached for him.

He pulled her close and gently kissed her again and again while keeping the mood light and non-threatening. He paused. "You're a quick study. Was that enough for now?"

"Um, well, I'd still like to see what it feels like to use our tongues. Can we try that?"

"Of course." After another tender kiss, he deepened it with his tongue. She mimicked his tongue movements, moaned, and draped her leg over his thigh.

Derek was lost in the moment until he heard a loud voice outside the door.

"Blaze? Are you in there?" Sam opened the door.

Derek and Blaze jumped up with her in front of him. Ross, Sam, and Mike were standing in the hall. Before anyone spoke, Duncan and Loren arrived.

Mike glared at Derek. "What the hell, Derek?"

"Relax, I was just teaching her how to French kiss." Derek matched his glare.

"Blaze asked *me* to teach her last night." Mike thrust his hands on his hips.

"And she asked *me* to finish the lessons." Derek crossed his arms.

Sam grabbed Blaze's hand and guided her to Loren. "Mom, take Blaze up to your room so we can have a serious talk with her."

Sam waited until they disappeared and turned to Mike and Derek. "Have you lost your minds? Did you forget what happened to the men in the Generals' Chamber?" Panic tinged her voice. "Ross, please talk some sense into them before they get themselves killed." She bit her lip and stormed off down the hallway.

Derek arched a brow and turned to Ross. "What does Wewelsburg have to do with Blaze, and why does your girlfriend think our lives are in danger?"

"Let's discuss this in the study before the MI6 agents arrive." Duncan beckoned them into the room and closed the door.

Ross glanced at Derek and Mike and shook his head. "Mike, it's time for you to tell us what you know about Wewelsburg. If you don't, Sam will."

Mike took a deep breath. "I thought you knew. Sam contacted the triplets telepathically while she was being tortured. They formed a psychic connection and saw everything through her eyes, including the three of us. That's why Sam asked us to wipe off the greasepaint."

"That's how Blaze recognized me this morning." Derek leaned forward. "Did the triplets have anything to do with the electrical storm and charred bodies in that room?"

Mike nodded. "You have to understand, they had to save Sam, so they channeled their power through her and fried the Black Sun Master and his soldiers."

"And yet you still gave her kissing lessons?" Ross asked, looking astonished.

"I wasn't going to refuse the hottest woman I've ever seen and maybe make her angry. She likes me, and I intend to keep it that way." Mike sat back.

Ross glanced at Duncan. "Help me explain to these randy fools why they're playing with fire, literally."

The butler entered with a bottle of Samalens Armagnac, a carafe of coffee, and a silver tray with cups, cream, and sugar. He poured the coffee and left.

Duncan added a shot of brandy to each cup and passed them out. Then he faced Mike and Derek seated on the couch.

"Gentlemen, I certainly understand your attraction to Blaze, but she isn't like other women. She has mental control over Earth's electromagnetic energy and can burn you to a cinder in seconds." He paused for effect. "And it's not just her you have to worry about. Her sisters can do it remotely through her or Sam. Think about *that*."

Derek rolled his eyes. "I don't know about Mike, but the lass is hot for *me* in a good way." He grinned. "I've given her no reason to hurt me."

Mike bristled. "She was hot for *me* long before she met you, and so is her sister, Luna, so I see no reason to think *I'm* in danger."

Ross shook his head. "It's like you both have forgotten everything you ever knew about women. And what's to stop her sisters from getting jealous and zapping you?"

Derek and Mike exchanged glances.

Ross stood and faced them. "The triplets have been held captive by an unknown race their entire lives. We don't know anything about how they think or how they might react to unfamiliar situations. Male/female interactions bring strong emotions to the surface. Are you willing to risk your lives for a few moments of passion? Worse, you might be risking our lives too."

Duncan nodded. "Look how jealous you two got over kissing the same lass, and you've shared mortal combat. You're brothers in arms. That's sacred. Now imagine goddesses with lethal powers getting jealous." He glanced from Derek to Mike. "Please tell me you understand the danger."

Derek put his hand on Mike's shoulder. "Sorry, mate, looks like we've both stepped in it. What do we do now?"

"I guess we'd better dial it down a few clicks and get to know her better. Any suggestions on how to answer if she asks for more *lessons*?"

Ross drained his cup. "You're both in the military, so the solution is simple. Explain you could get into a lot of trouble with your commanding officers if you misbehave with her. Your orders are to protect her, not to engage in romantic behavior."

"Plus, you don't want to upset Sam and Loren, who are very protective of her," Duncan said.

"Sounds reasonable." Derek nodded.

"Yeah, I think that'll work." Mike turned. "Sorry, Derek. You didn't know what's been going on. I behaved like a jerk."

"Hey, so did I. I'll buy you a drink later, and we'll put this behind us. I owe you free drinks for life anyway, remember?" Derek shook hands with Mike.

"Now that we've got this sorted, let's hope Sam and Loren are having the same success with Blaze." Ross placed his empty cup on the tray.

Someone knocked on the door, and Duncan opened it. Nigel and Trevor stood in the hallway.

"We'd like to resume our interview with Blaze. Where is she?" Nigel asked.

"The women had a bit of a tiff this morning. They're up in Loren's room smoothing things over. I suggest we have some tea and scones while we give them a little time to calm down." Duncan led them to a room with bay windows and stained-glass French doors that opened onto a terrace overlooking the North Sea. The doors were closed to a brisk January wind that rattled the glass.

Nigel poured a cup of tea and dropped a sugar cube in it. "We expect answers from Blaze about Poseidon's Sword. I hope that's not going to be a problem."

"Right, if the Americans want us to honor the agreement, we'd best get some answers to the important questions," Trevor said.

"I understand, gentlemen, but tread carefully. Blaze Conor can mentally control the Earth's electromagnetic energy. For everyone's safety, please don't anger her." Ross crossed his arms.

"Sam gave us the same warning last night," Nigel said. "I can see by the looks on your faces you're serious."

"Good, I'm glad we're all on the same page." Mike glanced at Derek.

"Why is everyone so upset?" Blaze crossed her arms as she plunked down on a rose velvet settee in Loren's bedroom.

"Your lack of experience with men could result in some serious misunderstandings. Sam and I are concerned." Loren gave her a motherly smile. "We just want you to be safe and happy, and for Mike and Derek to be safe too."

"But I enjoyed kissing Derek. His kisses are as good as Mike's, and they both make me feel so giddy." She grinned. "Why is this a problem?"

Sam strode in during Blaze's last comment. "It's a problem because they may expect a lot more than kisses."

Blaze straightened. "What do you mean by *more*? Deep conversation?"

Sam shook her head. "Not even close, and didn't you notice how upset they were that you kissed both of them?"

"Not really. Your mother whisked me away before they said much."
Better not tell them my sisters were psychically connected while I kissed Mike and Derek. They can't wait until we do it again.

"Men tend to be very competitive, especially over a beautiful woman like you." Loren glanced from Sam to Blaze. "Last night, you asked Mike to give you kissing lessons, then you asked Derek this morning." She sighed. "I know you didn't intend it, but your behavior caused jealousy between them."

"Also, what you don't seem to realize is men often hope sex will follow kissing," Sam said.

"Don't you have sex with Ross?"

Sam smiled. "Yes, but I love him, and we developed a relationship before we became intimate. It's foolish to dive into sex with someone you just met." Sam settled on the settee and took Blaze's hands.

"Why? Aren't kissing and sex supposed to be pleasurable? I've already missed so much." Blaze puffed out her lower lip.

Sam glanced at Loren. "Would you like to take that one, Mom?"

Loren nodded. "The kissing may excite you physically, but true pleasure comes from mutual romantic feelings. That's not possible with someone you just met." Loren arched her brow. "Understand, Blaze?"

"I felt plenty of pleasure kissing Mike and Derek. Their soft lips and hard muscles made my heart race. I almost forgot to breathe." Blaze closed her eyes and sighed.

"How much do you know about sex? Do you understand how easily you could get pregnant...or a disease?" Loren pulled a chair close to the settee and sat down.

"Pregnant? No, the Atlanteans taught me and my sisters science, chemistry, geography, world history, Atlantean history, telepathy, foreign languages, and many other things, but not much about sex. They expect us to remain virgins for our *execution* on Poseidon's Sword." Blaze shrugged. "Maybe getting pregnant will save us."

"Blaze, you're only twenty-four, and we're not certain the Atlanteans intend to execute you. You may have your whole life ahead of you. The last thing you'd want is to be tied down with a baby right away." Sam threw up her hands. "If you're going to act all wild and crazy, at least use birth control."

"Birth control?" Blaze tilted her head. "How does that work?"

"You know how babies are made, right?" Loren asked.

Blaze shrugged. "I've seen diagrams in books."

"This could take a while." Loren got up and pulled the servant's cord.

A few minutes later, Baxter knocked and entered. "How may I be of service?"

"Send up some tea, please, and tell Duncan we'll be here for at least an hour," Loren said. "Oh, and reassure him all is well, just a lot of girl talk."

"As you wish, Mrs. Starr." Baxter bowed and left.

Mom, Blaze, and I walked into the room where the men were seated at a long table.

Blaze blushed and took a few hesitant steps forward. "Mike, Derek, I'd like to apologize for my inappropriate behavior. I never intended to cause trouble between you." She bit her lip and cast her eyes downward. "I'm sorry."

Mike and Derek stood and smiled.

"That's okay, Blaze. We understand." Mike walked around the table and hugged her.

"No worries, lass. Join us for tea and scones." Derek pulled out a chair.

Mom slipped between them. "Yes, Blaze, sit beside Duncan, and I'll sit next to you." Mom took Derek's chair and slid his teacup and plate down a spot.

I walked around the table and sat between Mike and Ross, across from Blaze. "Mom, show Blaze how we put the strawberry jam and clotted cream on the scones."

Ben strolled in and took a seat beside Nigel after greeting everyone.

Duncan's mobile phone rang. He pulled it out of his pocket, and Blaze asked, "What's that?"

"It's a communication device called a mobile phone. Here, let me show you." He handed it to her and pointed at the screen. "Touch the green ANSWER button and answer the caller."

She pressed the button. "Duncan MacLeod's phone, Blaze speaking."

Duncan reached over and pressed the SPEAKER button. "So everyone can hear."

"*Blaze*? Is this a joke, or am I really speaking to the Goddess of Fire?"

"Who are you, and how do you know who I am?"

"My name's Lance Bowie," he said in a Texas drawl. "I'm a close friend of Sam's. We're both pilots with Luxury International Airlines, and I was with her when she found the artifact that has statues of you and your sisters on it. Are they with you?"

"No, they're still prisoners. I'm the only one who escaped the enclave."

"Is it in Petra?"

"No, the Himalayas. Why did you think Petra?"

"Because we found a hidden chamber there with pictures of you and your sisters."

"Oh, Sam hasn't told me about that one. I'd like to see it."

"I'd love to show it to you, but the king of Jordan might not let us in. We wreaked havoc there. I should warn you Sam tends to be a danger magnet."

Mike, Ross, and Derek laughed.

Blaze glanced at me. "What's a danger magnet?"

I leaned over the table and held out my hand. "Give me that phone." I grabbed it from her outstretched hand. "That wasn't funny, Lance."

"I thought it was funny." Mike elbowed her and grinned.

"Sam? I've missed you, babe. Happy New Year."

"Happy New Year to you too." I hoped Ross didn't read anything into the "babe" comment.

"How's my favorite captain? I can't believe one of the triplets is there. Y'all been havin' a good time?"

"Not unless being kidnapped several times and almost drowning is considered a good time."

"What? Who took you?"

I filled him in on what happened in Orlando and on Sweetwater's island in the North Sea.

"Oh, God, did Nicolai hurt you?"

"Just a few cracked ribs. Ross and his team rescued us." I took a sip of hot tea.

"Dang, woman, you sure do keep your boyfriend and the British military busy."

"Yeah, but after that ordeal, our government wanted me back in the States."

"Uh, were you involved in that pre-dawn attack at the Dover base? It was all over the news."

"Yep." I told him about Sweetwater's submarine.

"Holy crap, none of *that* was on the news."

"Neither was what happened next." I briefed him on the Black Sun and sinking their submarine.

"Was that when you almost drowned?"

"Yeah, but the Brits rescued us and flew us back here."

"What's the story on the Black Sun? I thought they were wiped out in Wewelsburg."

"So did I. Apparently they have another base."

"Well dang, are you safe now?" Lance's voice cracked.

"Yes and no. The Black Sun is out there, but I killed Nicolai, and Ross's team is guarding me now."

"You killed the giant psycho? That must've been an epic battle."

"Yep, *this* time, I'm sure the sonofabitch is dead."

"Dang, woman, you're ba-ad ass."

"Hey, is Jeff okay with me being off work? I'd hate to lose my job."

"He'd like you back ASAP, but he understands the seriousness of the situation. Hurry up and find Poseidon's Sword so our military can deal with it and you can come back to work. We all miss you."

"If everyone would stop bouncing me back and forth across the pond like a human ping-pong ball, maybe I could find the damn thing. Anyway, thanks for calling, give my best to everyone at work, tell them I miss them too, and have a Happy New Year." I ended the call and handed Duncan the phone.

Nigel cleared his throat. "Uh, Sam, you omitted the bit about the Black Sun last night. Explain yourself."

Oops.

The room fell silent. Mike nudged me, Blaze's eyes widened, and Ben gulped his tea.

My cheeks flushed as I glanced from Nigel to Trevor. "Gentlemen, I'm really sorry. My government ordered me not to tell you that part. I hate keeping secrets, especially from America's beloved mother country." I stared into my teacup as my cheeks burned hotter.

Ben took charge. "I'll take the blame for disclosing the Black Sun. Let's tell the government that I was exhausted and let it slip."

"You don't have to do that," I said.

"I want to. It's *my* fault we lost the artifact. If I'd kept it in the university's safe, it would still be there. Let me at least keep *you* out of hot water." Ben sighed.

Trevor said, "We'll play along with your story, provided you and Sam tell us the truth about Sweetwater and the Black Sun."

"Agreed." Ben turned to me. "Sam?"

"Sure, why not? The cat's out of the bag now anyway."

"We'd best retire to the study first for privacy." Nigel stood.

"Uh, that's not necessary. Almost everyone here already knows more than you do about what happened." I shrugged. "Sorry."

I gave the MI6 agents a thorough recap of everything from Dover up to our rescue in the South Atlantic, saying my first telepathic communication with Blaze had been when the professor and I were treading water—a partial lie about Blaze, but more than they knew before.

"Do you know where the Black Sun was taking you?" Nigel asked.

"To their home base where their Supreme Master intended to interrogate me about the triplets and Poseidon's Sword. His mental control over Earth's EME may be far greater than the Master on the submarine."

"If that's true, he could fry all our electronics," Nigel said.

"He's not telepathic, and neither are the others, so he can only control the electromagnetic energy near him. Otherwise, the Master in Wewelsburg Castle would've called upon other Masters for help, and they might've defeated us," Blaze said.

Uh oh.

Nigel and Trevor glared at me.

"Sorry, but I didn't tell my country about Wewelsburg either. It was too complicated to explain, and I didn't want to put the triplets at risk."

"My sisters and I telepathically used Sam to direct all the EME from the ley lines under the castle into Master and his men. We incinerated them to save Sam," Blaze said.

"Thank you, Blaze." Nigel sucked in his breath. "All right, Sam, continue your account of the Black Sun's submarine."

"Second Master fried Sweetwater's sub and killed everyone on board. It was terrifying. He tried to do the same thing to the American nuclear sub that was stalking them, but I killed him with the laser weapon seconds before he would've succeeded," Sam said.

"Oh, so that's how the American submarine near the Falklands was disabled?" Trevor asked.

"Yes, the Black Sun Vril Masters are extremely dangerous and won't be easy to defeat." I shivered just thinking about them.

"And they want the doomsday weapon?" Trevor asked.

"Yes, they tried to kidnap me three times during my round-the-world charter flight back in October. As I explained earlier, they too refer to me as the Golden Twin from the ancient prophecy and expect me to lead them to Poseidon's Sword."

"It would be helpful if you knew the location of their home base," Nigel said.

"As a show of good faith and to make up for my lies last night, I'll tell you something I haven't told anyone yet, not even the U.S. government. I saw the course line on the electronic map table in the Black Sun's submarine. They were headed to the Antarctic under the Ronne Ice Shelf in the Weddell Sea." I sat back.

"And the coordinates, can you remember them?" Trevor asked, his eyes bright.

"I didn't have time to memorize them—the damn sub was sinking. Sorry."

Nigel held off a moment. "Their base must be hidden inside the ice. Although no permanent residents live on Antarctica, numerous countries maintain research facilities with about 5,000 personnel during their summer, which is now, and around 1,000 during the harsh winter. Someone would've noticed a surface base."

Ross jumped in. "Do we have a research station near the target area?"

"Halley Station is on the Weddell Sea east of the Ronne Ice Shelf, and Rothera Station is on the Antarctic Peninsula west of it," Nigel said. "The Americans have Palmer Station near us on the peninsula, Amundsen-Scott at the South Pole, and McMurdo Station on the Ross Ice Shelf. McMurdo is the largest facility."

"A joint op would minimize the risk," Mike said.

"And how do you intend to defeat the Supreme Master?" I asked.

"That's a question for Blaze. She's the only one here with the same expertise as the Supreme Master." Mike glanced across the table at her.

"I have no way of knowing if my ability is equal to or greater than his. Also, we don't know how many Black Sun Masters share his abilities. We might be outnumbered to the extent that we'll lose the battle." Blaze locked eyes with me.

"Clearly, it's too early for a military solution. You need more intel." I finished my scone.

"The U.S. Navy could try sniffing around with a remote-operated submersible—maybe use the study of orca migrations as a cover story." Mike glanced around the table.

"We might have an ROV available at Halley Station, but that's something for our governments to discuss," Trevor said. "Before we take this to them, we'd like to hear what Blaze knows about Poseidon's Sword."

All eyes turned to Blaze.

She pulled a document from her pocket and waved it. "I want assistance from America to expedite declaring my sisters and me alive, restoring our citizenship, providing us with U.S. passports, and finalizing our inheritance. The official paper Captain Kingston gave us means nothing until the U.S. government fulfills their promise. I'll wait while Mike secures compliance with this document." Blaze nodded to Mike and smiled.

Mike's eyes widened. "Uh, okay, wasn't expecting that, but I see no reason why this can't be accomplished. I'll make the call." He pulled out a satellite phone and stepped out.

The group engaged in polite conversation while they waited for Mike's return. Thirty minutes later, he returned with a signed document declaring the triplets alive and verifying their status as U.S. citizens.

"I knew Duncan wouldn't mind if I used his fax machine." He

handed Blaze the papers. "And that's a legally binding order to expedite your passports and inheritance."

"Thank you, Mike." Blaze turned to the MI6 agents. "The weapon is housed in an obsidian pyramid. It can't be the pyramid in the Himalayas because that one is used as a power plant and worship center." She shrugged. "The only other obsidian pyramid I know of is on the ocean floor in the sunken city of Atlantis northeast of Cuba. That must be where it is."

"That narrows it down." Mike grinned at Blaze. "America will send a research sub and check it out."

Blaze's eyes widened. "Mike, promise me you'll never go there."

He leaned forward. "Why?"

"Atlantean legends say Poseidon created a monstrous creature with massive jaws to guard the city. The fierce beast has no equal."

Southern Indian Ocean

An elderly man with a Fu Manchu mustache gripped the railing on the stern of a one-hundred-foot Chinese junk. A tattoo of a dragon clutching a gold trident in its claws covered his right forearm. The same image decorated the main sail on the wooden ship.

It was summer in the Southern Hemisphere, and warm breezes billowed the sails as the sun trailed across the late-afternoon sky.

The ship's captain approached and bowed before speaking in Chinese. "Dragon Master, we have reached the target area south of Madagascar. Do you wish to drop anchor?"

"That won't be necessary. Just lower the sails. The orcas will arrive soon." The old man stared down at the smooth waves and breathed in the salty air.

Minutes after the sails were furled, several crew members cried out and pointed aft.

Tall black fins sliced through the water in circles near the stern. A bright glow underwater rose in the center of the orcas. A huge killer whale clutched the Atlantean artifact in its jaws, the lit end with the statues sticking out.

Dragon Master climbed into a dinghy hanging from the stern, and the crew lowered it onto the water. He sat calmly as the killer whales split from the circle, and the male orca delivered the artifact into his hands. Then the whales vanished into the depths.

He gazed at the three goddess statues on top, their hands holding crystal pyramids with one lit. "Ah, my lovelies, you have returned to me once again."

When he was back on deck, he said, "Captain Wu, raise the sails and set course for the Arabian Sea."

The captain bowed. "As you wish, Dragon Master."

A sailor brought him a bucket of fresh water. The old man carefully washed off the brine and polished every inch of the artifact. When he finished, he smiled.

The key to Poseidon's Sword was on its way home at last.

He carried the artifact into his stateroom and secured it in a velvet-lined case. Just as he started to close the lid, the light flickered once. Not certain of what he saw, he sat and watched it. Ten minutes later, he observed another brief flicker, but then it remained steady.

Had the saltwater damaged it? If so, the Atlanteans would have to move up the timetable.

SIX

Nigel Kingsley and Trevor Chambers flew back to London in a helicopter to follow up on what they had reported via encrypted phone to their boss at MI6.

As the senior agent, Kingsley began their report in the soundproof boardroom. "We have a brief window of opportunity to beat the Americans to Poseidon's Sword. Blaze Conor told us it's in the obsidian pyramid in the sunken city northeast of Cuba."

"She also said there's a monstrous sea creature guarding it, but that's probably bollocks." Chambers reached for the stainless-steel pot of hot tea in front of him.

"Let's hope it was a myth started to keep thieves away from the weapon. Our research subs are unarmed." MI6 Commander Pierce Brandon tapped the keys on a laptop, and a map of the area northeast of Cuba appeared on the wall-mounted plasma screen opposite the mahogany conference table.

Brandon pointed at a spot on the map. "Ever since the brief chat General Barnes had with Sir Lady Samantha almost two weeks ago, we've taken steps to investigate both possible weapon locations. We have satellites scanning for the Himalayan dead zone."

"And the underwater site?" Trevor asked.

"HMS *Kelpie* has *Isurus*, our research sub. They just arrived on station over the sunken city."

"Do the Americans have a vessel there too?" Kingsley asked.

"No, we think they were too busy looking for Sweetwater, the Black Sun, and then dealing with the attack on their nuclear sub. And Blaze Conor hadn't told them she thinks Poseidon's Sword is there."

"We definitely have a leg up on the Americans. The sooner we search that city, the better," Chambers said.

Brandon glanced at his watch. "*Isurus* is being launched as we speak. We should have an answer soon."

Kingsley hesitated. "Blaze Conor was genuinely concerned about the research team's safety. Should we warn them about the sea creature?"

Brandon shrugged. "What's the point? They can't defend themselves."

"We could send a message to *Kelpie* to be extra vigilant for possible attacks on *Isurus* by an unknown creature," Chambers said. "Might save time if they have to mount a rescue mission."

Brandon arched a brow and crossed his arms. "Seriously?"

"Blaze Conor has been straightforward and sincere in her chats with us. She wouldn't have given us such a vehement warning unless she believes the threat is real."

Kingsley nodded his agreement. "She begged Lieutenant Mike Starr to promise he wouldn't go there, and we know she's keen for him."

"All right, gentlemen, a warning message will be sent." Brandon punched a button on the desk phone and gave the command. Afterward, he said, "Now tell me everything you know about the Black Sun and their base in Antarctica."

USS LEVIATHAN, Key West, Florida

Commander Max Rowlin ran his hand over his short sandy hair as he read the urgent message. The tall thirty-five-year-old Texan was the youngest ship's captain in the U.S. Navy and the son of Sam's boss, Luxury International Airlines Chief Pilot Jeff Rowlin.

His 500-foot covert-ops research vessel was equipped with defensive missiles and high-tech electronics for espionage. It also carried two top-secret weaponized thirty-foot Scorpion submarine prototypes with clear canopies and a forty-two-foot research submarine. A four-man diving bell, Hardsuit 2000s for deep dives, scuba gear, and a ten-person decompression chamber fulfilled the needs of the research divers.

Rowlin strode onto the bridge and spoke to Executive Officer Vance Lowes, "We have our orders. Flank speed to that underwater city discovered northeast of Cuba. The Brits are already on station. Our objective is believed to be inside a huge obsidian pyramid." He shook his head. "And if that's not weird enough, our Scorpions have been tasked with protecting our research sub from possible attack by a monstrous creature."

"Nah, seriously?" The XO arched his brows.

He showed him the printed orders. "They're not joking."

Lowes, a laid-back fellow Texan and friend in his early forties built like an NFL linebacker, grinned and slapped Rowlin on the back. "All right, Captain Kidd, time to battle a real sea monster. Let's go kill the kraken." He hummed the theme song from *Pirates of the Caribbean*.

The Captain Kidd moniker wasn't meant to disparage Rowlin. His crew admired and respected him, even though he was younger than many of them. He'd proven his worth by earning several combat medals on past covert missions.

Rowlin keyed the intercom as soon as the USS *Leviathan* was underway from Key West. "SEALs and submarine pilots, report to the bridge."

He waited until all the men and one female sub pilot gathered on the bridge. "We have our orders. The weapon is thought to be inside a giant pyramid in a sunken city." He took a moment to look into their eyes. "Two wrinkles: The Brits are already on site, and we may have to engage a sea creature reputed to be enormous and deadly."

The group exchanged surprised glances.

"Do they know what it is, sir?" a research submarine pilot asked.

"Type unknown. The Scorpions are supposed to guard the research sub and be ready for an attack. That's all we know."

"Captain, are you certain it wasn't code to expect an enemy sub?" an African-American SEAL nicknamed Banger asked.

"That would make more sense, but no, the orders came straight from U.S. Fleet Forces Command. They don't play code games."

The communications officer burst in and thrust a paper at Rowlin. "Excuse me, Captain, but this is an emergency."

His eyebrows arched as he read the message. "This just got real, people. The British research sub, *Isurus*, was attacked by a sea monster reported to be almost three times its size and communications with them have ceased. Their support ship, HMS *Kelpie*, is now under attack and asking for help."

The SEAL team leader, Commander George Bern, stepped forward. His lean, ramrod-straight six-foot frame and intense hazel eyes radiated confidence from years of combat. "If it surfaces, we'll take it out with missiles and RPGs, but underwater, it's up to the Scorpions."

Lieutenant Jane Hoebich, one of the Scorpion pilots, asked, "Do we have any intel on what this thing looks like?"

Rowlin glanced at the printout. "The sub's interrupted final transmission described jaws the size of a double-decker bus filled with razor-sharp teeth."

She raised a brow. "Think they're exaggerating, sir?"

"The Brits aren't known for hyperbole. If anything, they understated the size."

Lowes shook his head. "Dang, we really do have to kill the kraken."

"All right, people, I want the Scorpions ready to launch the moment we arrive on site, SEALs armed for combat, and our research sub secured on board until we neutralize the threat." Rowlin turned to Lowes. "XO, sound the alarm for battle stations."

HMS KELPIE, Thirty Miles Northeast of Cuba

Captain Ian Brown of HMS *Kelpie* gripped the center console as his 150-foot research vessel rolled to the right. The unseen creature was ramming them amidships.

Could their steel hull withstand the vicious blows?

Isurus, their four-man submarine, was only thirty-two feet—no match for this. But a signal buoy had surfaced shortly after they'd lost contact with the sub. That meant someone was alive when the buoy was launched. He prayed the crew had survived and would be rescued by the Americans—if they could kill the beast.

A male voice with a Spanish accent blasted over the bridge speakers. "Attention, HMS *Kelpie*, this is Cuban Patrol Vessel 1545. We received your distress call and will arrive in five minutes. Acknowledge."

"This is HMS *Kelpie*. We're under attack by an enormous sea creature. Extreme caution advised," Captain Brown said.

"Understood. Cuban 1545 has a 50-caliber machine gun on the bow. We have your vessel in sight."

When the forty-five-foot Cuban gunboat was within one hundred yards, it slowed its approach.

The underwater ramming of HMS *Kelpie* stopped.

Captain Brown watched the nearby Cuban gunboat. He gasped when the monster attacked from underneath and bit the boat in two, dumping the crew into the sea.

Massive jaws full of sharp teeth shredded the screaming men and gulped them down. In seconds, everything was gone, except a bloody flotsam soup.

The captain's face paled, and his hand shook as he picked up the radio mike. "HMS *Kelpie* calling USS *Leviathan*. Do you read?"

"This is Captain Rowlin on USS *Leviathan*. We're ten minutes out. What's your status?"

"This is Captain Brown on HMS *Kelpie*. Situation dire. Warning: Do not proceed unless your ship is heavily armed. The beast devoured a Cuban gunboat with one bite. Acknowledge."

"USS *Leviathan* has 500 feet of double-hulled steel and heavy armament. It'll take a lot more than one bite to sink us. We've got your back, Captain Brown. ETA: six minutes. Do you have a visual on the creature?"

"Its jaws are big enough to bite a forty-five-foot boat in half. I haven't seen the rest of it. Our research sub estimated it's eighty to ninety feet. We're listing to starboard after its repeated ramming amidships."

"Understood. We have you in sight. Would you like to transfer your crew to my ship?"

"There's no way to do that safely until you kill that creature. Good hunting, Captain Rowlin. We're relying on you. *Kelpie* out."

MacLeod Castle

I waved goodbye to Blaze, Mike, and Derek as Ross started his Aston Martin. Our plan was to drive to his place and spend time alone, as promised by the U.S. government. I glanced at him. *So handsome! My ribs were still tender, but not enough to quell my desire for my hot Highlander. How did I get so lucky?*

"I hope you don't mind leaving everyone for a while," he said.

"Not at all. I want to be alone with you."

"I'd like that too."

"Good. It'll be more fun with just us." I squeezed his knee. "We'll make it up to them later."

"Works for me, lass." He accelerated down Duncan's curving driveway.

Soon we arrived at Sinclair Castle, which stood on a high hill surrounded by a deep, broad moat. A twenty-foot stone wall with ramparts encircled the outer boundary of the circular canal, and heavy wrought iron double gates opened inward via the same remote control that lowered the drawbridge. The ancient mechanisms had been modernized with electric motors.

Ross keyed the remote as we neared the gate.

"I like your security system," I said, marveling at the massive structures.

"It keeps out Viking raiders." He grinned as we drove over the ancient bridge and up the drive that curved back and forth to avoid a straight, steep climb.

A nice middle-aged couple who kept the household running smoothly waited outside the castle's oak entrance door.

Ross parked under the portico and popped the trunk. When he exited the car, his butler said, "I'll get the luggage, sir."

"Don't bother, John," Ross said. "They're just small overnight bags. You and Mary should go inside where it's warm."

John opened my door and offered his hand. "Welcome to Sinclair Castle, Sir Lady Samantha."

"It's good to see you and Mary again," I said. "Thank you for always making me feel like a princess. You're very kind."

Mary did a little curtsy. "It's always a pleasure to have you here."

Ross guided me inside and asked Mary, "Is the picnic lunch ready?"

"Aye, sir, and the horses are saddled and waiting in the stables. John fastened the basket and blanket behind Odin's saddle."

I looked up at Ross. "We're going riding?"

He smiled. "We should do something fun together, don't you think?"

"Sign me up. Horseback riding and a picnic sound good to me, but what will I wear?"

He held up a duffel bag. "I borrowed riding clothes and boots from your mother. She said you're the same size."

"Let's get changed and go while the sun is shining." I trotted up the stairs.

Fifteen minutes later, we headed for the back door.

Ross waved at Mary. "We'll be back in an hour or two, depending on the weather."

We strolled into the stables and spotted John holding two magnificent steeds. He beckoned me to a beautiful sorrel mare. "This is Valkyrie, a steady, good-tempered mount, and a champion eventer."

I rubbed her nose as she nuzzled me. "I didn't see her last time I was here."

Ross mounted Odin, his black stallion. "Valkyrie was a Christmas gift from Duncan. I think he was really thinking of you, since your colt Zeus won't be old enough to ride for a couple years."

Clouds, like scattered cotton balls, drifted in from over the North Sea as we set off down a dirt path behind the castle. Brisk January air turned my cheeks a rosy pink as I adjusted my riding helmet. Warm in a wool sweater under a down parka and woolen riding breeches borrowed from Mom, I savored the briny scent as waves crashed against nearby cliffs.

"This place is beautiful and so different from flat Florida. I love it here." I smiled, my gaze gliding across hills, valleys, and an angry sea.

"Aye, lass, but it's especially lovely in the summer. I'll take you sailing on Loch Ness, famous for the sea monster Nessie, but she's just a myth."

"Or maybe she's real, and she's careful to stay out of sight." I smiled, remembering my wild ride in Loch Ness with Charlie. We had never told anyone.

I eased up beside him and admired his broad shoulders and rock-hard thigh muscles bulging against his snug breeches.

Ross pointed to our left. "We'll take this path where that rise blocks the wind."

We turned onto a narrow path that wound down into a cozy little glen surrounded by thick bushes. A broad oak tree, stark and skeletal in its winter wardrobe, stood in the center like a big sun umbrella without its fabric.

He reined in Odin. "Let's stop here for our picnic." He dismounted and reached up to help me down from the tall mare.

My heart quickened when he placed his hands on my waist and effortlessly lifted me to the ground. Sandwiched between him and Valkyrie, I slid my hands up his chest.

He leaned down and kissed me, drawing me close. "Ah, lass, it's good to have you back." He turned and untied the blanket. "Help me spread this under the tree."

I grabbed one end and smoothed it over the ground.

He smiled and patted a spot beside him as he sat down. "I've been wanting to bring you here since last fall. This is the first time you haven't had injuries that prevented you riding."

"Sad but true. I haven't exactly been an ideal girlfriend." I sighed as I pulled off my black helmet. "I don't know why you put up with me. You could do much better."

He gazed at me in silence as though he was thinking it over. "Lass, I've never met anyone like you." He swept me into his arms and kissed me, thrusting his tongue into my mouth. "No one has ever turned me on the way you do, and God knows life with you is never boring." He grinned. "I've decided to keep you."

We rolled around on the blanket, entwined, his hands caressing my breasts. I wrapped my legs around him and devoured his lips in passionate kisses.

His mobile phone rang. Breathless, he said, "I have to answer this, lass. It might be the DSF." He fumbled for the phone in his jacket pocket. "Captain Sinclair."

Ross listened and then replied, "We'll head back now. Give us forty minutes."

He pocketed his phone. "Sorry, lass, they need us at MacLeod Castle to meet with some generals." He took a deep breath and helped me up.

"Are you *sure* we have to leave right now?" I nibbled his ear.

"Aye, lass, sorry." He drew me close for one last kiss. "Put on your helmet. We'll canter back."

USS LEVIATHAN

Max keyed the intercom for the Combat Information Center. "This is Captain Rowlin. Are all weapons operational and ready to fire?"

"Aye, Captain, missiles armed, deck-mounted weapons ready, and SEALs in position with shoulder-fired RPGs."

"And the Scorpions?"

"They're standing by in the launch bays, armed with mini torpedoes."

"I'm not releasing them until I see what we're up against. Put the sonar on active scan and ping the area. No sea mammals would be within fifty miles of this monster."

He paced in silence, waiting for sonar confirmation.

The speaker blared: "We have a target, Captain. Approximately eighty feet long, bearing one-five-zero and heading straight for us."

"Good, we're drawing it away from the Brits. Keep me updated on its location."

Rowlin pushed the speaker button on the communication console. "Attention: Dr. Kip Peterson, report to the bridge." He glanced at his

XO. "Maybe our resident PhD in marine biology can identify the creature if it shows itself."

The windows in the bridge rattled, and the XO's coffee splashed him when the beast rammed the ship on the port side.

"Shit." Lowes shook the hot coffee off his hand.

Rowlin scanned the sea with binoculars, hoping for a glimpse of the monster.

A tall, broad-shouldered man with a thick mane of short white hair and a full beard hurried onto the bridge. Rowlin thought he looked more like a Viking than a marine biologist.

"What can I do for you, Captain?" Dr. Peterson glanced out the windows.

"Ah, Kip, I'm glad you're here. I'm hoping you can identify what we're up against out there." He gestured toward the British ship.

The windows rattled, and more coffee spilled when the beast rammed the ship again.

"Sonofabitch." Lowes tossed the cup into the trash.

"Have you spotted it yet?" Kip scanned the sea.

"No, any suggestions?" Rowlin arched his brows.

"I noticed it hit the port side twice, so it probably dives under the ship and circles back for another attack. Position the SEALs on the starboard side. Have them wait two seconds after the next hit and then toss grenades over the side. See if that brings it to the surface."

"It's worth a try." He glanced at his XO. "Give the order."

When the next hit hammered the port side, the three officers stood by the starboard windows.

Seconds later, plumes of water erupted when the grenades exploded. The men on the bridge scanned the sea as the SEALs stood ready with RPG launchers.

A huge dorsal fin broke the surface, followed by an equally tall tailfin about forty feet behind it. Three rocket-propelled grenades missed the beast by inches as it dove beneath the waves. Seawater from the exploding grenades burst forth in heavy plumes.

Rowlin glanced to port and spotted a wake churning toward the much smaller British ship. "Kip, over there." He pointed.

The monster leaped from the sea and crushed the British ship's stern.

The marine biologist's eyes widened. "My god, it can't be real. I was sure that documentary on television was a hoax."

"Hold fire!" Rowlin yelled into the mike. "We can't risk sinking their ship."

The massive beast slid back into the sea and left the stern at the waterline.

"Captain, a fish that size with those unusual pectoral fins—it can only be Carcharodon megalodon." Kip pointed in the direction of the beast's last location.

"Speak English!" Rowlin said, frustrated.

"It's a prehistoric shark believed to have been extinct for more than two million years—a giant killing machine. No wonder the marine life in this area has become so depleted." Kip shook his head, mouth agape.

"Just tell me how to kill the mother." Rowlin balled his fists as the giant shark crashed down again on the stern of HMS *Kelpie*.

"There's only one option: Your Scorpions will have to draw it away and kill it with their torpedoes, but it won't be easy. That shark's fast, and it could destroy one of those subs with a single bite." Kip hesitated. "Could be a suicide mission."

"We'd better do something quick." Lowes pointed. "The *Kelpie* won't stay afloat much longer."

The British ship's crumpled stern was riding low and taking on water.

"I'm going down to the submarine bay. XO, you have the conn."

Lieutenant Jane Hoebich rechecked all her gauges in *Scorpion One* as she waited for the launch order. The curvy blonde was only five-foot-three —not the typical warrior. But she was an expert at mixed martial arts and the only female submarine pilot in Special Operations.

She glanced over her shoulder at her weapons specialist, Ensign Scooter McCoy, skinny and five-foot-six with a slight case of acne. "Are the fish ready to swim?" asking if the high-powered mini torpedoes were good to go.

"Yes, ma'am, same as last time you asked. Fired up to go hunting, huh?" His tone turned serious. "Uh, looks like the captain wants a word." He pointed at the catwalk between them and the other Scorpion.

Rowlin motioned for both sub crews to raise their canopies.

"What's up, Captain?" Jane removed her headset.

"I'm not gonna sugar-coat it." Rowlin glanced from her to the other pilot, Lieutenant Fred Lichten. "The creature we're up against is an eighty-foot prehistoric shark called a megalodon. It's fast and deadly—bit a Cuban gunboat in half, and now it's sinking the British support ship. We can't use our surface weapons without risking hitting the Brits. It's up to you. Torpedoes are our only option, but first you'll have to draw that monster away from the *Kelpie*."

"What are we waiting for?" Jane cocked her head.

"This might be a suicide mission. That meg could destroy your sub with one bite, maybe even swallow you whole." He looked into their eyes. "You deserve to know the score."

"Send me alone, Captain. Scooter has a family. I can handle the weapons." She glanced over her shoulder.

"Forget it. You're not going without me." Scooter crossed his arms.

"Count us in too," said Lichten, the handsome dark-haired pilot on *Scorpion Two*. "We'll take opposite courses and blast our floodlights on bright."

"Damn straight, Captain, I'll smoke that meg's ass." Lichten's weapons specialist, Ensign Bull Simmons, built like a fireplug, raised his meaty right hand in a thumbs-up gesture.

Rowlin paused a beat. "Ancient legends claim the meg was meant to guard the city, so if you speed down there with your lights blazing, you might draw it away from the British ship."

"Understood," Jane said. "We'll dive like we're attacking the sunken city and lure the shark to us."

Rowlin nodded. "All right, *Scorpions One* and *Two*, cleared for launch. Godspeed."

Jane glanced across at Lichten as they secured their canopies. They each gave the launch crew a thumbs-up signal followed by a salute.

The Scorpions dropped into the water simultaneously, and their hydrogen/oxygen fuel cells silently propelled them. The thirty-foot submarines resembled sleek little fighter jets with powerful mini torpedoes mounted under their short wings.

Jane banked left and dove for the bottom as Lichten banked right. "Keep your head on a swivel, Scooter. I want that meg's last meal to be a tasty torpedo, not us."

"It's so dark at the deeper depths it could be lurking just outside the range of our lights. Better do a slow roll on the way down in case it's under us in our blind spot."

"*Scorpion One*, comm check," the CIC communications officer said.

"*Scorpion One* reads you five-by-five." Jane heard the ship ask *Scorpion Two* the same question and receive the same reply. As she completed the roll, a massive black obsidian pyramid materialized in front of them. "Wow, that pyramid has to be about 500 feet tall."

"Watch out!" Scooter yelled.

The meg zoomed past them and slapped its tailfin against their submarine, knocking them into a sideways roll toward the top third of the giant pyramid.

Jane struggled to stop their rapid horizontal spin and avoid a fatal crash. Their floodlights reflected off the smooth obsidian blocks when she stopped the roll inverted a few feet from the apex.

"Whoa, that was close." Scooter exhaled a deep sigh. "Where'd the shark go?"

The meg streaked by as Jane rolled upright. "Damn, that beast is fast."

Turbulent currents from the giant shark rocked them as they dived for the bottom to look for cover.

The meg turned back to zero-in on them.

In seconds, their lights revealed a section of the city. Before that, Jane had doubted the ancient metropolis existed.

White marble buildings in spectacular hexagonal and circular designs glistened beneath them amidst gold statues of kings and queens, smaller pyramids, and two giant sphinxes. Beautiful sea-life sculptures abounded in areas that looked like they had been city parks. The 2,000-foot depth was too deep, dark, and cold for any sea life to grow on the smooth structures.

"Wow, this is unbelievable." Jane glanced in every direction.

She slipped their sub under a bridge between two identical twenty-story marble buildings encircled with columns shaped like giant women with their arms crossed. Still wide-eyed at the spectacular vista, she switched off their lights. The sub rocked violently after the shark zoomed overhead, its wake funneling between the towering buildings.

"Fred, where the hell are you? We're between buildings on the eastern side of this crazy city with the shark somewhere above us." Jane glanced over her shoulder.

"We have the meg at our twelve o'clock racing toward the black pyramid. We're in pursuit."

"Roger, we'll hug the bottom and head your way." Jane switched on the lights and focused on maneuvering between huge marble-columned buildings and magnificent statues. "I'd enjoy this fantastic view a lot more if we didn't have to worry about being swallowed."

"Watch out for that sphinx. Its front paws are dead ahead." Scooter chuckled. "Bet you never expected to hear those words in a submarine."

"Good thing the water's crystal clear. This is the most amazing obstacle course I've ever navigated." Jane's tense tone was filled with awe as their floodlights revealed more of the spectacular city with giant sphinxes guarding the central section, various-sized pyramids covered in gold, silver, and semi-precious gems, and the giant black pyramid standing sentinel on the northern edge of the ancient metropolis.

"Hey, isn't that *Isurus* at eleven o'clock next to that small gold pyramid?" Scooter pointed to their left.

Jane slowed and adjusted her course. "You're right, it's the British research sub. I'll maneuver close so we can look for any signs of life."

Simmons's voice boomed over the comm, "*Scorpion Two* has target lock on the meg—torpedo away."

As precious seconds ticked by, Jane pulled alongside the disabled submarine. She and Scooter scanned the porthole.

A face pressed against the three-foot-diameter glass. More smiling faces appeared. The four-man crew waved at them.

"*Scorpion One* has found *Isurus*. The crew is alive. Repeat: *Isurus* crew is alive," Jane reported.

"*Scorpion Two's* torpedo will hit the meg in three…two…shit! Its tail slapped it away. The torpedo is tumbling sideways." A loud boom reverberated through the water. "The torpedo impacted a building. Firing second torpedo now," Lichten announced. "We'll nail it this time."

Jane looked up ahead and spotted the huge shark swimming toward the upper portion of the black pyramid with *Scorpion Two* behind it, their floodlights illuminating the scene. A torpedo streaked through the water toward the megalodon.

Just when it looked like the giant shark would slam into the pyramid, it shot up over the top. The torpedo impacted thirty feet from the apex and left a gaping hole in the obsidian blocks.

Scorpion Two pulled up when the torpedo exploded. They glided above the apex, and the megalodon shot up from behind it and chomped down on the aft end of their submarine, shaking it back and forth in its massive jaws.

"*Scorpion Two* calling Mayday. The meg is biting our propulsion unit. Oh shit, we just broke loose. The pressure bulkhead is holding, but we're falling toward the pyramid. No control."

"*Scorpion Two*, this is Captain Rowlin. Do *not* blow your ballast. Fire your ballistic netting at the apex to arrest your fall."

"*Scorpion Two* is firing now." Three seconds later, Lichten said, "It worked. The netting stopped our fall, and we dropped into the hole from our torpedo. The big bastard can't reach us now. Thanks, Captain."

When the megalodon attacked her friends, Jane accelerated toward the giant shark. As soon as *Scorpion Two's* cockpit was out of the way, she yelled, "Cleared to fire."

Scooter keyed his mike. "*Scorpion One* has target lock—torpedo away."

The torpedo formed a foaming trail to the meg's jaws, still clutching the severed aft end of *Scorpion Two*. Seconds before impact, the shark dropped the power unit and dove to the side. The torpedo exploded in the heavy steel casing and propelled shards of twisted steel in every direction.

"*Scorpion One*, report in," Rowlin said.

"Either that shark's smarter than it looks, or it dropped *Scorpion Two's* aft end so it could come after us. Our torpedo hit what was left of the propulsion unit." Jane steered toward the charging megalodon, barely visible in their lights' outer reaches, but speeding into sharp focus.

"The British ship is taking on water, and the crew will be the meg's next meal if you don't find a way to kill it fast," Rowlin said.

"It's coming for us, Captain. This time, we'll send one straight into its gullet." Jane aimed her sub at the menacing monster and keyed the intercom. "Scooter, we'll have to time this just right. Fire a torpedo into its mouth at the last possible moment before I pull up. Don't miss or we're shark food."

"You know me. I never miss."

Jane estimated the closure rate with the megalodon. It wouldn't open its mouth until it was almost in biting range—a few seconds before impact. Maybe not enough time to pull up. A lot of lives were depending on them.

We're going to kill that beast, even if I have to drive straight down its throat.

Jane keyed the mike. "*Scorpion One* is on target. Its mouth is opening. Five seconds to impact—fire!"

"Torpedo away. Impact in two…one…"

A massive explosion triggered violent shock waves through the water.

SEVEN

MacLeod Castle

Ross and I strode into Duncan's castle. Ross had his mobile phone to his ear. "Aye, General Barnes, we're back." He glanced at his watch. "Understood, sir, we'll expect you in ten minutes."

The sound of a helicopter landing was followed by a knock on the door. Baxter stepped past us to open it.

U.S. Army General James Ryan charged through the door with his aide rushing up the steps behind him. His face was flushed from the frigid air as he removed his uniform hat and exposed a gray buzz cut. He handed his hat and coat to Baxter.

"Welcome to MacLeod Castle, General Ryan." Ross extended his hand.

"Ah, Captain Sinclair, haven't seen you since the joint battle in Wewelsburg last October." He shook Ross's hand and winked at me.

"Sorry about the Dover debacle, Sam. Good thing I have a hard head. I don't think I've ever met anyone who's been kidnapped as many times as you have. You must be exhausted."

"A few more days of R & R would certainly help," I said, hoping my time with Ross would be extended. "And thanks for shielding me with your body back in Dover."

"That was the least I could do." Ryan reached into his coat and handed me my passport, retrieved from a locker in Hogwarts Castle at Universal Studios. "This is yours." He pulled out two more. "Give these to the Scottish children who were kidnapped with you. You'll see them, right?"

"Yes, Charlie Moncreiffe and Emily Brown will stop by for a visit while I'm here. I didn't get a chance to say goodbye to them when your D-boys swooped in two weeks ago."

"Sorry. In retrospect, I should've left you here. Tell the kids their backpacks will be mailed to them." He glanced around. "Is Mike here?"

I nodded.

"Aye, General, he's waiting for you in the great hall." Ross turned. "Follow us."

Blaze walked up to Ross and me. "Oh, good, you're back."

Derek strode in.

I said, "This is General James Ryan of the United States Army."

"General, this is Blaze Conor, and I'm sure you remember SAS Lieutenant Derek Dunbar from the Wewelsburg battle." I nodded at Derek.

Blaze offered her hand.

Ryan gently took it. "Pleased to meet you."

Derek shook Ryan's hand.

Mike entered the foyer. "General Ryan, sir, we have everything set up in the great hall. We're expecting General Barnes momentarily."

The thumping blades of another helicopter echoed off the castle walls. A few minutes later, British General Brent Barnes, resembling James Bond in his perfectly pressed uniform, strode in with his aide three paces behind. After more introductions, everyone filed into the great hall.

Duncan stood in front of a large map of Antarctica pinned to a mobile corkboard. A tiny black flag marked the suspected location of the Black Sun base inside the Ronne Ice Shelf. Tiny U.S. flags marked the three U.S. bases in Antarctica while U.K. flags marked the two British bases. He nodded at the generals.

"Welcome, everyone, and please be seated. I'm Laird Duncan MacLeod, retired SAS commander, and the men on my left, Nigel Kingsley and Trevor Chambers, are MI6 agents. Kingsley will start the meeting." Duncan settled in his chair.

Nigel smiled at me. "Thanks to Sam, we know the approximate location of the Black Sun base. The ice in that region varies in thickness up to a thousand feet." He pointed at the black flag. "General Ryan, I believe you're aware a U.S. nuclear submarine experienced the destructive power wielded by a Black Sun Master."

Ryan nodded.

Nigel continued, "Well, their Supreme Master is thought to have even more power. Obviously, we can't conduct an attack using standard battle tactics."

Ryan glanced at the map, then to Nigel. "I agree this'll be tricky. Seventy percent of the Earth's fresh water is frozen in the Antarctic and must be protected."

"And we must safeguard the research stations operated by countries from around the globe." Barnes pointed at the red dots marking them. "A carefully planned surgical strike is the only way."

"Step one is pinpointing the Black Sun's exact location." Nigel gestured at the map. "We can try nosing around with a remote-operated submersible from Halley Station."

"That won't be necessary." Blaze glanced at everyone around the table.

All heads swiveled to her.

"Miss Conor, please explain." Nigel crossed his arms.

Blaze's tone was matter-of-fact. "During my twenty-three years in their custody, the Atlanteans taught me everything they know. The only way the Black Sun could have survived inside the ice all these years would be in a vertical, cylinder-shaped structure powered by Earth's electromagnetic energy, which they call Vril. Find an intersection where multiple ley lines cross, and that's where they're hiding." She paused.

"Their structure will have thick outer layers of insulation to prevent internal heat from melting the ice around them, and they'll have a cluster of air vents at the surface disguised as ice formations. Also, they'll have a horizontal cylinder connected to the base for their submarine pen, probably large enough for several subs. The subs are, no doubt, used to supply their base and carry out missions."

Ryan studied the map. "So, there'll be one place inside the Ronne Ice Shelf where several ley lines intersect, and that's where they'll be?"

Blaze nodded. "Correct."

"What are ley lines, and how do you know their complex is cylindrical?" Barnes asked.

"Ley lines, also called dragon currents, are paths of concentrated electromagnetic energy that crisscross the planet. Their society reveres that energy, which they call Vril. The most concentrated Vril will be at a major intersection of ley lines, and the most efficient structures for the use of Vril are circular or hexagonal." She shrugged. "Except for the obsidian pyramid, all the buildings in the Atlantean enclave are either circular or hexagonal." Blaze glanced at Trevor, who was tapping the keys on his laptop.

"I've got it," he said. "I pulled up a map of ley lines in Antarctica. There's only one spot where four ley lines intersect, and it's in the Ronne Ice Shelf." He turned to Duncan. "Do you have some string I can use to plot the intersection on the map?"

"Aye, Baxter will fetch it." Duncan summoned his butler.

Baxter hastened back with a ball of string and a pocket knife.

Trevor ran string to the latitude and longitude coordinates for the four-way intersection. The strings crossed close to the black flag, which he moved to the intersection.

I looked at Blaze. "Well, now that we know where they are, any ideas on how we destroy them without getting our soldiers fried by their Supreme Master?"

She didn't hesitate. "I know exactly how, but you and your mother aren't going to like it."

USS LEVIATHAN

Captain Rowlin trained his binoculars on the sea above the impact area. It wasn't long before the surface was covered with bloody chum from tons of shredded shark flesh.

He swallowed hard and keyed the mike. "*Scorpion One*, report status."

He waited a few seconds and tried again. "*Scorpion One*, this is Captain Rowlin, report status." He glanced at XO Lowes. "Keep calling."

Rowlin called HMS *Kelpie*. "Captain Brown, it's safe to abandon ship now. We're sending evacuation boats to assist."

"Thank you, Captain Rowlin. We'll launch the life boats, and I'll stand by the radio until I'm certain everyone is accounted for. Captain Brown out."

Rowlin turned to Lowes. "XO, see to it the *Kelpie's* crew is recovered as fast as possible so we can rescue the sub crews before they run out of air." He grabbed the mike and glanced at the floating chunks of bloody flesh. "*Scorpion One*, report in."

"*Scorpion One* reporting," Jane said. "The shock wave from the blast sent us tumbling backwards. I've never been so dizzy in my life. Judging by all the chum, I'm guessing we turned the meg into fish food."

"Affirmative. Good job. You had us worried. Now we need you to hook a cable on *Scorpion Two* and tow them aboard. We're stationed directly above the black pyramid." Rowlin paced as he spoke.

"Aye, Captain. We'll be in position in five minutes."

SCORPION ONE

Jane checked her submarine's systems, flipping switches and scanning gauges, as she headed for the other Scorpion tethered to the pyramid. Her neck and shoulders relaxed when she verified that everything was operational.

She hovered in front of the hole in the pyramid and radioed, "*Scorpion One* in position."

Jane glanced over her shoulder while keeping the sub stationary. "All right, Scooter, work your magic with the robotic arm and hook the cable to them."

"Sit back and watch a master at work." He used a joystick for the hinged arm to secure their tow cable's hook to *Scorpion Two's* tow bracket. "You know, it's a miracle we didn't end up in the monster's belly."

"We wouldn't have been there long. The explosion would've set us free from our Earthly bonds."

"Yeah, well I like my Earthly bonds." Scooter retracted the robotic arm and waved at *Scorpion Two's* crew.

"Me too," Jane said. She keyed the mike. "You guys doing okay over there?"

"We're good to go, Jane. Thanks for the hookup, Scooter." Lichten waved.

"All righty, Bull, disconnect the netting line." Jane backed away from *Scorpion Two*. "Blow most of your ballast, and we'll tow you to the sub bay."

Lichten flashed a thumbs-up signal.

The submarines ascended, and Jane towed *Scorpion Two* into *Leviathan's* moon pool where the support crew unhooked their tow line.

"We're in the lift. Thanks, Jane and Scooter." Lichten and Simmons saluted.

The captain broke in: "*Scorpion One*, assess the situation with *Isurus*. Find out how much air they have and see if you can assist them to the surface."

"Aye, Captain. We're on our way. *Scorpion One* out." Jane dove her sub toward *Isurus*.

Scooter pointed as they approached the stricken British submarine. "Look at the viewing port. They're holding a sign against the glass."

She eased closer to read it. "Oh no, they blew their ballast, but they're stuck in the muck with only six minutes of air left. Hurry and connect our tow cable to their nose fitting."

He manipulated the robotic arm and hooked their cable to the research sub. "All right, we're good to go."

Jane eased the Scorpion forward to take out the slack in the cable. She increased forward thrust to maximum power, but *Isurus* wouldn't budge.

"We need to break them free." She glanced around. "I have an idea." She keyed the mike. "*Scorpion One* to Captain Rowlin."

"Rowlin here, go ahead."

"We have *Isurus* on the hook, but they're stuck in the muck with about four minutes of air. Requesting permission to fire a torpedo into a structure sixty yards ahead to shake them loose with a shock wave."

"Whatever it takes, save them, Lieutenant."

"Aye, Captain. Stand by with the lifting crane. Time is of the essence."

"Understood. Surface on the port side, and divers will unhook you. Report when you're on the way up with *Isurus*."

She keyed the intercom. "Fire into that marble building at twelve o'clock and sixty yards ahead."

"Torpedo away. Let's hope this works."

"Hang on." She held the thrust at full power as the shock wave hit.

They were far enough from the blast to maintain control in the turbulence. Suddenly, they surged forward as *Isurus* broke free.

"It worked," Scooter said.

She keyed the mike. "*Scorpion One* is on the way up with *Isurus* in tow. It's going to be close on their air."

"Understood. SEALs will open their top hatch as soon as they break the surface. Look for the divers on the forward port side." Relief was evident in Rowlin's voice.

MacLeod Castle

Duncan summoned his butler. "Baxter, please ask Loren to join us."

My mind raced. How could my mother and I contribute to the mission?

When she arrived wide-eyed and tense, Duncan offered her a chair beside him.

I tried to ease the tension. "Hi, Mom. Blaze is helping the generals formulate a plan to destroy the Black Sun base, and apparently, it involves us." I glanced at Blaze. "Let's hear it."

She walked to the map and grabbed colored stickpins from the table, then stared at the black flag. "May I borrow a pen?"

Nigel handed her a red marker.

Blaze drew a red circle around the black flag. "This circle is approximately one-quarter mile from the center of the intersection where the base is located." She tacked four pins on the circle, equidistant from each other. "These mark the spots where we must stand to simultaneously direct the energy from the dragon currents to superheat the Black Sun base."

"And by *we* you mean you, me, and my mother?" I asked.

"And my sister, Luna."

That bombshell got everyone's attention.

"What?" Trevor said. "Aren't your sisters imprisoned in the Himalayas?"

"Yes, but Luna plans to escape soon. The Atlanteans don't know how I escaped or where I went. They only know I left during their worship ritual early in the morning. That's why she must go at night. She's waiting for a full moon later this month to see better for flying the paraglider she made." Blaze bit her lip. "It'll be a dangerous flight."

"Assuming she's unable to escape, do you have a backup plan?" Barnes asked.

"Wait a second." Mom raised her hand. "I don't know how to control Vril, and neither does Sam."

"You're both descendants of Atlantean goddesses, which means my sisters and I can telepathically use you as conduits, like we did with Sam at Wewelsburg Castle."

Uh oh. The generals and the MI6 agents glared at me.

Nigel stood and spread his hands on the table. "Sam, we agreed you wouldn't hold back information. Explain yourself."

I glanced at their red faces. "It wasn't my place to divulge it, and I couldn't explain how they did it anyway. The triplets saved my life. Disclosing their participation at Wewelsburg might've put them at risk. Now that Blaze has come forward, you can ask *her* for the details."

All eyes turned back to Blaze.

"My sisters and I used our telepathic and psychic connection to Sam and directed all the Vril into the men along the perimeter of the chamber. We mentally overpowered the Black Sun Master and defeated him."

I broke in. "The result was similar to what Second Master did to Sweetwater's submarine and the men inside. He tried to do the same thing to one of our nuclear subs, but I killed him before he could finish the job."

"With all due respect, Blaze, I don't like this," Mike said. "You intend to risk your life and the lives of my mother and sister? How can you be sure this'll work?"

"We'll have to practice connecting with your mother to prepare for the mission. Four ley lines intersect at the center of the Black Sun base, so we need four of us to focus the energy into the base. If we do it simultaneously, the result will be so swift and deadly, they won't have a chance to retaliate. They'll be too busy trying to deflect our attack."

Blaze shrugged. "The tricky part will be getting us off the ice before it breaks apart and tumbles into the void left when their cylinder city sinks." She returned to her seat between Mike and Derek.

Ryan leaned forward. "Their city will sink?"

"Their outer walls would have to be made of steel, similar to a double-hulled submarine, like the ones Sam said Sweetwater and the Black Sun had. That steel will be heated to the point of cracking and melting, which will release the trapped air inside. With no buoyancy and no ice to support it, the melted cylinder city will drop to the bottom of the sea. The surface ice nearby will crack and tumble into the void." She maintained her matter-of-fact tone. "That's why we must execute the plan on a day with good weather and time it perfectly for our escape."

"Are you assuming an insertion and exit via helicopter?" General Barnes asked.

"Yes, but with four helicopters for the pickup. One helicopter will drop us off and leave immediately to avoid drawing attention. And we can use the onboard GPS to drop us off at precise ley-line locations."

The men nodded to each other.

"This plan sounds like the surgical strike we wanted, Blaze, but how will you determine when it's time for the helicopters to pick you up?" Ross said.

"Once we're dropped off at the focal points, the mission won't take more than five minutes. The helicopters can hover at safe distances, about three miles away. When I feel the first vibration, we'll have maybe one or two minutes before the ice collapses. I'll light a flare, and the helicopters will race to our rescue."

"That's cutting it close." Mike frowned. "I suggest we outfit them with inflatable survival suits, just in case."

"The entire plan is based on the assumption that Luna will escape and join our mission," Barnes said. "Can someone else accomplish this if Luna doesn't make it?"

I turned to Blaze. "What about the Dragon Master? He gave me the artifact in Hong Kong. Members of his Dragon Society are supposed to be experts on dragon currents."

Blaze shook her head. "No, they're experts only on the *locations* of dragon currents. The Atlanteans formed the Dragon Society thousands of years ago. Through the centuries, they kidnapped young Chinese boys and brought them blindfolded to their enclave to train them. When they were old enough, they were sent into the world with specific missions. The Dragon Master's mission was to guard the artifact until you came for it."

"Why can't a Dragon Society member take Luna's place if she doesn't escape?" I asked.

"Because they can't control Vril or connect with us telepathically."

"Any chance you could find an Atlantean outside the enclave who'd be willing to help us? They have the same abilities as you, don't they?" Nigel asked.

"No, they all live within the enclave, and they don't have mental control over Vril," Blaze said.

"Then how were they able to harness electromagnetic energy to power their community?" Trevor asked, frustrated.

"They used their vast scientific knowledge from 200,000 years of existence." Blaze shrugged. "This shouldn't surprise you. According to my history lessons, a scientist named Nikola Tesla came close to harnessing Vril for free electricity in the USA over a hundred years ago. Too bad greedy businessmen stopped him."

"But if the Atlanteans don't share your control of Vril, how did they teach you to do it?" Mike asked.

"The techniques were recorded in their archives. They merely coached us to develop our natural abilities—abilities only descendants of Atlantean goddesses possess. I should explain those women they called goddesses were just women from a different race with unique abilities. That's why we don't look like the Atlanteans."

"When is the next full moon, and should we expect to find Luna riding an orca in the Arabian Sea?" Mike asked.

"Oh my, is that how you found Blaze?" Mom asked.

"An orca carried her to my boat, and I took her aboard the submarine that picked up my team," Mike said.

The Brits exchanged surprised glances.

"The next full moon is on January 23. Luna will contact me when she's free. Then we'll coordinate a plan to pick her up, probably on the Arabian Sea." Blaze glanced at Mike.

"Why aren't both your sisters escaping together?" Derek asked.

"Solraya must stay behind to fool the guards into thinking Luna is still there long enough for her to get far away. If they try to leave together, they'll get caught. I'm counting on both your countries to help us rescue Solraya once we've secured Poseidon's Sword."

"We have a research vessel over the sunken city now, and our sub has begun exploration," Nigel said. His mobile phone rang. "Excuse me, I have to take this call." He walked to the far end of the great hall.

Moments later, Nigel returned with a pale face. "Your warning about the sea monster proved accurate, Blaze. Our research sub was attacked and disabled on the seabed, and our support ship was sunk by an eighty-foot prehistoric shark called a megalodon. The Americans killed the beast and rescued our people. They're planning a joint search of the obsidian pyramid tomorrow. Finding an entry point won't be a problem because the Americans blasted a hole in it when they shot torpedoes at the giant shark."

"What if the torpedo destroyed Poseidon's Sword? I don't know what the weapon looks like. The archives didn't have any pictures of it," Blaze said.

"Don't worry, we'll send down Hardsuit divers and determine if it was or still is inside the pyramid," Ryan said.

"One more thing." Blaze waved a document. "No more waiting. I want our passports in hand and our inheritance completed before we leave for the Antarctic mission."

Ryan stiffened. "When Luna arrives, we can get pictures for your passports, but not Solraya's."

"Actually, you can take all three pictures when Luna arrives." Blaze pointed at me. "Sam can sit for Solraya. They look identical, and we can prove it."

"All right, show me the proof, and I'll make the arrangements."

Duncan said, "The proof she's referring to requires a long trek beneath the castle. Shall we have lunch first?"

"That's an excellent idea." Ryan smiled. "Thank you, Laird MacLeod."

"I don't know if I'll ever be hungry again," Mom said, looking worried. "Antarctica isn't my idea of a good time."

"I've got your back, Mom," Mike said. "I'll make sure you survive the mission."

"You'd better make sure everyone survives the mission." Mom bit her lip.

"Mrs. Starr, I can assure you that every precaution will be taken to ensure everyone's safety." Ryan squeezed her hand.

Mom sighed. "Well...okay, what's for lunch?"

"Grilled chicken over Caesar salads and Louis Latour Chardonnay," Duncan said.

EIGHT

USS LEVIATHAN

Captain Rowlin keyed the mike. "Cleared to lower divers." He switched to the in-helmet channel for the dive team. "Divers, descend back to back, and be on the lookout for sharks. That massive chum field two days ago attracted every shark within a hundred miles."

"Aye, Captain, but they probably aren't hungry after the feeding frenzy," Banger answered.

Two divers in Navy Atmospheric Diving System Hardsuit 2000s were winched over the side. The suits were operational down to 2,000 feet and were equipped with sixteen rotary joints and two thrusters. Tethered to lift cables with integrated power, data, and communication lines, the suits remained at one atmosphere regardless of depth.

Rowlin had assigned the British marine archaeologist, Dr. Richard Crenshaw, as dive buddy for Banger. He wanted someone familiar with ancient civilizations to help spot traps and boost diver safety after the recent chaos. Crenshaw had received ten hours of specialized training the previous day to prepare him for the Hardsuit dive.

"This is Captain Rowlin with a comm check."

Both divers responded in clear voices.

Lowes handed Rowlin a cup of coffee. "Relax, we killed the kraken."

"True, but the pyramid might be rigged with traps." Rowlin rubbed the back of his neck.

"I agree with Captain Rowlin. There's no telling what might be lurking inside." Captain Brown sipped a cup of Earl Grey tea. "On behalf of the UK, I'd like to thank you for allowing our man to participate in the dive."

"The four bottles of forty-year-old Scotch rescued from your ship were thanks enough." Rowlin shrugged. "And his expertise will enhance the mission."

"My crew and I will always be grateful for what you did." Brown shook Rowlin's hand.

"Banger here," the comm squawked. "Sharks are ignoring us. Plenty of meg chunks are still floating around. We're at 1,400 feet and descending. The pyramid's directly below us. Over."

"Keep a sharp lookout," Rowlin said. "More surprises may be waiting down there."

"Aye, Captain, we'll be ready. Banger out."

Banger engaged his suit's thrusters, which moved him around like astronauts during space walks. He gazed at the eerie burial site of HMS *Kelpie* planted upright on the sea bottom, barely visible in the gloom pierced by his brilliant auxiliary floodlight.

Thirty feet below the pyramid's apex, he led Crenshaw through the jagged hole 1,500 feet from the surface. Broken chunks of black obsidian littered the area, compliments of the torpedo explosion. As he glanced at his dive buddy, he couldn't restrain a smile, thinking their Hardsuits made them look like the Michelin man.

"I'm surprised the massive water pressure at this depth didn't destroy the pyramid when the torpedo hit it." Banger glanced around.

"All pyramids have airshafts, including this one. It would've slowly filled with water as it sank to the bottom thousands of years ago, equalizing the water pressure," Crenshaw said. "Switch off your floodlight. It's too bright in this confined space."

Their headlamps illuminated only a few feet of the clear water flowing into the dark, foreboding structure. Banger turned his head from side to side and surveyed every detail on the smooth lava-rock walls, looking for ancient traps as they stepped over debris and inched deeper along the passage into the pitch-black interior.

Crenshaw moved ahead of him before the passage narrowed, angling down into the darkness, the divers sandwiched between close walls with a ten-foot ceiling.

Crenshaw spoke into his voice-activated mike. "Good thing I'm not claustrophobic. We barely fit single file, and these black walls seem to be absorbing the light."

"I see gold trident symbols on the walls—maybe a sign we're on the right path." Banger's integrated camera filmed everything from inside his helmet.

"And the tridents are getting larger." Crenshaw stopped abruptly. "Bugger!" He raised his right arm.

Banger understood the signal to halt and peeked past Crenshaw. A glowing apparition rushed at them, leaving no chance for escape.

Both ducked as a bizarre nine-foot fluorescent fish with a wide mouth full of pointed teeth swept over them.

Crenshaw gasped. "Bloody hell!"

"I've never seen anything like *that*." Banger glanced behind him. "Good thing we started with forty-eight hours of air, because I just sucked down an hour's worth."

"Divers, what's happening down there?" Rowlin's voice filled their helmets.

"Relax, Captain. It was just a big, ugly, glowing fish. We're good," Banger said.

"How's Crenshaw?" Rowlin asked.

"I'm all right," the Brit said. "That toothy bugger gave us a bit of a fright."

"All right then, carry on and stay sharp. Rowlin out."

Crenshaw straightened and forged ahead at a snail's pace with Banger close behind.

After circling around the interior perimeter on a slight downward slant, Crenshaw signaled a stop. "Looks like a Z-shaped entrance hall. Could lead to something important."

"Onward, Doc. I'm right behind you."

The long, narrow Z ended at a solid wall with an open door on the right. "We've reached an entrance to an inner chamber about fifteen feet in diameter." Crenshaw stepped inside and waved Banger forward.

Banger hesitated. "Any signs of a trap?"

"Nothing so far." Crenshaw eased in a few feet. "Looks like that complicated entrance pathway prevented damage from the torpedo's shock wave."

Banger tapped his shoulder. "Should we be concerned about that glowing globe?"

"Only one way to find out." Crenshaw stepped forward. "Follow me."

Feeling protective of the civilian, Banger activated his thrusters and floated to the center of the room. He hovered near the glowing globe. "Holy hell! If you thought that fluorescent fish was scary, wait until you see this."

Banger took a step back and glanced around the strange circular room. A ten-foot golden statue of Poseidon stood guard along the opposite side of the curved wall. His right hand wielded a seven-foot gold trident. Three life-sized white moonstone statues of young women stood equidistant along the room's perimeter, all looking identical except for their hair and eye colors.

As Crenshaw approached, Banger waited behind the central sculpture—a four-foot gold dragon clutching a one-foot diameter crystal globe in its front claws. Inside the luminous globe filled with clear liquid, a large human-like eye with an iridescent-blue iris seemed to follow his movements, as though someone was looking through it remotely.

Crenshaw stared. "Is it just me, or do you get the feeling that eye is looking right at you?"

"Seems like it." Banger backed away from the globe. "That eye gives me the creeps."

"This is a scientific marvel. We should take it." Crenshaw moved closer.

Their headlamps died and thrust them into pitch-black darkness, except for the pale globe appearing to float in space.

"Shit. Can you still hear me, Crenshaw?" Banger checked the LED indicators in his suit and tried to switch on his floodlight. Nothing.

"Everything's working except my lights." Crenshaw hesitated. "What do you think about that globe with the weird eye?"

"I vote we leave it alone." Banger edged backward a few more feet.

Their headlamps burst to life and illuminated the room.

Banger stared at the floating eyeball. "That does it. The globe stays here."

"We have to take it. It's an important artifact." Crenshaw extended his graspers.

Their headlamps died again.

"Doc, for a guy with a PhD, you sure are acting stupid. The globe stays." Banger's tone was firm.

Their headlamps burned brightly again.

"Relax, I'm not taking the globe. I was just verifying the connection between our stated intentions and our headlamps." Crenshaw glanced around. "It's like it's watching and listening. This is mind-blowing."

"So, now what?" Banger glanced up and noticed an open four-inch diameter vertical shaft in the ceiling directly above the globe. It appeared to extend to the pyramid's apex. Something shiny glinted inside when he directed a light beam into it. He poked Crenshaw and pointed up. "We're definitely not taking *anything*."

A foot-long black eel, encircled by shiny gold bands, slithered out from underneath the globe, looking like a live piece of jewelry.

Crenshaw jumped back and stared downward. "I just saw that eel swim out from under there." He pointed at the opening in the floor under the globe, which lined up with the shaft in the ceiling. "Maybe these cylindrical ducts are meant to be energy pathways."

A loud thud reverberated inside the chamber.

Banger turned and pointed at the entrance. "We're in deep shit now."

A stone door had dropped down, sealing them in.

"Mayday! Dr. Crenshaw, calling *Leviathan*."

"Forget it," Banger said through their radio intercom. "Our cables are severed." He pulled his line and held up the severed end. "No electrical power or comm lines."

"We're trapped." Crenshaw thrusted to the door and searched for a control switch.

Banger's SEAL training kicked in, enabling him to remain calm. "Conserve your battery. Walk instead of using the thrusters and only speak when necessary. We still have plenty of air. I'll switch off my headlamp to conserve power while you search the perimeter for an exit."

"And if I find one, how'll we get topside without lift cables?" Crenshaw asked.

"When the dive master lost contact with us, he would've checked the cables and verified we're no longer attached to them. He'll arrange a rescue mission." Banger switched off his headlamp. "Don't worry, the CO_2 scrubbers in our oxygen tanks will ensure we have plenty of air."

Crenshaw took a deep breath. "Right then, you distract the eye while I look for a hidden control to open the door."

Crenshaw walked to Poseidon and studied him. He pulled on the trident with his grasper, but it wouldn't budge.

"Keep looking, Doc. You're doing fine." Banger kept his voice steady.

Banger decided not to divulge their worst problem. If their battery power ran out, they couldn't operate their suits or use their radios once they were outside. That meant no chance of rescue.

MacLeod Castle

Blaze sat across from Loren in Duncan's study. "I have to get you ready for the Antarctic mission."

"What if I can't learn telepathy?" Loren bit her lip. "I'm a lot older than you."

"You can do this. We're descendants of the same ancient race. Your daughter managed it with no training because the ability lies dormant within." Blaze crossed her legs. "We'll start with close-proximity telepathy. Once you master that, we'll increase the distance between us."

Loren sighed. "All right, what do you want me to do?"

"Close your eyes and listen. When you hear my voice inside your head, raise your hand." Blaze stared intently at Loren, her eyes narrowed in concentration as she telepathically yelled, *"Loren!"* repeatedly.

Nothing.

Loren shrugged. "I warned you, I'm too old to learn this."

"Nonsense, try again." Blaze continued calling Loren's name.

Several minutes passed before Loren finally raised her hand.

"Good, now say my name in your head." Blaze waited several minutes until she heard Loren call her name telepathically.

"Now concentrate on sending full sentences." Blaze watched her and waited. Several more minutes ticked by before she heard, *"Blaze, do you like chocolate?"*

"Well done, Loren. That came through loud and clear. Let's try a conversation."

Now that their telepathic connection was strong, the conversation flowed.

"Blaze, are you certain we can defeat the Black Sun in Antarctica?"

"Yes, we easily defeated their master in Wewelsburg. This time Solraya will channel through Sam, and I'll control my end and yours. Also, we'll have four powerful ley lines to draw from, compared to only two in Wewelsburg."

"You sound like you know what you're doing, and you don't want to die either. I trust you to get us through this." Loren opened her eyes and broke the connection.

"What happened?" Blaze tilted her head.

"Sorry, but I feel drained. Can we take a break?" Loren rubbed her temples.

"Yes, of course, this can be a bit tiring until you adjust. Next time, we'll try communicating from separate rooms." Blaze walked over and squeezed her shoulder. "You're a fast learner. Once you get better, it'll be fun."

"We could talk about the men right in front of them without them knowing." Loren laughed. "You're right, it *will* be fun."

Sam knocked and stuck her head in. "Sorry to interrupt, but Charlie and Emily are here, and they'd love to meet Blaze."

Blaze smiled. "Bring them in."

A darling eleven-year-old girl with brown curls and big blue eyes followed Sam into the room. An auburn-haired twelve-year-old boy with hazel eyes stood behind them.

Sam waved the children forward. "Blaze, I'd like you to meet the bravest children in Scotland, Emily Brown and Charlie Moncreiffe."

Emily curtsied, and Charlie kissed Blaze's hand.

"Children, this is Blaze Conor, also known as the Goddess of Fire." Sam grinned.

Emily giggled and Charlie bowed.

"We're also known as Dame Emily and Sir Charles." Charlie glanced at Sam. "But we only use our titles for special occasions."

"The children were instrumental in helping me last summer, so the queen honored them with titles," Sam said.

Blaze beamed. "I'm honored to meet such extraordinary young people."

Emily's face flushed as she asked, "Do you have super-powers?"

"Of course. Unscrew that light bulb and hold it out." Blaze pointed at a table lamp and waited for her to do it. Then she focused on the glass bulb, and it filled with light.

Emily stared open-mouthed at the lit bulb in her hand. "That was brilliant."

Charlie touched the bulb and glanced at Blaze. "How'd you do that?"

"I can control Earth's electromagnetic energy with my mind." Blaze smiled. "And I've been teaching Loren how to communicate telepathically. Sam can do it too."

"Really? Will you teach us?" Charlie asked.

Sam stepped in. "Sorry, but only descendants of an ancient race can do that." She draped an arm around each child's shoulder. "Let's let them get back to work now. And don't let me forget to give you your passports."

USS LEVIATHAN

Captain Rowlin paced on the bridge. "Any word from the divers?"

SEAL Commander George Bern shook his head. "The dive cables are severed, so no comm lines."

"Maybe the comms are inop. We've heard nothing but static since they entered that chamber." Rowlin stopped pacing.

"Dive ops tried winching them up. No drag from the divers—definitely severed." Bern glanced at his watch. "That chamber is blocking radio reception too."

Max keyed the intercom for the submarine bay. "This is Captain Rowlin. Is *Scorpion One* ready to launch?"

"Aye, sir, the crew is ready, and all systems are go."

"Cleared to launch Scorpion. Tell Lieutenant Hoebich to shine her spotlight into the pyramid and look for our dive team." Rowlin stared down at the sea.

Five minutes later, a call came over the loudspeaker. "*Scorpion One* is approaching the entry hole."

Rowlin grabbed the mike. "Roger, *Scorpion One*, find our divers."

XO Lowes walked in with two cups of coffee and handed one to Rowlin. "Any news?"

Before he could answer, he heard Jane's voice on the speaker. "*Scorpion One* is hovering about thirty feet below the apex. The dive cables are dangling over the entry hole. No divers in sight."

Rowlin stared into space. "We stopped reeling in the cable when there wasn't any drag. Any sign of them?"

"Negative. They must be trapped inside. May as well take up the cable."

Rowlin glanced at Bern. "Their air supply should be good, right?"

Bern checked his dive watch. "Forty-five hours of air remaining, but their suit temps may start dropping when the internal battery runs out. Their radios and thrusters need battery power too."

Rowlin keyed the mike. "*Scorpion One*, does it look like we should send in an ROV?"

"A small remote-operated vehicle could easily maneuver around in there."

"I'll send it. We need to know what happened before I risk losing another diver." Rowlin rubbed his chin and faced Bern. "What if we send it down with some C4, just enough to blow a door if it's closed?"

"We wouldn't know how close they are to the door. If the explosion penetrates their suits—"

Rowlin interrupted, "They'll implode." He sighed.

Fifteen minutes later, Jane called. "*Scorpion One* watched the ROV enter. It didn't take long to disappear inside. The passageway must turn."

Seconds passed in silence. Rowlin gulped his coffee.

"*Scorpion One* reporting. No joy on the ROV. Are you receiving video from it?"

Rowlin keyed the mike. "Affirmative. So far, nothing but a dark, curving hallway."

"Roger, *Scorpion One* standing by."

Scooter keyed the mike. "Captain, what if I blow off the apex with a torpedo? If I can hit the point, the falling debris should be minimal."

"There's no guarantee the divers have a clear path to the apex. Let's keep that as a last resort." Rowlin stared at the water, brainstorming a safe solution.

Several minutes ticked by as Rowlin and Bern watched the ROV feed.

"Looks like a dead end," Bern said.

"Isn't that a stone door on the right?" Rowlin said.

"If it is, that must be where they are." Bern stared. "Hey, it just opened, and the dive team is coming out."

"They look unharmed." Rowlin tried to hide the tension in his voice.

"Damn." Bern elbowed Rowlin. "The last one out got his backpack dinged when the door dropped down behind him. His suit might fail."

"*Scorpion One*, radio them to hurry out and grab the handholds along the sides of your sub. Bring 'em up fast. A recovery team is in the water on our port side." Bern rushed from the bridge.

"Aye, Captain, *Scorpion One* will be topside in ten minutes."

"Good work, *Scorpion One*. We'll be ready when you get here."

A half hour later, the dive team was safe on board and had replaced their sweat-soaked clothes with dry fatigues.

Rowlin paced while the medic checked them over.

"They're in good shape, Captain." The medic picked up his medical bag and left the conference room.

A sailor entered with a tray holding a large coffee pot, cream and sugar, mugs, and fresh doughnuts.

Captains Rowlin and Brown, Dr. Peterson, and Commander Bern settled across from Banger and Crenshaw at the long conference table.

"Let's start with how you opened that door and work backward." Rowlin glanced at Crenshaw and Banger. "We heard nothing but static after you entered the chamber."

Banger nodded at Crenshaw.

"We decided Banger would distract the all-seeing eye while I searched for a hidden control to open the door." Crenshaw sipped hot coffee and shot a glance at Banger.

"Hold on." Brown leaned forward. "Dr. Crenshaw, what all-seeing eye?"

"Sorry, Ian, but that will be difficult to explain. Let's start with the easy bits." Crenshaw grabbed a chocolate-covered doughnut. "Like I said, we searched the circular room. There were four statues along the perimeter—Poseidon, Solraya, Luna, and Blaze. At first, nothing seemed unusual about them."

He took a sip of coffee. "Then I took a closer look at the blond goddess nearest the door. Her diadem seemed thicker than the ones on her sisters' heads, and I discovered it was mounted on a circular track. I rotated it clockwise, and the door opened." He grinned and bit into the doughnut.

Bern faced his SEAL. "Banger, what was in that room?"

He shrugged. "Hard to explain, sir."

"Never seen anything like it." Crenshaw shook his head.

"Damn it, Crenshaw, you're the bloody archaeologist. Let's have it." Frustration tinged Brown's voice.

"In the chamber's center, a gold dragon sculpture clutched a glowing crystal globe with a big eye suspended inside." He sighed. "The eye watched us, like someone could see through it remotely."

Banger jumped in. "Yeah, our headlamps died when we discussed taking the globe. And when I told Crenshaw to leave it, our headlamps came back on."

Brown shook his head. "That could've been a coincidence."

"Which is why I tested it twice more with the same result." Crenshaw crossed his arms.

Rowlin narrowed his eyes. "Gentlemen, are you saying every time you verbally indicated your intention to take the globe your headlamps went out, and every time you said you'd leave it there your lights came back on?"

"Exactly, and when I pointed out the shafts above and below the globe, the stone door sealed us in and severed our cables." Crenshaw took another bite of his doughnut.

Rowlin searched the divers' eyes and found no deceit. "What about our main objective? Did you find Poseidon's Sword?"

A shrug. "We found a golden ten-foot statue of Poseidon holding a seven-foot trident. It didn't appear to *do* anything." Crenshaw glanced at the men across from him. "That pyramid was built by an ancient civilization whose technology was quite different from ours. What if that globe with the all-seeing eye *is* the weapon?"

Banger nodded. "It had its own light source, also impossible to explain."

"According to our intel on the artifact discovered by Samantha Starr a few months ago in Hong Kong, it was an obsidian pyramid with three goddess statues standing on top, each holding a small crystal pyramid. It housed a powerful laser weapon." Rowlin looked at the divers. "Did you see anything like that?"

Crenshaw thought a moment. "Come to think of it, the three goddess statues *were* holding crystals shaped like pyramids." Crenshaw turned to Banger. "Right?"

"Yep, and the shafts beneath and above the globe looked like they extended through the center of the pyramid." He tilted his head. "I recall Crenshaw saying the shafts might be an energy pathway right before the door dropped."

Rowlin shook his head. "I never dreamed my first mission on *Leviathan* would be this bizarre."

NINE

MacLeod Castle

Blaze and Mom continued practicing telepathy every day and expanding the distance between them. Later, I joined in from Ross's castle, adding to the fun.

"This is working out great for me," I said. *"While you practice for the mission, I get to enjoy time with Ross."* I snuggled against his shoulder as we lounged in bed. I savored the fact he was unaware I was having a telepathic conversation.

"And I get to spend time with Mike," Blaze said. *"I really like him."*

"Oh boy, looks like Ross is ready for round two. I'll have to sign off now. Have fun, ladies."

"Wait, what did you mean by round two?" Blaze's voice blasted in my head.

"I'll explain later. Gotta go."

After our second steamy afternoon delight, Ross nuzzled my neck. "What are your long-term plans, lass?"

I gazed into is deep-blue eyes. "Same as most people—marriage and children—but not right away, so don't bolt. I'd like us to have the chance to experience whatever normal life is once the Black Sun mission and search for Poseidon's Sword is over."

He smiled and stroked my hair. "Ever since I met you last summer, your life has never been normal. Do you really expect that to change?"

"Geez, I hope so. I wouldn't want to keep up that pace my entire life." I smoothed his jet-black hair. "What about you? Do you have a plan for the future?"

"Aye, lass, and it all centers around you." He kissed me softly. "Even though we live on opposite sides of the ocean, and major crises keep getting in the way, I can't imagine life without you."

"Good, because I intend to keep you." I decided it was time to lighten the mood so I nibbled is ear. "If you don't want to lose any body parts, now would be a good time to feed me."

He glanced at his watch. "Get dressed and I'll take you to my favorite pub. The food there is delicious."

Every so often while I was with Ross, I contacted Mom and Blaze telepathically, just to check in and see how they were progressing.

Eventually, Mom was able to contact Blaze's sisters in the Himalayas, just like I did. After she mastered talking to all three sisters at once, the five of us practiced connecting simultaneously, like we would during the mission in Antarctica.

The full moon was due in one week.

USS LEVIATHAN

Rowlin met in the ship's conference room with the same men who had convened after the divers escaped the pyramid's upper chamber.

"That massive storm system that stalled over us a few days really put us behind schedule." Rowlin glanced at Crenshaw and Banger. "Let's start with a status report from the divers."

"Forget about the room with the glowing globe." Crenshaw shook his head. "We can't find a way to open that bloody door from the outside."

Banger nodded. "We don't want to risk damaging the interior with explosives, and you know we lost one of our ROVs while searching narrow passages nearby."

"Gentlemen, I'm open to suggestions. The Pentagon brass is leaning on me hard. We struck out in the apex, but there must be some way to enter near the base." Rowlin opened a folder and handed out papers.

Kip glanced at the info. "These are diagrams of pyramids. Are we hoping to find similarities with the Atlantean pyramid?"

Rowlin nodded. "Emphasis on hoping. Anything look familiar?"

"The Egyptian pyramids at Giza look like the Atlantean one with their proportions based on the golden ratio." Crenshaw pointed at a diagram. "The Great Pyramid's entrance is fifty-nine feet above ground level, so it's possible the Atlantean pyramid is similar."

"Can we use a submersible ground-penetrating radar unit along the base to find the entrance?" Banger asked.

Kip frowned. "GPR doesn't work in salt water."

"So how do we find the door?" Rowlin glanced from Crenshaw to Kip.

Crenshaw tapped a spot on the diagram. "The entrance should be centrally positioned fifty-nine feet above the base, like in the Great Pyramid. The problem is each side of this pyramid is 786 feet long, and we don't know how much of its base is hidden under thousands of years of silt."

"Our research sub has advanced subsurface imaging." Kip sipped his coffee. "We'll look in the middle at the base and work upward."

"All right, but which side?" Rowlin ran his hand over his short sandy hair.

"The one in Egypt is on the north face. This one's oriented to the four compass points like the Great Pyramid, so let's start with the north side." Crenshaw gazed at the ceiling, like he was visualizing something. "A bigger problem will be excavating at a depth of 2,000 feet if the entrance is partly buried in silt."

Rowlin drained his cup. "Not really. We have the equipment for that —a modified Javeler hydraulic submersible dredge pump with accumulators for pressure equalization. It's effective down to 4,000 feet and is powered hydraulically with an ROV."

"Let's send down our research sub and find that entrance." Kip sat back, satisfied.

Crenshaw grinned. "You Americans have all the best toys."

Rowlin stood beside Bern and Kip as Crenshaw and Banger donned their Hardsuits.

Kip patted Rowlin on the back. "Not bad. It only took three days for our sub to find the entrance and an ROV to blow the door open and clear the debris."

Rowlin nodded. "I wish I could send you down with them, but we need over 2,500 feet of cable for each diver to reach the bottom and explore inside the pyramid." He faced Kip. "Sorry you have to wait. You can go once they find something."

"I understand. Besides, you might need the other suit for the rescue diver." Kip thumbed at a SEAL nick-named Ace who waited nearby.

Bern gestured at a winch. "This one's ready to deploy Ace if necessary."

Rowlin checked the monitor. "ROV shows water is clear at the dredge site. Divers are cleared to descend. Be careful down there."

"Right you are. No telling what we'll find this time." Crenshaw rechecked his gauges and snapped a few pictures of the sunken British research vessel as he descended.

"I wish our lights penetrated farther," Banger said. "I'd love to get the big-picture view of the city. Too bad we can only see the pyramid and shipwreck in the dark gloom."

"Maybe we can get a tour on the Scorpion later," Crenshaw said, snapping a picture of Banger.

When the divers reached the entrance, Banger said, "It's plenty wide enough to enter side by side, but let's take it slow and look for traps."

Their headlamps illuminated a wide dark passage straight ahead. The broad hallway was flanked by statues of Atlantean kings and queens wearing gold crowns and wielding gold trident scepters. The eight-foot statues were spaced every ten feet on both sides.

"These statues are magnificent." Crenshaw snapped closeups of the statues' faces as the divers eased into the infinite darkness.

At 300 feet in, Banger raised his arm. They stopped at a wide archway opening into a huge circular chamber 186 feet in diameter as measured by Crenshaw's laser measuring device mounted in his helmet.

Crenshaw checked the archway. "I don't see any trigger devices. Looks safe to enter."

Banger thrusted into an ornate room with a ninety-foot domed ceiling.

Crenshaw pointed. "Looks like there's an open four-inch cylindrical shaft in the ceiling's center. Probably the same one we found in that upper chamber." He used his thruster to float to the middle and survey the circular room.

Banger followed.

Crenshaw pointed his headlamp into the ceiling shaft, and it reflected even brighter. He glanced down. "Another shaft runs through the floor. See it, right under this huge orca sculpture?"

Banger looked from side to side before admiring the impressive sculpture. "Don't forget what happened the last time we commented on possible energy shafts."

Four orca statues balanced backs-to-backs on their tailfins, their heads bowed. An enormous diamond cut into a vertical rhombus nestled between their necks. The sharp tips pointed up and down toward the central shaft.

"That geometric-shaped diamond must be worth a gazillion dollars." Banger snapped several pictures.

"Maybe it's the laser weapon." Crenshaw studied the orca sculpture.

"Check those out." Banger pointed.

A hundred white marble statues of beautiful life-size women guarded the circular perimeter. Each held a pyramid-shaped crystal. Four statues sat on golden thrones at equidistant intervals between them. One was Poseidon, and the other three were the triplet Goddesses of Sun, Moon, and Fire.

Crenshaw floated along the perimeter and photographed each statue. "I think I discovered something important." He crouched to look at one of the statue's crystals then glanced between the statue on his left and the one on his right. He compared them to the statue on the throne between them, then looked out at the center sculpture. "Right, I'm rather sure about this." He thrusted to a statue on a throne directly across the room.

Banger joined him. "What's up?"

He tapped his integrated dive compass and pointed at a statue. "See how this statue is aligned with north? She's angling the tip of her crystal at that diamond rhombus. All four statues on the thrones are aligned with cardinal compass points and are aiming their crystals at the huge diamond."

"Right, the triplets are holding their crystals, and Poseidon's crystal is at the tip of his gold scepter, also pointing at the diamond." Banger moved closer to Crenshaw.

"And the orcas are positioned so there's only a clear path to the diamond from those four statues." Crenshaw pointed at the magnificent gem. "The rest of the statues are aiming their crystals toward a central point above the orcas."

Banger circled the perimeter and checked his findings. "You're right. It's as if they're all directing energy from their crystals either into the diamond or directly above it, all merging in line with those shafts that run through the center of the pyramid."

"This could be Poseidon's Sword." Crenshaw touched the brilliant gem with his claspers. "Look for a trigger mechanism."

A loud ping answered his comment.

They froze and waited.

Silence.

"The diamond might be the trigger." Crenshaw grasped the top point. "Maybe it rotates vertically to activate it." He tried to turn the massive diamond.

Another loud ping reverberated.

"Stop messing with that diamond," Banger yelled. "We should proceed slowly and study the room before we activate anything."

A razor-sharp trident about ten feet long dropped from a recess in the domed ceiling and speared Crenshaw's backpack, pinning him beside the orca sculpture. He jerked wildly, trying to break free.

Another trident brushed past his right shoulder, and the sharp tip embedded in the floor.

"Stop, you'll breach your suit!" Banger rushed toward Crenshaw.

Too late.

A trident dropped from the dome and pierced Crenshaw's helmet.

Air, blood, and guts erupted as his aluminum Hardsuit imploded under the immense water pressure.

Shocked, Banger stared at Crenshaw's crushed suit until he heard loud clangs echoing. He spun around.

Long tridents had dropped from recesses in the entrance archway, and their prongs had locked into grooves in the floor, barring the doorway.

"Mayday! Crenshaw's dead, and I'm trapped. Bring small explosives. Hurry." Banger shouted into his mike and zoomed to the door.

His heart sank when he discovered a trident had severed his cable. No comm. He had battery power and oxygen.

Gotta avoid spears while I wait for rescue.

He scooted under the archway as close as possible to the bars, seeking protection from deadly tridents as Crenshaw's dark-red cloud drifted past him.

God help me.

Atlantean Enclave

Clouds from the artificial tropical climate shrouded the Atlantean enclave hidden in the vast Himalayas. A full moon glowed through a milky swirl of cumulus clouds driven by air currents funneling through the high valley.

Luna peeked out her bedroom window and then hugged her sister, Solraya. "Wish me luck."

At 2:30 a.m., Luna pulled a heavy jacket from under her gilded canopy bed, shrugged it on, and checked the pockets for her goggles, gloves, wool ski mask, and gold coins. "All set."

Over the past six months, the triplets had stolen everything they would need from the Atlanteans.

"Be careful and give my love to Blaze." Solraya hugged Luna again. "I'll miss you."

"Don't worry, if everything goes according to our plan, we'll be together soon." Luna pulled on her gloves, climbed out the window, slid thirty feet down their handmade rope, and slipped into the shadows cast by clouds over the small village.

Dressed in black, she darted between dark buildings to an obsidian pyramid towering a hundred feet into the moonlit sky. A narrow stairway up the back side led to the top. Luna climbed slowly, cloaked in the pyramid's shadow where most of the wind was blocked.

The previous night, she had secured her black paraglider and an insulated cocoon to a gold platform at the apex of the pyramid, hidden from observers on the ground. Now she pulled on her wool ski mask and goggles, secured her hood over them, and spread out the paraglider. She buckled her harness and attached it to the silk glider, careful to arrange the risers just so. Then she pulled off her gloves and held them in her teeth.

She tugged the cocoon up to her armpits, fastened it to her harness, and pulled on her gloves. She yanked the risers to lift the paraglider and turned into the brisk wind. In an instant, she was airborne and rising above the black pyramid. Powerful air currents lifted her higher as she aimed for a tiny cluster of lights far beyond a narrow pass in the mountains.

The clouds dissipated, and the temperature plunged the moment she left the invisible zone surrounding the enclave. She'd never felt air that cold.

"This is exhilarating—the freedom, the cold air, the speed—I should've done this a long time ago. Blaze, thank you for having the courage to go first," Luna said telepathically.

Sam cut in. *"Pay close attention to the air currents. They can shift in an instant and slam you into a mountain. Concentrate on managing your lift and forward momentum."*

"Remember what I taught you after my flight, which was a lot easier than yours," Blaze said.

"The wind feels steady. Maybe it's not as variable at night."

"Don't count on that," Sam said. *"Expect anything and always be on the lookout for a safe place to land."*

"I hope I can stay up a long time. I love this."

"Our high valley acclimated us to low oxygen, but don't go too high." Blaze's voice sounded comforting. *"We'll stay with you until you land."*

Luna enjoyed the panoramic view of majestic mountains towering over a snow-covered valley glistening in the bright moonlight as she glided in silence, ever increasing her distance from the enclave.

Her paraglider shuddered and jerked up in the shifting air currents. A sudden gust turned her toward a jagged wall of granite.

"Oh God, I'm headed for a cliff!"

"Pull the control on the opposite side to turn back into the wind," Sam said.

Luna barely avoided sharp crags stretching out for her, but one tore her cocoon as she brushed past.

"My cocoon has a long tear down the left side, but I missed the cliff."

"Luna, you have to be ready for every wind shift," Sam said. *"One mistake could kill you."*

"Don't worry, I'm so pumped full of adrenaline my reflexes are razor sharp now."

Lifted and propelled by the howling wind, she sped toward her destination, a tiny village nestled beside a road to a small, distant airport. She remained vigilant as her paraglider rose, dipped, and barely missed rocky crags sharp enough to shred her. After almost two hours, Luna alighted on a narrow road.

"I'm finally on the ground. Thanks for keeping me company, Blaze and Sam."

"We're glad you landed safely," Blaze said. *"Contact us when you reach the Arabian Sea."*

Luna slipped out of her harness and rolled up the paraglider. The silk glider fit perfectly in the insulated cocoon she had worn for warmth.

She shivered as she headed toward the dim village lights. The valley was silent except for the relentless wind whipping through high mountains flanking the snow-covered dirt road.

A low rumble interrupted Luna's quiet hike. She stepped aside as an old Jeep emerged over a rise in the road. Bright headlights blinded her when it stopped in front of her.

TEN

USS LEVIATHAN

R owlin paced on the bridge. "Any update on the dive team?"

"Bad news," Bern said. "We just reeled in Banger's severed cable. Crenshaw's cable is hung up on something. No comms from either diver."

Rowlin called the moon pool's operator. "Launch an ROV to search for our dive team. I don't want to send another man down until I have some intel. And get the Scorpion ready. I want it fully armed."

"Aye, Captain, I'll have the ROV inside the pyramid in fifteen minutes."

Rowlin glanced at his watch and stared down at the placid ocean, gentle rollers masking the drama unfolding deep below.

Several minutes later, the intercom chimed. "Uh, Captain, you'd better come down and see this. Bring Commander Bern with you." The ROV operator's tone was grim.

"We're on our way." Rowlin turned to Lowes. "XO, you have the conn."

When Rowlin and Bern entered the moon-pool chamber, the ROV operator waved them over to a video screen displaying live feed. Banger stood behind bars. He pointed over his shoulder at Crenshaw's crushed suit, pinned beside an orca sculpture. Then he made a writing motion with his right clasper.

"This is a disaster." Rowlin turned to Bern. "Send Ace down with explosives."

Bern picked up the interphone and called the dive station on deck where Ace was standing by in a Hardsuit.

It wasn't long before he was reeled down with a bag of small, pre-wired explosives.

Rowlin and Bern watched him on the monitor. At the bottom, Ace used his thrusters to enter the pyramid. He ignored the magnificent royal statues and rushed down the wide passage to Banger.

He stopped a few feet in front of the barred archway where Banger waved frantically on the other side for him to hurry forward.

Too late.

Tridents dropped from the ceiling and pierced Ace's Hardsuit, pinning it to the floor. His body imploded along with his suit and obscured the crumpled metal in a dark cloud.

Hovering nearby, the ROV had captured the gruesome scene for Rowlin and Bern.

Banger made exaggerated writing motions again with his right clasper.

"Damn it, this shouldn't have happened!" Rowlin pounded his fist on the bulkhead.

Bern shook his head. "It's my fault. Banger signaled he needed to write something when the ROV first found him. I assumed he wanted us to send a diver with explosives and jumped the gun. I should've warned you to hold off on sending Ace down."

Rowlin sucked in his breath and squeezed Bern's shoulder. "I'm responsible, period." He nodded at the ROV operator. "Bring up the ROV so we can send it back to Banger with a slate and grease pencil."

The ROV returned in ten minutes. Rowlin and Bern watched its video feed as it headed back down to Banger armed with the slate. Upon arrival, its robotic arm struggled to angle the slate through the bars. Finally, it succeeded.

Banger grabbed the grease pencil with his right clasper, scrawled a note, and held it in front of the video camera: NEED OVERHEAD SHIELDS TO BLOCK TRIDENTS.

Rowlin stared at the monitor. "Have the ROV cut Ace's cable so we can reel it in, then send the ROV outside to avoid spears while we figure out how to make two trident-resistant shields." He glanced at Bern. "Any ideas?"

Bern rubbed his chin. "How many Kevlar vests do we have?"

"Enough for the entire crew." Rowlin's eyes brightened. "Oh, you're thinking of using some to build a shield thick enough to stop tridents?"

"It could work." Bern nodded. "We'll mount them on aluminum sheets with handles riveted to the underside for the divers' claspers."

"And I have a sharp sword we can use to field-test them." Rowlin grabbed the interphone and called the maintenance bay. "This is Captain Rowlin. I need two four-by-four sheets of heavy-duty aluminum with two metal handles riveted three feet apart on the under-side of each sheet across the middle. I'll be down with the rest of the parts. This is a rush job."

Himalayas

Three men approached cautiously from the Jeep and faced Luna in a semicircle.

"What are you doing out here in the middle of the night?" a man with a broad face and three front teeth missing said in Hindi.

Luna answered in perfect Hindi, thanks to her extensive education. "I'm on a long journey and need a ride to the airport."

Not sure how much to pay, she offered a gold coin to each man.

"Or we can take *all* your gold and sell you to the white slavers," a tall burly man on her left said. He yanked off her hood, goggles, and ski mask. "Ah, a real beauty."

"You don't want to do this." She stepped back. "It will end badly for you."

The men laughed. The one on her right snatched the sack from her and looked inside.

"You're making a big mistake." She glared at the men.

"Take off your jacket. We want a closer look, maybe sample the merchandise before we sell you." Broad face grinned with his hideous teeth.

"This is your last warning." Luna took another step back. "Don't make me kill you."

Broad face laughed and flicked open a switchblade. "Don't make me cut off your clothes."

He waved the knife. "Start stripping."

The men laughed.

Luna rushed backward and focused on her attackers. Steam rose from the ground beneath them. In seconds, a thick fog obscured the men as their screams pierced the night. Flames crackled through heavy mist as the surrounding snow melted into a stream of boiling water red with blood.

An acrid scent of burnt flesh tainted the air.

Five minutes later, frigid air currents quelled the steam. Three charred lumps smoldered twenty feet in front of the Jeep.

Luna bent over and wretched. She steadied herself and picked up her goggles, ski mask, and bag before walking around the human cinders.

She sighed. *Why wouldn't they stop threatening me?*

She tossed her bag on the back seat and climbed into the Jeep. Her hand trembled as she switched on the ignition. It didn't take long to figure out how to drive.

Soon she was winding down the mountain road to the remote airport.

USS LEVIATHAN

It took about fifteen minutes for Rowlin and Bern to finish making two shields covered with a double layer of Kevlar vests.

Rowlin picked up his Navy sword. "I hope this works." He stood over the shield and plunged the sword straight down with as much force as he could muster.

The sword only penetrated partway through the first layer of Kevlar.

Bern examined the result. "We have a winner, but the divers will have to guard against being knocked over by the tridents slamming into their shields."

"We'd better get this right. This is our last Hardsuit until new ones arrive via helicopter next week." Rowlin sheathed his sword.

Bern smacked his forehead with his palm. "I was so focused on making the shields that I forgot about diver qualification."

Rowlin faced him. "Explain."

"The Hardsuit 2000s are so new that we only had two SEALs trained in them, Banger and Ace." He shook his head and frowned. "We can't risk sending down an untrained diver, especially at that maximum depth and with all the hazards inside the pyramid."

Rowlin clenched his jaw. "We have a Hardsuit-qualified diver, but he's not a SEAL. He's a marine biologist—Dr. Peterson."

"Think he can handle this mission?"

"He's got at least thirty Hardsuit dives, some under treacherous conditions." Rowlin picked up the interphone. "Send Dr. Peterson to the maintenance bay."

"I'm betting he'll jump at the chance. I saw envy in his eyes every time the divers went down." Bern turned a shield over.

"He told me he's eager to get inside the pyramid. I think he can do this." Rowlin turned when he heard the bulkhead door open.

"Captain, Commander, how may I help?" Kip glanced at the shields.

"You're the only Hardsuit-qualified diver we have left. Crenshaw and Ace are dead, and we need to rescue Banger." Rowlin scrutinized him. "Are you up for it?"

"Yes, sir, send me in." He lifted a heavy shield. "What're these for?"

Rowlin explained the situation. "These shields will be the only things standing between you guys and the tridents."

"How long are the tridents?" Kip examined the shields.

"We estimate about ten feet," Bern said. "The ones in the domed ceiling drop from ninety feet, but the water slows them down a little."

"So, we'll brace for impact, move slowly, and make damn sure we don't stumble." Peterson looked at them. "When can I suit up?"

"They should be ready for you on deck." Rowlin offered his hand. "I knew I could count on you. Be careful down there."

Kip shook his hand and glanced from Rowlin to Bern. "One request: I'd rather not go down unarmed."

"No problem." Bern patted his shoulder. "With the captain's permission, I'll give you a ballistic speargun loaded with six spears."

Rowlin nodded. "I'm all for hedging our bets. Let's get moving."

Thirty minutes later, Kip spoke into his voice-activated mike. "I'm entering the pyramid. My shield is overhead, and Banger's shield is tethered to my utility belt." He glanced over his shoulder. "ROV is shadowing me." Sweat trickled down his face, more from nerves than heat.

His bright headlamp illuminated the royal hallway as he stepped deliberately, expecting a trident to hammer him any second.

Nothing.

His labored breath was the only sound in the eerie hall.

He took thirty minutes to walk the 300 feet to the circular chamber's archway. A trident slammed into his shield when he was five feet from Banger. Deflected by the Kevlar, the sharp spear clattered onto the floor, but Kip fell to one knee.

He sucked in his breath, stood, and edged up to the bars. Smiling, he waved and maneuvered the other shield through the bars to Banger.

"I sure am happy to see you," Banger said via his radio. Thanks for coming to save my ass. Hand me the explosives from Ace's bag and I'll blast free."

As Kip retrieved the explosives, tridents hammered him, barely missing the charges. He noticed Banger didn't raise the shield when he stood under the archway close to the bars, so he followed his lead on his side.

Banger worked with smooth efficiency as he rigged the bars to blow out. When he finished, he said, "Raise your shield and move over against a wall."

Kip backed away and was stunned by falling tridents. He dropped to one knee but quickly recovered and took cover by a wall.

The detonation triggered small shock waves, but the divers were braced. Banger thrusted through the archway as new tridents dropped.

His shield prevented them from forming another barrier, and they clanged onto the floor behind him, echoing off stone walls.

The divers stood beside each other and looked down the long hallway as tridents slammed into their shields.

"There seems to be an endless supply of these damn spears near the chamber." Banger glanced at Kip. "I think the hot zone ends a little farther down the hall. Ready to run the gauntlet?"

"Wait, I think something's moving just beyond our lights." Kip tried to discern what it was.

The ROV zoomed up to them and bobbed up and down, like a dog trying to get their attention.

Kip heard Bern's voice in his helmet speaker. "Warning! Something big is headed your way. We didn't get a good look at it."

"Understood, we'll proceed with caution." Peterson relayed the message to Banger.

"I have a bad feeling about this. Let's back up against the wall between those statues and turn off our floodlights." Banger eased up against the hallway wall beside the statue of an Atlantean king.

Kip backed in beside him, and they extinguished their lights.

The one-foot oval ROV floated nearby in water as black as sackcloth. Only its tiny position lights were visible as it sped fifty feet down the corridor and trained its floodlight toward the exit 250 feet past it.

A dark shadow crept closer. Kip recognized it when the ROV's floodlight illuminated it.

"I've been worrying about this ever since that megalodon attacked our ship. I was hoping I'd be wrong, but no such luck." Kip handed Banger the spear gun. "That's a baby megalodon."

"Baby my ass! It has to be over thirty feet." Banger briefly lit his headlamp and glanced at the spear gun. "This'll be like hitting him with pellets. Turn on your floodlight while I rig the spears with explosive tips. He probably won't notice us between these statues."

"Don't count on it. Light will draw him, and he can sense our heartbeats anyway." Kip looked at the approaching shark. "I have a better idea. Let's lead him into the circular chamber and stand flush against the walls on either side of the door."

"Oh, I get it. He'll get speared swimming through the entrance. I like it." Banger switched on his floodlight, slung the bag over his shoulder, and gripped his shield as he thrusted back to the chamber.

Kip followed close behind as tridents smashed into their shields. He turned and stopped along the right wall as Banger veered left. No tridents dropped while they were against the walls.

The ROV, now brightly lit, zipped into the chamber with the baby megalodon in hot pursuit. The ROV's floodlight extinguished as it hid behind the central orca sculpture in the vast room.

No tridents fell when the huge shark swam through the archway.

"New plan: We trick the archway mechanism into barring the door with tridents." Kip eased along the wall to the archway.

"We have to time this to the split second, or we'll be trapped in here with the meg." Banger inched toward the arch.

Kip hesitated and watched the ROV dodging the giant predator. "We'll back through side-by-side using our thrusters for one quick burst."

Banger eased beside him close to the arch. "Ready?"

"Hurry and count down." He pointed. "It's headed for us."

"Three, two, one." Banger activated his thrusters.

The two divers barely made it through the archway as an avalanche of tridents sealed off the doorway.

The baby meg smashed into the bars, and the tridents bent outward.

"I don't think those bars will hold him for long. Let's get the hell out of here." Banger zoomed down the long corridor.

Kip raced up beside him. "I hate to tell you this, but that shark may not be our worst problem. The parent we didn't kill might be nearby. We should proceed with caution."

"You're saying we've got a huge man-eater on our six and maybe an even bigger one waiting outside? At least the tridents stopped assaulting us." Banger's voice sounded faint.

"You've got another problem: Your battery is almost gone. Turn off your light and tether to my rear grommet so I can tow you." Kip handed him a line from his utility pack.

Kip called Bern once Banger was secured. "Peterson to base: I've got Banger on a tow line. His battery's almost dead."

"Understood. We lost feed from the ROV. What happened with the big shark?"

"We trapped it in the chamber, but it's about to break free. We need to hitch a ride on the Scorpion, but first can you verify the parent we didn't kill isn't roaming around down here?"

"I'll get the sonar operator to ping the area and then send down the Scorpion. Where do want to wait?"

"We're sitting ducks inside this entrance hall. I'll look for a nearby building with a door too small for the thirty-foot meg. Peterson out."

The sound of metal breaking reverberated down the hallway as Kip rushed outside with Banger in tow.

Gwadar, Pakistan

Luna paid the pilot ten gold coins. "Thanks for the fun flight. I loved it, and you can keep the paraglider. I won't need it."

He zipped the coins into an inside jacket pocket. "Wait a minute while I flag down a fuel truck, and I'll escort you to the terminal."

She walked under the high wing and around the odd-looking main landing gear, its long struts looking like legs with bent knees. "It's not that far. You don't have to walk me."

The pilot in his late twenties smiled and gazed longingly at the raven-haired beauty. "The guards will harass you if you walk in alone." He flagged down a fuel truck to fill the tanks in his Polish-manufactured single-engine PZL Wilga, its polished aluminum skin shining in the late afternoon sun.

"Oh, thank you. I don't want any trouble." Luna shrugged off her heavy jacket, perspiration moistening her skin in the warm, mid-70s coastal air. She followed him through an entrance door at the Gwadar International Airport terminal.

He walked with her to the exit and pointed. "You can get a taxi over there." He handed her a business card. "Call me if you need a flight back. I hope I see you again."

She waved goodbye and strolled to the taxi stand, where she read the posted fare to the port.

The first cabbie in line opened his rear passenger door. "Taxi,

Miss?"

She jumped in. "Take me to Gwadar Port. I can pay with something far more valuable than rupees." She flashed a 1.5-inch diameter gold coin.

The cabbie slid behind the wheel and turned to stare at the glittering gold. His eyes widened. "Make it three…no *five* gold coins."

According to a sign near the taxi stand, the harbor was nine miles away.

Luna frowned and opened the door. "I'm no fool. If you're going to be greedy, I'll take a different cab."

"No, no, I will take you. One coin is enough." He reached out his hand.

"I'll hold onto this until we arrive." She closed the door and sat back.

Twenty minutes later, through crowded streets and a mélange of offensive fumes, annoying horns, and roaring engines, they pulled up to the port. Luna stepped out and surrendered her coin.

Now, how to find the right boat? She scanned the bustling harbor, ignored the huge freighters and tankers, and headed for an area crowded with fishing boats.

Gulls squawked and swarmed around a small trawler tied nearby. Blood and fish guts littered the dock. A man perched on a barrel, mending a net.

Luna wrinkled her nose and stepped over the smelly innards. "Hello, is your boat available for charter?"

He glanced up at her, his eyes widening. "Uh, well, that depends. Where do you want to go?"

"About thirty miles out to sea." She stepped closer. "I'll pay you well."

"Lady, that's sixty miles round-trip, and fuel is expensive." He rubbed his fingers together in the universal sign for money.

"I'm only going one way, but, of course, I'll pay for the round-trip fuel."

He raised a brow. "You're going thirty miles out, and then what?"

"And then you'll return alone. That's all you need to know." She edged closer. "Will you take me?"

He rubbed his jaw and studied her. "It'll cost you $2,000 American, plus $1,000 to keep me quiet." He stood and dropped the net.

"Oh, I have something far better than dollars." She handed him a gold coin. "I'll give you another ten. They're worth way more than $3,000. Do we have a deal?"

He turned the heavy coin over in his hand with the same greedy smile as the cabbie's. "When do you want to go?"

"Right now." She held out her hand for assistance to board.

He hesitated. "It'll be dark soon, and my crew went home."

"We don't need them. Isn't your boat equipped for night running?" Luna pointed at fixtures housing flood and position lights.

He frowned at his watch. "I'll be late for dinner."

She flashed him more gold coins from her pocket. "Think about how many dinners these will buy. Let's get moving." The coins jingled in her pocket.

He ran his eyes over her and licked his lips. "All right." He held her hand too long after helping her board.

She pulled her hand away and tapped the cockpit console. "I'll show you where to go on this GPS unit once were underway."

He started the engines and released the dock lines. Screeching gulls circled as they headed out of the harbor.

Luna contacted Blaze telepathically. *"I hired a trawler captain to rendezvous with the submarine. We're on our way."*

"Does the boat have a GPS?"

"Yes, that's the first thing I looked for. Give me the coordinates."

Blaze told her where to meet the submarine. *"The U.S. Navy doesn't want the guy on the fishing boat to see their sub. When you reach the waypoint, jump into the sea and tell the captain to go home."*

"All right. I'll contact you when we get there. Can't wait to see you in Scotland and meet everyone." Luna entered the coordinates in the GPS and glanced down at the darkening sea as the boat plowed through gentle rollers.

Sunken City of Atlantis

Outside of the pyramid, Kip veered left with Banger in tow and scanned the water illuminated by his floodlight. Something deadly could be lurking just beyond his light's range, but the lethal shark stalking them took precedence.

Kip's sweat-soaked hair stood up on the back of his neck, a primeval warning as old as mankind. "Where should we go?"

"I remember a marble building about fifty yards ahead." Banger glanced at his compass and pointed. "That way."

"I'll use maximum thrust to get us there before the meg swims out." They surged into the inky void as his floodlight blasted a narrow tunnel of light.

A white marble building soon materialized. Kip rushed over the stone steps and propelled them through an open four-foot-wide entryway.

A loud thud behind them broke the tense silence. Kip shuddered and glanced over his shoulder. The baby meg's head had rammed the doorway a second after they entered. Luckily, it was too big to fit through.

"That was close." Kip towed Banger several feet from the door.

The shark repeatedly rammed its head in a frenzy, driving deep vibrations through the stone building.

Sweat ran down Kip's face and burned his eyes. "I don't think it can break through. Let's hope the surviving parent isn't out there." He glanced at Banger when he didn't hear a response.

Banger scribbled on his slate: Dead battery. Call for help.

Kip nodded. Dive Ops was listening to his voice-activated mike via his communication cable. He spoke to the SEAL in command. "Bern, we're in a marble building about fifty yards east of the pyramid's entrance. The baby meg is ramming the door, but it's too big to get in. Send the Scorpion to draw it away and blast it to bits."

"Understood. They're coming. How's Banger?" Bern was all business, like any SEAL during a mission.

"His battery's dead. He's writing on the slate. Uh, any intel on this monster's other parent?" Kip steadied his voice as the shark continued ramming the building.

"Nothing on sonar, but the Scorpion is fully armed just in case. Sit tight. We'll get you out of there. Dive Ops out."

Kip wrote on Banger's slate: Scorpion coming.

ELEVEN

Arabian Sea

S tars sparkled around a brilliant full moon as the trawler captain cut the engines. "Okay, this is it." He glanced around at the empty sea and grinned. "Time for some fun."

He reached for Luna.

She pushed him away. "No fun. I'm going for a swim, and you're going home." She handed him the gold coins.

He turned and locked the coins in a console compartment.

She contacted Blaze. *"I'm at the rendezvous point, ready to jump in."*

"Good, we're in contact with the sub. It'll be there soon. Send the boat away."

The captain licked his lips and pulled a blade from a recess in the console. "Take off your clothes." He waved the knife.

Not again.

She stepped backward. "Don't make me kill you. Take your gold and go home before it's too late."

He curled his lips into a snarl. "I'm not afraid of an unarmed woman. Obey me or I'll cut you."

Luna bit her lip and backed up to the stern rail.

He grinned and waved the knife. "You're trapped with no one to help you. Time to get naked."

Blaze's voice blasted in her head. *"Five minutes, Luna. Is the boat gone?"*

"No, the captain is threatening me with a knife. He ordered me to strip."

"Defend yourself and don't let him see the submarine."

"This is your last chance," Luna yelled. "Leave me alone and go home."

He thrust the knife at her belly.

She dodged the blade and punched his nose. Blood poured down his face.

"You'll pay for that. When I'm done having my fun, I'll sell you to the white slavers."

Blaze invaded her head again. *"One minute."*

"I'll be ready."

Luna turned and jumped into the sea. She kicked hard to flee the trawler.

"I'll chop you up with my propellers and let the sharks feast on what's left," the captain yelled.

He started the engines, shifted into forward gear, and began turning.

"Even though you're a bad man, I gave you a chance to live. Now it's too late," Luna yelled.

The water beneath the boat began to boil. Within seconds, the boat burst into flames. The fuel tank exploded, and a loud boom echoed on the water.

Luna ducked under before the blast's shock wave passed over. When she surfaced, burning flotsam littered the sea.

She shook her head and blinked salt water from her eyes. *Why didn't he do what I asked?* Her stomach churned.

A massive submarine surfaced behind her, and a wave from the displaced water splashed over her. She turned.

A man in a wetsuit dived into the water and swam toward her. When he was a few feet away, she recognized his face in the bright moonlight and glowing flames.

"Hello, Mike, it's good to finally see you in person." She managed a smile.

"My pleasure, Luna." He nodded at the flaming debris. "What happened?"

"The trawler captain attacked me. I had no choice." She bit her lip.

He pulled her close. "Are you okay?"

She sighed. "Why do men keep trying to hurt me? This didn't happen to Blaze when she escaped." She rested her head on his shoulder.

"Sounds like he got what he deserved, but I'm sorry you had to deal with that." He glanced at the trawler's charred remains. "I'm glad you're on our side. Put your arms around my neck, and I'll tow you to the sub."

SCORPION ONE

Jane and Scooter tightened their seat harnesses and saluted the moon-pool operator. Their sleek attack sub slipped into the water and silently dove toward the ancient city.

"Set our targeting sonar on active scan. Can't be any sea mammals down here with a meg on the hunt." Jane checked her heads-up display.

"Aye, Lieutenant, nothing so far." He swung their powerful floodlights around to different angles to probe the black depths.

After a few minutes, their lights illuminated sections of the magnificent city. They banked around a giant sphinx and zipped between gleaming white marble buildings.

"Don't expect a cake walk. That so-called baby is about the same size as our sub, and it's fast and deadly. Stay sharp." She maneuvered close to the bottom so the shark wouldn't surprise them from underneath.

"I'm always sharp," he said.

She pulled up and banked around a small golden pyramid.

He said, "Watch out for that big mermaid statue."

Jane swerved around it. She eased back on the throttle when their floodlights exposed the prehistoric shark. "There it is, ramming that doorway."

"We can't shoot and risk hurting the divers. We'll have to draw it away first." Scooter adjusted the range on his sonar. "An active ping will get its attention."

"Wait, we don't want that monster on our six. Is the harpoon loaded?" She silently hovered thirty feet behind the enraged beast.

"You want me to spear it?" He armed the firing switch.

"I'm assuming it'll run from the harpoon prongs embedded in its back, putting us on its six. Either way, we'll draw it away from the divers." Jane eased to within fifteen feet of their target. "Cleared to fire."

Scooter fired the harpoon into the meg's back behind its dorsal fin. The shark gyrated and shook. Then it fled upward and dragged the Scorpion behind it on a hundred-foot line.

"Release the harpoon line and fire the torpedo when you have target lock. I'll maneuver us clear." Jane steadied the sub behind the fleeing meg.

The big shark dipped, climbed, and turned, trying to break free of the sub. Just as Scooter got the target-locked tone, the harpoon tore loose.

The meg darted left.

"Damn, we had torpedo lock for a second before the prongs ripped loose," he said.

"No way in hell are we losing him. I'm sticking to his six like glue." Jane matched the shark's every move. "Smoke his ass, Scooter."

"I've got target lock. Torpedo away. Impact in three, two, one,…"

Jane banked hard right and dove for the bottom. A shock wave from the explosion rocked them. "Did we hit it?"

"I'd be drummed out of the Navy if I missed at that range. We just created another sushi buffet for the shark population." He patted her on the shoulder. "Nice piloting!"

"*Scorpion One* to base: The baby meg is fish food."

"Rowlin here. Good job. Now bring our divers up. We have a recovery team standing by on the port side."

"Aye, Captain, we'll bring them home. ETA five minutes." Jane dove to the marble building where the divers were hiding.

Scooter jabbed her shoulder. "Heads up, Lieutenant! Mommy's home, and she looks pissed!"

MacLeod Castle

Mike led Luna into the great hall, his SEAL team close behind. She bolted into her sister's arms. "Blaze, I wasn't sure if I'd ever see you again." They hugged.

"How was the trip?" Blaze grinned and stepped back.

"Except for those horrible men, everything was fun, especially the jet. The view was spectacular."

"Forget about the attacks. You're with good people now."

Luna glanced around. "This castle is beautiful, and I love the hearths with the blazing fires. Nice and cozy."

I stepped forward and took her hands in mine. "I feel like I already know you, Luna. We've talked telepathically so many times."

"Sam, you really do look exactly like Solraya." Luna backed away and smiled. "It's like my other sister is right here with me."

Mom slipped in and embraced her. "It's good to finally meet the person connected to the voice I've been hearing in my head."

After we finished fussing over each other, Luna met Duncan, Ben, Ross, Derek, the two generals, and the MI6 agents, while Ross's SAS team greeted Mike's SEAL team.

I noticed Derek kissed Luna's hand and locked eyes while her hand lingered in his. *Men.*

I turned and hugged Mike. "Good job, brother dear. I love it when a plan comes together. Did Matt get a chance to meet Luna?"

"He did. I think it was love at first sight, for him anyway." Mike grinned.

"He always was a sucker for dark-haired beauties. Did she say anything about him?"

Mike glanced around and lowered his voice. "She asked Matt to kiss her like I kissed Blaze." He shrugged. "I gave them a few minutes alone, and they were smiling when I returned."

I rolled my eyes. "Geez, you men never learn, do you?"

Mike winked. "I've learned a lot of things, Sis."

I punched his arm. "I hope you learned how not to get roasted."

Duncan tapped a knife against a glass. "Now that we're all here, let's be seated and begin the meeting." He waited until everyone settled into their chairs. "General Ryan, would you like to begin?"

Ryan stood. "Thank you, Laird MacLeod." He nodded at us women. "Ladies, the weather forecast is looking good for this week. We'll fly you down to McMurdo Station tomorrow. The UK has positioned an aircraft carrier on the northern border of the Weddell Sea. They'll provide the helicopters." He glanced at the British general. "General Barnes will explain the plan." Ryan sat down.

Blaze stood and interrupted. "My sister and I aren't going anywhere, because America did not honor its promise to issue our passports and assist us in receiving our inheritance."

Ryan's tone hardened. "We'll provide your passports after the Antarctic mission. We must act while we have a good forecast. I'm sure you understand."

"We understand we're non-persons with no country or legal rights." Blaze faced Ryan. "Our only leverage to return to America and live a normal life is our ability to help destroy the Black Sun and locate Poseidon's Sword. Once we accomplish that, you'll have no incentive to help us, and we'll be at your mercy."

Luna nodded. "We can always wait for another good forecast."

"But your inheritance will take time. You'll have to deal with courts and corporate lawyers from your father's company," Ryan said.

"Lawyers from Gold Trident Industries are en route from New York with their CEO, who happens to be the girls' uncle," Mom said. "Tim Conor has assured me that as long as the triplets agree in writing to allow him to continue running the company, he will transfer three quarters of the company's privately held stock to them. He said some of the other assets will take a little longer to sort out. He wants to do right by his brother's daughters."

Blaze nodded. "My uncle said once the lawyers examine the computer chips from our lockets, and verify we have valid ID from our passports, they'll execute the legal documents to finalize our stock transfer and begin processing the rest of our inheritance."

Luna stood. "We're not helping with anything until we have all three valid passports in hand and our inheritance documents." She settled back in her chair and crossed her arms.

Blaze and Luna glared at Ryan, the chandeliers buzzed, the lights flickered, and tension radiated throughout the great hall.

Ryan glanced at the vibrating lights and turned to his aide. "Set up the equipment for the passport photos." He turned to Blaze and Luna. "We'll email the photos to our London embassy and expedite the passports. We should have them by tomorrow morning in time for you to meet with the corporate lawyers and finalize your inheritance paperwork."

The buzzing stopped. The chandelier lights steadied. My muscles relaxed, and I exhaled.

"While we're waiting for my aide, let's finish the mission briefing." Ryan nodded to General Barnes.

Barnes glanced at the other women and me. "As promised, we'll do everything to ensure your safety and the success of the mission. Two Special Forces teams, SEALs led by Lieutenant Starr and SAS commandos led by Captain Sinclair, will provide security and rescue you out of the ice if necessary." He nodded at Ross.

Ross stood. "It's a long flight to Antarctica, so you'll rest at McMurdo. The next day, helicopters will take you to Rothera Station on the Antarctic Peninsula. We'll get you suited up in specialized survival gear. The suits have CO_2 cartridges for instant inflation, internal oxygen for two hours, GPS tracking devices, and strobe lights." He turned. "Mike?"

"We'll have one chopper drop you off at your individual ley-line positions." He glanced at Blaze. "This should be a swift in-and-out mission, no more than five minutes on the ice above the Black Sun's base. Helicopters will hover within three miles of each woman, waiting for Blaze's flare." Mike glanced at us. "Then the choppers will swoop in and pick you up."

Ryan stood. "Any questions?"

Mom raised her hand. "What about contingency plans?"

"Every helicopter will be equipped with a winch and a rescue diver. If you fall into an ice hole, inflate your suit and we'll get you out." Ryan glanced around.

"What if we don't kill Supreme Master quick enough?" Mom asked.

Blaze turned to Mom. "Our telepathic practice has made our

connections strong, and our combined power is absolute. Everyone inside that base will die in the first minute or two. We'll spend a few extra minutes to crack, melt, and sink the base, just to be certain we get them all. No worries, Loren, all will go as planned."

Ryan's aide returned. "Everything's ready to take the passport photos in the study."

Duncan stood. "Ladies, please return here when you finish the photos. My chef has prepared a delicious dinner with steak Béarnaise, new potatoes, and mixed vegetables. And we'll have plenty of Sam and Loren's favorite red blend, Opus One." He smiled at Mom.

I spied Luna and Derek locking eyes again and smiling.

Uh oh.

SCORPION ONE

Jane accelerated to a spot between tall buildings, settled on the seafloor, and cut their lights. She glanced up through their glass canopy and searched the eerie pitch-black water. "Did we lose her?"

Scooter studied the sonar screen. "Mommy dearest is right above us."

Huge jaws chomped on the roof of a nearby building and scattered stone blocks around them. The massive shark attacked the buildings with blind rage, savagely ramming and biting everything within reach. Its vengeful frenzy churned the water with turbulent currents rushing through the corridor between the stone structures in the ancient city.

"Attention Scorpion: This is the captain. Sonar picked up a seventy-five-foot creature in your vicinity, probably the baby meg's parent. Hold off on bringing up the divers until you torpedo that monster."

Jane keyed her mike. "It already found us, sir. We're pinned on the seafloor between two buildings. Can you draw it away so we can ride its six?"

The radio was silent a moment. "I have an idea. Sit tight, I'll get back to you. Rowlin out."

A small block hit the left wing and slid off the trailing edge. The beast continued hovering over them, ramming the roofs and showering the area with broken blocks.

"I sure hope the captain has a quick solution." Scooter pointed up. "We'll be buried in rubble if that monster doesn't stop soon."

"And there'll be no way to rescue us." She sighed.

We're counting on you, Captain.

USS LEVIATHAN

Rowlin called Kip. "Remain in the building. The baby meg's dead, but now the other parent is attacking the sub. Standby."

"Understood. Awaiting orders. Peterson out."

Rowlin called the SEAL commander in Dive Ops. "Bern, meet me down at the moon pool." He glanced at Lowes on his way out of the bridge. "XO, you have the conn."

"Aye, Captain." He saluted. "Time to kill another kraken."

Six minutes later, Bern strode into the submarine launch bay called the moon pool. "What's up, Captain?"

Rowlin stood beside the narrow twelve-foot tandem cockpit of *Scorpion Two*—all that remained after the first meg had destroyed the eighteen-foot section aft of the cockpit, including the wings. "Can you rig this to explode if the meg bites it? Enough C-4 to blow its head off?"

Bern put his hands on his hips and stared at the Scorpion's cockpit. "Oh yeah, no problem."

"Good. We'll rig it with enough batteries to power an array of floodlights. I want the beast to see it coming. We'll set it for slightly negative buoyancy for a slow descent." He opened the canopy. "Hopefully, the shark will investigate it and give *Scorpion One* a chance to maneuver behind it."

Bern nodded. "One way or another, there'll be a big boom and another meg funeral."

Rowlin nodded and called the chief mechanic with instructions.

Five minutes later, two mechanics walked in carrying boxes of wires and lights. Another sailor wheeled in a cart loaded with batteries. And Bern's SEAL team arrived with explosives and detonators.

Rowlin looked grim. "Get to work people. Time is critical."

The SEALs worked on the explosives, while the mechanics wired the floodlights. After ten minutes, Bern stepped back and stared, his mind apparently elsewhere.

Rowlin touched his shoulder. "What's up?"

Bern rubbed his chin. "I'd like to include a remote detonator as backup."

"Wouldn't that require visual confirmation on the target and an underwater detonation signal?" Rowlin shook his head. "Don't forget we lost our last ROV."

"We'll get confirmation from the Scorpion. I'll suit up and use a rebreather unit to prevent noisy bubbles and dive to a hundred feet. That depth will be sufficient to transmit the signal."

Rowlin hesitated. "You'll have nothing to protect you from that monster."

"The meg is focused on our attack sub. It won't even notice me almost 2,000 feet above it." His tone held firm. "I want to give our people every chance."

"Then I want antennas all over this. If the shark breaks one, I want six more that still work. Redundancy is our friend." Rowlin nodded at the workers. "Make it happen."

Scorpion Two's sealed cockpit crept down from beneath the USS *Leviathan*. Its lights were so bright that Rowlin could spot them from the bridge. When the lights faded from sight, he called Dive Ops.

"Confirm comms and send the diver down."

"Aye, Captain, the comms are good between the sub, the ship, and our diver," a SEAL in Dive Operations answered. "Diver away."

Rowlin paced as he listened in on the comm channel. Five lives depended on his plan.

"Commander Bern to *Scorpion One*: What's your status?"

"The meg is wreaking havoc above us. A huge stone block just landed on our left wingtip, pinning us down. Another one in the wrong place and we're done for." Jane's voice was tense. "Uh, I don't know what's happening topside, but the crazy mother just swam away."

"We wired *Scorpion Two's* cockpit with explosives and floodlights and sent it down," Bern said. "One bite will blow the shark's head off. I'm in dive gear at a hundred feet. Let me know if you see the meg near the bomb."

"Wilco, but why are you in the water? You could be its next meal."

"I have a remote detonator. Tell me if you see it close to the bomb, and I'll blast it to pieces."

Several minutes passed in tense silence as Rowlin paced the bridge. He keyed the mike. "Give me a sitrep. What's happening down there?"

"*Scorpion One* has the bomb in sight. It's about 300 feet above us and descending straight at us. Will it blow if it hits us?" Jane's tone was tight with tension.

"Where's the damn shark?" Bern asked.

"Oh God, it just swallowed the bomb, and it's swimming right for us!" Jane said.

TWELVE

Antarctic

The triplets' enjoyed a warm reunion with their uncle, who hadn't seen them since they were infants. Everything went smoothly with the lawyers, and their passports and inheritance paperwork were secured before the long flight to McMurdo Station. The stock transfer would happen that day, and the rest of their inheritance had been agreed to and was being processed. They were fortunate to have such a kind uncle assisting them.

After a good night's sleep at McMurdo, the strike group flew to Rothera Station on the Antarctic Peninsula and prepared for the mission to eliminate the Black Sun's base inside the Ronne Ice Shelf.

Mike scanned the women to check every detail of their specialized survival suits and tactical gear. "Your GPS trackers are on, but double-check them. Remember, if you fall into an ice chasm, pull the inflation cord and the suit will inflate. Switch on your oxygen supply when you close your faceplate. It's good for two hours, but the mission will be over in minutes."

Loren hugged him. "I'll be glad when we're done. I'm not exactly commando material."

Mike grinned. "Mom, all your kids are badass warriors. Who do you think gave us that fierce tenacity?"

"Your father, rest his soul." She kissed Mike's cheek. "I'm holding you to your promise to keep everyone safe, including you."

Sam rolled her eyes. "Geez, Mom, if a SEAL team *and* a SAS team can't keep us safe, no one can. Relax, we'll be fine."

Blaze nodded. "It'll be over before you know it."

"I think it'll be exciting." Luna grinned at Derek. "And afterward, the military will rescue our sister in the Himalayas so we can all be together again."

General Ryan strode in. "All right, ladies, I'm sending Lieutenant Starr in the helicopter that will drop you off at your ley-line coordinates. Remember to switch on the strobe lights on top of your hoods as soon as you're on the ice. We'll have four more helicopters nearby with SEALs and SAS soldiers at the ready. When Blaze gives us the flare signal, the helicopters will fly in and pick you up. Questions?"

Blaze glanced at her female team and gave Ryan a thumbs-up.

Mike waited while Ross hugged Sam. He saluted Mike before zipping his hood and trotting out to a waiting helicopter. Derek waved to the women before following Ross out the door. When the four helicopters lifted off for their designated holding zones, their rotors churned up clouds of swirling snow on the ramp.

Mike escorted Loren, Sam, and the Conor sisters into a fifth helicopter that would drop them off one by one at their assigned attack points and pick up Loren after Blaze's signal. He liked having a backup chopper in case one broke down in the extreme Antarctic conditions.

Sam sat between Blaze and Luna, and Mike sat next to Loren and held her hand.

Loren glanced at Mike. "How can you be so calm?"

"This is what I do, Mom, and this one will be a lot easier than most of my missions. You ladies are doing all the heavy lifting." He grinned and patted her hand.

"Well, that's reassuring." Loren rolled her eyes.

The pilot announced over the speakers, "Five minutes to zone one."

Mike rechecked his weapons. "Everyone, double-check your GPSs are on." He checked his mother's GPS on the back of her hood, then watched as Blaze, Sam, and Luna checked each other and gave him the thumbs-up.

"One minute to zone one," the pilot announced.

Mike moved to the door and waited for the signal. "Blaze, remember to zip your facemask into your hood and switch on your oxygen."

She nodded.

"Zone one, Blaze out," the pilot announced.

Mike opened the door when the helicopter touched down. "Switch on your hood strobe light as soon as you're out." He patted Blaze's back.

She jumped out into the swirling snow whipped up by the rotor blades. A second later, her flashing strobe pierced the white veil.

The Super Lynx continued around the imaginary circle to each drop point. Loren was last.

Mike helped her out into the balmy -15 $\circ$ F summer weather. "You can do this, Mom. I'll be back for you in about five minutes." He secured her mask, switched on her oxygen and strobe light, waved, and closed the cabin door.

As his helicopter headed for its holding zone, he glanced back at the solitary figure on the ice and prayed. He'd lost his father and younger brother several years ago and couldn't bear losing his mother or sister.

USS LEVIATHAN

Rowlin keyed the mike. "Detonate, detonate now!"

Everyone waited for an explosion.

Nothing.

"The signal can't reach the bomb unless the meg opens its mouth," Bern yelled into his facemask mike.

"*Scorpion One*, deploy a signal buoy," Rowlin ordered.

"Buoy away," Jane announced.

Scooter said to the shark, "Open your big mouth."

The signal buoy shot upward as the prehistoric shark dived at the sub. As the buoy approached it, the beast snapped at it.

A massive explosion set off shock waves through the water.

Flotsam from the submarine cockpit littered the surface, intermixed with bloody flesh and guts from the monster.

Rowlin keyed the mike. "*Scorpion One*, report."

Jane's excited voice filled the speakers. "Score: *Leviathan* three, megalodons zero, but our left wingtip is pinned under a stone block. Do you still have a Hardsuit diver on comm?"

"Affirmative. Turn on your lights so he can find you."

"Tell him to bring something to lever that block off our wing. *Scorpion One* out."

Rowlin answered a call from Dive Ops and put it on speaker. "Captain, we haven't heard from Commander Bern. I put two divers in the water to look for him."

"They'd better find him before an armada of sharks arrive for the megalodon buffet." Rowlin scanned the sea with his binoculars.

Lowes sidled up. "They'll find him. The shock wave probably stunned him. Good thing he wore a full facemask."

Rowlin rubbed the back of his neck. "I'll be glad when we have everyone back on board. This day has been a bitch." He picked up the mike and called Kip.

"Hello, Captain. We heard the big boom. I hope that was the end of the last meg." He sounded chipper.

"Affirmative, but we need your help. *Scorpion One* is pinned under a stone block. They want you to lever it off. Look for their lights about fifty yards east of you."

"No problem. We'll grab a few tridents from the pyramid and free them in no time. Tell them to expect us in ten minutes. Peterson out."

Rowlin cracked his knuckles while waiting for updates from the search team and *Scorpion One*.

Lowes scanned the sea. "Think more of those giant buggers are out there?"

"God, I hope not. At this rate, we'll never figure out if that pyramid is housing the weapon." Rowlin sighed. "The Pentagon expects results —and soon."

A SEAL from Dive Ops announced over the bridge speakers: "Captain, we found Commander Bern. Sharks were circling him. We had to use bang sticks on them so we could pull him into the RHIB."

"Is everyone safe aboard now?" Rowlin asked.

"Aye, Captain, the doc just checked Bern. He's conscious, but a little disoriented."

"Good, keep watch for more sharks. We still have to recover the Hardsuit divers when the sub brings them up. And Banger may be getting cold. His battery ran out almost an hour ago. Work fast when he surfaces." Rowlin stared out at the deceptively placid sea.

"Aye, Captain, we'll be ready. Dive Ops out."

"Peterson to base. We retrieved six tridents, and we're on our way to the sub."

"Understood. Be careful. That city is full of surprises." Rowlin glanced at his watch.

Lowes touched his shoulder. "Don't worry. Banger's body heat will keep the suit warm long enough to get him topside."

"I hope you're right. We've lost too many men today. Once we get our divers and sub crew on board, we'll have to deal with Crenshaw's and Ace's remains."

Lowes shook his head. "Not much left after their suits imploded. We can leave them where they are and call it a burial at sea with a memorial service on deck. Or we can retrieve their crumpled suits for a land burial."

"I'll ask Ace Rivera's family which they'd prefer after they've been notified of their loss. Captain Brown will do the same for Richard Crenshaw's family." Rowlin sighed. "That part of my job never gets any easier."

"*Scorpion One* to base. The divers used tridents to lever the stone off our wingtip. We're free now and towing up the divers. Where do you want them?"

"Drop them off on the port side amidships. A recovery team will reel them in while you proceed to the moon pool. They'll winch Banger out of the water first and get him out of that Hardsuit."

Antarctic

Blaze spoke to Solraya, Luna, Mom, and me telepathically. *"I'll direct energy through Loren's ley line and mine, Solraya will channel through Sam's ley line, and Luna will handle her own. Remember to hold your positions until I fire the flare. Ready?"*

I answered, *"Ready,"* along with the other women.

Blaze began the countdown. *"Three, two, one, now."*

I imagined powerful energy waves converging on the Black Sun base 500 feet beneath the surface ice and superheating their towering steel cylinder-shaped community.

I trembled. Would their Supreme Master retaliate before we could kill him?

The ice shuddered under my feet, but I held my position. What was happening below? Was Supreme Master dead or was he mounting a counterattack?

A thick fog formed over the attack zone a quarter mile away and rapidly spread to us, a problem which we hadn't anticipated. Foot-deep water from melted ice sloshed around me in the first two minutes.

No matter how hard I tried to remain calm, my heart raced from not knowing the big picture. Would I burst into flames if the Black Sun counterattacked? If the ice collapsed faster than anticipated, how would the chopper find me in the thick fog?

The melted water lapped at my knees. Finally, a faint red glow from Blaze's flare penetrated the fog. Oh God, that meant the ice was about to disintegrate. *Where was my helicopter?*

Loud crunching heralded the crumbling ice mass encasing the Black Sun's base, indicating a giant clump of molten steel that had once been a multi-level city had plunged into the depths and left a huge void in the ice.

In seconds, the surface ice broke apart and tumbled into the widening divide as chasms spiraled outward, and escaping steam thickened the fog. Thundering rotor blades reverberated through the moist air, the decibels ever increasing.

My zone was on the north side with the Weddell Sea five miles behind me. Our attack must've generated heat along my ley line because the fog and melting ice seemed to track a straight line to the sea —another thing we hadn't anticipated.

I slogged through hip-deep water to escape the expanding ice chasms, praying the rescue helicopter would save me in time. Rotor blades thundered all around me in the heavy fog, but I couldn't spot a helicopter.

A loud splash followed the deep cracking sound of a massive ice chunk plummeting behind me. I glanced over my shoulder as a ten-foot tsunami from the displaced water crashed into me. I yanked my inflation cord and twisted onto my back as the forceful wave propelled me along the stream of melted ice on the northern ley line.

The high-speed wave swept me into the Weddell Sea, and the momentum slammed me into towering icebergs. Helpless in the strong current, I spun around. My head banged against a protruding ice crag, and I blacked out.

Ross checked his watch and scanned the sky. He spotted the flare Blaze fired the moment it appeared above the thickening fog hanging over the recovery zones. He keyed his mike. "Flare! Begin evac."

All the helicopters and soldiers were on the same tactical frequency. Ross heard the pilots acknowledge the command as his chopper headed toward Sam's zone.

A loud boom, followed by smoke and clanking, signaled the catastrophic failure of their left engine. It had exploded and severed the fuel and oil lines. Flames engulfed the engine.

The integrated fire extinguishers failed to put out the fire even after the fuel on that side had been shut off. Smoke filled the cabin, and the pilot was forced to land.

Ross heard his pilot call: "Chopper Three has an engine fire. Chopper Four, pick up Sam in zone three. Acknowledge."

Chopper Four's pilot acknowledged the command as Ross's helicopter slammed onto the ice. Ross jumped out with a fire extinguisher and listened on the comm as he blasted the fire.

"Chopper One has Blaze and will pick up Chopper Three's team. Heavy fog in pickup zones."

Ross prayed for the announcement of Sam's rescue as he extinguished the flames.

"Chopper Two has Luna. Proceeding to Chopper Three's location to render aid."

"Chopper Five has Loren. Waiting for Chopper Four's report."

"Chopper Four reporting: Heavy fog, no joy on Sam. Request Chopper Five assists in search and rescue. Repeat, no visual on Sam. Ice chasm expanding in center of zone three."

Ross keyed his mike. "Get a fix on Sam's GPS and look for her strobe."

Mike's voice broke in, "Our rotor wash blew a hole in the fog, but there's no GPS signal or strobe in view. She must be under the ice, and it's blocking her signal. I've got my dive gear on and will be on the winch in five minutes."

Ross tried to steady his voice. "Thanks, Mike. I'll hitch a ride to zone three and lend a hand." He paced on the ice, oblivious to the cold.

When Chopper One landed, Ross jumped aboard and leaned in to the pilot. "Take me to Chopper Five to pick up Loren. I'll stay and help while you fly her and my pilots back to base."

"Understood, Captain Sinclair." He waited for Ross's pilots to board and then sped back to where Choppers Four and Five were searching for Sam. "Chopper One has Captain Sinclair. He wants to swap places with Loren so we can fly her to base."

"Roger, Chopper One, land on our six and we'll send her to you," Chopper Five's pilot responded as he touched down near the ice hole.

Ross leaned close to Blaze. "Contact Sam telepathically and find out where she is."

"I've been trying." Blaze bit her lip. "No answer."

"If you reach her, tell her I'm coming." Ross jumped out.

Ross met Loren halfway between the helicopters and gave her a hug. "We'll find Sam, don't worry."

Loren grabbed his arm. "I'm counting on you to bring back Sam *and* Mike."

Ross yanked her behind him as a huge leopard seal lunged at them. Loren screamed.

Ross blasted it with his MP7 and pushed Loren toward Chopper One. "Hurry! The ice is splitting."

Strong hands pulled her inside as Ross plowed through the deepening water to Chopper Five. He climbed aboard a second before the ice split.

The chopper lifted off and maneuvered over the center of the ever-widening ice hole. Mike waited by the door in his dive gear, ready to be lowered into the icy maelstrom.

"I'll operate the winch." Ross crouched beside the controls. "That way, the copilot can keep a lookout for Sam."

Mike nodded and signaled the pilot. The chopper hovered in position.

"Watch out for leopard seals," Ross said, his hand on the winch control. "They're desperate to escape the chaos."

Mike patted a large dive knife strapped to his right calf. "Send me down. I'll try to pick up her GPS on this waterproof tablet, but I might not get a signal under the ice. I hope I'll see her strobe." Mike scooted to the edge of the open door and hung his flippered feet down. He nodded at Ross and dropped over the side.

Ross lowered him down at a smooth, quick pace and left slack in the cable when Mike entered the water. While they hovered, he watched Mike swim between churning chunks of ice. Sam couldn't be deep in her inflated suit. She'd be close, trapped under the ice, or crushed and pushed beyond reach.

"I looked for her light in the dark first and then with my dive lights on bright, but no GPS signal or strobe in view," Mike reported through the voice-activated mike in his full-face mask. "The ice is churning me like I'm in a blender. No sign of her." He sighed. "Better bring me up before I get crushed."

Back on the chopper, Mike pulled off his mask. He rubbed his face with a towel and slipped off the BC vest and tank. "Damn, it's cold down there. Thanks for the help, Ross."

Ross hesitated. "Give it to me straight. Any chance she's alive?"

"A slim one if she fell into the chasm, but maybe she ran away from the hole, and her GPS is inop." He turned to the pilot. "Fly slowly along the northern ley line so we can look for her strobe light." He squeezed Ross's shoulder. "We'll never see her red suit in this heavy fog. Let's hope her strobe is working."

The helicopter inched along the stream of melted water while Ross and Mike searched from both side windows.

Ross called to the pilot, "Anything on her GPS?"

"Sorry, sir, nothing."

"Choppers Two and Four, report," Ross said.

"Chopper Two searched the eastern quadrant inside and outside the fog area. No joy."

"Chopper Four searched the southern quadrant. No GPS signal or visual on her strobe, so we moved to the western quadrant. Nothing there either."

"Understood. Return to base. Chopper Five will continue searching north to the Weddell Sea," Ross said.

When they reached the sea, they cut across to Rothera Station, landed, and climbed out.

"Maybe that stream washed her into the sea." Mike walked beside Ross.

"I'll contact the carrier and ask General Barnes to deploy the search-and-rescue helicopter." Ross's voice cracked.

"Let's take a chopper to the ship. I want to be ready to dive in when they find her." Determination filled Mike's eyes.

"Why don't you give your SEALs a turn when we chopper out to the ship?"

"Good idea. No reason for me to freeze my ass again. I'll direct the rescue from the SAR helicopter." Mike bit his lip. "She'll be out there. She has to be."

When Ross and Mike entered Rothera Station, Derek, Loren, and the Conor sisters were waiting for them. Their expectant expressions plunged to despair when Sam wasn't with them.

Loren burst into tears. Blaze and Luna encircled her in their arms. Derek rested a comforting hand on Ross's shoulder.

Mike pushed in. "Don't cry, Mom, we'll find her. I think Sam was swept out to sea." He glanced at Blaze and Luna. "Any luck reaching her telepathically?"

Blaze's eyes turned downcast. "She isn't answering."

"Oh." Mike sucked in his breath and glanced at Ross. "Please keep trying and call us if you contact her. We're flying out to the carrier to assist in the search."

General Ryan joined the group. "Any news?"

"No, sir. With your permission, Ross and I will take our teams to the carrier and help search the Weddell Sea."

"Permission granted. Go find her." Ryan returned the men's salutes.

Mike rushed to change clothes and prep his team. In less than ten minutes, both teams were en route to HMS *King George*. They landed fifteen minutes later.

Mike, Ross, and Derek checked in at the Action Information Center on the British aircraft carrier, which was midway along the northern boundary of the Weddell Sea. General Barnes was aboard, directing the Black Sun mission.

"General, have we picked up Sam's GPS signal?" Mike kept his tone neutral.

"Nothing yet, Lieutenant. We've got a submarine guarding the area in case the Black Sun managed to launch one of their subs before we destroyed their base. If her GPS is sending a signal underwater, our sub will detect it."

"And if she's floating on the sea?"

"Weddell is the most dangerous sea in the world, littered with icebergs. Can't take the ship in there, but we can send the SAR helicopter." He glanced at the plasma screen. "No GPS signal so far." Barnes touched Mike's shoulder. "Did you see anything unusual in the chasm?"

"No, but I noticed a strong flow of melted ice water running north —could've swept her out to sea."

Barnes glanced at his watch. "If you're right, we should pick up her GPS or see her strobe soon."

"My SEALs are ready for a water rescue, sir." Mike stared at the screen on the wall, eager to see the blip from Sam's GPS.

Ross stepped forward. "General Barnes, the women haven't been able to contact her telepathically. That means she was knocked unconscious—or worse. Her GPS unit may have been smashed if her head hit the ice. With your permission, I'll place my men on four mission helicopters to scan the Weddell Sea. Finding her visually may be our best option."

"Excellent suggestion, Captain Sinclair. I'll give the order." Barnes grabbed a mike and called Flight Ops.

"Thank you, sir, I'll accompany my men to the flight deck." Ross saluted Barnes, nodded at Mike, and zipped out the door with Derek to gather his team.

THIRTEEN

USS LEVIATHAN

Captains Rowlin and Brown and Commander Bern settled across from Kip and Banger at the conference table.

Rowlin started the meeting. "We've reviewed the dive video from your integrated cameras and read your official reports." He glanced from Kip to Banger. "I deeply regret the loss of lives, and I appreciate your contributions to the mission, gentlemen. Now the key question: Is Poseidon's Sword inside that circular room?"

"Maybe. The Atlanteans went to great lengths to protect that huge chamber." Banger shrugged. "Everything went south when Crenshaw tried to rotate the diamond rhombus."

Rowlin glanced at Kip. "Your opinion?"

"That room contained similarities to the prototype that Samantha Starr discovered—the same goddesses holding pyramid-shaped crystals. But it was on a much grander scale with Poseidon and a hundred statues aiming crystals at or above the rhombus." He glanced at Banger for confirmation.

"But it's inside, instead of on top of the pyramid," Banger said.

S. L. MENEAR

"There are energy pathways below and above the rhombus, and Crenshaw spotted a reflector way up in the channel above the rhombus. I think it's meant to magnify the energy and reflect it downward, possibly to blast into the seafloor beneath the pyramid."

Rowlin frowned. "Why downward?"

Bern turned to him. "Captain, if I remember correctly, a mighty earthquake swallowed Atlantis. It's possible a massive laser shot could trigger a shift in the tectonic plates."

Brown straightened. "My God, if those plates merge, they could push Atlantis up to the surface and send 1,000-foot tsunamis in every direction."

"That would wipe out Florida, the Bahamas, island nations, the entire Eastern seaboard, the Gulf Coast, and coastal cities across the Atlantic." Rowlin shook his head. "Millions of people would die, and property damage would be in the trillions."

"It would devastate our country." Bern shook his head.

"Another detail of interest: The pyramid sits on the intersection of six ley lines. Could be important," Kip said.

"We need more intel before we jump to conclusions." Rowlin pulled out his secure SAT phone. "Miss Starr is a pilot with Luxury International Airlines, and my father is their chief pilot. He'll know how to contact her. We need to show her our findings and get her opinion."

Banger cocked his head. "Uh, Captain, doesn't the military have her contact info?"

"I'm sure they do, but I'm not in the mood to deal with need-to-know and chain-of-command bullshit." He dialed the number, waited a few seconds, and heard his father's deep voice.

"Max, good to hear from you, Son. How's the *Leviathan* treating you?"

"She's saved many lives recently, but that's a story for later. I need help from one of your pilots, Samantha Starr. She found an artifact a few months ago, and we need her eyes on something we found related to it. How can I contact her?"

"I hope you found Poseidon's Sword so she can come back to work."

Max rubbed his chin. "I'm not sure what we found. That's why I need to talk to her."

"You need her and Professor Ben Armitage. He figured out how to fire the prototype. Last I heard, they were in Scotland—long story. Lance talked to her New Year's Day. You can contact her through her SEAL brother, Lieutenant Mike Starr, or her SAS boyfriend, Captain Ross Sinclair." He recited the SATCOM numbers.

Max jotted down the numbers. "Thanks, Dad."

"Ask her to bring Blaze, the Goddess of Fire. She's in Scotland too. Obviously, this is all top secret," Captain Jeff Rowlin said in his smooth Texas drawl.

"Dad, my ass is on the line with the joint chiefs, and you've been more helpful than you can imagine. I owe you big."

"Happy to help, Son. Keep me posted and give my best to Sam."

"Sam?"

"Captain Samantha Starr, my favorite lady pilot. Everyone calls her Sam."

"Oh, right. Thanks, Dad." Rowlin switched off the SAT phone and smiled at the expectant faces around the table. "Gentlemen, things are looking up. We may soon be hosting a goddess."

HMS KING GEORGE

Mike paced beside the Royal Navy Sea King SAR helicopter on deck. He intended to direct the water rescue if they found his sister. His earbud kept him informed on the radio frequency.

He glanced at his DOXA dive watch. Five minutes of air left for Sam. He bit his lip and willed her to be found.

Ross's voice blasted into the radio. "Attention, search-and-rescue divers. We have a visual on Sam. A pod of orcas is pushing her toward the ship. She's about 300 yards off the starboard bow at the ship's two o'clock."

"Understood. SAR on the way," Mike answered.

He joined two SEALs in dive gear in the Sea King. They rechecked their gear en route to the rescue location.

Ross's helicopter hovered above Sam to mark the spot. When the Sea King approached, Ross's chopper moved away and hovered nearby to observe.

"Don't worry about the orcas. They're friendly," Mike told his divers. "She's been saved by killer whales before. Go get my sister."

The divers leaped into the sea and swam to Sam, who resembled Gumby in her bloated air-filled suit. The orcas abandoned their charge and vanished into the depths. In minutes, Sam was harnessed to a winch line and reeled aboard.

Mike pulled her in and unzipped her face mask. He felt for a pulse. *It's strong. Thank God!*

He lowered the winch line to retrieve his divers while he checked Sam over. He found a large lump on the back of her head, and her GPS and strobe light had been smashed.

He turned his attention to helping his divers aboard. The pilot returned to the aircraft carrier where Ross's chopper landed behind them.

Mike's men helped him wrestle the cumbersome survival suit off Sam.

"Good, no blood seeping through her long underwear. Let's get her on the stretcher." Mike lifted her shoulders, careful to keep her head up.

Ross reached their helicopter before she was lifted out. He froze when he saw her inert body.

"Relax, Ross, she's alive—no blood, strong pulse—she'll come around." Mike pushed out the stretcher. "Help us carry her to the hospital deck."

Mike and Ross waited outside the door while the doctor examined Sam.

Neither spoke, each lost in thought.

The doctor strode out. "You can see her now. She's awake but groggy, probably has a concussion. Other than that, she's in good shape."

Mike and Ross rushed to her side. Her bed was elevated to help her sit up. She managed a weak smile as they flanked her.

"Ross? Mike?" She blinked.

They nodded.

"Two of my favorite men." She coughed, so Ross held a glass of water to her mouth. She drank slowly and nodded. "Thank you."

Ross bent down and kissed her softly. "You had me worried, lass."

"Yeah, you had everyone worried, Sis, especially when Mom and the sisters couldn't reach you telepathically." Mike hugged her.

"Easy!" She groaned. "I must've bounced off every iceberg in Antarctica. Just my luck, my ribs had finally stopped hurting and now this."

Mike shook his head. "I should've known you'd need a helmet and body armor. Gotta live up to your code name, Danger Magnet." He chuckled.

"Very funny. So where did you find me?" She glanced from Ross to Mike.

"In the Weddell Sea. Orcas pushed you toward our ship." Mike grinned.

"I guess I have Blaze and Luna to thank for that. Have you talked to them?"

Mike and Ross exchanged blank glances. "We were so worried about you that we forgot to call them. Better do it now. Mom's been crying." Mike pulled out his cell.

When his mother answered, he said, "Sam's alive and well, safe aboard the aircraft carrier."

"Thank God, I was so worried. May I speak to her?"

"Of course, hang on a sec." Mike handed the phone to Sam.

"Hi, Mom, I'm okay. Just a few bumps and bruises from bouncing off icebergs."

"We were worried when you didn't answer our telepathic calls. I guess you were knocked unconscious. Blaze and Luna sent orcas to look for you."

"Mike told me orcas pushed me toward the ship, but I don't remember anything after my head hit the iceberg until I woke in the ship's hospital. Sorry I made you worry."

"It's not your fault. I'm just grateful you were rescued. We'll request a ride to the ship so we can see you. Rest now. I love you."

"Love you too, Mom, and thank Blaze and Luna for me. I'll see everyone after I have a nice, long nap." Sam handed the cell back to Mike. "I'm sure I have you two to thank for my rescue." She smiled at Mike and Ross.

"Ross found you, and my SEALs fished you out of the sea. I've lost count of how many times he's saved your sorry ass. You sure picked the right boyfriend." Mike grinned and patted Ross's back.

"I'll have you know there's nothing sorry about *her* arse." Ross winked at her.

"You should get a medal for the most rescues of a foreign national in a six-month period." Sam took another sip of water.

"You're the only reward I need, lass." Ross kissed her and smoothed her hair. "Now get some rest and we'll check on you later."

"And don't worry, I'll warn everyone not to hug you." Mike leaned over and kissed her forehead. "Sweet dreams, Sis."

USS LEVIATHAN

Rowlin switched on the satellite phone and dialed Mike's number.

"Lieutenant Mike Starr. Who's calling?"

Rowlin introduced himself and explained why he was calling.

"Any relation to airline pilot Jeff Rowlin?" Mike asked.

"He's my father. That's how I got your number. Can you help me out?"

"If you think you've found Poseidon's Sword, I'm authorized to give you whatever you need," Mike said. "Besides Sam and Ben, we have two of the goddesses now, Blaze and Luna. My SEAL team will escort them to your ship. General Ryan is running the American op from this end. I'll get him to sign off on this, and we'll hop a jet to the Key West Naval Air Station and then chopper out to your ship."

"Great. How soon can you be here?"

"Uh, it'll take a while. My sister took a nasty fall today and sustained a concussion. The doctor will probably want to keep her overnight for observation. And, except for Ben, we're all a lot farther away from you now than when we were in Scotland. I'll send Ben from Scotland ASAP."

"Understood. Sorry about your sister. Send me the ETAs as soon as you can. I appreciate this, Lieutenant."

"Hey, we're all on the same team. I'll look forward to meeting you." He hesitated. "One more thing: Brief your crew to behave in a non-threatening manner at all times around the goddesses. They're total babes, but they're lethal." Mike signed off.

Rowlin stared at the phone. "Well, gentlemen, turns out we'll be hosting *two* goddesses, Blaze and Luna. Anybody know which one Luna is?"

Kip grinned. "According to Samantha Starr's report on the proto-type, Luna is the moon goddess—raven hair and deep-blue eyes."

"Remind me again what Sam and Blaze look like." Rowlin looked expectantly at him.

"Sam is identical to the sun goddess—golden hair and turquoise eyes. Blaze has flaming red hair and emerald-green eyes befitting a fire goddess." Kip smiled. "Meeting them will be a unique experience."

"Or a deadly one. Lieutenant Starr says we're to behave calmly and passively around them." Rowlin shook his head. "Sea monsters, lethal goddesses, and an ancient weapon in an underwater city. This is one weird mission."

McMurdo Station, Antarctic

Ross stood beside Derek and Loren as they watched the Gulfstream jet depart with Mike's SEAL team, Sam, and the Conor sisters.

He sighed and stared at the fading jet.

Loren squeezed Ross's arm. "What's wrong?"

"I don't like her going somewhere dangerous, especially when I won't be there to protect her." Ross frowned.

Derek squinted at the jet. "Mike's team will keep her safe."

"I hate to see her leave so soon after getting a concussion." Loren bit her lip. "I hope she'll be all right."

Ross glanced down at her. "She's usually sad to leave me, but she looked excited this time."

"Few people have ever seen the sunken city of Atlantis. This is the chance of a lifetime for her." Loren smiled. "Don't worry, Sam is never happy to leave you. It's just that she's eager to see the legendary city."

"I guess you're right." He gestured across the ramp. "Looks like our ride to Scotland is ready." Ross led Loren and Derek, accompanied by his SAS team, to the waiting jet.

As they began their long flight home, Ross had the uneasy feeling that Sam was headed into terrible danger.

FOURTEEN

Military Gulfstream Jet

Mike watched Sam, Blaze, and Luna smirk and grin while occasionally glancing his way.

He crossed his arms. "Enough, ladies, it's rude to talk telepathically in front of others." He raised a brow at Sam. "And shouldn't you be napping, Sis?"

"I slept before and after the fuel stop. Now that we're almost there, I'm too excited to sleep." Sam glanced out the passenger window. "Looks like we're descending."

Mike looked at the three smiling women. "After we land, take a few minutes for a pit stop. Then we'll board the chopper and fly to the ship."

Blaze tilted her head. "Mike, please explain pit stop."

"Oh, sorry, I forgot you don't know slang. It means using a toilet. The airport bathroom is a lot bigger than the one on this airplane. You might want to freshen up before we board the helicopter and land on the ship. Understand?"

Blaze and Luna nodded and smiled.

Twenty minutes later, their jet landed and taxied to the parking ramp.

Two Navy Seahawk MH-60R helicopters waited nearby.

"All right, ladies, meet me by the Romeos in ten minutes." Mike pointed across the ramp.

"The what?" Luna said.

"Oh, sorry, that's the nickname for those helicopters." He pointed again.

Sam chuckled. "The military has nicknames for almost everything."

Sam, Luna, and Blaze made a quick stop in the bathroom while their bags were loaded, then gathered around Mike and his team.

"They don't want all of us on the same chopper. Sam and Luna will go on that one with three of my men." He pointed to his left. "And Blaze and I will take this one with the rest of my team."

A crewman on each helicopter outfitted them with life vests and helmets. An hour later, they landed one at a time on the helipad of the USS *Leviathan*.

———

Rowlin left Lowes in command on the bridge while he went to the helipad to greet their guests. Ben had arrived the day before and made fast friends with Kip.

The first helicopter landed, and three SEALs escorted Sam and Luna onto the deck where Rowlin stood. He exchanged salutes with the SEALs and smiled at the ladies. It was too noisy for introductions with the rotor wash blasting them.

The bags were carried below decks so the chopper could take off. Soon the second chopper landed, and a blond Navy lieutenant emerged with Blaze and his SEALs. The bags were offloaded, and the second helicopter departed. Rowlin waited until the noise subsided.

He saluted the lieutenant and his SEALs. "Lieutenant Starr?"

"Yes, sir, and this is my sister, Sam. That's Luna, aka the moon goddess, and that's Blaze, the fire goddess."

The women smiled.

Rowlin kissed each woman's hand in turn and welcomed them

aboard. "I have refreshments in the conference room where a few people are eager to speak with you. Follow me." He led them into the ship and down passageways.

"In here." He waved them into the conference room where he introduced them to Commander Bern, Kip, Banger, and Captain Brown. "And you already know the professor."

The women greeted Ben, settled in seats across from Rowlin, and grinned.

Blaze and Luna flanked Mike. "Now, ladies, we've been over this: No talking telepathically when other people are present. Care to share?"

Blaze's green eyes twinkled. "Um, well, we couldn't help noticing how young and handsome Captain Rowlin is, especially compared to the generals we've worked with."

Luna interjected, "The other men here are handsome too."

Sam rolled her eyes. "Forgive them, they don't get out much."

Rowlin smiled. "Maybe you could remind my wife what a great catch I am."

"We might need to gather more intel first." Luna smirked.

Mike sighed. "All right, ladies, settle down. This is an important mission briefing."

"Captain Brown's research ship was sunk by a megalodon," Ben said.

"Sorry you lost your ship," Blaze said.

Sam glanced across at Rowlin. "We haven't heard the details."

"An eighty-foot prehistoric shark attacked everyone who came near the underwater city." Rowlin gestured at the coffee, soft drinks, and sandwiches. "Help yourself."

Blaze reached for a ham-and-cheese sandwich. "We were told you killed it."

"One of our attack submarines blew it apart with a torpedo. Later, a thirty-foot baby megalodon attacked our divers, and then its mother showed up. She was about seventy-five feet. We believe we've eliminated all of them, but sonar is keeping a close watch just in case."

"Good, I'd rather not dive with sea monsters lurking in the depths. I've had enough close calls to last a lifetime." Sam poured a glass of spring water.

"Mike told me about your concussion. How's your head feeling?" He'd noticed the lump on her head when he followed her into the room.

"It doesn't hurt unless I touch it. I'll be good to go by tomorrow." Sam smiled at Rowlin. "I assume you want me to dive down there to check out whatever you found?"

"Yes, but first Kip and Banger will describe the circular chamber inside the pyramid so you can compare it with the prototype. We're hoping it's Poseidon's Sword." He nodded at Kip.

The marine biologist described everything he'd seen and shared his conclusions. "Banger has a few things to add. He and a marine archaeologist who was killed entered a chamber near the top of the pyramid. Banger?"

"The weird thing about the upper chamber is a glass globe with a large human-like eye floating in it. We felt like somebody was watching us remotely through that eye." Banger described the room and everything that had happened there.

Sam asked, "Kip, did a megalodon kill the marine archaeologist?"

Kip hesitated and turned to Rowlin, who nodded approval. "I guess Banger should explain. He was there when it happened." He gave Banger a nod.

"Dr. Richard Crenshaw was speared by tridents that dropped from the ceiling in the big circular chamber." Banger shot a glance at Brown.

"Sorry to hear that," Sam said. "What triggered the tridents?"

"I'm not certain, but I think it's because he tried to rotate the diamond rhombus." Banger stared at his coffee. "He was trying to activate the weapon."

Sam faced Rowlin. "Don't you think we should figure out what it does before we switch it on?"

"We now have a theory, and if we're right, we won't ever activate it." He focused on the women's faces. "We're thinking it might be designed to fire a powerful laser into the seafloor and trigger an earthquake that will compress the tectonic plates and push Atlantis up to the surface."

Expressions of alarm registered on their faces.

"Ladies, you look upset. I assumed goddesses from Atlantis would want their famed city to rise again." Rowlin watched their reactions.

Luna looked at him. "No, Captain Rowlin, we're not Atlanteans. We're descended from another race that lived among them and whose women were regarded as goddesses because of their unusual abilities."

Blaze interjected, "The remnant of Atlanteans kept us prisoners in their secret enclave in the Himalayas. Solraya is still imprisoned there. *They* want their city to rise again. *We* want it to remain buried beneath the sea."

"And we want the U.S. military to rescue our sister." Luna glanced at Blaze.

"Sounds reasonable." Rowlin slid pictures across the table. "Ladies, take a look at these and tell me if you think this might be Poseidon's Sword."

"Captain Rowlin, I need a word with you concerning another matter while the ladies look over the pictures." Mike slid back his chair and stood.

Rowlin nodded. "Excuse us." He led Mike out the door. "This way."

Rowlin and Mike entered a small office with a desk and three chairs. "Have a seat." He settled behind the desk as Mike sat across from him.

"All right, Lieutenant, what's so important it can't wait until after the meeting?"

"General Ryan instructed me to brief you about the sisters as soon as possible." Mike sat back and glanced at his hands. "It's complicated."

"Hey, I think I could believe almost anything after everything I've experienced since my ship arrived over the sunken city." He pulled a bottle of Glenfiddich and two glasses from a desk drawer. "Whisky?"

"God, yes, and I think you're going to need a shot after I tell you about the triplets."

He poured two doubles and slid one across the desk. "I'm listening."

"The triplets—Solraya, Luna, and Blaze—have mental control over Earth's electromagnetic energy. They can draw energy from a ley line to incinerate their target." Mike took a swig of whisky.

"What targets?"

"People, ships, entire communities, whatever." Mike downed his drink.

"So, you're warning me they can fry my ship at will?" Rowlin crossed his arms.

"Not only that, but they can do it telepathically through my sister or mother if one or both are in the target area. I was there when the women wiped out an enemy base with the help of my mom and sister."

Rowlin downed his drink. "Should I be worried?"

"So far, they seem to be on our side, but it could turn fatal in seconds if anyone threatens them. I'm having a light romance with Blaze, and her sister, Luna, likes my twin brother. Our plan is to keep them in romantic bliss while our country figures out what to do with them long term."

"Now I understand why you told me to be non-threatening around them." He pushed his glass in circles on the desk. "I sure hope they aren't quick tempered."

Mike shook his head. "They don't seem to be. Just try to avoid any misunderstandings that might trigger an attack. I'll run interference and keep things as calm as I can."

"What about your sister?" Rowlin raised a brow. "She seems close with them."

"Sam treats them like the sisters she never had. They listen to her and follow her suggestions."

"They must have a lot to learn after being locked away in the Himalayas most of their lives." He smiled. "Was Blaze's first kiss with you?"

Mike nodded. "And Luna's first kiss was with my brother, Matt. He's a Navy fighter pilot stationed on the USS *Lawrence Lee* in the Med."

"I'll make a call and have him sent here ASAP. We need all the help we can get to keep those women happy and calm. I'm not about to have my first ship incinerated." He stood. "We'd better return to the meeting."

"Oh good, you're back." Sam glanced up from the pictures on the table. "I think this may be Poseidon's Sword, and the triplets agree, but we need to see it in person to be sure."

"How do you know your sister in the Himalayas agrees?" Rowlin settled across from the women.

"Mike scolded us about it when we met you—we speak with each other telepathically." Blaze shot a glance at Mike.

Ben cleared his throat. "Based on my experience with the prototype, I agree with the women, and I wouldn't worry about accidentally firing the weapon."

"Why not?" Rowlin sat back.

"The prototype required several steps. First, the crystals had to be activated." He nodded at Sam. "They filled with light when she touched them. Then I had to rotate the diadems on the statues' heads to release the crystals from their grasp and insert them into slots at their feet. Only then would the laser fire."

"The circular chamber is different from the prototype in size and design, but the principle appears to be the same," Sam said. "I'm guessing the diamond rhombus somehow magnifies the crystals' energy, but the only way to be sure is to activate the crystals and surmise the rest. Obviously, we won't fire the weapon." She hesitated. "The little prototype was so powerful I used it to sink a submarine."

Rowlin exchanged glances with Bern and Mike. "You can't touch the crystals with your bare hands at that depth, so how do you intend to activate them?"

"While you were gone, Commander Bern told us about the Hard-suits. They're metal, which conducts electricity, so Sam should be able to send her body's electromagnetic energy into the clasper and touch it to a crystal. Right?" Blaze searched the men's faces for confirmation.

Kip joined in. "Salt water is an excellent conductor, so I think it increases the odds that Sam may be able to activate a crystal with her internal energy."

"Does Sam have dive experience?" Bern asked.

"She has a PADI Master Diver rating and about 240 dive hours." Mike smiled at his sister. "No Hardsuit experience, but she's a fast learner."

"Faster than you, frogman." Sam grinned.

"We can probably have you trained in eight hours." Bern glanced at Rowlin. "With the captain's permission, we'll start tomorrow."

"Sounds good," Rowlin said. "And that will give you a little more recovery time from the concussion."

"Captain, may as well save time and train all three of us together. Chances are Blaze or I will need to visit that chamber to determine how the weapon works," Luna said.

He turned to Bern. "Can you train all three?"

"Sure, Banger will do most of it, but Luna and Blaze aren't divers, are you?" He glanced from one sister to the other.

"No, but we were raised to be one with the sea. We're quite comfortable in the water." Blaze turned to Luna.

"Right, we can do it. We should be ready to go down if they find something unexpected." Luna smiled at Rowlin.

Captain Brown checked his watch and stood. "It was lovely meeting you ladies." He nodded at the men. "Gentlemen, thank you for everything. It's time for me to escort Dr. Crenshaw's remains back to England." He saluted.

Rowlin, Bern, and Mike returned his salute.

"Safe travels and thanks again for the Scotch." Rowlin walked him to the door and turned to Luna. "Uh, Luna, I forgot to tell you Mike's brother, Matt, will be joining us tomorrow in time for lunch." Rowlin watched her face. "I imagine you'll be happy to see him."

Luna grinned. "Oh, yes, very happy."

"Good. We'll get you settled in your cabin now. You can rest and relax for a few hours and then join me in the wardroom for dinner this evening." Rowlin stood.

"What if we get bored?" Blaze asked. "Can someone give us a tour of the ship?"

"My Executive Officer, Lt. Commander Vance Lowes, will show you around. Use the interphone in your room to call me, and I'll arrange a tour." He led them to their quarters.

After seeing to his guests, Rowlin joined Lowes on the bridge.

"How'd it go with the goddesses? Are they total babes like Lieutenant Starr said?" Lowes arched his eyebrows.

"We have a potentially lethal situation with the so-called goddesses." Rowlin relayed Mike's information.

"Dang, why is there always a downside with beautiful women?"

Rowlin shrugged. "They might request a tour today. If so, I'm sending you. I want you to meet them and get used to being around them, but be careful not to seem threatening in any way." He hesitated. "And don't be surprised if they flirt with you. Just keep it light. Mike and Matt Starr are trying to accommodate their desire for romance. Matt will be here by noon tomorrow."

"Fine with me. Let the Starr brothers end up like beef jerky. I have a hot li'l cowgirl waiting for me back in Texas. No danger of incineration, but she has a big ol' six-shooter, and she can shoot flies off a watermelon at twenty paces." He grinned. "Like I said, always a downside."

The intercom buzzed. "Captain, the ladies are requesting a tour," the communications officer said.

"Understood. I'm sending the XO down to guide the ladies." He turned back to Lowes. "This ship is my first command, and I'm very fond of her, so be your usual charming self with the ladies and keep my ship safe."

Lowes saluted. "Aye, Captain, Officer Charming will save the day." He sang the words to "Witchy Woman" as he exited the bridge.

Rowlin shook his head. *What would Dad think if I told him about all this?*

Lowes introduced himself to Sam and the Conor sisters, taking care to charm each woman with a kiss on her hand. "Would you like to start at the top deck and work down from there?"

Blaze nodded at Sam and Luna. "That sounds fun. We'll follow you."

He led them along a gangway and up several steep stairways, glancing back occasionally to check on them. "If you ever get lost, just ask a crew member for directions."

Luna grinned. "That won't be an issue. We have perfect memories."

Lowes stopped and cocked his head. "Sam too?"

Sam shook her head. "No, not me, but I can always follow them."

He gestured for them to gather close. "We're about to step out on the forward deck. Stay close to me and remain vigilant. There's a lot of activity out there, and I don't want anyone getting hurt. Any questions?"

The women eyed his upper body and grinned.

"Uh, ladies, is there a problem?" He crossed his arms.

"Ooh, now they look even bigger." Luna reached up and squeezed his right bicep.

He arched a brow and glanced at Sam.

"Um, they were just admiring your big muscles. Captain Rowlin is a bit leaner." Sam grinned. "I'm sure you wouldn't begrudge them some manly eye candy. These women have been locked away their entire lives."

He straightened. "Far be it from me to deny you ladies my manliness. Feel my muscles any time you wish." He grinned and opened the door. "Shall we proceed?"

Blaze squeezed his left bicep as she walked by. "Let's go."

After touring the forward and aft decks, Lowes led them up to the bridge and stuck his head in. "Permission to bring visitors on the bridge, Captain?"

"Permission granted." Rowlin smiled and waved the women forward. "Are you enjoying the tour?"

Blaze and Luna hooked their arms through Lowes's arms and grinned.

Sam rolled her eyes. "They're enjoying your XO's muscles."

Lowes shrugged and smiled. "Hey, I'm just trying to keep everybody happy."

Luna sidled up to Rowlin. "Tell us about your ship. What are its capabilities?"

"Most of that's classified, but it can keep you safe, even from megalodons." He pointed out controls that would interest a pilot. "It's about as complicated as the cockpit of a Boeing airliner. Right, Sam?" Rowlin turned to her.

"Very similar to the Boeing." She smiled. "Maybe you should let me drive."

Blaze interrupted, "Captain, are we allowed to visit the place where they control the weapons?"

He frowned. "Sorry, it's off limits, but how did you know about that?"

"We've been on two aircraft carriers so far, American and British." Blaze smiled sweetly.

Rowlin arched a brow. "And did they let you visit their control centers?"

"We didn't have enough time." Blaze gave her flame-red tresses a toss and pursed her lips.

"Sorry, ladies, I'd love to show it to you, but I'm sure you wouldn't want to get us in trouble." He locked eyes with Lowes. "The XO will show you our dive center and then our moon pool. They're both interesting, and you'll be using the dive center soon." He smiled and escorted them to the door.

After the tour, Lowes returned them to their cabin in plenty of time for the women to freshen up before dinner with the captain.

FIFTEEN

Sam and the Conor sisters spent the next morning in the dive center, learning how to use the Hardsuit 2000's hand-operated metal graspers and thrusters controlled by foot pedals.

"The microphone is voice-activated, and the video camera operates on a continuous loop," Banger said and tapped the backpack. "An oxygen rebreather unit provides forty-eight hours of air, and a battery provides backup in case the power cable gets severed."

Commander Bern assisted Banger with the training. Every now and then, Blaze and Luna would look at them and grin.

Bern shook his head. "Ladies, you're acting like you've never seen a man before."

"That's because they haven't seen men like you until the past few weeks." Sam arched a brow. "You should be flattered. They don't act like this around all men."

"Let's try to stay on topic. You're all learning this faster than expected. My main concern is whether you'll feel claustrophobic in the suit at depth and then panic." Bern glanced at the smiling women. "Well?"

"The suit has a viewing port, so I'll be fine, no panicking," Sam said.

"I'm eager to dive down there and see if it's really Poseidon's Sword. Then I can get back to my airline job."

"We're excited about going down too." Blaze nodded at Luna. "And we never get claustrophobic."

"That's true. Mother Ocean is our friend." Luna smiled at Bern.

He glanced at his watch. "Time to break for lunch."

Matt strode in and smiled at the women. He was dressed in the tropical short-sleeved white Navy officer's uniform that made most women swoon.

Luna rushed forward with a big hug. "Matt, it's good to see you again."

"The pleasure is all mine." He sneaked a kiss on the nape of her neck. "Blaze, Sam, good to see you."

They grinned and planted kisses on his cheeks.

Matt introduced himself to the SEALs. "So, how's the training going?" He glanced from Bern to the women.

"We're ahead of schedule." Sam smiled at Bern.

Matt studied the Hardsuit 2000. "Are you sure you'll be okay in one of these, Sis?" He turned to Sam.

She grinned. "I'm looking forward to it. The thrusters will make it feel like flying."

"Yes, but you'll be secured inside a metal suit with only a small viewing port. I know how you hate tight, closed-in spaces." He raised a brow and focused on her expression.

Sam jutted out her chin. "This is different. I just don't like caves. I'll be fine."

Bern stepped in. "Sam, if you're claustrophobic, you need to admit it right now. This is serious."

"I do *not* have claustrophobia. It's a cave phobia." Sam glared at Matt. "I'll prove it. Put me in the suit right here and put a bag over the viewing port. Leave me in there as long as you deem necessary." She turned to Bern. "This way there's no risk, and you'll be satisfied I won't panic."

Matt glanced at Bern. "Do it. If I'm right, this won't take long." He touched Sam's shoulder. "Don't be angry, Sis. I'm your big brother. It's my job to keep you safe."

Mike sauntered up and glanced around at the tense faces. "Now what?"

"Our sister insists the Hardsuit 2000 won't give her claustrophobia." Matt nodded at the massive metal suit.

Mike's eyes widened. "Oh, right, I forgot about the caves."

Sam threw up her hands. "Enough! Put me in the suit so we can settle this."

Bern waved Banger forward. "All right, let's do it." He glanced at Sam. "We'll leave you in it during our one-hour lunch break. A Dive Ops crewman will keep watch over you."

Sam glared at her brothers until the helmet swallowed her face.

Bern did a comm check. "Can you hear me, Sam?" He studied her face through her faceplate.

"Loud and clear. As you can see, I'm fine. Now cover my helmet and go enjoy lunch."

Mike draped a towel over her helmet and checked his watch. "This won't take long." He glanced at Matt.

Luna grasped Matt's arm. "Let's go."

"All right, but we'll be called back before we're halfway to the wardroom."

Bern made one final call before they left. "Sam? How're you doing?"

"I'm fine. Save some food for me."

An hour later, the Starr brothers and Conor sisters returned from lunch with Bern and Banger.

Mike snapped off the towel like a magician and peered through the glass. "Her eyes are closed. Is she unconscious?"

Bern grabbed the mike. "Sam, talk to me."

She opened her eyes and yawned. "I had a nice nap, but now I'm really hungry. I hope you brought me something."

The group exhaled a collective sigh of relief.

Bern and Banger freed her from the Hardsuit, and Bern checked her pulse and pupils.

"Her vital signs are normal." Bern turned to the crewman on watch. "Any problems while we were gone?"

"No, sir, she slept like a baby." The crewman smiled at Sam.

"That settles it. I'm good to dive tomorrow." She smirked at her brothers. "*See*? Just because I hate caves doesn't mean I'm claustrophobic. Now where's my lunch?" Sam glanced around.

Matt held out a sandwich and a can of cola. "No hard feelings?"

"No, we're good." She kissed his cheek and looked for a place to sit with her lunch.

Bern stood between Matt and Mike. "Better safe than sorry, so thanks for speaking up."

The twin brothers smiled at their sister as she attacked her sandwich.

Mike turned to Bern. "Problems tend to follow her wherever she goes, so expect the unexpected."

"Yeah, she'll probably get kidnapped by mermen." Matt shook his head.

The following morning, Sam and Banger donned their Hardsuits. Bern made one final call as the divemaster lowered them over the ship's side.

"Divers, comm check."

"Loud and clear," Sam said.

"Five by five," Banger replied.

"No megs on sonar, but keep a sharp lookout. Call when you enter the pyramid."

A few minutes later, Banger reported, "The water is clear with no sharks in sight."

After ten minutes, Sam said, "The city is coming into range of the external lights you added to our suits. The view is spectacular. I see pyramids, sphinxes, and white marble buildings. It's all so beautiful! The large white-columned building might be their Hall of Records. And the obsidian pyramid is right next to us. We're descending down its north face." Her tone radiated excitement.

A few minutes passed.

"We're in front of the pyramid's entrance," Banger reported. "Permission to enter?"

"Permission granted," Bern said. "Be careful and remember to hold the shields over your heads."

"Understood, entering pyramid now." Banger's voice tightened.

"Ooh, look at all the Atlantean kings and queens." Sam couldn't contain her excitement.

"I'm glad you're enjoying this, but keep a firm grip on your overhead shield. None of us want you speared by a trident." Banger's tone was serious.

"Chances are that won't happen. I'm the Golden Twin. The security system is probably programmed to accept me." Sam sounded calm and confident.

"That would be a refreshing change from my reception on every dive here, but don't count on it."

After several minutes, Banger pointed. "There's the entrance to the circular chamber. We're entering the zone with all the security measures. Brace for falling tridents." His voice tightened again.

No tridents dropped.

Banger's video relayed Sam thrusting ahead of him into the chamber.

"Hey! You were supposed to follow me." Banger tapped her helmet.

"Sorry, it won't happen again." She turned. "Wow, look at that orca sculpture with the giant diamond in the center." She thrusted to it.

Banger followed her. Their video cameras sent all the images to the ship. Sam reached out and touched the diamond rhombus with her clasper as Banger yelled, "No!"

"Sorry, but I don't think anything will happen," Sam said. "My touch is supposed to activate the crystals."

The diamond filled with a brilliant light that shot light beams in every direction. Shiny gold tiles embedded in the walls at angles reflected the light to specific crystals. In seconds, crystals held by the hundred non-deity statues along the room's circumference became illuminated.

A low, steady hum resonated as light sparkled around the brilliant diamond rhombus, and the statues directed their light beams to merge above the orca sculpture.

"Huh, that was dumb luck." Sam looked around the chamber.

"Emphasis on the word dumb," Banger said in a sarcastic tone.

"Touching the diamond activated the crystals—probably saved us a lot of time, considering how many crystals are here," Sam said.

Still no tridents.

Sam dropped her tethered shield and studied the opening in the ceiling above the orcas. She looked down and noticed the opening beneath the sculpture. "Banger, I think I know what this is."

"You damn well better! Now turn this off and pick up your friggin' shield."

Bern's voice broke in. "What's happening? Did Sam activate the weapon?"

"Don't worry. If I'm right, this is only half of Poseidon's Sword. This room setup is the repeater that magnifies the laser after the other half sends it here." She pointed at the energy pathway in the ceiling. "The laser comes up through the floor, passes through the diamond, shoots up that pathway to be reflected back into the diamond, and its power is magnified when it fires into the seafloor."

"Maybe, but turn it off now in case you're wrong." Banger's tone was firm.

"Yes, Sam, turn it off," Bern said through the comm line.

She looked around the chamber. "Uh, I don't think I can do that. The prototype could only be turned off *after* it was fired. Sorry." She studied the orca sculpture. "We should send Blaze or Luna down here. They might figure out how to switch it off."

Four hours later, after debriefing Banger and Sam, Kip and Blaze had their turn in the obsidian pyramid.

"Now, Blaze, remember, don't activate anything without discussing it first." He led her into the circular chamber.

Dazzled by the sparkling lights, Blaze stopped near the central orca sculpture and studied the layout of the room. She edged closer to the illuminated diamond, careful not to touch it. "I don't need this." She dropped the shield tethered to her suit.

"You can't be sure. Better to be safe." He pointed. "Hold it over you."

"Kip, the tridents aren't meant to spear goddesses from Atlantis. I'll be fine, but you should probably keep holding your shield." Her voice was calm.

"Maybe, but how do the tridents know who's under them?" His voice tightened.

"Relax, I'm safe here." She used her thrusters to circle the room and study the statues. The deity statues were the only ones with unlit crystals. She stopped in front of the Goddess of Fire. "This one looks like me." She reached out with her clasper and touched the statue's crystal.

The crystal filled with brilliant light and shot a light beam straight into the diamond rhombus, which in turn shot light beams into the crystals held by Poseidon and the other two goddesses, illuminating them. In seconds, the diamond became so brilliant it seemed as bright as the sun.

"Oh shit, what did you do?" Kip turned away from the diamond.

"Nothing, I just touched my statue's crystal." She glanced around. "I agree with Sam. This is definitely a repeater."

"You weren't supposed to touch anything!" Bern yelled through the comm.

"Sorry, I did it without thinking. Nothing ever happened when I touched crystals in the enclave."

"Can you see a way to turn it off?" Kip moved close to her as the low humming ramped up to a high-pitched whine.

"Banger said Crenshaw twisted Solraya's diadem to open the door in the upper chamber. Let's check all the goddesses for moveable diadems." Blaze moved closer to her statue's head. "This one isn't on a track."

"I'll check Luna while you check Solraya." Kip moved toward the moon goddess statue.

A few minutes later, they met near the middle.

"No rotating diadems. Maybe Poseidon has the off switch." Blaze floated to his statue as Kip followed.

They gently tried moving his scepter with no success. His crown was firmly affixed to his head, and his trident wouldn't move either.

He glanced around the room. "Any chance the control is on one of the hundred non-deity statues along the perimeter?"

"Only one way to know. I'll check the fifty on this half, and you check the other side." She pointed.

Forty minutes later, they met in the middle.

"No luck. Sam was right. It won't turn off until after it fires." She studied the orca sculpture. "I think we're done here. Nothing more we can do until we locate the other half of the weapon."

"Do you think it's in one of the smaller pyramids in the city?" He moved toward the door.

She hesitated. "More likely, it's in that big marble building with the white columns. Let's look there." Blaze surged ahead of him.

"Wait for me." He hit his thrusters and caught up with her.

Their objective was eighty yards from the obsidian pyramid. Ten minutes later, they were at the entrance.

Peterson turned to her. "Shields up."

She let out an audible sigh and raised her shield.

When they entered, their cameras sent video of the magnificent library to the ship. Gold vaults lined the outer walls and encircled a huge statue of Poseidon standing in the center. The building must have been designed to protect its contents from salt water because gold never corrodes.

"So, is the weapon here?" He looked around the impressive room with its high ceiling.

"This is their Hall of Records. Those vaults house a treasure trove of scientific information. I read about this place in the Atlantean archives." Blaze looked at the engravings in the ancient Atlantean language. "All their knowledge is preserved here."

"What about the weapon? Where else should we look?" He moved toward the door.

"I changed my mind. The weapon isn't here. The Atlanteans would've placed it over one of the ley lines that intersect underneath the obsidian pyramid. Could be thousands of miles from here. Time to go topside." Blaze followed him out the door.

Kip called Bern. "You heard what Blaze said. Do you concur, or should we keep searching?"

"We'll bring you up and discuss future searches. Move clear of the buildings, and we'll reel you in." Bern's voice had an edge to it.

Blaze glanced at Kip. "He sounds angry. I hope I'm not in trouble."

"Let's concentrate on our ascent and worry about that later." He checked his shield's tether.

As they rose slowly, the magnificent city receded into the inky depths.

Bern called the divers when they were 400 feet below the surface. "There's an unknown submarine approaching from the south. Let me know when you see it."

"I hope it doesn't run through our cables." Kip glanced around.

"We're trying to contact the sub, but no response so far," Bern said.

"I see it!" Blaze's voice jumped an octave. "It's coming straight for us. Looks about forty feet long with a viewing port in the nose."

"It's slowing and easing closer." Kip's voice hardened.

Captain Rowlin joined the conversation. "Peterson, can you see anyone in the sub?"

"We're facing the nose port. The crewmen are wearing uniforms. I see red logos with four assault rifles crossed on a skull."

"Mike just told me that's the logo for Lord Sweetwater's company, Predator International," Rowlin said.

"While we were looking at the crew, they grabbed us with dual robotic arms."

"They're cutting our cables," Blaze said.

"Understood," Bern said. "*Scorpion One* will be there in a few minutes."

Kip's voice tensed. "They're accelerating away with us. Warn the Scorpion not to—"

Rowlin keyed the mike. "Say again, Peterson."

No reply.

"This is *Scorpion One*. Target in sight heading south. The submarine cut their dive cables and is holding the divers with twin robotic arms."

"Stop that sub," Rowlin commanded.

"We can't use torpedoes without harming the divers, but we might be able to disable their propeller with our harpoon," Jane said. "Firing now."

"This is Peterson. We switched to radio comms. They have us in their grasp and could crush us if they don't like what the Scorpion does."

Jane's voice amped up. "*Scorpion One* just took out their propeller. We're moving in for the kill."

"Wait! The robotic arms just clamped down. Any tighter and we're Jell-O," Kip said.

"Don't worry, the arms will fail in the open position," Jane said. "We placed a small mine amidships. Detonation in three, two, one—"

A violent blast rocked the enemy submarine, and the extreme water pressure caused it to implode. The robotic arms opened and dropped the divers as a cloud of air bubbles burst from the crushed submarine. The crumpled lump of steel sank from sight.

"Divers, use your thrusters to separate so we can slide in between you. Then grasp our side rails so we can tow you topside." Jane maneuvered the Scorpion between them as they steadily sank.

"Peterson is clamped onto the starboard rail." He glanced left. "Blaze, use your claspers to grab the port rail."

"I've got the left rail," Blaze said. "Take us up, Scorpion."

SIXTEEN

Blaze and Kip changed into civilian clothes after shedding the Hardsuits. They joined Sam, Luna, the Starr twins, Captain Rowlin, and XO Lowes on the bridge. The women hugged Blaze.

"Did you find out where that submarine came from?" Blaze asked the captain.

Rowlin handed her binoculars and pointed. "We believe it was launched from that freighter owned by Lord Edgar Sweetwater's company, Predator International."

The communications officer burst in and handed Rowlin a paper. "From U.S. Fleet Forces Command, sir."

Rowlin read the message and swore under his breath.

"What's wrong?" Blaze touched his arm.

"My SEALs are ready to go, but we've been denied permission to board the freighter." Rowlin shook his head. "Apparently, Sweetwater has excellent lawyers."

"I thought he drowned when the Black Sun attacked his sub base," Sam said. "He dived in and never surfaced."

Mike shrugged. "You never saw his body, and the SEALs didn't find him there."

Blaze edged closer to Rowlin with her binoculars trained on the

196

freighter. "Are you certain Sweetwater ordered the attack on us from that freighter?"

"Everything points to him, but we can't force them to leave the area because they're in international waters." Rowlin balled his fists.

Blaze lowered the binoculars. "Captain, would you like us to destroy that ship for you? After all, they did try to kill me."

Rowlin stiffened and faced her. "I understand how you feel, but innocent crew members could be aboard that freighter. The submarine's crew tried to kidnap you and Dr. Peterson, and they paid for it with their lives."

Mike joined the debate. "Blaze, is there a way to melt their engines without causing an explosion in the engine room?"

She glanced at Luna. "We can melt their engines, but I'm not sure what the end result would be."

Lowes jumped in. "What about melting their propellers into big lumps welded to the drive shafts? That would render them dead in the water, no matter how strong their engines are."

Rowlin stared at the freighter. "That would force them to be towed to port." He glanced at Blaze. "Can you do it? Melt the screws?"

Blaze nodded. "I'll need to be where I can see the propellers so I don't overdo it and accidentally destroy the ship. Put me in the Scorpion with a pilot. When I'm close enough to see the propellers, I'll melt them."

Rowlin keyed the intercom. "Lieutenant Hoebich, report to the bridge." He glanced around. "We'll explain the mission to the Scorpion pilot."

Lowes stared at the freighter. "The water is crystal clear. Better not let their crew spot our sub."

Jane entered the bridge and stood at attention.

"At ease, Lieutenant. I have an unusual mission for you." He nodded at Blaze. "This is Blaze Conor. She'll accompany you in the Scorpion." He gestured at Jane. "Blaze, this is Lieutenant Jane Hoebich, one of our best submarine pilots."

Blaze frowned. "No offense, but don't you have any male pilots? It's not a competency issue. It's just that I've spent all my life exclusively with women. I'd prefer a man with me in the submarine."

"What the hell, Blaze? I thought you liked me." Mike frowned.

"Relax, darling, you're my guy. I'd just prefer some male company on the mission." Blaze kissed his cheek.

Mike glanced at Rowlin and turned to Jane. "Maybe Lieutenant Hoebich doesn't want another pilot taking her submarine."

Jane shrugged. "Fred's been like a caged animal since the meg destroyed his Scorpion. I don't mind if you send him, Captain."

Blaze leaned into Jane and whispered. "Is Fred good looking?"

"He's the epitome of tall, dark, and handsome. And he's a good guy," Jane whispered.

Blaze gave Rowlin a hopeful look. "Jane doesn't mind if I go with Fred."

Rowlin sighed and keyed the intercom. "Lieutenant Lichten, report to the bridge." He focused on Blaze. "This is serious business, Blaze. I'm counting on you to behave like a dependable warrior during the mission."

A handsome man in his late twenties entered the bridge. His eyes widened at all the women.

Rowlin made the introductions and explained the mission. "I realize this sounds bizarre, but I can assure you we're dead serious."

Lichten glanced from the almost-identical women to Rowlin and then focused his attention on Jane. "I've been a bit stir crazy since I lost my Scorpion, so I have to ask, is this for real or are you guys playing with me?"

"Hey, nothing should surprise you after the megalodon and the sunken city. I can assure you, this is as real as it gets." Jane pointed at the freighter. "They sent a submarine that grabbed Dr. Peterson and Blaze—almost killed them."

"Can't send our SEALs to investigate." Rowlin shook his head. "Friggin' lawyers."

"Is your Scorpion ready to launch?" Lichten asked Jane.

"Ever since the first meg attack, we've stayed ready." She nodded at Lichten. "You're good to go."

"In that case, I'm ready if you are, Miss Conor." He offered his arm. "May I escort you to the moon pool?"

Blaze squeezed his arm. "Call me Blaze."

Mike rolled his eyes. "Geez, this is a combat mission, not a date."

"True, but Blaze is a civilian, and she deserves every courtesy." Lichten smiled and saluted as he led her out.

Rowlin shook his head. "It'll be a miracle if my Navy career survives this crazy Atlantis mission."

Lichten leaned over and helped Blaze secure her seat harness. "Any questions?"

"What weapons do we have for close-quarters combat where I can't use Vril?" Blaze glanced around the narrow cockpit.

"This sub isn't designed for that." He pointed at a weapons control panel in front of her. "These are the firing controls for our mini torpedoes, and that one fires a harpoon. We also have magnetic mines we can place on a boat's hull with our robotic arms, but that's it. Why can't you use Vril?"

"If we're close to the concentrated energy, we'll get fried too. Don't worry, I'll call in a pod of orcas for backup, you know, just in case."

His eyes widened. "A pod of orcas, really?"

She nodded. "They'll obey my commands."

"Um, okay, should we wait for them or launch now?" Lichten tightened his harness.

Blaze closed her eyes. After a minute, she said, "They'll be near the freighter in fifteen minutes. Let's go." She put on her headset.

"All righty then." He closed and secured the canopy. "Powering up Scorpion now."

After a systems check, he flashed the moon-pool operator a thumbs-up, followed by a salute. *Scorpion One* slid into the water and silently dove beneath *Leviathan*.

"We'll go deep and come up under them so their crew can't see us." He checked his sonar screen and steered to the coordinates for the freighter.

Ten minutes later, Blaze looked up through the clear canopy. "There it is."

The dark shape of a 400-foot hull loomed above them.

"I'll ease us under it near the aft end. How close do you need to be?" He pulled back the throttle on the silent propulsion system.

"About thirty feet forward of the propellers. I need to see them, but we don't want to be too close." She waited as they eased aft. "Right here is perfect. Hold it steady while I focus on melting the props."

Rowlin called the Scorpion. "Lichten, give me a sitrep."

"We're in position, and Blaze is doing her thing."

"Call when it's done. Rowlin out."

The water around the freighter's propellers churned into a bubbling cauldron as the metal props glowed bright red.

A minute passed. "I'd better stop before the heat spreads to the entire ship." Blaze waited until the water calmed to see her handiwork. "Good, the props look like metal blobs."

Fred called *Leviathan*. "Mission accomplished, Captain."

Before Rowlin responded, heavy netting dropped onto the Scorpion and ensnared it. Lichten tried to pull away, but the netting tightened. Scuba divers encircled their submarine.

Lichten keyed the mike. "Mayday! *Scorpion One* is ensnared in heavy netting. They're trying to reel us into their moon pool."

"Use your robotic arms and cut the net," Rowlin said.

Lichten tried the robotic arms, but they were pinned against the hull. "The arms are trapped in the netting, Captain." He looked over his shoulder. "Uh, Blaze, better call in your orcas."

The net line was slowly reeling in the Scorpion. Divers in full face-masks hovered above the sub's canopy and smirked at them, looking confident they were helpless.

"They're here." Blaze pointed at a pod of orcas that rose from below them and attacked the divers.

In seconds, the killer whales' sharp teeth ripped the men to pieces. A dark-red cloud engulfed the submarine.

The sub's backward motion stopped after a big orca chewed through the line that had been reeling them in.

Scorpion One fell away from the freighter, but Lichten was unable to gain control because of the tight netting.

"Blaze, can you order the orcas to tow us back to *Leviathan*?"

"The orcas will grab mouthfuls of netting and tow us back," Blaze said.

"I'll blow our ballast once we're clear of the freighter. Our divers can cut off the net when the orcas leave." Fred swallowed hard as a severed leg bumped against their canopy.

Rowlin's voice filled their headsets. "*Scorpion One*, what's happening down there?"

"Blaze called in a pod of orcas. They killed the enemy divers and bit through the line that was reeling us in. We're still trapped in the net, but the orcas are towing us back to *Leviathan*. We'll need divers to cut us free."

Brief silence.

"Call us when it's safe for our divers," Rowlin answered.

"Aye, Captain, *Scorpion One* will call when the orcas are gone." Fred said to Blaze, "Huh, I bet even the captain wasn't expecting *that* one."

Sam, Blaze, and Luna were seated at the conference table with Captain Rowlin, the Starr lieutenants, and other key personnel.

"After what we did to that freighter, Rear Admiral Ashby, who's in command of the Atlantic fleet, might pay us a visit." Max gave the women a stern look. "If she questions you, be very careful what you say. And don't mention anything about the orca attack."

"Now, about the dive. Ladies, I know you're not in the military, but your orders were simple: Don't touch anything in the pyramid unless we approve." Rowlin glanced from Sam to Blaze. "You failed to obey that simple order, and now we have a dangerous situation."

Sam glanced sideways at Blaze and back to Rowlin. "I can't speak for Blaze, but I got caught up in the moment. Everything was so spectacular my enthusiasm got the best of me, but in my defense, the diamonds on the prototype never illuminated when I touched them. I'm sorry."

"We have a major problem if you're right about the circular chamber being a repeater." Rowlin studied their faces. "Now that you ladies activated it, the Atlanteans might be able to fire the laser weapon through a remote ley line that connects with the repeater and kill millions of people."

"And destroy a sizeable portion of our country," Bern added.

Blaze sat back and smiled. "Gentlemen, you can relax. There's no way the Atlanteans can fire the weapon."

Rowlin leaned forward. "And why is that?"

"The weapon can't be fired without the key, and *she* is sitting right here beside me." Blaze grinned at Sam.

Rowlin sat back and crossed his arms. "Sam is a person, not a key. Explain."

"Sam is the Golden Twin. Ancient prophecy refers to her as the *key* to Poseidon's Sword. The Atlanteans need Sam's unique electromagnetic energy to activate the weapon. *She* is here with us, so *they* can't fire the weapon, and *you* can relax." Blaze smiled.

Rowlin narrowed his eyes. "All right, Blaze, suppose you explain what you were doing in that Hall of Records? How did Sam know about it, and why did you go inside when you knew the weapon wasn't there?"

Sam glanced at Blaze. "I'll go first. I recognized the white-columned building from Plato's account of Atlantis."

"And I read about it in the Atlantean archives." Blaze shrugged. "I admit I knew the weapon wouldn't be in there, but I couldn't pass up a chance to see the famed Hall of Records. Sorry."

"As long as you're coming clean, why don't you admit you activated that chamber on purpose and explain why you did it?" Rowlin glanced from Blaze to Sam.

"Honestly, Captain, I just got caught up in the moment and didn't think." Sam shot a look of desperation at her brothers.

"Uh, Captain Rowlin, Matt and I know our sister well. What she said is consistent with lots of other stuff we've seen her do." Mike shook his head.

"Yeah, she tends to be a danger magnet." Matt shrugged.

Sam rolled her eyes.

Blaze focused on Rowlin. "I admit I touched it on purpose, but not to activate a weapon. I was curious to see if my energy would affect the crystal held by my statue. Nothing like that ever happened when I touched crystals in the enclave's temple, so I didn't expect that one to light up."

Rowlin sighed. "How certain are you the other half of that weapon is on a remote site?"

The three women made eye contact, and Luna spoke for the first time. "The circular chamber is definitely a repeater designed to receive the initial energy from one of the ley lines that intersect underneath the pyramid. We should search along those ley lines, or dragon currents as the Atlanteans call them, and look for sites that were significant to their realm."

Ben spoke up. "I might be able to help with that. I studied the prototype, and it had a map engraved into the obsidian pyramid with gold tridents marking sites. The other half of the weapon might be at one of those locations."

"We can compare the sites to the ley lines under the chamber and see which one is on a connecting ley line." Sam smiled at Ben. "Do you remember where the sites were?"

"I took copious notes. There's six: Egypt in the vicinity of the Great Pyramid, Santorini, the Himalayas west of Kathmandu, the Yucatan, Bimini, and Scotland under MacLeod Castle."

Kip punched a few keys on his laptop. "Eureka, all six are on ley lines that intersect here."

"We know it's not the one in the Himalayas because Luna and I were there," Blaze said. "Maybe we should search the nearest sites first."

Rowlin stared at the ceiling in thought. "Bimini is easy. I'll send you in with the SEALs dressed as civilians on a dive vacation. The Yucatan will require some stealth. I'm sure our government won't want Mexico to know what we're looking for. The jungle there is dense in many areas. That mission will require more planning."

Ben nodded. "We've seen the chamber under MacLeod Castle, no weapon. And I can tell you from experience the Egyptians won't allow us to search anywhere near the Great Pyramid. A second Hall of Records for the Atlanteans is supposed to be under the Great Sphinx of Giza's right paw, but no one is allowed to excavate there."

"I've been to dive sites in the Aegean, including Santorini," Kip said. "We could play tourists there, no problem."

"It would be nice if at least one thing about this mission was simple." Rowlin made eye contact with the military men. "Bimini is the easiest place to exercise our military muscle without making too many waves."

"I'll get my SEALs ready." Bern turned to Rowlin. "Do you want the Starr brothers to tag along?"

"We need all the help we can get to keep these women under control." Rowlin narrowed his eyes at them. "Ladies, I'm counting on you to avoid international incidents. Please, it's imperative you follow orders this time. All right?"

The women nodded.

"While we're working out the logistics, I'll send the women to Key West with Mike and Matt to shop for tropical clothes. Have fun, but stay under the radar." Rowlin glanced at the Starr brothers. "You know what I mean."

SEVENTEEN

Key West, Florida

Although it was high season in Florida, a small group from the Midwest missed their flight because of a blizzard, so the Navy was able to book three rooms at the Hyatt Resort on the water near Mallory Square and Duval Street.

"How should we divvy up the rooms?" Mike asked when they checked in mid-afternoon.

Sam grabbed a key. "You and Matt take one room, the Conor sisters can stay together, and I'll take the last room, just in case Ross comes for a visit."

"Works for me," Matt said. "Let's get settled and meet back here in fifteen minutes to go shopping."

Blaze grinned at Mike. "It'll feel good to get out of these long-sleeved tops and jeans from Scotland in this hot weather."

The group entered the elevator for the short trip to the top floor of the waterfront resort.

Mike showed Blaze and Luna how to use the key card to open their room door.

Blaze followed Luna inside and said, "We have water-view rooms with balconies."

Sam opened her door. "Nice room." Her balcony overlooked turquoise-blue water glistening under bright sunshine.

Matt grinned. "All right, ladies, see you downstairs."

Ten minutes later, the twins entered the lobby and waited for the women, who arrived together.

Mike took Blaze's hand. "Our mission is to walk a couple blocks to Duval Street and buy some tropical vacation clothes, including swim trunks for us and bikinis for you ladies."

Luna grabbed Matt's hand, and Sam walked beside him on his right. It wasn't long before they reached the shops on Duval Street.

"Ooh, look at all the pretty clothes." Luna pointed at the store windows.

A tall, slender man wearing flamboyant makeup and hot-pink short shorts zoomed by on Rollerblades, followed by a woman covered in multi-colored body paint wearing a thong bikini. She flaunted a bright-blue buzz cut and blue lipstick.

"Wow, what country are they from?" Blaze asked.

Mike laughed. "They're Americans. Key West is a diverse community with lots of artistic types."

"Yeah, it's like taking a fun vacation on another planet." Matt nodded at a passing elderly woman wheeling a baby carriage filled with three toy poodles sporting pastel-pink highlights in their fur.

"I want the electric-blue bikini in that window." Sam pointed at it.

"I hope they have one in red." Blaze followed Sam into the store.

Mike shot a glance at Matt as they followed Luna inside. "This'll be fun. We'll get a bikini fashion show as they try them on."

"We should be sipping margaritas while we watch." Matt grinned and grabbed two pairs of Hawaiian-print swim trunks. "These'll do." He handed one to Mike.

The twins grabbed a few shirts, jeans, shorts, and khaki pants to complete their wardrobe, but didn't try them on. They knew their sizes and didn't want to miss the show.

Mike settled in a chair next to Matt. "We're ready, ladies. Bring it on."

Blaze was first in a red bikini with matching stiletto sandals. Luna followed in an electric-green floral bikini and green stilettos, and Sam walked out with an armful of clothes.

"I'm not modeling for my brothers. That'd be weird." Sam handed the clothes to the salesperson. "I want all these, and he's paying for it." She pointed at Mike.

Blaze spun around and smiled. "Well? What do you think?"

"I think you look like a goddess." Mike grinned. "Let's see what else you picked out."

Luna leaned toward Matt. "You didn't say anything. Don't you like my bikini?"

"Oh, sorry, I love it. I could look at you in that all day." Matt arched his brows. "Show me the other stuff you chose."

An hour later, Mike and Matt were loaded down with shopping bags bulging with clothes and shoes charged to the U.S. Navy.

Mike flagged down a bicycle-powered rickshaw big enough for six passengers. "All aboard." He dropped the shopping bags on top and in front of an empty seat. "We'll take the bags up to our rooms and find a fun place for dinner."

Sam frowned. "I feel like a fifth wheel. Maybe you four should go without me."

Before Mike could answer, his cell played, "All My Exes Live in Texas." He grinned at Sam. "Perfect timing. Lance is calling." He hit SPEAKER and handed the phone to Sam.

"Hi, Lance, bet you didn't expect me to answer Mike's phone."

"Sam, darlin', how're you?"

"Lonely. We're in Key West, and Mike's with Blaze, Matt's with Luna, and I'm all by myself."

"Holy crap, *two* of the triplets are there?"

"Yep, a lot has happened lately."

"Well, dang it, Jeff told me you were in the vicinity, and I was hoping we could get together and catch up."

"Any chance you can get here in time for dinner? I feel awkward dining with two couples."

"Shoot yeah, I'm in Miami with the L-39 jet I bought last week. I can be at your hotel in about an hour. Where're you staying?"

S. L. MENEAR

"The Hyatt Centric close to Duval Street."

"Tell your brothers I'm taking you to dinner. See you soon."

Sam grinned and handed the phone to Mike. "Thanks, now I have a dinner date with Lance." She grabbed Mike's wrist and glanced at his watch. "I'd better hurry and get ready."

Mike texted Lance and then said, "I'll get a rental car and meet him at the airport. I want to see his new toy."

Matt nodded. "Those older generation fighters are way cool. I'd love to fly it and compare it to my modern F/A-18."

"We'll fly it tomorrow. Don't make him late for dinner. I'm hungry." Sam rushed into her room.

Mike crossed his arms. "Why does she seem excited to see Lance? She has a boyfriend."

"Give her a break. She deserves some fun after all she's been through," Blaze said.

"Yes, let her have a little fun." Luna nodded. "Then we can enjoy some romance without feeling guilty about Sam." She winked at Matt.

Mike gave Matt a sideways glance and grinned. "You're right, ladies. Tonight, romance will rule the evening." He ran his eyes over Blaze. "Wear that sexy red-floral sundress for me."

"And the matching red stilettos, of course." Blaze gave him a come-hither look. "Find us a romantic restaurant, darling."

Luna nuzzled Matt's neck. "And I'll wear that strapless navy sundress you like."

The sisters grinned and dashed into their room.

Mike draped his arm around Matt's shoulder. "Well, brother, I think we might get lucky tonight. That is, if we don't mess up and get turned into beef jerky."

Matt shook his head. "Not funny. I thought bedding a goddess would be epic, not deadly, like going to bed with a black widow."

"Good thing we're adrenaline junkies." Mike grinned.

Matt shrugged. "We might not live to regret this, but if we do score, you and Blaze take our room, and I'll sleep in Luna's room."

"Sounds like a plan. I'll get us reservations at a good restaurant." Mike followed his brother into their room.

Lance glanced over at Mike during the drive to the hotel in their rental car. "So, uh, what do the goddesses look like?"

"Blaze and Luna?" Mike grinned. "Like goddesses, you know, beautiful faces and perfect bodies."

Matt leaned forward from the back seat. "Actually, they look exactly like Sam, but with different hair and eye colors. It's bizarre how much they resemble her."

"Yeah, and be warned: They communicate telepathically, so we never know if they're talking about us," Mike said.

Lance glanced from one brother to the other. "But not Sam, right?"

"Wrong, she has the ability too." Mike shrugged. "They taught her."

"And remember, they can fry you to a cinder in seconds, so don't piss them off," Matt said.

"Why do the beautiful ones have to be so dang dangerous?" Lance shook his head. "I've lost count of how many times your sister almost got me killed."

"And yet here you are, taking her to dinner." Mike laughed.

"I admit I have a thing for Sam. Can't help it. She really gets under my skin. But I'll never pry her loose from Ross. She's in love with him." Lance sighed.

"Maybe, but she seems really excited about seeing you." Mike pulled into the hotel parking lot.

"Yeah, she made us promise not to mess with your fighter jet until tomorrow so we wouldn't be late for dinner." Matt patted Lance's shoulder.

"I was surprised she didn't ask to fly it. The L-39 was supposed to be bait to lure her to me." Lance shrugged. "All's well that ends well."

"She said we should all fly it tomorrow," Matt said. "Apparently shopping makes her hungry, so she's in a hurry for dinner."

"Tomorrow's good. Mind if I grab a shower and shave in your room and ditch this flight suit for some dinner duds?" Lance grabbed his small overnight bag as he exited the car.

"No problem." Mike checked his watch. "We have fifteen minutes."

Lance dabbed on some cologne and glanced in the mirror. "Well, this is as good as it gets. I'm ready to roll."

Mike handed him his overnight bag. "Here's the plan: Pretend you changed at the airport and ask if you can stow your bag in Sam's room. Matt and I want to keep our options open with Blaze and Luna tonight."

Lance grinned. "Understood. I'll keep Sam busy so you guys have a shot with the sisters. Lead the way."

They knocked on Sam's door, and Lance's eyes widened when she opened it. She was wearing a short-sleeved, electric-blue, low-cut, snug dress with matching stiletto sandals.

When she saw Lance, she smiled and hugged him. "It's so good to see you, Lance. I've missed you." She kissed his cheek. "Umm, I love your cologne."

Mike laughed. "Well, this is off to a good start. Mind if he stows his bag in your room while we have dinner?"

"No problem." She waved him in and smiled at her brothers.

Lance shot the men a victory glance and deposited his bag on a chair near the bed.

"Let's not keep the goddesses waiting." Mike gestured at the door. "Shall we?"

Lance offered Sam his arm. "Ready, darlin'?"

She took his arm. "I can't wait for you to meet Blaze and Luna. You've already seen their statues."

"And their pictures on murals." Lance grinned. "According to your brothers, it'll be like meeting two versions of you."

Lance and Sam waited a few steps back while Mike and Matt knocked on the sisters' door. Lance glanced at Sam and sucked in his breath, trying to quell his thundering heart. Moments later, Blaze and Luna emerged looking sexy in their new dresses.

The sisters seemed to focus on Lance's liquid-green eyes for a long moment before appraising the rest of his lean, muscular six-foot-two body. They grinned and arched their eyebrows at Sam.

Mike said, "Come on, ladies, no fair speaking telepathically. Now behave yourselves and meet our friend and Sam's coworker, Lance Bowie."

Lance took each woman's hand in turn and kissed it. "It's an honor to finally meet two of the famous triplets. I hope I'll meet your sister soon."

The women glanced at Sam and laughed. "It's like you've already met her. She looks exactly like Sam."

"Lucky me, two gorgeous blondes. It's always good to have a spare." He chuckled.

Sam playfully punched his arm. "Forget it, cowboy. You'll be lucky if you can handle one."

He grinned. "I can live with that." He draped his arm around her. "Time to dine. I've been told you're really hungry."

Sam nodded. "Ravenous—must be from all the fresh sea air."

"Our rental car awaits." Matt beckoned them to the elevators and took Luna's hand.

After a short drive, they entered a charming waterfront restaurant with a nautical motif. The maitre d' led them past statues of mermaids and sea creatures to a round table for six on the water's edge. Candles bathed the table in soft light as a full moon rose in the clear night sky.

Lance pulled out a chair for Sam. When their eyes met, he felt like she was seeing him in a new light—not looking at him the way she looked at colleagues. *I might finally have a real chance with her.* He noticed a gentle breeze had spread goose bumps on her arms, so he draped his arm around her.

Sam snuggled against him. "Ah, you always feel so warm."

Lance noticed the other couples grinning at him. He shook his head. "It sure is weird being surrounded by women who look like Sam."

The waiter handed them menus and asked to take their drink orders.

Mike said, "Dare we allow these women to have wine?"

"I don't know." Matt nudged Luna playfully. "They're already grinning a lot. Maybe we shouldn't stoke the fire."

"I say throw caution to the wind and party hearty." Lance gave a thumbs up to the men.

"Come on, guys, be brave and bring on the wine." Sam turned to the waiter. "Let's see your wine list."

The waiter handed the list to Lance, who asked, "Are we having surf or turf?"

Blaze and Luna exchanged confused looks and turned to their dates.

Mike explained, "Lance asked if we're having seafood or steak so he'll know what kind of wine to order."

Luna looked across at Lance. "What are you having?"

"Well, darlin', I'm a Texas boy, so red meat is part of my DNA, but I'm willing to go for the steak and lobster combo if y'all have a hankerin' for white wine."

"I like to try new things. Why don't we order red and white so we can sample several things on the menu?" Blaze looked at Mike for his opinion.

"Good idea." Mike nodded to Lance. "Order a merlot and a chardonnay."

Lance opened the wine menu and angled it at Sam. "See anything you like?"

"It all looks good. You choose." Sam planted a soft kiss on his cheek.

"Dang, who are you and what've you done with Sam?" Lance shot a glance at her brothers and grinned.

"She took a hard blow to her head recently." Matt chuckled. "Maybe the concussion switched her preference from Scotsmen to Texans."

"That'd be a medical miracle I'd gladly welcome." Lance leaned over and kissed the top of Sam's head. "Yeah, we're definitely ready for some wine."

As the evening progressed, Lance noted the sisters became more intimate with Mike and Matt, slow dancing close, cuddling, and sneaking kisses. When their group was ready to return to the hotel, it was obvious the other couples intended to spend the rest of the night alone.

He walked Sam to her room, and she handed him her key card.

When he opened the door, she said, "Would you like to come in?"

and walked across the room to set her handbag on the dresser. She turned. "There's a mini bar here if you'd like a drink."

Sam's never done this before. Maybe she and Ross broke up, and she didn't tell her brothers because they're good friends. Lance locked the door's deadbolt. "What would you like to do now?"

She strolled over to him and slid her hands around his neck. "Oh, I don't know, what would *you* like to do?"

Lance swept her into his arms, his heart pounding, and kissed her like the world was about to end. He dipped her in a dramatic, swooning Hollywood kiss, his tongue teasing, and slowly brought her up. His arms trapped her against his muscled physique. "How about that?" he said in a hoarse whisper.

"Hmmm, I'm not sure." Her breath came in short spurts. A naughty glint lit her eyes as she pulled his face close. "You'll have to do it over and over until I decide."

Lance unleashed months of pent-up passion, driven by a deep desire to win Sam. He pinned her against the wall and lifted her dress over her head. Her erect nipples teased his chest when she yanked off his polo shirt. His lips burned into hers as he carried her to the bed.

They tumbled onto the silky sheets and rolled around in a heated game of foreplay, his tongue fencing with hers as his hands explored and caressed her curves.

She reached back, and her fingers found the light button in the headboard. The room plunged into darkness with faint light filtering through the sliding-glass doors facing the sea.

Lance took his time, wanting their lovemaking to be so mind-blowing it would erase any memory of Ross's touch. Sam was breathless and as turned on as he was, yet she seemed tentative, as if something was holding her back.

Does she have mixed feelings because of Ross?

Lance was comfortable taking the dominant role. When he felt her moist body trembling beneath him, he gazed into her passion-crazed eyes and slid inside her. He felt a slight resistance as he thrust deeper into her.

She gasped and went rigid, but then she relaxed and lifted her pelvis against him.

Wild with desire, his brain was incapable of rational thought as their bodies exploded in simultaneous ecstasy.

He rolled her onto his chest, and they languished in each other's arms. After a brief nap, he was ready for more. She welcomed his love-making, reaching for him again and again. They finally drifted into a deep sleep in the wee hours of the morning.

When dawn filled the room with a warm glow, Lance woke and gazed at the naked beauty beside him. His eyes swept over her flawless form, and he froze when he spotted blood on the sheets.

No way Sam was a virgin. But he did feel something on the way in. What the hell?

Her left side was beside him, and he focused on her left breast. No scar. He checked her right breast, even though he was sure the knife wound had been in the left one. No scar there either. He checked her left arm. There should've been two bullet scars, one on her left shoulder and one on the inner side of her left bicep. No scars anywhere.

Holy crap, this isn't Sam. I should've known she'd never cheat on Ross. Sono-fabitch, this has to be Solraya...unless Sam used a special scar removal treatment. Yeah, maybe that's it. Can't be Solraya. But what about the blood? Maybe her period just started. I have to be sure. If this isn't Sam, that means Sam's in big trouble, and I'm in deep shit.

Lance eased out of bed and took a shower. After a quick shave, he dressed and checked on Sam/Solraya.

Her eyes flitted open, and she smiled and sat up. "Where're you going? Come back to bed." She patted the empty spot beside her.

"Sorry, darlin', the airline called. I have to run out for a quick turn-around flight. I'll be back soon, though." He kissed her tenderly. "Last night was magic."

EIGHTEEN

Key West International Airport

Lance took a cab to the airport, not sure what to do. If the woman in his bed *wasn't* Sam, he had to be careful not to tip off her or her sisters that he knew the truth.

Lance pulled out his cell and called Ross. Only one way to be sure who he'd slept with, and that was to ask Sam's boyfriend who'd seen her naked recently.

"Lance? How are you?" Ross answered, surprised.

"Ross, ol' buddy, I wish this was just a friendly social call, but I'm afraid this may be a life-or-death situation. You're not going to like my questions, but you're the only one who can solve this puzzle." Lance tried to steady his voice.

"What's going on?" Ross's voice hardened.

"I have good reason to believe that Solraya is masquerading as Sam."

"Why do you think that?"

"Uh, there's no easy way to say this, sorry." Lance hesitated. "I slept with Sam last night, and this morning in the daylight, I noticed she didn't have any scars on her left arm or left breast. Did she still have the scars the last time you saw her?"

Ross paused a long time before his strained voice answered, "Part of me wants to kill you, but it took guts for you to call me, and this could be critical." He sighed. "Sam still had all her scars a few days before she flew to Florida. Last night, was she covered with fading bruises and were her ribs sore?"

"No bruises, no sore ribs, and another thing: She looked at me like she was seeing me for the first time, and, uh, she acted like a virgin in bed. Uh, I think I felt her cherry break, and a little blood was on the sheets." Lance hesitated. "Ross, I admit I have a thing for Sam, but she's always been fiercely loyal to you. I should've known last night was too easy. Shit, I'm sorry about this. I feel like a total dick."

"I worried something was wrong after we fished Sam out of the Weddell Sea," Ross said. "She wouldn't sleep with me—said she was too sore. I assumed the concussion and other injuries were just too much for her."

"Was there a time she was out of sight when they could've made the switch before you rescued her?"

"Aye, she was lost for almost two hours. Plenty of time to make the switch." Ross paused. "The only boat spotted in the area was a Chinese junk sailing east toward the Indian Ocean."

"This whole dang adventure started when we met a Chinese guy in Hong Kong who called himself Dragon Master. He's the one who gave Sam the artifact with the obsidian pyramid and goddess statues on top."

"Bloody hell, the bastards must've taken Sam and replaced her with Solraya. All three goddesses are together now, and God help us if they find out we know. I've seen what they can do."

"Uh, it may be worse. Mike and Matt slept with Blaze and Luna last night," Lance said. "They're all lovey-dovey, thinking everything's great."

"And it didn't bother them that Sam was cheating on me? I thought they liked me," Ross said, his voice bitter.

"They don't know we slept together, and I'm sure they would've had your back if they hadn't been thinking with their dicks."

"You need to meet with them away from the women to clue them in. The Atlanteans must've taken Sam to their enclave in the Himalayas. We have to figure out a way to deal with this without ending up a pile of cinders."

"Ross, the real Sam is the only one I care about. I'll do anything to make this right and help you rescue her. Swear to God."

"We've got to keep a tight lid on this or we're all dead and maybe millions of people too. Meet secretly with the Starr brothers and call me when you're together. In the meantime, I'll meet with my DSF, General Barnes."

"I'll get back to you ASAP, and Ross, I'm truly sorry about this."

"Help me get her back safe. That's all I care about."

Next, Lance called his friend and chief pilot at Luxury International Airlines, Captain Jeff Rowlin. "Jeff, I need your help. Sam's in a life-or-death situation."

"When is she not?" Jeff chuckled. "What's she got herself into this time?"

"I can't discuss it on an unsecured line, but suffice it to say we're talking end-of-the-world, Armageddon-type bad shit."

Jeff's tone turned all business. "What do you need?"

"Didn't you tell me she was working on something with your son?"

"Yeah, she was on his ship. Is he okay?"

"He's fine. She was in Key West with her brothers, Blaze, Luna, and me. I need to contact Max so I can ask him to call Mike and Matt. It needs to look like the military is calling them away from the women. They have no clue what's really going on, and I can't risk calling them myself and tipping my hand. I'll explain later."

"Where are you now?"

"The civilian airport in Key West."

"Give me a few minutes to reach Max on his ship. Then go to the Naval Air Station where a Navy Seahawk will take you to the USS *Leviathan*. You can brief Max in person. Then he can send for the Starr brothers, and y'all can sort this out together."

"Good idea. Thanks, Jeff."

USS LEVIATHAN

An hour later, Lance unbuckled his seat harness after the Seahawk landed on Max's ship. He ducked out of the helicopter and spotted him waiting nearby.

Lance offered his hand. "Max, how the hell are ya?"

Rowlin shook his hand. "I'm not sure until I know what the big emergency is. Follow me." He led Lance to his private stateroom.

"It's a bit early for a snort. Care for a beverage?" Rowlin opened a small refrigerator.

"A bottle of water, thanks." Lance twisted off the cap and took a long drink.

Rowlin sat back. "All right, let me have it."

"Well, Sam isn't really Sam. She's the sun goddess, Solraya. I talked to SAS Captain Ross Sinclair, Sam's boyfriend. He thinks they made the switch during the two hours Sam was lost in the Weddell Sea."

"Wait, back up. How do you know she isn't Sam?"

"Uh, I slept with her last night." Lance explained the physical differences between the two women. "Turns out, I had sex with Solraya, and Mike and Matt have no idea she's not Sam. They've been too busy romancing Blaze and Luna."

He stared at him a moment. "Did the Starr brothers sleep with the Conor sisters?"

"Yep, and they were still in bed when I left this morning. We need a plausible reason to pull them away from the sisters so we can tell them what's going on." Lance emptied the water bottle.

"This is far worse than you realize. Does Captain Sinclair know where they took Sam?" He keyed the mike for the ship's speakers. "XO, report to the captain's stateroom."

"Probably the Atlantean enclave in the Himalayas."

"That means we're about to become toast unless we can figure out a way to buy some time." He keyed the mike again. "Commander Bern, report to the captain's stateroom."

Minutes later, XO Lowes walked in, followed by Commander Bern.

Rowlin gestured to chairs. "Gentlemen, have a seat. This is Lance Bowie. He's a pilot at the same airline where my dad works." He waited until they all shook hands. "We've got a serious situation, and I hope to hell we can find a solution."

The men settled across from him, looking alert and combat ready.

"Solraya Conor secretly replaced Samantha Starr before the women arrived on our ship. We've been hosting all three goddesses from the Atlantean enclave, and we aided them in powering up the pyramid under us so it'll be ready to receive and magnify the energy beam sent by Poseidon's Sword."

"Shit, this'll be a career-ending screwup." Bern shook his head.

"More like a world-as-we-know-it-ending screwup," Rowlin said.

"If they fire that weapon, Atlantis will rise and send monster tsunamis in every direction, killing millions." Lowes shook his head.

"Don't they need Sam to activate the weapon?" Bern asked.

"That's why they took her. The triplets have steered us away from the pyramid in the Himalayas all along because that's where the weapon is. And now the Atlanteans have Sam." Rowlin sighed. "And if the triplets realize we know the score, they'll fry us."

"What weapon?" Lance asked, confused.

Rowlin filled him in. "Obviously, this is top secret."

"Understood." Lance exhaled. "This is some serious shit."

Bern glanced from Lance to Rowlin. "Do Mike and Matt know about this?"

"No, they spent the night with Blaze and Luna. I need you to bring three SEALs with you, but not Banger, and keep an eye on the triplets while Mike and Matt fly back to our ship. Tell them all is well and that I just need to finalize the plans for Bimini with them."

Lowes asked, "Where was the fake Sam while the brothers were in bed with the goddesses?"

Lance cleared his throat. "Uh, she was in the sack with me. That's how we know she's not Sam—no scars and a bunch of other differences."

"Who knew bedroom skills might end up saving the world?" Lowes shrugged. "Hey, if you hadn't nailed her, we wouldn't know they've been deceiving us." He gave Lance a thumbs-up. "Good work."

Lance shrugged. "That was the easy part. Now we have to figure out how to not end up looking like overcooked meat at an all-night barbeque. Any suggestions?"

"We need to stall them so our military can find Sam before they fire that weapon." Rowlin turned to Bern. "We'll take them to Bimini as planned and pretend to search there." He nodded at Lance. "I want you with us. Ever served in the military?"

"I was a fighter pilot in the Air Force," Lance said. "Got an honorable discharge about a year ago and went right to work for your dad at Luxury International."

"What was your rank when you left the Air Force?" Rowlin asked.

"I made captain a year before I left."

"Good, I'll get you recalled for temporary duty at your old rank and have you assigned to my command," Rowlin said. "Don't worry, you'll only be back in the military long enough to complete this mission—a few weeks at most."

"This way the airline will have to grant me a military leave of absence, which means they can't fire me for being off work," Lance said.

"That's right," Rowlin said. "We'll be in civilian garb for this, acting like tourists to fool the Bahamians. Your job will be to keep Solraya happy in the sack so she won't get bored and kill us all."

"Nothing like potentially lethal sex to give a guy friggin' performance anxiety. Dang, I wonder if I can get PTSD from this?" Lance quipped.

"You'll get F-R-I-E-D if you upset her, so keep your cool." Rowlin turned to Bern. "Get your men together and fly to Key West ASAP. I'll put in a call to Mike and order him and his brother to meet your chopper for a quick trip out here. Dismissed."

Rowlin stood. "XO, you have the conn while I deal with this. Lance and I will meet with Ben, Kip, and Banger in the conference room while we wait for the Starr brothers. Send them in when they arrive."

In the conference room, Captain Rowlin introduced Lance to Ben, Kip, and Banger and waited for everyone to settle in their chairs. He briefed them and asked for ideas on how to prevent the impending disaster.

Ben spoke first. "We may have more time than you think. An orca took the artifact from us in the Southern Atlantic. It's possible that artifact, combined with Sam's inner energy, is the key to firing Poseidon's Sword."

Rowlin shook his head. "We can't assume that. Even you thought it was a prototype for the much larger weapon."

"We've been wrong about a lot of things. We believed the triplets were working against the Atlanteans. Now it appears they've been complicit all along." He straightened. "I assume you know the triplets sent orcas to save us when the submarine sank. What if they commanded an orca to take the device and deliver it to a ship which then delivered it to the enclave?"

Rowlin narrowed his eyes. "An orca took the artifact from you?"

"Yes, while we were treading water." He grabbed a bottle of water and took a swig. "And another thing: Their original plan was to fire the weapon on the winter solstice at the end of this year. If they move up their timetable, they'll wait until a similar day with astrological significance, such as the March equinox or summer solstice."

Rowlin pulled up a calendar on his smart phone. "Let's assume worst-case scenario. When is the March equinox?"

"March 21." Ben licked his lips. "That gives us three weeks to keep them busy looking at the wrong sites while the military finds that enclave in the Himalayas. If we can get Sam back, they can't fire the weapon."

"Maybe not." Kip glanced around the table. "Now that the repeater is armed, couldn't one of the triplets take Sam's place in the Himalayas to fire the weapon?"

"No, according to the prophecy, the Golden Twin is the key to Poseidon's Sword. She alone can fire the weapon." Ben sat back.

"What if she refuses? They can't force her to do it, can they?" Banger asked.

Ben frowned. "Actually, they can. Her touch activates the weapon, so all they have to do is tie her to it."

Banger's eyes widened. "I have an idea. She's telepathic, right? Ask her mother to contact her and find out where she is."

Rowlin shook his head. "If only it were that simple. They're probably drugging her so she can't call for help telepathically."

Banger nodded. "That would make sense. They have to keep her alive, but they can keep her too drugged to function mentally."

"Yes, but they'll have to let the drugs wear off before they need her to fire the weapon. Otherwise, the drugs will alter her inner energy." Kip narrowed his eyes. "We'll have a brief opportunity to contact her when she gains mental clarity."

"I hate to say it, but we may have to kill Sam to save millions." Rowlin clenched his jaw. "Obviously not my first choice, but the many outweigh the one."

"What if we kill the triplets?" Lance searched their faces.

"Easier said than done. Unless we take them all out simultaneously, even one survivor can instantly fry us, and it won't change the outcome. The repeater is already armed." Rowlin shook his head. "Sorry, I know you and Dad are fond of Sam."

"Fond?" Lance bit his lip. "I friggin love her. There has to be another way."

"What if we destroy the obsidian pyramid here?" Kip glanced at the others. "Wouldn't that solve the problem?"

Rowlin shook his head. "The repeater is just insurance—overkill. I checked with experts on ley lines and seismic activity. If they fire a massive burst of energy into that intersection, the tectonic plates will smash together and push Atlantis to the surface anyway. The repeater simply accelerates the process."

"And if we blast this pyramid to hell, the triplets will realize the jig is up and fry us." Banger shrugged. "Gentlemen, we're in deep shit."

As if on cue, Mike and Matt walked in. They looked surprised when they saw Lance.

"Lieutenants, grab a chair. I'm sorry, but we have bad news about your sister," Rowlin said. "As you might've guessed, Lance spent the night with Sam. Only it wasn't Sam, it was Solraya." He briefed them.

Mike glanced at Matt. "We'd noticed some small things, but we thought it was because of her concussion."

"If the triplets find out we know, we're toast. How the hell are we going to fix this?" Matt glanced around the table.

"We have to stall for time and fool them while our military searches for Sam. She's the key." Rowlin paused. "They can't fire the weapon without her."

"And that presents another problem." Mike glanced at the men. "The enclave is protected by a dead zone. Nothing electronic works there, and if an aircraft flies over it, they'll crash, so recon flights aren't an option."

"We could send a drone, but its systems would stop working before it could transmit data." Rowlin tilted his head back. "I guess we could narrow down the location based on where the drone goes dark."

Lance straightened. "I just remembered I'm supposed to call Ross while we're all together so we can coordinate our plans."

"Ross knows?" Mike asked.

"Yeah, I called him to verify Sam still has the scars." Lance shook his head. "That was beyond awkward, but he said he suspected something might be wrong before she left Antarctica."

Matt glanced from Mike to Lance. "Does he hate you now?"

"Not totally." Lance sighed and shot a glance at Rowlin. "He said all will be forgiven if I help him get her back safe."

Mike's eyes widened. "Oh shit, the military intends to kill Sam to stop the weapon, don't they?" He focused on Rowlin.

"Only as a last resort, so let's find her in plenty of time before the March equinox." Rowlin handed Lance an encrypted satellite phone. "Call Captain Sinclair and put him on speaker."

Ross's voice filled the speaker. "I briefed General Barnes, and he said our military is redoubling efforts to locate the enclave. SAT imagery is hampered by constant cloud cover over large portions of the Himalayas." Ross paused. "Radar coverage in that area twenty-three years ago was spotty at best, so we can't use old air-traffic records to determine exactly where the Conor's jet crashed. What's the plan on your end?"

"We're going to buy time and distract the triplets by staying with the original plan to search for Poseidon's Sword at sites in Bimini, the Yucatan, and Santorini." Lance sighed. "I don't know how I'm going to pull this off now that I know I'm with Solraya and not Sam."

Ross's voice hardened. "You'll give an Academy Award performance because Sam's life depends on it, that's how. I'm counting on you to keep your word and help me rescue her."

Rowlin moved the satellite phone closer to him. "Captain Sinclair, this is Captain Rowlin from the USS *Leviathan*. Solraya knows Sam has a strong connection with you. Would it help if you took Lance's place?"

"I'm not keen on cheating on my woman, and it wouldn't work anyway. Solraya avoided intimacy with me because she knew I'd notice their differences. She's happy with Lance. Let's keep it that way."

"I hope the UK understands the absolute need for secrecy as we deal with this. The fewer people who know, the better." Rowlin kept his tone firm.

"No worries there. After what we saw them do in Antarctica, we intend to exercise extreme caution. We're telling our recon pilots only that we're looking for a large black pyramid with major historical significance. They'll use ground-mapping radar to find it beneath the clouds."

"What about the dead zone?" Rowlin said. "You could lose your airplanes."

"We considered that. The pilots are equipped with cold-weather survival gear and rations. If they have to punch out, we're counting on them to hike in close enough to pinpoint the enclave's location before hiking back out to activate their GPS locator beacons."

Matt spoke up, "The ejection system might not work in the dead zone."

"True, but millions of lives are at stake. It's a chance we have to take." Ross paused. "Captain Rowlin, you have my number. I've been designated liaison officer. Let me know if there's anything the UK can do to assist you."

"Understood, Captain Sinclair, we'll keep each other in the loop."

"I'm counting on America to do everything possible to rescue Sam. I realize taking her out may be the only way to prevent a catastrophe, but let's agree to make that our last resort," Ross said.

"We haven't forgotten Sam's a national heroine on both sides of the pond. We'll save her if we can. Talk to you soon." Rowlin switched off the phone.

He glanced around the table. "I'll have Commander Bern bring the triplets back to the ship, and we'll head for the Bahamas. I've arranged to lease a 120-foot yacht with a dive platform to help us keep up the tourist façade. Remember, be your most charming selves around the women. Think of them as suitcase nukes with hair triggers."

Rowlin turned to Kip. "You'll have a major role in the dives, looking for anomalies that might lead to an unexpected discovery underwater. There's a remote chance we're wrong about the weapon being in the Himalayas, so we're still going to treat each search as a serious mission."

"I'll do my best, Captain." Kip shrugged. "Who knows? We may find more artifacts connected to Atlantis now that we know where their continent used to be."

Ben cleared his throat. "Uh, Captain, I'd like to return to Harvard if I'm not needed here anymore. I'm supposed to be teaching classes."

"Of course, Professor. I'll arrange a military transport for you." Rowlin stood. "Let's get this show on the road."

Rowlin entered the bridge and saluted his XO. "Commander Lowes, I'm leaving to procure the yacht for our covert mission in Bimini. You have the conn. Take good care of my ship while I'm gone and see to it Professor Armitage gets a ride home."

"Aye, Captain, I'll keep everything shipshape and ready for action." Lowes returned the salute.

Rowlin made a brief call and then descended the stairs to Dive Operations, where the SEALs waited in civilian clothes. "Gentlemen, I conferred with the joint chiefs, and they agreed we need to keep the triplets alive and well. If the Atlanteans lose contact with them, they might assume the worst and fire the weapon immediately. Forget about looking for opportunities to take them out."

Commander Bern glanced at his men. "Understood, Captain, we'll keep them safe."

"Bern and Banger, come with me in the RHIB. We'll secure the yacht, return after nightfall, and pick up everyone."

NINETEEN

BLUE WATER QUEEN

Rowlin pulled alongside the USS *Leviathan* at 7:10 p.m. and idled the yacht's engines while three SEALs boarded with Kip, the Starr twins, Lance, the triplets, and a ship's cook. He waited while their bags and dive gear were loaded aboard, then saluted and pulled away.

Lance joined him on the bridge. "How do the controls feel?"

"This beauty handles like a dream—twin diesels, side thrusters, the works." He grinned. "I still prefer my Navy ship, but this is fun." He set course for their initial dive site.

After they dropped anchor on site, he gathered the group of fourteen. "While we're playing tourists on a dive vacation, we'll stick to first names to make things seem casual." Max reminded everyone of their first names. "This yacht has ten staterooms, plus crew quarters, so we'll be able to accommodate everyone comfortably. Ladies, you have the option to take separate rooms or share rooms with Mike, Matt, and Lance."

The women exchanged glances.

Blaze stepped forward. "We'd like to share rooms with our men." She grinned and took Mike's arm.

"That leaves enough staterooms for everyone except the cook. Sorry, Ted, you'll have to use the crew quarters. Let's get everyone settled and meet in the dining room for a late dinner." Max grabbed his bag and led them below.

Fifteen minutes later, the group settled around a long dining table. Ted had brought platters of cold cuts, breads, and salads from the ship to expedite their first meal on *Blue Water Queen*. Everyone passed the platters around family style.

Max addressed the SEAL team leader from the head of the table. "George, I want you and your SEALs to train Blaze and Luna for scuba diving." He glanced at "Sam." "How long has it been since your last scuba dive?"

She gave Max a blank look. "Um, a long time, I guess. Can't remember exactly."

"George will see to it you get a thorough refresher course." Max shot a look at George. "Train in the shallow water over the area called the Bimini Road. It's believed by some to be the remains of a city."

"Why don't they know for certain?" Luna turned to Kip.

"The bleached coral looks like square blocks in a straight line, like a road, but many scientists argue it's a natural coral formation." Kip shook his head. "I've never seen coral grow in square shapes, but that's the scientific world for you—narrow-minded dolts."

"Judging by how fast you ladies learned how to use the Hardsuit, we can probably have you ready for scuba diving after one day of training." George glanced at Matt and Lance. "Mike's a SEAL, but what about you guys? Are you certified for scuba?"

"I have a deep diver certification with PADI, and it's current," Matt said.

"So do I." Lance grinned. "In fact, my last dive was two weeks ago at the same little cove in Hawaii where Sam found this Rolex for me." Lance raised his left wrist to show off the Submariner dive watch.

"That was damn generous of you, Sis." Mike admired the valuable watch.

"Lance is worth it." "Sam" planted a kiss on Lance's cheek.

"While the women train, Kip and I'll scout around with the ROV in the deeper water." Max took a bite of his sandwich and nodded at Kip.

"The shallows have been explored to death, but we might find something in water too deep for scuba diving." Kip glanced at Max. "I assume if we do, we can bring in *Leviathan* and dive in the Hardsuits."

Max nodded. "Whatever it takes to find that weapon."

The next morning, George had the women practice with their snorkels and then remove and don their scuba gear while underwater. The triplets seemed relaxed and comfortable in the ocean, showing off for the SEALs.

"Well done, ladies," George said when they surfaced at the end of the drills. "Let's take a fifteen-minute break. Hand us your BC vests with your tanks."

"We'll be back in a few minutes. Woo hoo!" Blaze yelled as the men transferred the scuba gear to the yacht's dive platform.

George turned in time to catch the triplets riding away on dolphins. They wore their masks and snorkels and held on when the dolphins dived underwater. Moments later, the dolphins leaped up with the women gripping their dorsal fins.

"This is fun!" Luna yelled.

"Sonofabitch!" George said as he watched them. "They weren't supposed to engage in unauthorized activities."

Banger shrugged. "Well, this must be their idea of a break."

"Sam" rode up to the men and gestured at a waiting dolphin. "Come on, Banger, it's fun."

George nodded at him. "Better keep an eye on them."

Banger grabbed the dolphin's fin and surged after them.

George shook his head. "This would never happen in the Navy." He looked up at the sun deck where the Starr twins and Lance lounged in deck chairs, laughing.

Himalayas

A British pilot descended over the cloud-covered Himalayas in his Typhoon Eurofighter jet. His specialized radar, added for this mission, painted the landscape in ground-mapping mode. So far, nothing was pyramid shaped.

"Discovery One to base," the pilot said into his helmet mike.

"This is base, go ahead Discovery One."

"Clouds are obscuring mountains at angels twenty and below. No pyramid on ground radar."

"Roger, Discovery One, continue the search northwest."

"Discovery One, wilco." The pilot studied the radar while maintaining 30,000 feet, high enough to safely clear the mountains northwest of Mount Everest as he flew at a reduced speed of 500 mph.

As the minutes ticked by, his display screens suddenly went blank and his engines flamed out. The radio stopped working. His cockpit fell silent, except for the whistle of air rushing over his canopy.

The dreaded dead zone.

He activated the ejection system as the Typhoon's nose dropped.

Nothing happened.

He was trapped inside a fly-by-wire fighter with all systems dead.

No control.

No hope.

He envisioned his wife and children during his last seconds before the jet smashed into a mountain. The explosion reverberated through the snow-covered peaks.

SAS Base, Dundee, Scotland

Ross called Rowlin on the secure satellite phone. "Captain Rowlin, how's it going in Bimini?"

"It's been interesting. Commander Bern trained the triplets on scuba gear, then had to corral them when they took off riding dolphins. They're quite comfortable in the water. How's it going on your end?"

"We lost our recon jet over the Himalayas about a hundred miles northwest of Kathmandu. No contact with the pilot. We're sending in Gurkha units to look for him and the enclave, but it's a huge area to search in treacherous winter conditions. We'll try to narrow down the search grid with drones. I'll keep you updated."

"Thank you, Captain Sinclair. I'll do the same."

Bimini

After six days of exploring dive sites, *Blue Water Queen's* crew hadn't made any discoveries. The group gathered around the dinner table for a hot meal of baked grouper and steamed vegetables.

"I think it's time to move on and search the Yucatan," Max said.

"I agree." George reached for the breadbasket. "There's nothing here."

Blaze frowned and nudged Mike. "Can't we do something fun before we leave the area?"

Mike made eye contact with Max. "If Max gives his approval, we'll take you, Luna, and Sam to dinner at a beautiful casino resort on Paradise Island in the Bahamas tomorrow night."

"I want to go." Luna raised her hand.

"Me too, we need a break." "Sam" stared at Max with pleading eyes.

Max looked around the table. "All right, I'll need a little time to coordinate plans for exploring the Yucatan anyway. Mike, Matt, and Lance will accompany the women, but no gambling." He shot the men a stern look. "Just dinner and return."

"Great, we'll enjoy a gourmet dinner while keeping a low profile." Matt grinned and nodded at Max.

"I'll contact the dockmaster there and see if we can get a slip. Then you won't need to take the RHIB, and we can get provisions for the next leg of the cruise." Max slid his chair back and strode to the bridge.

"Will they have a slip big enough for us?" George asked.

"Are you kidding?" Mike laughed. "This yacht will probably be one of the smaller ones. That place is full of rich high rollers."

A few minutes later, Max returned to the table. "Everything's set. We have a slip scheduled for 6:30 p.m. tomorrow with a midnight departure."

"That will make it easier to wear pretty dresses for a nice dinner." Blaze grinned. "I'll wear my red satin dress."

Luna and "Sam" chimed in on what they planned to wear.

"Whatever makes you ladies happy." Lance made eye contact with Mike and Matt.

"You'll love the saltwater aquarium integrated throughout the resort." Matt squeezed Luna's hand. "They even have a pyramid with a water slide through a shark tank."

"Sounds like a fun place." "Sam" leaned in to kiss Lance's cheek.

TWENTY

Paradise Island Resort

A t 6:30 p.m., Max slid *Blue Water Queen* into a slip between a 230-foot yacht flying the Saudi flag and a 180-foot yacht flying the UK flag. Ten minutes later, Lance, Matt, and Mike strolled down the gangway with the triplets and followed a long, manicured path. They entered the resort's expansive lobby with a thirty-foot ceiling and spectacular décor mimicking a designer's image of ancient Atlantis.

"Wow, look at that giant glass ceiling sculpture. It has to be at least twenty feet in diameter." Blaze pointed at a multicolored hand-blown glass light fixture hanging high above them.

"I think it's meant to mimic a coral reef." Mike pointed. "If you look through that port over there, you'll see part of the fantastic salt-water aquarium that winds through the resort."

The women gathered in front of the window as a manta ray glided past, followed by grey reef sharks and colorful tropical fish darting in and out of the coral formations.

As they wandered through the beautiful Atlantis-themed casino, Mike directed their attention to a formal restaurant with a huge viewing port for the aquarium.

"Ooh, let's have dinner there." Luna's eyes widened. "It's so romantic."

"Hang on a sec while I check with the maitre d'." Mike strode over to a man standing at a podium and had a brief conversation. He returned with a smile. "We have a table for six right in front of the viewing port at 7:30."

Blaze kissed him. "Well done."

"The tunnel over there is lined with viewing ports." Matt pointed. "We can follow that through to the outdoor area."

Matt led the group through the tunnel, pausing along the way to watch the varied sea life. Eventually, they emerged into a courtyard with an ancient-looking pyramid temple.

"That pyramid looks high." Blaze tilted her head back to gaze at the top. "And that's a steep slide."

"Let's go around." Mike led them to the side of the pyramid where a massive glass wall exposed the depths of the pool at the base of the slide. Huge nurse sharks rested atop a Plexiglas tube that was an extension of the waterslide and fed into a lower pool beyond the shark tank.

"Sam" laughed. "The sharks are looking down through that tube, like vultures waiting for their prey to slide through."

Lance grinned. "That's their daily entertainment. Nurse sharks are the only kind that don't need to swim constantly to breathe, so they can just drape themselves over the tube and enjoy the view."

"Yeah, they look a lot like giant catfish." Mike pointed at an eight-footer.

"They also look well fed." Luna laughed. "Probably wouldn't even bother anyone who jumped into their tank."

"Yeah, too much effort." Matt glanced at his watch. Time to head back for dinner.

They strolled back through the viewing tunnel to the restaurant.

At dinner, Mike, Matt, and Lance sat with their backs to the viewing port so their dates could enjoy the aquarium.

Mike glanced at the table to his left. "I think those men are from the Saudi yacht docked beside our boat."

"Their head cloths are dead giveaways." Matt chuckled.

"Right, smart ass, but those ghutras just mean they're from the

Persian Gulf, not that they're from the Saudi yacht." Mike arched a brow.

"Could be loads of Arabs in a place like this." Lance glanced around the room.

Blaze peeked at the nearby men and focused on Mike. "Why do you care?"

He frowned. "I don't like the way they're looking at you."

Blaze took his hand. "Sounds like you're jealous. I like it."

"It's more than that. Attractive young women are kidnap targets for the sex slave market, although it's unlikely to be a concern in a classy place like this. I'm just being protective."

"Yeah, we don't want anything bad to happen to our ladies." Lance kissed "Sam's" hand.

"Our knights in shining armor." Luna grinned at Matt.

The waiter arrived with their entrees, and conversation quieted as the enticing food stole their attention.

Twenty minutes later, Blaze patted her lips with a linen napkin and glanced around. "Anyone know where the ladies' room is?"

"Yeah, over there behind the giant urns." Mike pointed.

"I'll go with you," Luna said.

"Me too." "Sam" stood.

Lance stood and pulled back her chair. "Why do women always go to the restroom together?"

"To help each other primp and talk about our dates." She grinned and followed Blaze and Luna.

Mike watched them disappear behind the urns and settled in his seat. "Looks like the Arabs are leaving."

One of the Arab men signed a credit-card bill and followed the other men out.

Lance sighed. "Well, so far so good with the triplets. I hope we don't screw up and get fried." He stabbed the last piece of steak with his fork.

"Yeah, our military had better hurry up and find that damn weapon." Mike took a sip of wine. "Sam's life hangs in the balance."

"So do ours." Matt emptied his wine glass.

Lance glanced at his Rolex. "How long has it been since they went to the restroom?"

"About ten minutes. You know how women are." Mike checked his DOXA dive watch. "We'll wait five more minutes. Then we'll go find them."

The women didn't return.

"You guys search the casino while I check the ladies' room." Mike strode around the urns and waited until a woman exited the restroom. "Excuse me, ma'am, I'm looking for my girlfriend. Did you see a redhead in there?"

"No, I was alone. Sorry." She smiled at him and walked away.

Mike pushed through the door to confirm the room was empty. He texted Matt and Lance with the bad news.

Mike read Matt's return text: *No luck in the casino. Meet us at the boat.*

Mike rushed down to the docks and found Matt and Lance staring at an empty slip where the Saudi yacht had been docked.

BLUE WATER QUEEN

Max looked up from an intel report on the Yucatan. "What do you mean they're gone?"

"They went to the restroom in the restaurant and never returned. The Arab men at the next table left right after the women, and now their yacht is gone." Mike sucked in his breath. "They've been eyeing the triplets."

Matt glanced at the SEALs. "Anybody see the Arabs board their yacht?"

The men shook their heads.

George clenched his jaw. "We were checking our equipment for the next mission."

Max pulled out his SATCOM and called XO Lowes. "A 230-foot Saudi yacht left the dock beside us about a half hour ago. Track it and call me when you find it." He set down the satellite phone and addressed his men. "I want this ship ready to depart in five minutes. I'll call the dockmaster with our new departure time."

Blue Water Queen had just cleared the harbor entrance when Max received a call from his XO.

"Captain, we've located the Saudi yacht. She's twenty miles southwest of your position. What are your orders?"

"Put *Leviathan* on an intercept course and send the Seahawk to pick up our SEALs so they can board that ship." Max glanced at George. "Gear up for combat."

"Aye, Captain," Lowes said. "*Leviathan* will intercept the Saudi yacht and send the Seahawk to pick up the SEALs."

Max faced Mike after George had left the bridge to get his men ready. "Go with the SEALs and recover the triplets."

"Aye, Captain." Mike rushed out.

"Uh, Max, I think we're missing something here." Lance stepped forward.

"Let's hear it." Max pushed up the throttles and scanned the instrument panel.

"How could the Saudis kidnap the triplets? The women would fry their asses and stroll back to us like nothing happened."

Max paused, thinking. "They could've been drugged with quick stabs from syringes to appear like sloppy drunks, barely able to walk. I'm guessing they need their full faculties to control Vril."

Matt nodded. "Or they decided to ditch us so they could carry on with their mission to raise Atlantis."

The thumping blades of a Seahawk echoed off the water.

"We'll find out soon enough." Max throttled back and idled the yacht while the SEALs boarded the helicopter.

MacLeod Castle

"*Mom!*" the word reverberated in Loren Starr's head as she lay awake trying to fall asleep.

Loren sat up and scanned the darkened room. "Sam?"

Duncan woke. "Loren, what's wrong?"

"Uh, I'm not sure. I heard Sam yell for me, but she's not here." Loren leaned over and switched on the nightstand lamp.

"*Mom! Help! The Atlanteans kidnapped me!*" Sam's voice invaded Loren's head.

Loren stiffened, closed her eyes, and concentrated. "*Where are you?*"

"The enclave in the Himalayas. They're keeping me drugged, so I don't have much time before the next dose. Solraya is pretending to be me."

Loren opened her eyes and glanced at Duncan. "Call Ross. Sam is talking to me telepathically. Tell him to hold while I get more info." Loren closed her eyes. *"Why did they kidnap you?"*

"They need me to fire Poseidon's Sword on the March equinox. The triplets are helping them. Sorry I got this so wrong. I thought the triplets were victims, not mass murderers."

Loren bit her lip. *"How can we find you?"*

"I'm in a high valley in a remote area—no civilization in sight. There's a lake beside their little village and a big black pyramid in the center of town. All their buildings are round or hexagonal, and the weather is tropical. The lake isn't frozen even though it's the height of winter. Oh god, here they come with another syringe full of drugs!"

"Sam? Sam, talk to me!" Loren heard nothing more. She opened her eyes and repeated everything to Duncan and Ross, who was on SPEAKER.

"Look for a patch of green with a blue lake and a black pyramid in the middle of snow-covered mountains. There's bound to be a thick layer of clouds over them if it's as warm as she said," Duncan said.

"Right, we forgot about the patch of green the surviving flight attendant mentioned seeing when the Conor's jet crashed in the Himalayas. That has to be the key to finding them. We'll search for a temperature inversion." Ross's voice telegraphed excitement. "I'll get right on this. Let me know if Loren hears from Sam again."

"Keep us updated as well. Good luck, Ross." Duncan set his mobile phone on a nightstand and pulled Loren into his arms. "Ross filled me in while you were talking to Sam. They already knew Solraya switched places with Sam, and they've been trying to find Sam while Mike and Matt are pretending all is well with the triplets."

"They seemed like such nice girls." She shook her head. "It's hard to believe they would help the Atlanteans kill millions of people." Loren fought back tears. "What's going to happen to Sam?"

"Don't worry. Ross will move Heaven and Earth to rescue her." Duncan kissed her.

"I hope you're right. I have a bad feeling about this." Loren buried her face in his chest.

Saudi Yacht

Six SEALs rappelled down ropes from the Seahawk and landed on the yacht's deck. In minutes, the ship was dead in the water with the crew and passengers secured in the lounge while they searched the ship.

Twenty minutes later, Mike waved George to the side. "Commander Bern, we've completed a thorough search of the vessel and found no evidence the triplets were here." He sighed. "Sorry."

George faced the Saudi prince and made up a story. "Your Highness, on behalf of the U.S. government, please accept my sincere apology in this case of mistaken identity. A yacht similar in size left Atlantis within minutes of this one with three kidnapped Americans aboard. I sincerely regret this inconvenience. We'll release your boat now."

The prince scowled. "Your intrusion is insulting and inexcusable. I will make a formal complaint to our ambassador. Now get off my yacht!"

George led his team onto the bow. The Seahawk hovered as the team members hooked themselves to ropes. The SEALs dangled from the helicopter as it flew back to the USS *Leviathan*.

Paradise Island Resort

While the SEALs were flying back from the Saudi yacht, Max took the cook back to *Leviathan* and had the gear and luggage transferred. He returned *Blue Water Queen* to the leasing agent and took Matt and Lance in the rigid hull inflatable boat to Atlantis. They docked, cleared customs, and walked up the path to the resort's lobby.

"Let's check if the triplets took a taxi before we waste time searching the resort again." Max strode to the doorman. "Did you see three beautiful women in their mid-twenties this evening?"

"Oh, yeah, mon," he said without hesitation. "Three hot babes. Dey ask for taxi to airport about three hours ago." He grinned, exposing a diamond-embedded gold tooth.

"Thank you." Max slipped him a $10 bill. "Call us a cab, please."

"Right away, sir." He stepped out and waved one forward. "Here you are, mon." He opened the back door.

Max jumped into the front passenger seat while Matt and Lance slid into the back.

"Take us to the airport," Max said as he fastened his seatbelt in the old Ford Crown Victoria taxicab.

The cabbie glanced at his watch. "Whatever you say, mon, but it'll be midnight by the time we get there. The airlines don't fly after midnight. Maybe you wait until morning?" His hand hovered over the meter button.

"We need to get there now." Max sat back and crossed his arms.

"Okay, mon." The driver hit the meter and accelerated down the road to the bridge to Nassau.

They made good time in the sparse traffic to the other end of the island. In forty-five minutes, the taxi pulled up to a mostly dark airport terminal.

Max turned to Lance and Matt. "Looks like they're shut down for the night." He pulled out his satellite phone. "I'll have our security people check the flight manifests for this evening." He glanced at the driver. "Take us to the general aviation terminal." Max made the call to his ship.

When they pulled up to Odyssey Aviation Bahamas, Max said, "Wait here, we won't be long."

The three men walked into a luxurious lobby furnished with over-stuffed leather furniture, beautiful oil paintings depicting island scenes, and colorful tropical plants. A lone man perched behind a teak desk.

"We're in hot water with our girlfriends," Matt said to the clerk.

"Yeah, we lost track of time in the casino and missed the private flight." Lance shrugged.

Max slid a $20 bill across the desk. "I hope you can help us out. Did you see three beautiful women about three hours ago?"

"Yeah, mon, never saw anything like that in all my years here." The man shook his head.

"What do you mean?" Max edged closer.

"Three corporate jets left within minutes of each other, and each jet took on three beautiful passengers. What are the odds?" He opened his hands.

"Did the same company own all the jets?" Max asked.

The man behind the desk checked his computer and nodded. "Gold Trident Industries owns the Gulfstream, Lear 55, and Citation X."

"And was there a blonde, a brunette, and a redhead on each jet?" Max asked.

"Yeah, mon, how'd you know?"

"Did you get a close look at them?" Max leaned in.

"I wish. They looked hot from a distance."

"Sounds like they played a trick on us because we missed their flight," Lance said.

Max sighed. "Do you have a record of the destinations?"

The man tapped a few keys and checked the screen. "Yeah, mon, all three flew to Fort Lauderdale Executive Airport."

"Thanks, you've been a big help." Max slipped him a $10 bill and turned to Matt and Lance. "Let's go."

They hurried out to the waiting taxi.

Seven-foot-six twin women with angular faces and lean, muscular bodies stood beside the cab, their long jet-black braids hanging down their backs.

The cab driver sat slumped over the wheel with his forehead against it.

"Gentlemen, we've been waiting for you," the twins said in unison.

"I don't think we've been introduced," Max said. "I'm Max." He nodded at the men. "And this is Lance and Matt."

"I'm Rutya, and this is my sister, Daitya."

"Unusual names. Where are you ladies from?" Max asked.

"We're named after twin Atlantean islands." Rutya arched a brow and focused on Matt. "Where is your brother?"

"Far away on a Navy ship. Why?" Matt hooked his thumbs through his belt loops.

"Our job would be easier if he was with you." Daitya ran her eyes over the men and licked her lips.

The women edged a few feet closer, illuminated by the bright security lights. Barefoot, they wore matching black stretch pants and black sleeveless tops. A giant shark swam over a black pyramid in a tattoo on Rutya's left shoulder while a dragon clutched a gold trident on her right shoulder. Daitya, who stood to her left, sported the same tattoos on opposite shoulders.

Max noticed each woman had one blue eye and one brown eye, though on opposite sides, like the tattoos. "And what is your job?"

Daitya's voice was a strange, deep timbre. "The goddesses have become too fond of you. We can't have you distracting them from their mission."

Lance turned on the charm. "Now ladies, we'd hate to see you end up a pile of ashes. What do you think they'll do if they find out you messed with their men?"

The women reached behind them and pulled out eight-inch daggers with jeweled hilts.

"They don't know we're here. You'll be the victims of violent muggings. Such a shame." Rutya grazed the knife across her left arm and licked the blood. "We promise to make it quick if you don't resist. Otherwise, it will be slow and painful."

"Accept our offer." Daitya cut her right arm and licked the blood. "We're Atlantean master assassins. No one has ever survived us." She behaved like a cat playing with a mouse.

Max glanced at Lance and Matt and shrugged. "Okay then, may as well get this over with." He stepped forward. "Me first."

Rutya stepped back. "You may have him, Daitya. I know how you love the taste of blond men."

Daitya licked her lips, flexed her long legs, and executed a lightning-fast spinning heel kick aimed at Max's head.

He ducked and took the hard blow on his shoulder. Her power kick knocked him to the ground, and his head slammed onto the pavement. Dazed, he lifted his head and looked around.

Matt shot a sideways glance at Lance. They separated and rushed Rutya, flanking her. She was ready with a spinning kick that hit their heads and sprawled them on the pavement.

Daitya surveyed the men. "These pretty boys aren't much of a challenge. I assumed the goddesses would choose mighty warriors." She sheathed her knife. "May as well have some fun."

"Good idea. I love the sound of breaking bones." Rutya slipped her dagger into a leather sheath behind her back.

The men jumped to their feet. Max ducked another kick from Daitya and landed a hard kick to her skinny torso. When she doubled over, he moved in for a knockout punch. But she straightened, blocked his fist, and hammered her fist into his jaw.

Max recovered and rammed his head into her sternum, tackling her. As she fell backward, she pulled out her dagger.

Meanwhile, Lance and Matt sparred with Rutya. Her longer reach gave her an advantage, but they outnumbered her. Lance kept her busy while Matt maneuvered behind her. Just when it looked like they had her, she knocked them down again with her long legs.

Max blocked Daitya's attempt to slash his throat, and he drove his fist into her windpipe. Gasping for air, she tried to stab him in a carotid artery while her powerful thighs squeezed the air out of his chest.

He clamped onto her right wrist and twisted it until he heard the bone crack. Her wrist went limp as she clawed at his eyes with her left hand. Max blocked her, snatched the dagger from her right hand, and slit her throat.

Lance and Matt rolled in opposite directions when Rutya turned to look at her sister.

Max squinted as Daitya's blood sprayed his face. He wiped his eyes and sprang to his feet.

"Noooo!" Rutya charged Max, and Lance and Matt flanked her from behind.

Max was ready for her long reach. When she tried to kick him in the head, he ducked and sliced her Achilles tendon with the dagger.

The wound spiraled her into a blind rage.

"Arrggghh!" She lurched and raised her knife at Max, dragging her right foot.

Lance swung his leg into her good ankle, and she tripped forward. Max grabbed her knife wrist and twisted it while plunging Daitya's dagger into her heart. Blood poured from her chest as her blade clanked onto the pavement. He yanked out the dagger, and she dropped face-first.

Max leaned down and checked for a pulse. Nothing. He turned and found Lance and Matt staring at the bottom of her bare feet. He raised a brow. "What?"

Matt tilted his head to the side. "There's a pictorial map tattooed on the bottom of her left foot."

"Drag her twin over here." Max turned Rutya over.

Lance deposited Daitya beside her, and Max held her right foot next to Rutya's left foot.

Max pulled out his cell. "That's both halves of the picture." He snapped photos and texted them to his ship with orders to decipher the location.

Matt studied the foot tattoos. "Maybe it's a picture of their Himalayan enclave."

"Or a map to Poseidon's Sword." Lance shook his head. "Dang, they were vile women." He patted Max's back. "Good job taking them out. Jeff never told me you were such a badass."

Max shrugged. "I've seen my share of combat."

"What are we going to do about this mess?" Matt glanced from the bloody women to Max's blood-soaked shirt.

"Check the cab driver. If he's dead, see if his shirt is clean." Max pulled off his shirt and used the back of it to wipe the blood off his face, chest, and hands.

Matt returned with a floral-print shirt. "The driver's dead—broken neck, poor bastard. I feel bad he got sucked into this."

"I hope he didn't have a family." Max handed Lance his bloody shirt. "Put this in the trunk along with the driver." He took the clean shirt from Matt and put it on.

Matt faced the building. "What about the security cameras? Should we destroy the footage?"

Max stood with his hands on his hips. "The Pentagon brass are going to be so pissed off about us losing the triplets, they might leave us here to hang. We'd better deal with this now." He glanced around. "Put the assassins in the trunk."

"Good thing this old Ford has a huge trunk," Lance said.

After they hid the bodies, they walked back to the general aviation terminal.

Luck was on their side. A downpour rinsed off the bloody pavement as they ducked inside.

Max lowered his voice. "Distract the guy behind the counter while I locate the security room and erase the footage. If they don't know a crime took place, they'll never check the tapes. And buy me one of those T-shirts they sell behind the counter."

"All righty." Lance and Matt brushed themselves off and sauntered over to the night clerk while Max pretended to head for the men's room.

When Max found the locked security room, he heard someone coming and ducked around a corner. He peeked and spotted an airport guard entering the men's room.

Max waited until the guard left. He picked the lock with his Leatherman tool and erased the footage from the past hour. Then he took a few minutes to scroll through the video. He couldn't pick out the triplets because all the women wore similar clothes, hats, and dark glasses. Sighing, he deactivated the security cameras and locked the door on his way out.

Max waved to Lance and Matt, and they walked out to the cab. Matt handed him the new shirt.

"Thanks." Max changed and dropped the cabbie's shirt in the trunk. "Let's go."

Lance slipped into the driver's seat with Max beside him and Matt in the back seat.

Matt leaned forward as they drove away. "Any ideas how to dispose of the cab and the bodies?"

"Yeah, park somewhere where there's no friggin' cameras and put the cabbie in the driver's seat and the women in the back seat. Then torch the car." Max glanced back at Matt. "I'm keeping the daggers."

"Okay, but how do we get back to our boat?" Lance turned onto the highway to Nassau. "Can't call a taxi and leave a record we were in downtown Nassau in the middle of the night."

Max shrugged. "We'll improvise."

Lance shut off the headlights and eased the cab down a dark alley leading to a deserted lot several blocks from Nassau's harbor. All was quiet at 3:07 in the morning.

Max got out and gently closed the door. "You guys move the bodies into position while I rig the car."

Lance popped the trunk, and Max grabbed the discarded shirts. He shoved part of the driver's shirt into the gas tank and waited for it to soak up gasoline. Then he draped it over the dead man after Lance positioned him behind the wheel. Matt and Lance arranged the twin assassins on the back seat and closed the doors.

Max glanced at the men. "Ready?"

They nodded.

Max pointed. "Meet me behind that old wood building we passed two blocks from here. I'll wait five minutes before I torch the car."

"We aren't smokers. How will you light it?" Lance asked.

Max pulled a butane lighter from his pocket. "I never go anywhere without it. I've been on enough missions to know the value of a reliable lighter. Besides, I enjoy a fine cigar now and then." He pointed. "Now hoof it."

Lance and Matt ran up the alley and turned right. Max glanced at his watch and twisted his bloody shirt into a cloth fuse. When the time came, he shoved part of the shirt into the tank and lit the exposed end. He bolted down the alley and rounded the corner just as the car exploded. He kept running until he reached the rendezvous point.

"Mission accomplished," Max said before leading Matt and Lance to the harbor. "Now we need to find another place that doesn't have security cameras."

They crouched behind an ice machine and surveyed the dock area for hidden cameras.

Lance pointed at dinghies tied up along the shore. "They must be for the sailboats moored out there. The ones with gas motors are noisy. Do you see one with an electric motor?"

"That dinghy has one, but first we need to disable that camera." Matt pointed at the corner of a nearby building. "It's aimed right at the dinghies."

Max threw a rock at the camera and broke the mount on one side.

He tried another rock. That time, he nailed the camera lens and shattered the glass.

"Dang, Max, where'd you learn to throw like that?" Lance shook his head.

"Football. I was a quarterback at Annapolis." Max glanced around. "Let's go. Keep your heads down."

The dinghy with the electric motor was chained to the dock, so Max unscrewed the mounts and transferred the motor to a large wood dingy with oars. "We need a 12-volt battery. Look for an old car without an alarm system."

Lance found an unlocked VW bus from the sixties. "This'll do." He popped the hood and disconnected the battery. "Got it."

Max connected the battery to the electric motor while Lance and Matt climbed aboard, untied the line, and cast off. Max twisted the handle to the right and steered away from the docks.

They headed slowly across the dark harbor to Paradise Island. Huge cruise ships towered in the distance as the calm water shimmered under the stars, and cool sea air soothed their scrapes and bruises.

Fifteen minutes later, Max pulled up to a rock seawall half a mile from the resort's marina.

"We'd better get out here to avoid the security cameras." Max waited as Lance and Matt clambered up the rocks. "Matt, keep a tight hold on the bow line until I get out."

Max unscrewed the motor mounts and lifted the motor. He smashed the propeller into the dinghy's wood bottom. A loud crack signaled his ploy was successful. He jumped out.

Matt released the rope, and Max shoved the dinghy into the wide passage between Nassau and Paradise Island.

Lance stood atop the sea wall. "The current's pushing her out, and she's taking on water. She'll sink in a few minutes."

"Let's head back to the marina. We'll clear customs and return to the ship." Max led them down a path between two bungalows. A main path ran along the inland side of the buildings, and the men ambled back to the resort's docks.

An hour later, they boarded *Leviathan*.

Mike met them aboard. "I have big news, but did you find the triplets?"

"Come with us to CIC to discuss everything." Max led them into the ship.

At the ship's nerve center, Max approached the communications officer. "At approximately 11:00 p.m., three jets owned by Gold Trident Industries—a Gulfstream, Lear 55, and Citation X—left the Nassau airport and flew to Fort Lauderdale Executive Airport. I need to know what they did after they arrived."

"Aye, Captain, I'll get right on it." The communications officer turned back to his computer.

Max turned to Mike. "The triplets ditched you guys and flew out on a jet owned by their company. They obviously planned the whole thing."

Matt briefed Mike on the details of the three jets but didn't mention the rest of the night. "What's your big news?"

Mike grinned. "Mom called. Sam contacted her telepathically and described the enclave. We might be able to find it with her clues."

"Did she say a lake was beside the village?" Lance asked.

Mike's jaw dropped. "How did you know that?"

Lance glanced at Max.

Max pulled out his cell and selected a photo. "We found a pictorial map." He held it out to Mike.

Mike tilted his head and squinted. "Is that somebody's feet?"

"We'll discuss that later. Does this look like what Sam described?" Max scrolled through the other shots for Mike.

"According to Mom, Sam said the village is beside a lake in a high valley in the mountains, and the enclave's climate is tropical, even though it's winter in the Himalayas." Mike pointed. "Isn't that a palm tree?"

"That's probably a clue about the climate anomaly." Max smiled. "Maybe we can find them before they fire that weapon."

The communications officer handed Max a printout. He read the paper and sighed. "The jets parked at Banyan Air Service and refueled. A private limo met the airplanes. No record of whether any passengers boarded the limo or where it went. Then all three jets departed. The

Gulfstream is en route to Los Angeles, the Lear landed in New York, and the Citation is bound for Seattle." Max shook his head. "My career is toast."

Matt squeezed Max's shoulder. "Don't give up yet. We're all in this together, and I'm betting that map will redeem us."

"My money is on the limo. If we find out where it went, we can nab the triplets," Mike said.

"And get fried to a cinder for your trouble?" Max shook his head.

"Maybe not." Lance grinned. "Remember, the evil twins said the triplets were too fond of us."

Mike crossed his arms. "What evil twins?"

"Eh, that's a conversation for later. We haven't had time to formulate a story for the Navy to explain how we got the map." Max gave Matt and Lance a stern look.

Matt glanced at his watch. "We'd better arrange for Homeland Security to meet the Gulfstream and the Citation when they land on the West Coast. The Lear already landed in New York, so it may be too late to do anything but investigate there."

"I'll make the calls, and we'll meet in my cabin for a serious debrief over some Scotch," Max said.

TWENTY-ONE

Possum Kingdom Lake, Texas

L una gripped the steering wheel on the classic '57 Chevy they'd purchased through a website. She turned onto a gravel driveway to a log cabin. The sisters exited the car and breathed in the fresh scent of pine trees and lake water.

Blaze grinned and patted Solraya on the back. "Good work, sister dear. Lance's lake cabin is the perfect spot, and he'll never suspect you had a reason for asking him about it."

"And this old car doesn't have any tracking devices installed in it." Luna grinned.

"Let's check out the dock." Solraya led the way around the cabin and down the hill to a huge winding Texas lake.

Wood slats creaked from their steps on a 60-foot pier lit by a brilliant full moon reflecting off the calm lake. Water lapped at the pilings as the silence was broken by an occasional splash from a fish snatching an insect off the surface and crickets calling from the forest.

Solraya dropped her zippered bag on the pier and glanced at her DOXA dive watch, which she had purchased in Key West during her impersonation of Sam. "It'll be dawn in less than an hour. Let's get the signal flares ready."

Blaze unzipped a long leather bag and pulled out several flares. "We'll light one when we hear it. Then we'll keep lighting them until it zeroes in on us." She passed some to her sisters. "Big Spring isn't too far from here."

"Too bad they can't come now." Luna grinned. "I can't wait to see it."

"It looked fabulous in the pictures on the Internet." Solraya sat on a bag bulging with cash. "It'll be perfect for us."

Luna and Blaze settled on their bags and enjoyed the panoramic view of the vast moonlit lake with distant cliffs hugging the far side.

USS LEVIATHAN

In his stateroom, Max sipped Balvenie Caribbean Cask Scotch brought over from HMS *Kelpie* and sighed. "My intel team said the triplets weren't on either of the jets that landed on the West Coast."

"That means they got off in Fort Lauderdale or flew to New York." Mike drained his drink. "What do you want to do? Split up and check both places?"

"They obviously put a lot of thought into this," Lance said. "My guess is they got off in Fort Lauderdale and sent all three jets out as diversions so we'd waste a lot of time looking for them."

Matt jumped in. "Lance could be right. Florida is close to the sunken city. Could be they found a way to sneak back there."

"And do what?" Max shook his head. "If they sit over the site in a boat, we'll spot them. And they'd get wiped out in the tidal wave when the island rises to the surface."

Lance sucked in his breath. "Maybe they bought a submarine. They've got enough money."

"Or they could rent one of those tourist submarines." Max pulled out his phone and typed in the search box. "There's one in Key West."

"Could finding them really be that easy?" Mike said.

"We'll know in a minute." Max picked up the interphone and called his intel officer. "I need to know immediately whether anyone has rented or bought that tourist sub in Key West—the one that holds fifty passengers." He listened a moment. "I *know* what friggin' time it is! Send a cop to wake up the owner. Say it's a matter of national security." He inhaled a deep breath and rapped his fingers on the desk.

"There's another possibility." Matt sipped the smooth whisky. "They could rent an amphibious aircraft with long-range tanks and circle over the city on the day it's scheduled to surface."

Lance nodded. "Yeah, after the sea settles down, they can land on the water and taxi onto shore."

"They'll need pilots and a place to hide until the March equinox next week." Max swirled his whisky. "Could they have rented one in Fort Lauderdale?"

Max's phone rang. "Rowlin here. You're sure? Okay, thanks." He hung up and sighed. "Nobody bought or rented a submarine in Key West."

Mike pulled out his smart phone and tapped the keys. "There's a Lake Amphibian and a Cessna 182 on floats for rent in Fort Lauderdale. Neither has high-capacity fuel tanks."

"I'll check Miami," Max said.

"Hell, let's check the whole state." Matt stared at his phone as he scrolled.

A knock broke their concentration. "Captain, sir, we got a call from the Key West Naval Air Station. There's a guy at their gate who claims to have an important letter that must be delivered to you ASAP. What should I tell them?"

"Have security hold the delivery guy and confirm the envelope is safe. If it's safe, fly him here right away." Max waved him out. "I wonder if the triplets sent it."

"Maybe." Lance shrugged. "Don't forget the evil twins were worried they liked us too much."

Mike glanced from Lance to his brother. "Who the hell are the evil twins?"

Max set down his glass. "Female assassins from the Atlantean enclave. They were sent to kill you, Matt, and Lance because you were distracting the triplets from their mission."

"So what happened?" Mike raised his eyebrows. "Where'd they ambush you?"

Max told Mike everything and drained his drink. "We're not sure what we're going to tell the Navy."

"And they were really seven-and-a-half feet tall?" Mike said.

"Yep, big mothers." Lance nodded. "Ugly too."

"When the Atlanteans realize their assassins failed, they'll send more." Mike glanced at Max. "Shouldn't we bring Naval Intelligence into the loop and try to grab whoever the Atlanteans send next?"

"Maybe, but I'm not sure we should give the Navy details of the twins' demise and disposal." Max made eye contact with Matt and Lance. "We definitely broke a few laws when we destroyed the evidence."

"Yeah, but that map will be our redemption." Matt drained his glass. "Now maybe we can locate the enclave and rescue Sam."

Possum Kingdom Lake

An hour and a half after dawn, a deep droning in the distance interrupted the sisters' solitude.

Luna jumped up. "Quick, the flare!" She turned to Blaze.

Blaze already had one in her hand. She lit it and swept it side to side as the throaty roar of two Pratt & Whitney R-1830 14-cylinder Twin Wasp radial piston engines grew louder.

"There it is." Solraya pointed and waved her arms.

A parasol-winged amphibious aircraft almost 64 feet long flew over the cliffs and circled the lake, preparing for its approach and landing.

The triplets waved flares on the end of the pier as a beautiful Consolidated PBY Catalina kissed the water and headed toward them.

"Ooh, it's so big," Luna said.

"And pretty." Blaze dropped her flare in the lake.

The women stepped back as the engines died, and the aircraft drifted to the end of the pier. The copilot jumped out and steadied the seaplane against the pier while the women boarded.

In minutes, the engines restarted, and the PBY accelerated for take-off. It rose gracefully above the serene lake and turned southeast.

Blaze slipped into the cockpit and stifled a yawn. "How long until we reach our destination?"

The captain glanced over his shoulder. "Several hours. Why don't you stretch out on one of the comfortable sidewall sofas and take a nap?"

"Sounds great. Wake me when we're thirty minutes out." Blaze turned and disappeared into the cabin.

TWENTY-TWO

USS LEVIATHAN

Aknock on the stateroom door was followed by an ensign with an envelope in his hand. "Captain, this just arrived on the chopper with the delivery guy. It's addressed to you, sir."

Max tore open the envelope and pulled out the letter. "It's from the triplets." He read aloud:

Dear Captain Rowlin,

This is for you, Mike, Matt, and Lance. We apologize for any trouble we have caused you.

Our situation is complicated. After we escaped the enclave, we convinced the Atlanteans we're working for them, but we're not. It was just a ploy so Solraya could switch places with Sam. Sorry, but it was the only way for our sister to join us. Sam's noble sacrifice will be honored in world history books that will chronicle the new world order under our rule.

At dawn on the March equinox, we'll send Vril through Sam, and the evil Atlanteans will perish when Poseidon's Sword is fired. We modified the weapon so it will vaporize their enclave when massive amounts of concentrated energy blasts into the dragon current.

The magnificent remnants of Atlantis will rise for our benevolent rule, and the world will change forever.

We want our men to rule with us, so please arrange for Mike, Matt, and Lance to be flown inland to safety and remain there until the day after the March equinox. We're sorry we can't save your ship, but you and your crew can fly inland too. And there's still time to evacuate all the coastlines if you hurry.

We don't want to hurt anyone, but any attacks on us will be met with deadly force. Resistance is futile.

Join us on Atlantis. Men like you and your crew will be rewarded in our new realm.

The 200,000 years of technology recorded in the Hall of Records will benefit the entire world. Electrical power will be free to everyone, provided by the dragon currents in Mother Earth.

All nuclear weapons will be rendered inoperative and sealed inside their silos. All weapons, including military aircraft, ships, and vehicles, will be destroyed. No more wars. No more divisive religions. Everyone will worship Poseidon and his three goddesses.

We hope to see you soon after Atlantis rises.
Solraya, Luna, and Blaze

Max looked up at the men. "Well, gentlemen, how do you feel about sharing thrones with the triplets?"

"Screw that. We need to find them and end their rule permanently." Lance drained his glass.

Max waved the letter. "Time to question the guy who delivered this." He called and ordered a master-at-arms to bring him to his stateroom.

When the young man was ushered in, his eyes were wide with panic.

Max glanced at the guard. "Remove the cuffs." He pointed at a chair as the prisoner rubbed his wrists. "Have a seat."

The man's hands shook as he eyed the men and settled in a chair.

"What's your name?" Max asked as he poured Balvenie into a glass and handed it to him.

"Joe...Joe Morgan. I...I didn't do nothin' wrong—just delivered the letter. Why am I here?" His hand shook as he lifted the glass to his lips.

"Relax. We know you're not a criminal, but this letter involves national security. Help us out with truthful answers to a few questions, and the chopper will take you back to your car." Max smiled. "First, tell us how you got this letter."

"I'm a limo driver. Three beautiful women paid me $10,000 in cash to drive from Palm Beach International Airport to the Key West Naval Air Station and see to it this letter was delivered to Captain Max Rowlin on the USS *Leviathan*. I guess that's you."

Max nodded. "And what were the women doing at the airport?"

"They chartered a Citation X and left right after they paid me." He tugged at his collar.

"Where did they go?" Max poured the men another round of Balvenie.

"I don't know." Joe shrugged.

"What's the name of the charter jet company?" Max pulled out a pad.

"Lux Jets. They're based at Atlantic Aviation on the general aviation side of the airport." Joe gulped the whisky.

Mike glanced at Max. "May I ask a question?"

He nodded.

"Why didn't you just pocket the money and toss the letter after they left?"

Joe pulled down his collar and revealed a heavy metal chain with a Master padlock. "They locked this around my neck to keep me honest. I don't know how they control it, but they can make it so hot it burns me.

They gave me a painful demonstration." He pulled the chain down half an inch to show the burn marks. "They said they'd burn right through my neck if I tried to remove the chain and didn't deliver the letter." He drained his glass. "Please, can you get this off me?"

Max called the maintenance bay and asked for a bolt cutter. "No worries, we'll cut it off. Thanks for your cooperation."

As soon as the chains were cut, Max sent Joe back to Key West on the helicopter.

"I'll ask Homeland Security to get the charter jet's destination." Max yawned. "Better try and grab a few hours of sleep. I have a feeling this is going to be a rough day for all of us."

Early that afternoon, an ensign entered the bridge and handed Max a document. "Captain, this is from Homeland Security."

Max sucked in his breath as he read the papers. "Sonofabitch!" He turned to his XO. "Things just got a whole lot worse. Call the Starr brothers and Lance Bowie up here."

Ten minutes later, the three men straggled in, their eyes bloodshot from lack of sleep.

"Judging by the look on your face, the news isn't good," Mike said.

Max faced the men. "Homeland Security tracked down the triplets. They flew from Palm Beach International to Graham Municipal Airport in Texas."

Lance straightened. "Graham can accommodate jets, and they're close to Possum Kingdom Lake."

The XO nodded. "I like to fish there."

"Did you ever talk about that lake with Solraya?" Max asked Lance.

"Yeah, she asked me where I like to go on my days off. I told her about my lake cabin." Lance shook his head. "Didn't think talking about that would matter."

"Well, they paid cash at the airport for a classic '57 Chevy they'd prearranged to buy through the Internet and drove away." Max accepted a fresh cup of coffee from a sailor.

"Smart, no way to track that old car." Mike took a coffee from the tray.

"The investigators asked locals around Possum Kingdom Lake if they'd seen anything unusual. Turns out a PBY Catalina landed there early this morning, picked up three women, and headed southeast." Max took a sip and glanced at Lance. "And their Chevy is parked in *your* driveway."

"There aren't many PBYs in flying condition." Matt helped himself to a cup. "Should be easy to find out who owns it."

"You're right." Max glanced at the document in his hands. "Turns out that one came from Big Spring, Texas. The owner agreed to lease it to the triplets for two weeks."

Lance said, "I know that guy. He'd never rent out his airplane."

Max pointed at a line on the paper. "For $50,000 in cash, he will."

"Dang, they have the seaplane they need to circle over the sunken city now." Lance gulped his coffee.

Mike glanced at the paper Max was holding. "Did Homeland find out where they went?"

Max nodded. "They had to state their destination when they got clearance to cross the Air Defense Identification Zone." He sighed. "They landed in Havana Harbor."

"Cuba? Shit, we'll never get to them now." Mike shook his head.

"I guess we'll have to wait until they're circling over Atlantis and blow them out of the sky with a long-range missile." Matt stared out to sea. "That way they won't see the jet that fired it." He turned to Max. "I'd like to volunteer to fly the fighter that ruins their day."

"We have fighters stationed in Key West." Max raised a brow. "Think that's far enough away, yet close enough for a hit?"

"It's perfect. They'll never see it coming." He glanced at Lance. "No way that old PBY has target radar, right, Lance?"

Lance nodded. "I've been in its cockpit. No target radar."

Max looked up, thinking. "Those women know all about our military. They'd know about threats like long-range missiles from fighters, ships, or submarines."

An ensign entered and handed a paper to Max. "A message for you from SECNAV."

Max clenched his jaw as he read it. "More bad news. They're sending in a carrier group. The triplets can fry the carrier and support ships simultaneously."

"Thousands will die." Matt bit his lower lip. "You don't have enough clout to tell the secretary of the Navy not to send those ships."

Mike nudged Matt. "General Ryan has seen the sisters in action. He'll convince SECNAV to recall the carrier group." Mike faced Max. "Call him, Captain."

Max grabbed the encrypted satellite phone and made the call. When he finished explaining the situation to the general, he hung up and paced.

Matt sucked in his breath. "Did he agree to contact SECNAV?"

Max nodded. "I hope it's not too late. The carrier group is only fifty miles from here."

The satellite phone rang. Max listened to the caller and said, "Yes, Rear Admiral, I'm certain. Tell them to turn around and steer east at flank speed." He listened. "How close? Your ships are toast if they enter that boiling water."

Max turned to the men on the bridge. "That was Rear Admiral Ashby. She said an area of boiling water is in front of their ships. It's littered with dead fish, but it smells like a seafood grill because the hot water cooked the fish. General Ryan warned her to turn around, and she called me to verify our bizarre story is true."

The satellite phone rang again. Max snatched it up and listened. "Can you stay ahead of it?" He hesitated, thinking. "If you hold flank speed and continue heading away from here, you might survive this. I suggest a thirty-degree turn so you're not over the ley lines they're using." He disconnected and glanced at the men. "The boiling water is following their ships. So far, they're staying about three hundred yards ahead of it."

"The triplet's letter said they intend to destroy all weapons of war." Mike sighed. "What if they do it now, before they raise Atlantis?"

"Then we're screwed." Lance turned to Max. "Time to call in the miracle man."

The Starr twins and XO Lowes glanced from Lance to Max.

"Who's that?" Mike said.

Max smiled. "My dad. He has a knack for solving difficult problems."

TWENTY-THREE

Luxury International Airlines, Palm Beach International Airport

C hief Pilot Jeff Rowlin answered his phone.

"Hi, Dad, how are things at the airline?"

"Uh oh, I know that tone." Jeff leaned forward. "What's wrong, Son?"

"I'm in deep shit. Actually, we all are, and I'm hoping you can help me figure a way out before it's too late."

"So, Lance wasn't kidding when he described his predicament as end-of-the-world, Armageddon-type bad shit?"

"Yeah, that about sums it up. Can you get down to Key West and hop a chopper to my ship?"

Jeff glanced at his Ball Engineer Master II Aviator watch. "I can be on your ship in about three hours."

"Good, but first you need to send all your airliners to airports in Kansas, Colorado, Nebraska, or anyplace far inland and not near a river that connects to the coast. Get everyone you care about out of Florida in case we can't fix this. Make up a story to convince them to leave. I'll see you soon, and thanks, Dad."

Jeff hung up and stared at the phone. *What could possibly be this bad?*

Something that would only affect the coast and connecting rivers. Tsunamis? He shook his head and picked up the phone.

After making all the arrangements advised by his son, he messaged his flight crews laid over in foreign countries and rerouted them to airports in the U.S. Midwest.

Satisfied he'd done all he could, he grabbed his "go" bag and headed for his personal airplane, a rare, highly modified two-seat F8F Bearcat with a Wright R3350 radial engine, a custom four-bladed prop, and long-range tanks. After checking everything, he pulled the prop through several turns on the venerable World War II fighter and climbed in to crank up the powerful engine.

USS LEVIATHAN

Right on schedule, Jeff climbed out of a Seahawk helicopter onto the helipad where Max waited for him. He gave him a quick hug.

"Thanks for coming, Dad. Lance and the Starr twins are waiting for us in the conference room." Max led the way.

After everyone exchanged greetings with Jeff, he settled in a chair and glanced around at all the glum faces. "All right, let's get right to it. What's the big emergency?"

Jeff sat back and listened as the men filled him in on everything that had happened and what was about to happen if they didn't find a way to stop the triplets.

An ensign knocked and handed Max a document. Max dismissed him and read the paper.

"All our fighters stationed in Florida, including Key West, have had their landing gears melted into the pavement. The Romeos too. The Seahawk on our ship is the only one still operational." Max shook his head. "Sorry, Dad, looks like we'll be incinerated next. I shouldn't have brought you here."

Jeff crossed his arms. "Those so-called goddesses must assume their men are still here. They might disable your weapons, but there's no way they'll incinerate your ship."

Max turned to Lance, Mike, and Matt. "We know the triplets communicate telepathically, but can they read minds too?"

"If they could read minds, Solraya would've fried me the morning I figured out she wasn't Sam." Lance shook his head and shuddered.

Jeff turned to Lance. "Are you up for joining me on a dangerous mission in one of the world's slowest airplanes?"

"Heck, yeah." Lance grinned. "What's the plan, boss?"

"Do you have an operational RPG launcher and several RPGs?" Jeff asked Max.

"I did. Let me check with the SEAL commander and ensure they still work." Max called Commander Bern.

A few minutes later, Bern walked in and took a seat at the table. "I checked all the launchers and RPGs. They're good to go. What's the mission?"

Max turned to his father, who said, "We need a Trojan horse, something lethal that appears benign. What could be less threatening than a Piper Cub on floats?"

"Brilliant. If the women see it, they'll ask the pilots if it's dangerous." Lance grinned. "The pilots will say it's harmless and never suspect we're carrying RPGs."

"I'll go with the pilot and fire the weapon," Bern said.

"I appreciate you volunteering, but this needs to look like a civilian op," Max said. "The triplets had time alone in Key West, and later after they ditched us, to set up a well-paid spy network. We can't take the chance someone will tip them off about a military op in a Cub. Better to use my dad and Lance. I already recalled Lance into active duty, but the triplets don't know that, and Dad is still active in the Navy Reserve."

Jeff nodded. "We'll launch a couple hours before dawn. When we spot them circling over the underwater city, we'll wait until they're in a turn away from us. Then Lance will hold it steady while I climb out on the right float and fire an RPG up their ass."

"Be careful the blowback doesn't light that old fabric-covered airplane on fire," Matt said.

"No shit. I never said this would be easy." Jeff shook his head. "And we won't have enough fuel to fly all the way back to Key West."

"Fuel won't matter if you fail, but if you succeed, my ship can rescue you and hoist the Cub aboard." Max grinned. "We have a heavy-lift crane that won't even strain itself on a little Cub."

"I'll give you a practice session with the RPG launcher before you leave the ship," Bern said.

"Uh, aren't we forgetting something?" Mike crossed his arms. "Where will you get a Cub on floats and position it in time for the mission?"

Jeff grinned. "Our friend, Madman Martino, has one, and he's at a float-plane fly-in in Key Largo. Lance and I will borrow the Cub, and he and Martha can fly to safety in my Bearcat. Problem solved."

"Great, Dad, let's get this ball rolling. Train with Bern, and then I'll have my Seahawk fly you and Lance to Key Largo and bring David and Martha to Key West. With any luck, the Seahawk will make it back to the ship. I'd like to have it available for contingencies." Max called the flight deck on the interphone and arranged everything.

When he hung up, he said, "I'd better call Captain Sinclair and ask if they're any closer to finding that enclave." Max grabbed the satellite phone and dialed Ross's number.

TWENTY-FOUR

SAS Base, Dundee, Scotland

R oss paced in his office, holding a satellite phone against his ear, as he listened to the update from Captain Rowlin.

Rowlin wrapped up the briefing with a question. "Have you located the enclave?"

"We think we've found it. There's a climate anomaly about a hundred miles northwest of Kathmandu, and it's in a dead zone. We've lost two drones there. A Gurkha unit hiked in to reconnoiter. We lost them too. It must be the right place." Ross sighed. "That's the good news."

"What's the bad news?"

"Our governments are talking to Nepal and India about getting permission to bomb the enclave. It's close to Chinese territory. No telling what the Chinese would do if they knew about the Atlanteans." Ross stopped pacing.

"The Chinese would allow Atlantis to rise and wipe out a significant portion of our countries. Better keep them out of this," Rowlin said.

"Easier said than done. They have spies everywhere." Ross settled in his desk chair.

"Uh, any chance your team will be sent on an attack-and-rescue mission before they bomb the shit out of the place?"

"Only if the initial bombing mission fails. You know the drill: They're sacrificing Sam to save the world. I'm convinced we can do both, but nobody at the top cares what an SAS captain thinks." Ross couldn't hide his bitterness.

"They won't need to bomb it if the Cub mission succeeds," Rowlin said.

"If your father destroys the triplets, the timing will be so close you won't be able to stop the bombs on the other side of the world. Besides, the Atlanteans don't know they're about to be vaporized. If you eliminate the triplets, the Atlanteans will still use Sam to fire the weapon." Ross sighed. "I'm pushing hard for my team to go in. It's the only way to save the woman I love regardless of what happens on your end."

"Don't forget the UK will be in the direct path of a monster wave, along with Portugal, Spain, France, the west coast of Africa, and the northern coast of South America," Rowlin said.

"Right. Ireland will block most of the wave from Scotland, but England will be hit in large population areas like London. The UK won't risk that to save one life, even if she is a national heroine here and in America. I understand their thinking, but I don't have to like it."

"I have a bad feeling the triplets might know another way to raise Atlantis if the bombs wipe out Poseidon's Sword." Rowlin hesitated. "We'd better succeed in eliminating them."

"I agree with you, Captain Rowlin. Let's hope the mission to bomb the enclave fails so the triplets will proceed with their original plan. Then the military will have to send in my team while they come up with Plan B."

"My father and Lance are on their way to get the Cub and fly it to Key West. Let me know what happens on your end. I hope you get Sam back, Captain Sinclair."

"We're all in this together. I'll do my best to save the day in Nepal while you take care of business near Cuba."

C-17 Globemaster Jet

The next day, Ross called Captain Rowlin on the satellite phone while he was en route to India. "The bombing mission failed. Their electronic guidance systems went haywire in the dead zone protecting the enclave, and the missiles impacted nearby mountains. Now they're planning a mission to drop low-tech bombs from a B52 flying high enough to avoid the dead zone."

"Did your team get the green light to go in ahead of the bombs?" Rowlin asked.

"Aye, but it'll be tight. This time they'll drop MOABs rigged to detonate on impact."

"The Mother of All Bombs? I watched one detonate in Afghanistan from twenty miles away. There's a reason it's named Massive Ordnance Air Blast. It left a huge crater and filled the sky with dirt. The ground shook like an earthquake. I can only imagine what several of those would do."

"They'll destroy the entire village and leave a giant crater. We'll only have a few minutes to swoop in with paragliders after a HAHO jump, grab her, and clear the area before everything goes boom."

"A high-altitude high-open jump?" Rowlin said. "What altitude will you open your chutes?"

"At 20,000 feet. The enclave's in a valley at 15,000 feet. The tricky part will be navigating through the cloud cover without hitting a mountain. We plan to follow part of Blaze and Luna's route when they flew out of the enclave, but in reverse." Ross squirmed in the upright troop seat in the Boeing C-17 Globemaster. "How's it looking on your end?"

"Well, tomorrow's the March equinox, and my ship is unharmed so far. My dad and Lance are ready to launch in the Cub tomorrow morning at zero dark thirty. They'll have to start well before sunrise to arrive in time to shoot down the triplets before they zap Sam at dawn."

"I'm counting on Lance to keep his promise and kill those bitches. Then, with a little luck, I'll snatch Sam off the top of that pyramid before they fire Poseidon's Sword, and we'll clear the enclave before the MOABs hit."

"Geez, that sounds like a *Mission Impossible* movie, but we're all counting on you. Millions of lives hang in the balance. If you save Sam, you save everyone, so that's a win-win," Rowlin said.

"Aye, but just to make things more exciting, Chinese troops are headed for the Nepal border near our target zone. The failed bombing mission caught their attention. If I manage to save Sam, we still have to land where a helicopter can pick us up. If the Chinese grab us—I don't want to think about that." Ross sighed. "I hope we'll talk again tomorrow after the mission, Captain Rowlin. If not, it's been a pleasure working with you."

"The pleasure was mine, Captain Sinclair. Godspeed."

MacLeod Castle

"Mom, I hope you can hear me. Please answer." Sam said telepathically.

Loren was awake in the wee hours of March 21, the vernal equinox as many called it in the Northern Hemisphere, too worried to sleep.

"Sam? Is that you?" Loren rubbed her eyes and glanced around the dark room.

"Yes, Mom, I don't have much time. They let the drugs wear off because they affect my electromagnetic energy, and they need me to fire Poseidon's Sword today."

Loren poked Duncan. "Wake up, Sam's talking to me telepathically. Call Ross." She switched to telepathy. *"What time are they planning to fire it?"*

"At dawn over the sunken city, which will be late afternoon here. I know about the military's attempt to bomb us. The dead zone saved us, but next time they'll use low-tech bombs. I'm sorry I'll never see you again, Mom. I sure do miss you, Ross, my brothers, Duncan, everyone. I never dreamed all this would come from finding that stupid artifact in Hong Kong."

"Wait a second, Duncan wants me to ask you something. He has Ross on the phone." Loren turned her attention to Duncan.

"Ask her if she knows what happened to the Gurkha unit the military sent there," Duncan said, holding his satellite phone to his ear.

Loren asked, and Sam said, *"The Atlanteans spotted them climbing up toward the enclave and sent an avalanche into them. No survivors."*

Loren relayed the info to Duncan, who told Ross.

Duncan listened to Ross and then spoke to Loren. "Ross said to tell

Sam he's coming for her. He plans to pluck her off the pyramid in the nick of time and fly away with her in his paraglider. Tell her to wear warm clothes if she can."

Loren relayed Ross's message to Sam.

"Mom, tell Ross not to come. I don't want him to die. I started this mess. No point losing him and his team because of me. I'd rather die knowing he'll be okay."

Loren took the SATCOM from Duncan and relayed Sam's message to Ross. She listened to his response, smiled, and handed the phone back to Duncan. *"Ross said to tell you he's going to save your sorry arse whether you like it or not because if you die, half the world dies with you, and he's not keen on living without you."*

"Well, okay then, I'll try to con them into letting me wear warm clothes and hope my hero saves the day. But I'll contact you again when I'm on top of the pyramid, just in case that doesn't work out. I love you, Mom. Give my love to Ross and Duncan."

"I love you too, Sam. Don't give up. Ross will save you. He always does."

Loren buried her face in Duncan's chest and sobbed. "I just want her to be safe and happy. That shouldn't be too much to ask."

Duncan wrapped his strong arms around her. "Don't cry, lass. Ross will save her."

TWENTY-FIVE

Predawn in Key West

The antique Piper Cub didn't have an electrical system and was intended for day use only. Jeff and Lance hired a forty-five-foot fishing boat with powerful spotlights for their night departure. It ran alongside them and lit their way as they taxied on the pontoons out of the dark harbor. The boat kept pace to their right and illuminated their takeoff path so they could avoid hitting floating debris.

After liftoff, Jeff checked the hand-held GPS as Lance lowered his night-vision goggles, climbed to 500 feet, checked the compass, and turned to a southeasterly heading for the submerged city. Jeff reached around Lance's right shoulder from the rear tandem seat and handed him the pre-set portable GPS that showed their course to the target area.

They'd been briefed that *Leviathan* would idle in place thirty miles east of ancient Atlantis so the triplets wouldn't see it.

Jeff listened to Max on the satellite phone he'd brought along. "So far, so good at our end. No boiling seawater. We show your flight on course and on schedule. You'll arrive about thirty minutes before dawn. No PBY on radar."

"Thanks, Son. Keep us in the loop."

Jeff yelled to be heard over the loud engine. "Max said we're on course and should arrive in about an hour. The PBY isn't airborne yet."

"Good. That agrees with our portable GPS. I'm guessing the PBY will arrive maybe fifteen minutes before dawn." Lance stretched. "The sunken city is only about thirty miles from the northeast coast of Cuba."

"In case they show up early, I'll load the RPG launcher as soon as we arrive on site." Jeff glanced over his shoulder at the duffel bag holding the rocket-propelled grenade launcher and three RPGs.

He shook his head. *Stupid to bring three. If I miss with the first one, the triplets will fry us, and the extra RPGs will trigger a bigger explosion.*

Lance glanced over his shoulder and grinned. "I hope you're feeling lucky today. I remember Sam saying she could be flying a fully armed F/A 18 against you in a Piper Cub armed with a BB gun, and you'd still find a way to shoot her down. Kinda like the way you splashed those terrorists' L-39s into the Med with our unarmed 767."

"That *was* lucky. I hope that luck carries over to this morning. We'll only get one shot." Jeff hesitated. "How do you feel about flying fifty feet above the water when the time comes?"

"Why so low?"

"If the blowback from the rocket launcher catches the Cub's fabric, we can splash down to put out the fire. I promised David we'd take good care of his Cub."

"Hah! Like *that's* our biggest worry." Lance shook his head. "Yeah, I can hold her at fifty feet, no problem. Just make damn sure you don't miss."

"Roger that. No missing. How close should we fly?"

"I'm not sure." Lance looked over his shoulder at Jeff. "If we ease up to a hundred yards away, think that'll be close enough to nail them?"

"Geez, I hope so. A PBY is a decent-sized target. I'll hit them when they're making the turn away from us during their circle pattern over the sunken city." Jeff checked his watch. "Then they won't be able to see the RPG streaking toward them."

"The fate of millions of people rests on one shot, so no pressure." Lance chuckled, trying to ease the tension.

"Thanks for reminding me." Jeff stared out at the dark ocean as the horizon lightened. "You know it's funny, Sam always manages to add major excitement to our lives no matter where she is."

"Yep, Sam sure is a danger magnet. I hope Ross saves her." Lance's voice cracked.

"I'm betting on it, and he's counting on us to eliminate her dark alter ego, Solraya, and her sisters." Jeff cracked his knuckles as if posturing for a fist fight. "I'll be damned if I'll let those evil bitches wipe out Florida and our airline's base in West Palm Beach. Dang it, I like living there."

Lance glanced at his Rolex Submariner. "The sky's brightening. We'll be on site in twenty minutes."

"Good thing those harpies are waiting until dawn." Jeff stretched. "It'll be easier to target them in daylight."

Lance checked his watch one more time. "I wonder how things are going on Ross's end?"

C-17 Globemaster Jet

Ross rechecked his gear and glanced at his self-winding watch. He'd replaced the battery-powered one that wouldn't work in the dead zone. He frowned. Headwinds were slowing the flight and shaving precious minutes off his mission time.

Derek patted his shoulder. "Relax, we'll save her. We always do."

"Too bad we can't use anything high-tech on the assault. We'll have to rely on basic combat skills." Ross hesitated. "No way to know what we're up against." He ran his hands over the combat knives strapped to each hip.

"Our weapons will work, just no laser sights." Derek checked the magazine on his MP7 submachine gun.

The five-minute warning horn blared, and a red light glared above them.

Ross stood and faced his team seated along the sidewall. "Final gear check. Prepare to jump."

Ross and his three teammates rechecked their equipment, moved to the rear door, switched on their oxygen, and closed their helmet visors.

272

"Comm check," Ross said. Three voices answered in his earpiece under his helmet.

"Remember, our GPS units and radios will only work for the initial approach through the mountains and after we leave." Ross glanced at the GPS display on his right wrist. "We'll lose everything electronic when we penetrate the dead zone, so keep a tight formation."

The pilot depressurized the cabin before the huge aft loading door opened and exposed the snow-covered Himalayas below. A horn blared, and the green jump light illuminated.

Ross took two running steps and dove into the frigid high-altitude air, followed by Derek and the rest of the team.

Himalayan Enclave

I sat strapped to a gold throne in the Atlantean temple. A gold statue of Poseidon faced me from his throne on the opposite side of the circular room. Two empty thrones flanked me in a group of three meant for the triplets. Images of Atlantis and the triplet goddesses decorated the curving walls. There were no windows, but I sensed my captors were coming for me soon.

Ever since I'd found that Atlantean artifact, I'd been driven by a desire to learn my true destiny. And now, after everything I'd been through, I couldn't believe my purpose in life was to fire a weapon that would kill millions of people.

Screw that! Time to change my destiny. I'd find a way to kill myself first. Maybe God wouldn't count suicide against me if my motive was saving lives.

A stone door swung inward, and ten Atlantean men in long black robes paraded in. They were eight feet tall with long bony fingers and cadaverous, elongated faces. Gold crowns festooned with tridents and images of the sun, moon, and fire adorned their heads.

They filed toward me in a solemn procession.

My stomach churned. *Oh God, this is it.* Maybe I'd get a chance to jump off the pyramid. The sides were steep, like a tall, narrow triangle. A fall from one hundred feet would solve the world's problem. *Can't lose my nerve.*

The leader approached me. "Golden Twin, your day of glory has arrived. You will be memorialized in our archives for this momentous occasion."

One of the men unclasped the leather strap from the grommet in the floor beside my throne and gripped it, the other end secured around my right wrist. Another did the same with my left wrist strap.

The group formed a semicircle facing me, the leader in the center.

"Must we keep your feet bound and drag you, or will you behave yourself?" the leader said.

"I won't give you any trouble. Resistance is obviously futile." *I'd have a better chance of jumping off the pyramid with my feet free.*

"Good. No point in dishonoring yourself. We promise to revere your memory." He waited as they freed my feet, then turned and led the procession toward the temple door.

The two guards holding my wrist straps flanked me. Three men led, and the other five marched behind us single file.

I needed to try for warmer clothes in case Ross somehow saved me. The air outside the enclave's artificial climate could be subzero.

"Wait, don't you have clothing for me that befits the occasion? A long, fancy robe, perhaps?" I arched my brow. "I want to look special."

The leader turned and ran his eyes over me. He clapped his hands, and a woman stepped into the temple. "Bring the ceremonial robe. Hurry."

She rushed out and soon returned with a glimmering golden robe.

The leader took it from her and turned to me. "Put one arm through at a time and no tricks." He nodded at my two guards.

One guy let go and allowed me to put my hand through the right sleeve. Then he grasped the strap again before my left arm was released. Once both arms were in the sleeves, they pulled the robe over my head. It covered me from my neck down to my feet.

My armpits moistened and sweat beaded on my forehead in the tropical heat as my body temperature rose under the heavy silk robe woven with genuine gold thread.

The leader turned. "Now we must hurry."

The men ushered me outside and up the narrow cobblestone street toward a black pyramid looming over the village. I breathed in the scents of tropical flowers as a warm breeze washed over me. Sweat trickled down my back.

We began the steep climb up the pyramid's staircase as my captors towered around me. They weren't taking any chances.

I contacted my mother. *"Mom, can you hear me?"*

"Yes, Sam, are you okay?"

"I'm on my way up to the top of the pyramid. One way or another, it'll all be over soon. I hope you and my brothers are somewhere safe from tsunamis."

I swallowed a lump in my throat. *"This is all my fault. I'm so sorry. I love you and promise I'll do whatever I can to stop them from firing Poseidon's Sword."*

"Don't do anything crazy. Stall for time. Ross is coming."

"I can't count on that. Millions will be saved if I can find a way to die before they use me to activate the key."

"No, Sam, let Ross save you. Please!"

"There's no guarantee he'll succeed. Once the key is activated, it'll be too late. I have to do the right thing. Goodbye, Mom."

We had reached the platform on top of the pyramid.

My hands trembled, my legs wobbled, and my breath came in short spurts.

Can't lose my nerve.

TWENTY-SIX

Airborne Over Atlantis

L ance put the Cub in a slow turn and gradually descended, glancing at the altimeter. He leveled off at fifty feet above the ocean.

"When the PBY pilots spot us, maybe they'll think we're doing recon for a deep-sea fishing charter." He glanced back at Jeff. "Time to lock and load."

Jeff checked his watch. "Fifteen minutes until dawn. I don't see them yet." He pointed south of their position. "I hope that storm isn't coming this way." Reaching behind him, he lifted the duffel onto his lap.

Lance stared at the approaching squall. "Damn, looks like it is."

Jeff pulled out the shoulder-mounted launcher for the rocket-propelled grenades and balanced it on his lap atop the duffel bag. He loaded an RPG and zipped the bag shut, then put it behind him. "Ready." He checked the launcher's targeting computer.

"Here they come." Lance pointed at an aircraft approaching from the southwest.

As the big amphibian closed the gap between them, Jeff said, "Looks like it's flying at about 2,000 feet."

"That'll give them a margin of safety above the tsunamis." Lance held the stick with his knees as he lifted binoculars to his eyes and adjusted the focus. "Yep, that's the PBY from Big Spring. Too bad we have to kill the pilots. They're good guys."

"I hate it, but there's no other way." Jeff focused on the incoming aircraft. "They're almost half a mile above us. Better close the distance a little. Ease up to 500 feet."

"Roger that." Lance added power and started a gradual climb as he turned toward the PBY Catalina that had started to circle.

The amphibious seaplane turned and headed straight for them.

"Uh, looks like they're coming for a closer look."

"Let them come. Pull your baseball cap down so the triplets can't recognize you if they're using binoculars." Jeff draped his windbreaker over the RPG launcher. "When they get close, keep your head down while I smile and wave."

Lance dropped the binoculars that hung from a strap around his neck and pulled down his ball cap so the brim covered half of his face.

Minutes later, the PBY passed by 1,500 feet above them and fifty feet to their right.

Lance rocked the wings in a friendly gesture as Jeff waved.

The PBY rocked its wings and turned away, headed for its circuit over the sunken city.

"We're not roasting, so I guess we passed scrutiny." Jeff looked at his watch again. "We'll let them establish their holding pattern over the city. That way, we can anticipate the timing on their turns away from us. Keep easing closer."

"Shit, the storm is coming." Lance pointed at the downpour approaching fast from the south.

Jeff checked his watch. Six minutes before dawn. "We'd better take them out before that squall hits."

"They're on the inbound turn. We have to wait until they turn outbound so they can't see the RPG streaking at them."

"That squall better not hit before then." Jeff opened the horizontally split door on the right side. The top half swung up and locked in the open position while the bottom half dropped open flush with the

277

cabin. He unbuckled his seatbelt and slung the launcher's strap over his shoulder.

A few light squirts hit the windshield in advance of the storm. Lance glanced right. "Shit, now the float's wet. Be careful. It'll be slippery."

Jeff shrugged. "Nobody ever said this'd be easy."

"PBY turning away now," Lance yelled.

Jeff grabbed the wing strut and stepped onto the right float. His foot slipped off, but he held onto the strut and righted himself. He had maybe five seconds.

With one arm hooked around the strut, Jeff crouched and swung the launcher into position on his shoulder. He activated the targeting computer and put the crosshairs on the PBY's left-wing root as it started its curve back toward them. The instant he heard the target-locked tone, he fired the rocket-propelled grenade.

As the rocket streaked toward the target, the fiery blowback hit the lower right side of the fuselage and lit the fabric on fire. The recoil upset Jeff's balance, and his feet slid off the float.

At that moment, the squall hit with full force and pummeled the light aircraft with driving rain and violent air currents.

"Hang on, Jeff, I'll put us on the water as fast as I can."

Jeff let the launcher drop from his shoulder and wrapped both arms around the wing strut as the floatplane pitched up and down in the blinding rain.

Lance wrestled the aircraft through the turbulence and searched for the ocean's surface in low visibility, trying to land parallel to the waves to avoid flipping over.

The RPGs in the duffel bag were close to where the fabric had caught fire. Would the rain put out the fire, or would the fire set off the grenades?

A shock wave from a violent explosion rocked the Cub seconds before it splashed down. It almost nosed over in a wave as the propeller tips sucked up spray from the frothy sea.

Lance glanced over his right shoulder. The fire was out, but Jeff was gone. He cut the engine so the airplane wouldn't pull away from wherever Jeff was. Rough seas combined with wind and driving rain pitched and rolled the aircraft.

"Jeff! Where are you?" He eased out onto the float and strained to see through the rain as salt water stung his eyes.

A mighty wave jostled the floatplane and knocked him into the sea.

Lance surfaced and gasped for air before pulling himself onto the pitching pontoon. After pausing to catch his breath, he struggled up to the open door and grabbed the portable radio from inside to call *Leviathan.*

"We're five minutes out," Max said. "We got under way right after the PBY disappeared from our radar."

"Great, just don't run over us in the poor visibility." Lance dropped the radio on the seat.

The rain stopped, and Lance wiped his eyes.

"Hey, how about giving me a hand up?" Jeff swam to the pontoon.

"Dang it, Jeff, you about gave me a heart attack." Lance offered his hand.

"All's well that ends well. At least, I hope it did." Jeff climbed aboard. "Any news from the other side of the world?"

"No, but I don't see any tsunamis." Lance glanced around. "At least, not yet."

PBY Catalina Seaplane

Minutes earlier, the triplets connected telepathically with Sam.

"Sam, we're sorry it had to be this way," Blaze said. *"We admire you and will ensure your sacrifice is memorialized."*

"What are you going to do?" Sam asked.

"At dawn here, in exactly five minutes, the Atlanteans will position you above the weapon. We'll send massive amounts of electromagnetic energy through you into Poseidon's Sword," Luna said. *"When the weapon fires, it will raise Atlantis and vaporize the enclave, leaving us to rule the new world."*

"Your new world will be a lot smaller after tsunamis destroy islands, coastlines, and millions of innocent people. Please don't do this!" Sam pleaded.

"We must fulfill the prophecy. Thank you for helping us," Solraya said. *"We'll never forget you."*

An explosion blew off the PBY's left wing and propelled a fireball into the cockpit. In the brief seconds before their deaths, the triplets had to either risk channeling the Vril into Sam before she was positioned over the weapon, or fulfill the ancient prophecy by alternate means.

Ever faithful to the Ancients, the triplets decided to lock their minds together in unity and complete one final task.

TWENTY-SEVEN

The Enclave, Earlier

W arm wind swirled around me at the narrow apex. The leader and my two guards stepped with me through an opening onto a gold disc fastened over the pyramid's tip as a platform. The rest of my escort waited on the steps.

I wiped the sweat off my face with my sleeve. The odd key I had found in Hong Kong months ago that I thought was a prototype awaited my special touch.

Destiny.

A seven-foot woman with black braided hair held the artifact and scrutinized me with her strange-colored eyes, golden irises flecked with red.

"As you can see, one crystal is already lit," the leader said to me. "You must've touched it before the orca took it from you in the South Atlantic."

"Yes, I was trying to ensure it would be found if we dropped it."

He beckoned the woman with the weird eyes forward. "Golden Twin, this is Rena. She has the honor of assisting you. Do not resist. Her combat skills are second to none."

"Don't worry, I understand this is my destiny." I hoped they'd believe me.

I sucked in my breath and peered down. The ground looked so far away, and the entire Atlantean population had gathered around the pyramid's base.

Gentle waves from a large mountain lake lapped at the shore. Tropical wind carried the scent of jasmine bushes blooming throughout the village. My nostrils flared, taking it in.

A lovely day to die.

"I have no intention of dishonoring myself in my final moment of glory." I nodded at my wrists. "Please, release me and allow me to finish this with dignity."

"Of course." He waved at the men holding my wrist straps. "We'll perform the unbinding ceremony."

The guards lifted my hands up and held them straight out in front of me.

"Now, Golden Twin, close your eyes while they release your straps." He stared at my face, waiting for me to close my eyes.

Could getting free really be this easy? I closed my eyes and waited. Hard objects brushed my fingers.

I opened my eyes. All three crystals on the ancient key glowed with brilliant light. They had tricked me.

The leader rotated the key and aimed it at a three-inch diameter slanted opening three feet from the center of the solid-gold platform. He locked the crystals in their slots and activated the laser. Without ceremony, he fired it into the opening.

A panel slid open in the platform's center and revealed a bread-plate size hole. Grinding heralded the opening of the obsidian apex beneath the platform. An enormous glittering diamond rose up into the hole. The leader deactivated the laser and handed the key to one of the men on the steps.

Despondent, I groaned as my chest muscles squeezed the air out of me.

I waited for the end. I had failed, and millions would die.

Nothing happened.

I turned to the leader. "Did the weapon fire?"

"We had to use your key to unlock it first. Now you must complete the final step." He glanced down at a giant sundial mounted on the roof of a nearby building. "It is time to begin the ultimate task." He pointed. "Stand over the diamond with your feet on the gold footprints on either side." The leader retreated to the steps.

Thank you, God. One last chance to save the world.

I behaved like a meek lamb heading for the slaughter. The men guided me forward. My unsuspecting captors told Rena to kneel and prepare to remove my shoes.

I used the slack in the straps and yanked the men backward. They stumbled and fell behind me off the small platform. I had counted on them pulling me down with them. Instead, they released my straps and fell to their deaths.

The triplets' voices invaded my head and distracted me. We had a brief telepathic conversation about their plans to raise Atlantis, destroy the enclave, and rule the world. I was unable to dissuade them.

Our telepathic conversation ended abruptly.

Rena's fiery eyes widened, and she jumped up.

Waves of intense psychic energy immersed me. Images and data reeled through my head so fast that I didn't have time to decipher them.

Stunned, Rena stared at me, her mouth open.

The psychic-energy flow ended as suddenly as it had begun. I took a deep breath. *Now or never.* I plowed into Rena as hard as the short distance allowed. Her wide eyes told me she wasn't expecting *that* maneuver. I buried my face in her chest as we shot off the platform.

We seemed to hang in the air for an instant until something slammed into my back. Maybe there was another reason for Rena's wide-eyed surprise. She growled and reached around me.

Her warm blood sprayed my face and dripped down my chest. She dropped away as strong arms gripped me.

"I've got you, lass. Help me buckle you into the harness." Ross held me with one arm as he slipped the harness over my right arm and shoulder. He switched arms and did the same on my left side.

I was so relieved to hear his voice and feel his arms around me, it was all I could do not to go limp. I steeled myself and buckled the chest strap. Now I couldn't fall away.

"Ross, love, I can't believe you're here. You saved me—again."

"You're not saved yet, lass. We have a long way to go, but first we need to fly behind that mountain peak before the bombs explode."

"Bombs?"

Staccato blasts from automatic weapons echoed off the mountains. I glanced around. Ross's team was firing MP7s from paragliders at Atlanteans wielding crossbows. Arrows zipped past us. One pierced the hem of my robe.

In seconds, a frigid Himalayan winter replaced the enclave's warm tropical air.

I gasped like I'd been sucker punched. My lungs ached, so I breathed through my nose to lessen the shock.

We made a sharp right turn around a mountain peak, and hell rained down behind us. I clamped my hands over my ears as the air vibrated with each massive explosion echoing through the pass. Air turbulence funneled into us and jostled us up and down.

Ross and his three teammates stayed on task and navigated through the mountains. A flat, open area appeared, bordered by a slope on one side, a sharp rise on the other side, and a narrow valley ahead and behind us.

"That's a good LZ, lads. Activate your EVAC signals." Ross maneuvered us down. "Get ready to land, Sam." He expertly flared the chute and gently dropped us on the snow.

We turned toward the falling chute and unbuckled our harnesses. I helped Ross roll up the fabric and secure it under some rocks while his men did the same. We didn't want them to blow into a helicopter's rotor blades.

A deep thundering grew louder. Could that be our rescue helicopter?

"Ross!" Derek nodded toward the downward slope about 300 yards away.

The snow flowed uphill. But it wasn't snow. Soldiers dressed in white —hundreds of them—climbed up the slope like ants swarming an ant hill.

Ross focused his binoculars.

"Bugger, it's the Chinese army!"

Ross stared at the swarm of soldiers. Red shoulder patches of Chinese flags with five yellow stars emblazoned their white uniforms.

He glanced around. "No cover. We have to slow them down before the helicopter arrives."

Sam froze and stared at the distant soldiers.

Ross squinted through his binoculars. "That's odd. Looks like steam rising in front of them. It's getting thicker by the second, and the snow is melting."

His men crouched and waited, but none of the soldiers pierced the thick veil of fog.

The ground shuddered with such force that Ross's team fell to their knees. A deep, thunderous roar echoed off the mountains.

A Super Lynx helicopter zoomed in behind them and hovered a foot above the snow.

The thunder wasn't from the rotors.

Ross jumped up and spotted a foamy wall of water rushing toward them through the pass. "Bloody hell!"

He grabbed Sam's arm and pointed. "The bombs must've blown away the part of the mountain holding the lake."

Everyone saw the deadly chaos rushing at them and dove into the chopper. They were barely inside as the pilot started a climb and turned away from the onslaught.

The engines screamed as the rotors clawed the turbulent air. Water splashed the chopper's skids as Derek slammed the door shut. "That was close. Think they'll shoot us down?"

Ross peered down the slope. "They're too busy trying not to drown."

Derek sighed and leaned against the door. He focused on Sam. "Are you all right? Your face and chest are covered with blood."

"No worries, Derek. It's not her blood." Ross pulled out a handkerchief. "I had to slash her attacker's neck."

Sam was shivering so hard she couldn't speak. The freezing weather had penetrated her ceremonial silk robe.

Ross wiped the blood off her face and stared into her eyes. "Sam? It *is* you, isn't it?"

She nodded.

"It was the strangest thing. Right before I swooped in and caught you, your body glowed inside a brilliant halo." He cocked his head. "And now your eyes…they're different."

"W-what's different?" she asked through chattering teeth.

Ross leaned closer. "Your eyes were always aqua blue, but now they're studded with deep blue and emerald green."

He squinted. "Never seen anything like it." He caressed her cheek. "How do you feel, lass?"

"B-b-better than y-you could ever imagine," she stuttered.

She gazed into his eyes, pulled him close, and kissed him with the deep intensity of a long-anticipated first kiss.

EPILOGUE

Captain Rowlin and Commander Bern watched as a crane on the USS *Leviathan* gently lowered the Piper Cub onto a flatbed truck parked beside the docked ship. Rowlin supervised the operation from the deck, as Jeff and Lance secured the floatplane to the truck bed.

"What will they do now?" Bern asked.

"Dad has an aircraft maintenance shop in the hangar at his home in a private airport community in Palm Beach County. He'll take the Cub there to repair the fabric."

"Is Lance going with him?"

"Dad will drop off Lance at the civilian airport so he can fly his L-39 back to Palm Beach International. Then he'll drive out to Dad's house and assist with the repairs."

Jeff and Lance looked up and gave exaggerated salutes before they climbed into the truck's cab. Rowlin and Bern returned their salutes.

Rowlin smiled proudly. "My father played a key role in saving the world as we know it."

Bern nodded and chuckled. "He also saved your Navy career and made you look like a genius to the Pentagon brass."

"No shit!"

"For you, Captain." An ensign handed Rowlin a sealed envelope. "Orders from Rear Admiral Ashby."

"Excuse me, Commander Bern." Rowlin took it and walked up to the bridge. XO Lowes turned and stood at attention when he entered.

"At ease, XO." Rowlin waved the envelope. "New orders." He scanned the document and swore under his breath.

"That bad, huh?" Lowes waited for the bad news.

"We've been ordered back to the sunken city. Our mission is to defend the site, deactivate the weapon inside the pyramid, recover the Hall of Record's contents, and secure the intel." Rowlin shook his head.

"Oh good, so nothing difficult." Lowes rolled his eyes. "Apparently, Washington thinks you can do anything now that the triplets have been eliminated."

"The Cubans had their eyes on us because our ship was close to them for so many weeks." Rowlin keyed the intercom. "Send up two coffees."

"And they're wondering how we melted the propellers on Sweetwater's ship, not to mention the incident with the orcas." Lowes shook his head. "Probably think we have a new weapon."

"And they've got to be wondering what happened to the PBY." Rowlin sighed. "And no way all that happened without drawing Russia's attention."

"Don't forget the Chinese. Their spy network has to be working overtime on why we bombed the Himalayas and what we've been doing over here. They'll probably send a submarine to sniff around. So will the Russians."

Rowlin nodded. "Yeah, well, our Navy already has a nuclear sub patrolling the area. Whoever recovers the Atlantean archives will have a huge technological advantage."

"Great, another mission for *Leviathan* with enormous, long-term significance."

Rowlin stared at the tranquil sea, his mind racing. "We're not going back there until I get another Scorpion to replace the one we lost, plenty of mini torpedoes and ROVs, several Hardsuits with qualified divers, two SEAL teams, underwater archaeologists, and a shitload of other stuff I haven't even thought of yet."

"What about Sam? Are you going to ask her for help?"

Rowlin heaved a big sigh. "Dad won't be happy about that. He wants Sam back at work, but she's the only one left alive with knowledge about the Atlanteans and how their weapons work."

"Mike and Matt are en route to Great Britain to rendezvous with her. They aren't going to like this either."

"And don't forget Ross. He just got her back. He'll want to keep her with him as long as possible. Can't say I blame him."

"Yeah, but we'll need all the help we can get on our new *Mission Impossible*."

"I'll ask Professor Armitage to join us. It'll take at least a month, maybe more, to get everything we need. Ross can keep Sam until then." Rowlin rapped the paper against the console.

"So…what are you going to tell your dad?"

"He'll be busy getting his airliners back to base, rearranging their flight schedules, and repairing the Cub. That'll give me time to come up with a plan he can live with." Rowlin turned and grabbed a cup of coffee off a tray offered by a sailor.

"We're assuming Sam will agree to join our mission." Lowes snatched the other cup off the tray and took a sip. "What if she refuses?"

"There's only one way to find out." Rowlin picked up the satellite phone. "She should be back in Scotland by now."

STRANDED

A SAMANTHA STARR THRILLER, BOOK 4

Four hours into our charter flight to Rio de Janeiro, the sky ahead turned dark and stormy. Turbulence jolted the Boeing 767 jumbo jet like we were driving down a road covered with deep potholes.

I switched on the seatbelt sign and keyed the PA system. "This is your captain speaking. We've got a little bumpy air associated with thunderstorms along our route. Nothing to worry about. Just keep your seatbelts fastened while we navigate around the weather. Flight attendants, secure the cabin and take your seats."

A monster seventy-five-thousand-foot thunderstorm blocked our flightpath over South America near Brazil's northern border with Venezuela. The dark sky around it flashed with multiple lightning bolts.

I spotted an opening right of course. "Tell ATC we need to divert thirty degrees right to avoid that big boomer."

Lance made the call, and ATC responded, "Luxury five-one-five, turn right to heading one-eight-zero for weather avoidance."

"Luxury five-one-five is turning right to one-eight-zero," Lance replied in his Texas twang.

As soon as we passed the storm, we got clearance to turn back on course and deviate as necessary to avoid storms along our route. It was a time of day with little air traffic on the airway.

"I'll go around this next one to the east." I banked left as Lance made the call to ATC.

Our jet rose and fell in the turbulent air like a boat going over waves in the ocean.

He finished the call and glanced at me. "All this deviating is cutting into our drinking time in Rio."

As I curved around the storm, I caught a whiff of something no pilot ever wants to smell on an airplane. "Is that smoke?"

"Smells like it might be electrical," Lance said. "Not sure where it's coming from."

I glanced behind him. "Multiple breakers are popped. Tell ATC we're investigating a possible in-flight fire and ask them to open a route to the nearest suitable airport. I'll check with the flight attendants."

I keyed the interphone to call the lead flight attendant.

Nothing. The interphone was dead.

My gut tightened as I hit the call bell three times in rapid succession.

"No radio response, not even on the standby radio," Lance said.

"Don't reset any breakers until you check the electronics bay. I hope we don't have a fire."

Barbi hurried into the cockpit. "What's wrong, Captain?"

"We're smelling a little smoke here in the cockpit. I need you and Tiesha to conduct a thorough cabin search to rule out a fire. Get back to me ASAP."

"I didn't smell any smoke in the cabin, but we'll check everything."

Right after Barbi left the cockpit, the autopilot disconnected.

"Autopilot failure. I'm taking over manually," I said, my hands gripping the yoke.

"We're not getting any warning lights, but the system could be compromised." Lance unbuckled his harness, moved to the back of the cockpit, donned a smoke/O2 unit, and grabbed a fire extinguisher.

"Be careful down there. I'll keep us away from storms."

He disappeared below while I waited several minutes in the silent cockpit.

No radios. No cell phone coverage. No autopilot. Plenty of lightning flashes, turbulence, and whiffs of that damn smoke.

Lance climbed up through the floor hatch and pulled off his oxygen mask. "We've been sabotaged."

My cheeks flushed with anger as I glanced back at him. "What did you find?"

"Someone must've entered the electronics bay after my preflight walkaround and rigged devices with timers. They fried our autopilot, all the comm and nav radios, the transponder, and our navigation computers."

"Is there a fire?"

"No fire, just some residual electrical smoke," he said, wiping black smudges off his hands with a napkin. "This was a professional job. We're in serious shit."

He clutched the side of the empty observer's seat as turbulence pitched us up and down.

"What about repairing at least one comm radio?"

Lance stowed the smoke/O2 unit as he said, "No way to fix it. All the circuits are melted."

"We're over the friggin' Amazon basin in the middle of nowhere." I held up my cell phone. "We can't even get a cell signal, which begs the question, why sabotage our avionics but not start a fire?"

"Or why didn't they destroy the airplane with a bomb?" He slid into his seat as another sharp jab of turbulence jolted the jet.

"Maybe we just haven't found the bomb yet." I bit my lip.

Barbi burst in, her eyes wide and her voice tinged with panic. "No fires in the cabin, Captain, but I think I found three bombs!"

Page Ahead to Purchase This Title

STRANDED
Available in eBook or Paperback From Your Favorite Online Retailer or Bookstore

ACKNOWLEDGMENTS

As always, I'd like to thank my Lord and Savior, Jesus Christ, for my many blessings.

I can't say enough good things about The Islander Grill & Tiki Bar in the Palm Beach Shores Resort on Singer Island in Florida. Owners Niko and Mel Bujaj ensure the food is always delicious and reasonably priced, and the staff is warm and attentive. They provide a fun atmosphere with different musical entertainers each night, many of them recording artists. It's a delightful place to dine and dance. The gourmet food, fine wine, and fabulous entertainment stimulate my creativity, and I've written many chapters there.

My favorite daytime place for writing is the covered oceanfront deck and restaurant at the Singer Island Hilton. The food and service is always superb, and the fresh sea air has never failed to boost my creative flow. I've spent so much time there, I have their menu memorized, and I think of their friendly staff as family.

Thanks to Aeronautical Engineer and Naval Architect Richard W. Metz for the golden ratio calculations, to Marine Biologist Kevin E. Peterson for advice about orcas, sea life, and underwater devices, and to my brilliant editor, Susan Bryant.

Special thanks to American Airlines B787 Captain Jeff Rowland for helping me brainstorm the scene where an RPG is fired from a Piper Cub floatplane. Jeff's friend, David, has a Cub on floats, Jeff had one with wheels, and I had a Piper Cub Special. Fun little airplanes.

Many thanks to proofreader Suzanne Berglind and to the Singer Island Writers, my treasured little critique group of multi-published authors. Thanks a million, Fred, George, Richard, and Tina.

AFTERWORD

"It is a mere question of time when men will succeed in attaching their machinery to the very wheelwork of nature." Nikola Tesla, 1856 - 1943

Dragon currents/ley lines are rivers of electromagnetic energy (Vril) that flow through the earth and crisscross the planet. Many of them intersect but probably not where I put them in my books.

The underwater city exists, but it is actually just beyond the western end of Cuba, and it doesn't have everything I described in my book. My theory is that Cuba was once part of the vast continent of Atlantis before it sank into the Sargasso Sea.

The Black Sun was a cult formed by prominent Nazis during World War II. They studied Vril to achieve mental mastery of it. The Black Sun was rumored to have a base inside the ice in Antarctica that they supposedly built before the war ended.

Except for a few structures in the underwater city near Cuba, all things Atlantean in my books are a product of my imagination.

The U.S. Navy uses Hardsuit 2000s to rescue submarines. The suits also have many commercial uses. Although I imagineered the USS *Leviathan* and the Scorpion submarines, similar vessels probably exist in the Navy.

Triple Threat is a work of fiction. The weapon, Poseidon's Sword, is a product of my imagination and may or may not be scientifically feasible. (Hey, I can't be an expert on everything.) Any inaccuracies in the book are unintentional and solely the responsibility of the author.

The airplane on the front cover is a Consolidated PBY Catalina amphibious seaplane similar to the one the triplets leased.

The record for highest altitude and longest distance flown in one flight in a paraglider is 26,575 feet and 140 miles in 2016 in the Karakoram Mountains, which form the western side of the Himalayas.

I hope you enjoyed *Triple Threat*. Samantha Starr, her relatives, and friends will return for many more adventures.

ALSO BY S.L. MENEAR

The Samantha Starr Thriller Series

Flight to Redemption

Flight to Destiny

Triple Threat

Stranded

Vanished

Life, Love, & Laughter: 50 Short Stories

ABOUT THE AUTHOR

S.L. Menear is a retired airline pilot. US Airways hired Sharon in 1980 as their first female pilot, bypassing the flight engineer position. The men in her new-hire class gave her the nickname Bombshell. She flew Boeing 727s and 737s, DC-9s, and BAC 1-11 jet airliners and was promoted to captain in her seventh year.

Before her pilot career, Sharon traveled the world as a flight attendant with Pan American World Airways.

Sharon also enjoyed flying antique airplanes, experimental aircraft, and Third-World fighter airplanes. Her leisure activities included scuba diving, powered paragliding, snow skiing, surfing, horseback riding, aerobatic flying, sailing, and driving fast cars and motorcycles.

Her beloved timber-shepherds, Pratt & Whitney, were her faithful companions for almost fourteen years, and she enjoyed riding her beautiful black and white paint stallion, Chief.

Sharon has flown many of the airplanes in her debut novel, *Flight to Redemption*, *Flight to Destiny*, *Triple Threat*, and *Stranded*, Books One through Four in her *Samantha Starr Series* featuring a woman pilot.

www.slmenear.com

 facebook.com/slmenear